DEADLY
HARVEST

DEADLY HARVEST

A DETECTIVE KUBU MYSTERY

MICHAEL STANLEY

BOURBON
STREET
BOOKS

An Imprint of HarperCollins*Publishers*
www.harpercollins.com

HarperCollins books may be purchased for educational, business, or sales promotional use. For information please e-mail the Special Markets Department at SPsales@harpercollins.com.

FIRST EDITION

Designed by Michael P. Correy

Library of Congress Cataloging-in-Publication Data is available upon request.

ISBN 978-0-06-222152-0

13 14 15 16 17 OV/RRD 10 9 8 7 6 5 4 3 2 1

For Alice Mogwe and Unity Dow
Who fight the battles we just write about.

The peoples of southern Africa have integrated many words of their own languages into colloquial English. For authenticity and color, we have used these occasionally when appropriate. Most of the time, the meanings are clear from the context, but for interest, we have included a Glossary at the end of the book.

For information about Botswana, the book, and its protagonist, please visit http://www.detectivekubu.com. You can also sign up there for an occasional newsletter and to become a Facebook fan.

CAST OF CHARACTERS

Words in square brackets are approximate phonetic pronunciations. Foreign and unfamiliar words are in a Glossary at the back of the book.

Bengu, Amantle   Kubu's mother [Uh-MUN-tleh BEN-goo]

Bengu, David "Kubu" Assistant superintendent in the Botswana Criminal Investigation Department [David "KOO-boo" BEN-goo]

Bengu, Joy   Kubu's wife [Joy BEN-goo]

Bengu, Tumi   Joy and Kubu's daughter [TOO-me BEN-goo]

Bengu, Wilmon   Kubu's father [WILL-mon BEN-goo]

Betse, Dikeledi   Orphan girl. Sister of Lesego [Dick-eh-LEH-dee BET-seh]

Betse, Lesego   Orphan girl. Sister of Dikeledi [Leh-SEH-go BET-seh]

Big Mama   Owner of the BIG MAMA KNOWS ALL *shebeen*

Demene, Wilson   Rough character [Wilson Duh-MEN-neh]

Dlamini, Zanele   Forensic expert [Zuh-NEH-leh Dluh-MEE-nee]

Gobey, Joshua   Nephew of Tebogo Gobey. Head of police diamond division [Joshua GO-bee]

Gobey, Maria   Tebogo Gobey's wife [Maria GO-bee]

Gobey, Tebogo   Deputy commissioner of the Botswana Police [Teh-BOW-go GO-bee]

Gondo   Witch doctor [GON-doe]

Khama, Samantha   First female detective in the Botswana Criminal Investigation Department [Samantha KAH-muh]

Koma, Constance   Lesego and Dikeledi Betse's aunt and guardian [Constance KO-muh ("o" as in English word *or*)]

Koslov, Helenka   IT expert in the Botswana Police

Mabaku, Jacob   Director of the Botswana Criminal Investigation Department [Jacob Mah-BAH-koo]

MacGregor, Ian   Pathologist for the Botswana Police

Maleng, Tombi   Daughter of Witness Maleng [TOM-bee Muh-LENG]

Maleng, Witness

Father of Tombi Maleng [Witness Muh-LENG]

Marumo, William "Bill"

Charismatic opposition party politician [William "Bill" Muh-ROO-moe]

Mogomotsi, Segametsi

Real teenager killed for *muti* in 1994 [Seh-guh-MET-see Mo-go-MOT-see ("o" as in English word *hot*)]

Molefe, Sunday

Rough character [Sunday Mo-LEH-feh ("o" as in English word *hot*)]

Nono

Young girl [NON-o]

Oteng, Jubjub

Bill Marumo's girlfriend [JOOB-JOOB o-TENG]

Owido, Mabulo

Tanzanian [Muh-BULL-o o-WEED-o]

Pilane, Jake

Doctor. Neighbor of Bill Marumo [Jake Pi-LAH-neh]

Pitso, Jacob

Freedom Party candidate

Rampa, Kopano

Undertaker [Ko-PAH-no RUM-puh]

Serome, Pleasant

Joy Bengu's sister [Pleasant Seh-ROE-meh]

Sibisi, Bongani

Professor of ecology at the University of Botswana [Bon-GAH-nee See-BEE-see]

Tibone, Robert   An assistant to Kopano Rampa

Tobogo, Tole   Partner of Constance Koma

Van der Meer, Kees   Professor at the University of
Botswana [CASE fun-der-MEER]

Part One

SOMETHING WICKED

"By the pricking of my thumbs,
Something wicked this way comes."

MACBETH, ACT 4, SCENE 1

ONE

As she walked home, Lesego's head was full of Christmas. She knew her sister would save some of her tips and buy her a small present. Lesego had no money, so she was making Dikeledi a doily from scraps of red material left over from her needlework class. She was trying to embroider "Dikeledi" across it in blue, but she'd made the first letters too big, and the whole word wouldn't fit neatly. She frowned. She was going to have to start it again.

Lesego was carrying a cloth bag heavy with shopping and another with her schoolbooks and, even though it was a threadbare hand-me-down, her school uniform was hot. She was already tired when she came to the steep hill leading to her aunt's house in the upper section of Mochudi. She sighed, and her eyes followed the road upward, causing her to miss her footing. She stumbled, nearly dropping her shopping. The two potatoes she'd bought rolled from the top of the bag toward the road, and her shopping list, which had been shoved between them, fluttered into the weeds on the side of the road. She gave a small cry and scurried after the potatoes; her aunt would be furious if she lost anything. Just as she retrieved the fugitive vegetables, a red Volkswagen pulled over and stopped next to her. The driver leaned across and opened the passenger door.

"Hello, Lesego," he said. "Jump in. I'll give you a lift up the hill."

She gave a grateful smile and wrestled her shopping and schoolbooks into the car. "Hello, rra. It's very kind of you. It's a long hill." He smiled back, put the car into gear, and started on the road up. There was a click as he engaged the door locks. Lesego took no notice. She looked around.

"This isn't your usual car."

"You're very observant, Lesego. My car is at the garage. They loaned me this one while they service mine."

She nodded, wondering about people who were so rich that they could just lend you a new car with no trouble. But she thought it would be rude to say that, so instead she pointed at her supplies.

"I got everything my aunt wanted except the two sweet potatoes. They were too expensive—and old as well—so I bought two ordinary potatoes instead, which were cheap. Do you think she'll be cross?"

"I'm sure she won't be. It was a sensible decision."

She nodded, relieved.

When they reached the top of the hill, she turned to the driver.

"You can drop me here if you like, rra. I can walk home now. Thank you."

But the car started to move faster now that it was on the level.

"Let's go for a short drive first," he said.

"Where's Lesego?"

Dikeledi looked down at her bowl of gravy with a few kidney beans floating in it. She hoped the question wasn't meant for her, but her aunt looked directly at her: "Dikeledi, I asked you where Lesego was."

"I don't know, Aunt," Dikeledi said in a frightened voice. "She didn't come back from school."

"She didn't bring the shopping, either. I gave her money." This seemed to offend Constance Koma the most. *"Where is she?"*

Dikeledi glanced around the table desperately, looking for rescue. But the boys were silent, their eyes downcast. Surprisingly, it was Tole who came to her aid. The children were supposed to call him uncle, but between themselves they had other names for Constance's partner, with his bad breath and groping hands.

"Who cares where she is, Constance," Tole said. "She probably stayed over with a friend. We'll give her a good hiding when she gets back. Teach her a lesson." He reached across the table, pulled the dish of *pap* toward him, and dug into it with his fingers. "Let's eat."

"We haven't said grace yet!"

Tole hesitated, still holding the lump of *pap*.

"For-what-we-are-about-to-receive-may-the-Lord-make-us-truly-thankful-Amen." He dipped the ball of *pap* into his watery gravy and slurped it into his mouth.

The boys started to eat the same way, and Dikeledi joined in, hungry despite her worry for her younger sister. Her aunt scowled at her but said no more.

Soon the food was all gone.

"The *pap* was burned," Tole said. "And there wasn't enough."

"If you got off your ass and found work, we'd have more," Constance said.

"Don't talk to me that way!"

Constance just looked at him. After a few moments he shoved back his chair and stalked out. They all knew where he was going—to the Bootleggers Bar. He would come back drunk, and Dikeledi wished they could lock the door of the room where she and the boys slept. Putting it out of her mind, she jumped up and started to clear up the dishes. The *pap had* burned, and the pot would be hard to clean. As she scoured it, she worried about her sister. It was really late now, and a ten-year-old girl shouldn't be out.

At first Dikeledi couldn't sleep. When she did eventually drift off, her sleep was fitful, and she muttered and tossed, disturbing the boys lying alongside her on the same thin foam rubber mattress. Suddenly she sat straight up and screamed. The oldest boy reacted at once, covering her mouth with his hand. If they woke Constance or Tole, they'd all get a beating. Dikeledi struggled free.

"Oh God," she said. "It was so awful, so real. I was lying on a table, tied down. It was dark but I saw a knife. A huge knife. It stabbed down, here and here and here." She pointed to parts of her body. "Oh God!" She started to sob.

"It was only a bad dream, Dikeledi. It's okay. Careful, or you'll wake them."

Dikeledi just shook her head and went on crying.

* * *

The next morning there was still no sign of Lesego. Dikeledi left early, tense with worry, and walked to the café in town where she had a part-time job, serving customers for tips and a few pula. Slipping out at about eleven, she walked to Lesego's school, which had its morning break then, and found two of Lesego's friends. They both told the same story: Lesego left straight from school to go shopping. No one had seen her since. Dikeledi hurried back to work, sick with fear.

She left the café as early as she could, determined to persuade her aunt to go to the police. Perhaps it was not too late.

"Go away, Dikeledi," Constance snapped. "Lesego probably skipped school and knows what'll happen to her when she gets back home."

Dikeledi tried again and received a slap for her trouble, so for the moment she gave up and started on her chores.

By the next day it was clear that Lesego wasn't coming back, and Constance gave in to Dikeledi's pleading. She brought Dikeledi with her to the police, as if to prove her concern to the girl.

The duty constable listened to the full story before he asked any questions.

"Has she ever done this before? Disappeared for a few days?"

"Never. Now she's run off with my money. That's the thanks you get. I took the girls in when their mother died of AIDS. What could I do? They had no father, either. At least no one who'd claim them." Her hand tightened on Dikeledi's shoulder as if she thought she might also vanish. "And this is the thanks I get. She runs away with my money!"

"How much money did she take?"

"Twenty pula."

The constable frowned. "She won't get far on that."

Constance glared at him. "Twenty pula is a lot of money to me!"

The constable nodded. "So you believe she ran away from home. Where would she go? Does she have other relatives here?"

Constance shrugged. "Everyone has relatives. I don't know."

"Have you asked them if they've seen her?"

"Tole—that's my man—asked around. He knows everyone. No one's seen her."

The constable had run out of questions. "I'll file a missing-persons report."

Dikeledi burst out, "Please, can you look for her? I'm sure something awful has happened. Something really awful. I'm so scared." Tears ran down her face.

"Don't worry, Dikeledi," the constable said. "We'll look very hard. We'll find her. The police here are very good. We'll find her for you."

As he watched them go, the constable wondered if they would find the girl or if she even wanted to be found. Maybe she had run away from the hard-faced Koma woman. But perhaps the sister was right. It wouldn't be the first time something awful had happened in Mochudi.

The next day Dikeledi slipped away from work early and went home past the police station. The same constable was on duty, and she asked him whether they had found anything.

"We asked at the school. They said she was there that day, then she left to buy some things and walk home."

Dikeledi nodded. She knew this.

"We found a shopkeeper who remembers her. She wouldn't buy sweet potatoes even though they were big and fresh. But she bought other stuff. Then she left."

Dikeledi nodded again, waiting.

"We haven't found anyone who saw her after that."

Dikeledi shook her head. "But someone must've. She would've walked up the hill. To get home."

The constable hesitated, then said kindly, "Dikeledi, perhaps she decided not to go up the hill. Maybe your aunt is right. Maybe she did run away. Would she have a reason to?"

Dikeledi just shook her head, thanked him, and left.

She stopped outside the police station wondering what to do. Lesego might have run away from Tole and Constance—Dikeledi could understand that—but she'd never do it without saying goodbye to her sister. Never.

Dikeledi wandered around for a while and spoke to a few more people, but she learned nothing new. Eventually she gave up and headed for home. But when she came to the hill, she stopped. There was no other way for Lesego to get to their aunt's house. She *must have* been here. Dikeledi scanned the area. It looked the way it always looked. Houses clustered at the base of the hill, then clinging to the road as it climbed. On the edge of the road ahead, a couple of Coke cans, candy wrappers, two cigarette packets, a number of plastic shopping bags, and a grubby scrap of paper. She caught her breath. She recognized the handwriting at once even from a distance, the bottom loops of the *g*'s bulging out in the telltale script. She grabbed the paper, her heart pounding. It couldn't be a coincidence. She was meant to find this! She checked it for a message, but it was only Lesego's shopping list. She felt a surge of disappointment, but at least she knew Lesego *had* been here. She shouted and ran back toward the police station.

Dikeledi didn't recognize the man at the front desk, but she blurted out the story to him. He found the constable she'd spoken to earlier. He was eating a sandwich, and wasn't pleased to be disturbed.

"What is it now, Dikeledi? What do you want?"

"Look. I found her shopping list! Where the road goes up the hill. That proves she was there and something happened to her."

The constable carefully examined the piece of paper on both sides. He shrugged.

"Are you absolutely sure it's hers? Anyway, she could've dropped it on the way *down* the hill in the morning. And even if she was on her way back, it's only a few hundred yards from the shops. Maybe she threw it away when she decided she wasn't going home." He shook his head. But when he saw the girl start to cry, he added: "I'll get one of the men to look around there and see if we can find anything else." He pushed the list back at Dikeledi.

Dikeledi grabbed the paper and left, hopeless, ashamed of her tears. She walked home up the hill with the list tucked into her dress. She knew that the list meant something, despite the constable's dismissal. One day it would be important. Until then, she wouldn't tell anyone else about it. Certainly not her aunt. Not even the boys. No one.

It was several days before she had the courage to return to the police station. Again there was nothing new, and she forced herself to wait another week before she went back. The constable grew tired of her and became short and unhelpful. It was clear to Dikeledi that the police were no longer working on the case.

A week went by and Christmas came. Dikeledi and Lesego had always celebrated together. In the past, they found happiness together with their small, secret gifts. But with this lonely Christmas, Dikeledi finally gave up.

She knew she would never see her sister again.

TWO

It was the Tuesday morning after the four-day Easter holiday. Assistant Superintendent David "Kubu" Bengu drove to work with a smile on his face and a song in his heart. Actually the song was in his throat—Rossini's "Largo al factotum" from *The Barber of Seville*. He loved the piece with a passion, often startling other drivers with his slightly off-key, booming rendition. In some ways he saw himself as the factotum of the Criminal Investigation Department.

Just after passing the Game City mall, Kubu turned right off the Lobatse road into the Millenium Park offices of the CID. Every day that he came to work, he was grateful that the detectives had their offices at the foot of Kgale Hill—a wild enclave with the city lapping around its base, a rocky outcrop of natural bush that offered walks with wonderful views and provided homes for baboons, small buck, and other wildlife. Not that Kubu had ever been very far along the walks; his bulk and general belief that the best exercise involved lifting something delectable to his mouth rather dampened his enthusiasm for clambering up the hill. Nevertheless, as he squeezed himself out of his old Land Rover in the narrow parking bay, he could enjoy the wildness of the hill above him and hear distant calls from the baboons.

Kubu had spent a quiet weekend with his wife and daughter, and had particularly enjoyed the pleasure three-year-old Tumi had given his parents when they were all together on Easter Sunday. They were besotted by her.

He had barely walked into his office, however, when he realized that the day was not going to be a quiet one. There were already four messages on his desk.

The top one read, "The Director wants to see you—immediately." The word *immediately* was underlined many times. The director's assistant was not shy about making a point.

The second was from his wife, Joy, reminding him not to forget to pick up Tumi at noon for her doctor's appointment. He felt a twinge of irritation. Stop nagging, he thought. You told me about it as I was walking out the door.

The third message read, "Detective Khama would like to speak to you." Kubu raised an eyebrow. Samantha Khama was new to the Criminal Investigation Department and the only female detective. Kubu had met her briefly when she joined the CID a few weeks earlier, but he hadn't worked with her on any cases. Already the rumor mill was active, with people whispering that she disliked men and was possibly a lesbian. This was a dangerous reputation to have in a country where same-sex relationships were illegal. What did she want? he wondered.

The final message was in his own handwriting—he'd left it for himself on Thursday afternoon, before the long weekend. It had but one word on it—"Funeral."

"Sit down." Director Mabaku was not known for his pleasantries.

Kubu carefully lowered his considerable frame into the armchair that faced the desk. Mabaku took a folder from the stack on his desk and opened it.

"What do you know about Bill Marumo?"

Kubu frowned. Marumo was a charismatic politician who had defected from the ruling Botswana Democratic Party to found the Freedom Party. Disgruntled voters were flocking to him, and pundits were beginning to think that he could become a real threat to the BDP. But Kubu didn't think much of Marumo, regarding him as an upstart with no respect for tradition. A crowd pleaser with no substance.

"He's getting a lot of attention. Swaying a lot of voters. Even Joy's talking about supporting him." He rolled his eyes. "And as for Joy's sister, Pleasant, she and her husband—they've actually joined his party."

"Who would want him dead?"

"He's dead?" Kubu gasped.

"I didn't say that! I asked who would *want* him dead."

"Obviously the BDP would be delighted if he went away. There's no other real opposition. But they'd never do anything as stupid as that." He paused. "I don't know much about him otherwise. He may have some private enemies. Why? What's happened?"

"There was a dog's head at his front door this morning. And a message smeared on the door in blood. Here's a photo."

Kubu looked at the print. The words "your next" were scrawled across the door. The writer had obviously dipped his hands in the dog's blood to write the warning.

"At least we know whoever wrote the message wasn't well educated," Kubu said with a smile.

Mabaku didn't appreciate the joke. "I want you to dig around and see what you can find. Marumo will see you at his house at noon. The address is on the back of the photo. This had better not be the BDP's doing!"

"Has Forensics been there?"

"Yes. Your friend Zanele Dlamini had her people there right away. She may still be there. The head was only found two hours ago."

Kubu heaved his large body out of the chair.

"And, Kubu," Mabaku growled, "this is very important. I want to know what's going on. And quickly. Report to me when you get back."

"Yes, Mr. Director."

It's going to be one of those days, Kubu thought as he walked back to his office. How am I going to pick up Tumi, take her to the doctor, *and* be at Marumo's house at the same time? I'll bet Marumo will be an hour late anyway. Maybe I should get Tumi to the doctor half an hour early and hope he can see her right away. I may even be at Marumo's on time—fifteen minutes late at most.

He shook his head. He knew it was wishful thinking. The doctor liked to talk about criminal behavior with Kubu and always dragged out Tumi's appointments when he was there. If Marumo was on time, and he, Kubu, was late, Mabaku would banish him to a distant village like Tshwane or Shakawe, where he'd be far from his family and the food would be inedible.

No. He'd better reschedule Tumi's appointment for later in the week. Joy would not be happy.

He sat down behind his desk with its orderly piles and picked up the phone.

"Joy Bengu, please. It's her husband speaking." He held the phone away from his ear to minimize the noise of shouting children. Joy worked at a day-care center.

After a few minutes, she came to the phone.

"Hello, my dear," Kubu said in his most loving voice.

"Don't tell me you can't take Tumi to the doctor!" Joy's voice was not loving.

"Something's come up, and the director's made an appointment for me at noon. There's nothing I can do."

"Since when has the director made your appointments? You know I can't take Tumi today."

"I feel terrible about it, my darling. I hadn't forgotten." He paused. "Confidentially, a threat was made against Bill Marumo this morning. Mabaku's given it top priority. I'm sure the commissioner is worried that people will accuse the BDP of intimidating the opposition. It could all blow out of control if it's not well handled. I'm sure that's why he wants me involved."

"Is Marumo all right?"

"Yes. It was just a threat. I'll tell you about it later. Promise me you won't tell Pleasant. It's really confidential at the moment." Joy and her sister Pleasant were inseparable. They shared everything, sometimes to Kubu's embarrassment.

Kubu sensed the reluctance in her voice as she promised.

"I'll call the doctor and reschedule."

He heard Joy sigh. "I'll do it," she said. "And you'd better make sure that nothing happens to Marumo. He's going to save this country, if anyone can. And don't forget the funeral. You'd better pick us up at three. And you promised to think about the little girl. Will you do that?"

"Yes, dear. I will. Thank you, dear." Kubu was indeed grateful.

Before Kubu could settle down, there was a knock, and a short, thin woman walked in, her police uniform hiding any hint of femininity.

"Good morning, Assistant Superintendent," she said. "I'm Detective Khama." She extended her arm to shake hands, touching her right forearm with the fingers of her left hand in the respectful way.

"Ah, yes. We met the day you arrived." He was surprised by the firmness of her grip. "Please sit down. How are things going?"

"Thank you for seeing me. It's been a hard two weeks—so much to learn. So much bureaucracy. I'm glad I took all those computer courses. I can see some of the older detectives really struggling."

"I'm one of them!" Kubu smiled. "So how can I help you?"

"Rra, I've been assigned—"

"Please call me Kubu. Everyone does. I've had the nickname since I was about fourteen. A friend of mine told me that I wasn't a David—my real name—but a Kubu. I was really upset at first at being called a hippopotamus, but soon everyone was using the name, and it actually made me feel a little special. I came to like it. Now I barely know my real name."

"That's a nice story. As I was saying—"

"You're older than most of our new detectives. What did you do before coming here?"

"Ever since I was a teenager, I wanted to be in the police. But my family is poor, so I couldn't go to university. And I'm small, so they didn't want to take me as an ordinary constable. So I worked for seven years as a secretary in a law firm so I had enough money to get a degree through the University of South Africa."

Kubu nodded, impressed. UNISA was a correspondence university, and the degrees were challenging. Samantha must have been very focused.

"That's impressive. But how did you get into the CID?"

"I made an appointment with the commissioner of police and told him I wanted to be a detective. He wasn't very helpful at first, but when I pointed out there were no women in the CID, and the constitution gave women equal rights, he changed his mind." A glimmer of a smile flitted across an otherwise impassive face.

I'm sure the conversation didn't go quite like that, Kubu thought. Maybe that's where the rumors started. Taking on the commissioner of police!

"We always need new blood." He hesitated. "And new perspectives. I'm sure you'll be a great asset. Now, how can I help you?"

"Director Mabaku gave me this case. It's my first. I'd like as much help as I can get. I want to do well, and everyone says you're always willing to help. So here I am."

Kubu nodded. "Tell me about it."

"About four months ago, a young girl, Lesego Betse, disappeared in Mochudi. I'm told you know the town well."

"I was born there, and my parents still live there."

"I'm from there, too. Anyway, the local police never found any trace of her. After a while they assumed she was dead and cut back the effort to look for her. Then a bit later they declared the case cold and stopped looking altogether."

"Hmm. I wonder why the director gave you a cold case. He should've given you something straightforward to cut your teeth on—a grocery-store robbery or a holdup at a gas station."

"I asked for it."

Kubu stared at her for a few moments. "A cold case is the hardest to tackle, even for experienced investigators. You could be setting yourself up for failure."

"I know it's a risk. But I've sacrificed a lot to become a detective, and I want to make a difference."

"And I admire that, Samantha. But sometimes it's better to take things a little slowly. Take time to learn the ins and outs of the business. I was lucky. I hung around detectives while I was getting my degree. I learned more from that than I did at university. Experience really does make a difference."

"Assistant Superintendent, you're a man. I don't think you understand what it's like to be a woman in a man's world. All we ever hear is to take it slowly, not to rock the boat. You know what that means? It means men don't want to change, and anyone who pushes, threatens their cozy lifestyle."

"Not all men are like that . . ."

"Women who complain are branded as nuisances. I hear what the other detectives are already saying about me. 'A troublemaker,' they say. They resent an intrusion into their male club. How do you think it feels? I want to make a difference for women. To give crimes against them the same attention as the police give crimes against men. Is that unreasonable?"

Kubu sat quietly, pondering the truth of what Samantha had said.

"Kubu," she said in a quieter voice. "I'm told you have a daughter. Do you want her to be a second-class citizen? What if she wants to be a detective, and then is treated like me? Could you sit back and do nothing?"

"Samantha, I appreciate what you want to do. But I think you'll have more chance of success if you get to know the other detectives first and earn their respect. Then they'll listen to you. Change is always a slow process. Nobody who joins the force and immediately rocks the boat accomplishes what they want. They get people's backs up."

Kubu felt the atmosphere chill. "And I was told you would be sympathetic, that you weren't like the others! But you're the same, aren't you? In favor of women's rights in words, but not in action."

Kubu felt a flush of anger. Nobody talked to him like that, let alone someone new. She didn't know him; didn't know what he believed. Look at his relationship with Joy. They were equals. He took a deep breath. "I do want to help. I'm going to get a cup of tea for myself. And then we can talk. Can I get one for you?"

"No, thanks."

A few minutes later Kubu returned. He opened the bottom drawer of his desk and pulled out a tin of mixed cookies. "I'm on a diet, actually. So I only eat these on special occasions. Welcoming a new detective is one of those." He picked out his two favorites and offered the tin to Samantha, who refused. "In fact, it's two special occasions, as you're our first lady detective." He extracted two more cookies. He carefully replaced the top and slid the tin back into the drawer.

"I do want to help, so let's get to work. I remember reading about the case you're talking about. My mother was very upset. She thought it was another Mogomotsi case. You know about that one? Segametsi Mogomotsi was fourteen when she disap-peared while trying to sell oranges to raise some money for a church excursion. Her dismembered body was found months later."

Samantha sat perfectly still for several moments, eyes unfo-cused. "I know about it. It was also in Mochudi." She looked into Kubu's eyes. "The government was forced to call in Scot-land Yard to take over, but never made their report public. Why do you think that was? Because high up *men* in Botswana were involved. That's exactly what I'm talking about. Justice for some, a blind eye for others. Who cared that a little girl was murdered for body parts, when the reputation of *men* had to be protected. The same thing may have happened to Lesego Betse, and the trail is fresher."

What happened to her that makes her so intense? Kubu wondered. He made a mental note to ask his mother whether she knew Samantha's parents.

"We need to keep all the possibilities in mind," he said. "With no word after four months, we have to assume she didn't just run off. Someone abducted her. That could have been for a variety of reasons. It could have been for sex, or to take her out of the country and sell her as a sex slave. There have been cases of that. The fact that we haven't found a body suggests that might be the case."

"Or it could be a witch doctor who's taken her. For *muti*."

Kubu nodded. "In any case, this is how I would proceed."

For the next hour Kubu gave Samantha insights about un-dertaking such an investigation—the people she should speak to, the evidence she could trust, the evidence that might be unreliable, and the hostility she would encounter, both from people she would question and from Betse's family, who likely thought the police had not taken the investigation seriously. He also suggested that she check on unidentified bodies of children that had turned up since December. If she could find Lesego's body, that would be her best break.

Eventually Samantha stood up to leave.

"I hope you're successful," Kubu said. "Let me know how it goes. Come and see me anytime. Cases like this need to be solved."

She thanked him and left.

Kubu sat quietly for several minutes, reflecting on what had just happened. The CID will never be the same, he thought. I just hope that what emerges is a better place.

THREE

Kubu glanced at his watch. He had about an hour and a half before his meeting at Marumo's house. He turned on his computer and went to get another cup of tea while it booted. As he walked back into his office, he heard the familiar Windows start-up sound. Ignoring his e-mail, he went straight to the Internet. Google is my friend, he thought as he typed in "Bill Marumo." He had more than seventeen thousand hits in a fraction of a second. I'll start with Wikipedia, he muttered. He picked up his pen and started to take notes.

"William Mishingo Marumo. Born Maun 11/11/1972.

"Only child. Father killed in mine accident in 1984." Kubu wondered whether it had happened in Botswana or South Africa.

"Graduated Maun Secondary School, 1990. BA (Honours) Political Science, University of Botswana, 1995. Member of

Student Representative Council, 1993–1995, president 1995."
That's where he got started in politics, Kubu mused.

"Mochudi, January 1995: arrested in protests against alleged police cover-ups in investigation of ritual murder of Segametsi Mogomotsi."

Kubu put down his pen. Now there's a coincidence, he thought. Not half an hour ago Detective Khama and I were talking about the murder of Segametsi Mogomotsi, and now I read that Bill Marumo was arrested in the ensuing protests. He scratched his head. It's impossible that the two are related. Still, he felt a niggle of discomfort. He really didn't believe in coincidences.

He continued to browse the numerous reports about Marumo—newspaper articles in all of the Botswana newspapers, blogs, and even some coverage overseas.

"Junior reporter at the South African *Sunday Times*, 1996–1998. News reporter Botswana Radio, 1998–2000, then Botswana TV, 2000–2004." Kubu made a note to check what types of programs Marumo had worked on.

"Joined the BDP in 2002. Elected to parliament 2004 representing BDP in Gaborone West-North constituency. Left BDP 2008 to found Freedom Party. Charismatic speaker and fundraiser. Only Freedom Party representative in 2009 elections."

Kubu read some of the reports of rallies and speeches Marumo had given in his reelection campaign, as well as a number of editorial comments. Even after the election, Marumo had managed to stay in the public eye. He'd worked feverishly to support his candidates in two by-elections, although both had lost badly in the end. In parliament he constantly challenged the government's "same old way" approach, and he wrote a weekly column in *Mmegi* newspaper.

There was no doubt that Marumo was getting a lot of attention with his attacks on what he called the BDP's arrogance and lack of sensitivity to the plight of ordinary people. But even more than his attacks on the government, he was gaining supporters with his message of hope. He called for sharing the prosperity of Botswana, claiming that there was enough money to uplift all, to reduce the incidence of AIDS, to improve education, to create jobs, to protect retirement. His slogan: "Believe in yourselves, and we can change the world!"

Sounds like Obama, Kubu thought.

As Kubu drove to Marumo's house in the upscale suburb of Phologolo, he hoped that the interview wouldn't last long. He was feeling hunger pains and wanted to put them to rest. He was about to turn into Pela Crescent, where Marumo lived, when he was stopped by a couple of policemen.

"Assistant Superintendent Bengu, CID," he said opening the window and showing his badge.

"Okay, rra. Please park on the street. It's that house up there."

As though I could miss it, Kubu thought, seeing a crowd of people and two television trucks.

Kubu looked around as he heaved himself out of his old Land Rover. An upper-middle-class suburb. Very little traffic. Nice trees. Secluded. A low probability that anyone would have seen whoever left the dog's head, he thought. But if someone did see something, there was a decent chance they'd pay attention.

He walked to the house and skirted the crowd, which was in a semicircle around the gate to the driveway. Marumo was standing on a chair, pumping his hand in the air. Camera flashes were reflecting off his sweating face. "Whoever did this—they won't silence me," he shouted. "The people want change, and nobody is going to stop us."

Kubu walked up to a man standing behind Marumo and whispered in his ear: "Assistant Superintendent Bengu for a noon meeting." The man looked at Kubu but did nothing.

"Tell him!" Kubu hissed.

The man pulled a piece of paper from his shirt pocket, scribbled something on it, and handed it to Marumo, who had paused to take a drink from a bottle of water.

"Ladies and gentlemen, that's all for now. Thank you." Then he added sarcastically, "The government has sent its ace detective to solve this great mystery." He jumped off the chair and extended his hand to Kubu. "Nothing personal," he grinned. "Couldn't resist taking a shot at the government."

"It sounded more like a shot at me," Kubu replied without a smile. "Can we go inside?"

"I'm reasonably familiar with your political career," Kubu said after they had settled down in the living room. Kubu liked the feel of the plush leather chair that he'd lowered himself into. "Do you think it's at all possible that the BDP would try to intimidate you by leaving a dog's head at your front door?"

"Of course. They're very nervous about the gains we're making. They'll be in real trouble at the next elections if they continue to lose support." He took a deep drink from his water bottle. "It was a BDP supporter all right but, even if you find who did it, you'll never be able to tie it to the party. They couldn't afford any connection to come out. That would be a disaster for them."

"Do you think the threat is serious—you know, the 'your next'?"

"No. My party would tie it to the BDP. If it is the BDP be-hind it, killing me would backfire. Besides, it won't happen." He took another swig of water. "I'm well protected."

"You have bodyguards?"

"Oh, no. It's my destiny to be president. Nobody can stop that."

What arrogance, Kubu thought.

"Is there anyone else who might want to kill you? Ex-business partners, ex-girlfriends?"

Bill shook his head.

"Have you ever had an affair with a married woman?"

Bill didn't flinch. "No, never. That wouldn't be good."

"Do you owe anyone money?"

Again Bill shook his head. "It can only be politics related. I'm sure of that."

Kubu read through his notes and was satisfied he'd written down all the important facts.

"When did you find the head?"

"I didn't. My girlfriend did. I was working out in the back room, and she leaves for work around seven. When she opened the front door, there it was. When I heard her scream, I came running. It was disgusting."

"What's her name?"

"Jubjub Oteng."

"Did either of you hear anything or see anything?"

"No. We were up at six, so it must have been left during the night."

"And the gate? I see you've got an electric gate across the driveway. Was it open?"

"No. We always shut it at night. If the government spread the wealth around a little more, there wouldn't be so much car theft."

"So, whoever left it must've climbed over the wall."

"That's what the lady detective said this morning. They found footprints as well, next to the tree at the gate. She thought whoever it was scaled the wall to get in and used that tree to get out."

Kubu frowned. "Lady detective?"

"Very attractive woman. Didn't ask many questions, but poked around and took a lot of photos . . ."

"Oh! You mean Zanele Dlamini. She's not a detective. She's from Forensics."

Bill shrugged.

"Well, thank you for your time, Rra Marumo. We'll be in touch if we learn anything." Kubu struggled out of the low sofa. It's like a sports car, he thought. Nice to be in, hard to get out.

"I think it looks like something that a witch doctor would do—or someone imitating a witch doctor. You know, a spell for bad luck," Kubu said. "Do you believe in that sort of thing?"

Marumo smiled. "No, Superintendent. I do not. We live in the twenty-first century now. That's stuff of the past. The country would be better off if it paid more attention to accurate information than to the rantings of old men and women who think they've got special powers. Have you been to a *kgotla*? Chiefs and their advisers—all ancient—invoking the spirits to help them mete out justice." He shook his head. "No, we must move our country into the present. Make it energetic. Make our people energetic, not lazy as they are now. Then the country will prosper. Everyone will improve their lot. Have a roof over their heads, and food on the table."

He can't get off his soapbox, Kubu thought. I wonder if he's still on it when he's in bed with his girlfriend.

"Rra Marumo, please call me if you are suspicious of any-one. Or if you remember something you've not told me." Kubu shrugged. "But on the basis of what you've said, I don't have anything to go on—unless Forensics found something useful, like fingerprints that we can match. But I doubt they will, un-fortunately."

Marumo nodded.

"And you may want to hire a night watchman. That may be enough to scare off anyone who wants to do this again. Or put barbed wire on the wall and the gate, like your neighbors."

Kubu handed him a business card and shook his hand. "I hope something like this doesn't happen again."

He started to leave, then stopped. "Please ask your lady friend to call me as soon as possible. I'm sure I won't learn any-thing new—but you never know."

As he walked back to his car, Kubu thought the chances of finding who'd left the dog's head were slim. He shook his head. He remembered when politics in Botswana were clean. And that wasn't long ago.

"I hope this isn't a sign of things to come," he muttered to himself.

FOUR

By the time he'd navigated around the crowd of reporters and was heading back to Millenium Park, Kubu was ravenous. Mabaku would just have to wait for his report; Kubu needed lunch. He settled for the Wimpy at Game City and had steak, eggs, and chips, but skipped dessert because he was pushed for time. Then he rushed to see Mabaku and was glad to find him free. He had to fetch Joy at 3 p.m.

Mabaku glanced up from the paperwork that seemed to be swallowing his desk and waved Kubu to a chair. "What did you find out?"

"Not much. I haven't had a chance to check with Zanele, but there are no obvious clues."

"Do you think it was political?"

"It was political all right, but not necessarily the BDP. The smaller parties fight even more bitterly between themselves."

He hesitated. "Frankly, I wouldn't be surprised if Marumo set it up himself for the publicity."

Mabaku's eyebrows shot up. "What? Decapitate a dog and leave it for his girlfriend to find? That's pretty extreme."

Kubu shrugged. "He's a born showman. He was performing for the reporters when I arrived. And we only have his word that his girlfriend, Jubjub, found the thing. I want to question her about that. He's not at all worried, either. Apparently he's destined to be president of Botswana. No one can stop him. Can you believe the arrogance of the man?"

"Kubu, I know you dislike him, and I can't say his politics appeal to me much, either, but he *could* become president of Botswana. We have to take this seriously."

Kubu nodded. "I'm going to follow up with Zanele once she's had a chance to look through what they collected. And we'll go door-to-door around the area to see if anyone saw anything. And the dog's a mongrel. No hope of tracing it unless someone comes up with the rest of the body."

"Well, keep on it."

Kubu climbed to his feet, but Mabaku had a question on a different topic.

"Have you spent any time with Detective Khama? I suggested she chat with you to get some guidance."

"Yes, actually I spoke to her this morning. She's on the lost-girl case from Mochudi. A bit much for a novice, I'd say."

"Maybe you can keep an eye on her. Mentor her a bit. Give her some tips."

"I haven't really got the time to mentor a new detective, and I'm not sure she'll listen."

Mabaku paused. "Is that how she came across? It can't be easy for her settling in here as the only woman detective.

She's very persuasive and talked me into letting her take on that case, but I know some people wouldn't mind seeing her in trouble with it. Give her a chance, Kubu."

Kubu said he'd see what he could do. He hesitated and then turned to another matter.

"Mr. Director," he said. "Is it true that Deputy Commissioner Gobey is retiring?"

Mabaku stared at him for a few moments. "Yes. As of the beginning of June, I'm told."

"Will you be the new deputy commissioner?"

"It's impossible to know what the commissioner will do. There'll be others in the running, too. I'm not sure I really want the job, in any case."

"You're the best man for the job, Director. I'll be very disappointed if you don't get it. You deserve it."

"Thank you, Kubu. If I get it, it may open an opportunity for you, too."

Kubu looked at the sea of paperwork threatening to drown the director's desk. "Thank you, Jacob, but I'm happy with my role as detective."

Kubu checked his watch and left in a hurry. It was already a quarter to three.

As he drove, Kubu thought about Seloi, the young woman whose funeral he was about to attend. She was the older sister of one of Joy's charges at the day-care center and hardly more than a child herself. They were orphans; their parents had already succumbed to the same killer. Kubu fumed. How had this been allowed to happen? Why had Seloi not been on a stable regimen of antiretroviral drugs? Why had she been allowed to waste away before their eyes? What crack had opened in Botswana society for these unfortunate people to fall through? Now Seloi's little sister Nono—also HIV positive from birth—had lost the last of her family and was alone in a frightening world.

Joy and Tumi were waiting when Kubu arrived. He kissed Joy, and picked up Tumi to receive a big kiss and a huge hug around his neck. This, Joy would say with amusement, was the only part of Kubu's anatomy that the three-year-old could reach around. Kubu would just laugh.

Once Tumi was settled in the car seat, they headed to the cemetery. The traditional and religious parts of the funeral had already taken place; only the actual burial remained.

"What did you do today, Daddy?"

"I was at work, darling." Kubu didn't think Tumi would want to hear about a severed dog's head.

There was a moment of silence, and Joy took her opportunity.

"Did you think about what we discussed, Kubu? About Nono? There's no one to look after her, now her sister's dead. She's with a distant relative now, but they don't want her. They're very poor, and there's no room, and they can't afford another mouth to feed. They say she has to leave."

"I didn't have much time today, darling, with all the fuss about Marumo." He hesitated. "The social services—"

"Will just dump her somewhere. She'll lose her friends and the people at day care—the only people who still care about her. That's all she has left, Kubu. She's only four. If we can just look after her for a few weeks, a month at the most, we can find her a proper home. And Tumi loves her."

"Please, Daddy. Please can Nono visit us for a while?"

So Joy had enlisted Tumi in this plan, too. Well, he couldn't deny that the child desperately needed help, and who else could she turn to?

"I suppose we could do that," he said at last. Joy leaned over and hugged him, and Tumi yelled with pleasure from the backseat.

When the excitement died down, it was quiet for a few minutes while Kubu negotiated the traffic. Joy checked her watch. "I hope we're not late for the funeral."

Tumi piped up. "What's a funeral, Daddy?"

"Where we go to say goodbye to people who've left us. Like Seloi."

"Where has she gone?"

Joy said nothing. She'd had this all day; it was Kubu's turn.

"She's died, Tumi. Gone to another place."

"Mummy says she's with Jesus."

"Yes, I'm sure that's right."

"Can we go, too? To Jesus?"

Kubu glanced at Joy imploringly, but she just smiled.

"One day, darling. Not yet. We've a lot of fun to have together first."

"Why must we wait?"

Joy took pity on Kubu. "We have to wait till we are called, darling. Now let Daddy drive. The traffic's bad."

The cemetery was several acres of grassless sand, with mounds in straight lines like soldiers on parade. The graves of the more affluent had an awning supported by a metal frame. A few had elaborate gravestones, but most were inexpensive wooden crosses. The area where the burial was to take place had many small mounds—a sad reminder of the scourge of AIDS.

There was quite a crowd of mourners at the graveside, many of whom had made the traditional walk from the girl's home. Kubu and Joy greeted the few people they knew and took the opportunity to socialize. Tumi was somber, clinging shyly to Joy's dress. She kept staring at the open grave with the large pile of sandy soil next to it.

After about half an hour the undertaker arrived, driving a black pickup truck with the coffin, covered by a black cloth, strapped down on the back. The undertaker parked as close to the grave as possible—still about a hundred yards away—and climbed out of the cab. His white shirt was sweat-stained, and he mopped his face with a handkerchief. While he straightened his tie and struggled to put on his jacket, he shouted for some strong men to come to help him.

At the sight of the coffin, the women gathered around the grave and started to cry out and ululate. Some wept.

Kubu watched as four fit-looking men headed for the truck. The undertaker untied the coffin, carefully folded the black shroud, and slid the cheap pinewood box toward the volunteers. The men struggled to lift the coffin to their shoulders and carried it along the sandy path to the graveside. By the time they rested it on the waiting ropes slung across the hole, they were breathing hard. The wailing rose to a crescendo as they braced the ropes and lowered the box into the ground. Kubu glanced at Tumi, but she seemed intrigued, rather than frightened. He could just imagine the questions ahead.

Most of the mourners threw a handful of soil into the grave, and then they all waited while the men filled the grave and topped it with stones. The wailing died down, and people started to talk again. Joy went off with Tumi to comfort Nono.

Kubu found himself standing next to the undertaker, who was watching the final stage of the burial with proprietary interest.

Kubu said, "I suppose you have a lot of funerals for young people these days."

The man nodded. "I'm sorry to say we do. It's the plague. AIDS. The government should do something to stop it."

Kubu was irritated. Why was it always the government that had to take action? Why couldn't people help themselves and each other? But he just nodded.

The undertaker introduced himself. "I am Kopano Rampa, rra. Professional undertaker and director of Funerals of Distinction."

Kubu turned to the pompous little man and replied with the same formality, "I am Assistant Superintendent David Bengu of the Criminal Investigation Department."

Rampa took a step backward. "The police? Is there a problem?"

Kubu relented. "Not at all. My wife is a friend of the deceased. The funeral went quite well, I thought."

"Yes, thank you, rra." But Rampa seemed to have lost interest in the conversation. "Well, I'd better finish things up here. Please excuse me. It was good to meet you." He moved off and started loading the truck.

Kubu shrugged, then went to find Joy. It was time to take Tumi and Nono home.

FIVE

Detective Samantha Khama climbed the steps to the third floor of the Social Sciences building at the University of Botswana. The staff offices were on the upper floors, but she wasn't sure she was in the right place. Spotting a receptionist, she asked for help.

"I'm looking for Professor van der Meer. He's an anthropologist. He's writing a book . . ." Her voice trailed off because the secretary was nodding.

"Do you have an appointment?" she said. "Professor van der Meer is very busy." She obviously took the casually dressed policewoman for a student.

"Yes. I'm Detective Khama of the Botswana CID. Tell him, please."

The woman's attitude changed, and she guided Samantha to the professor's office. He rose to greet her and extended his hand. She shook it, touching her right forearm with her left hand in respect. He did the same unselfconsciously. He must have been in Africa for some time, she thought. He had frizzy red hair and a light complexion that was freckled by the Botswana sun. A half-buttoned shirt and khaki shorts completed a casual image.

He looked at Samantha appraisingly and offered a friendly smile, which the policewoman did not return.

"*Dumela*, Detective. Kees van der Meer. I am very pleased to meet you. I want to help you," he said in labored Setswana.

Samantha replied in English. "Thank you for seeing me, Professor. It's good to meet you, too."

Relieved, Van der Meer switched languages. "Actually, I hope I *can* help. I'm not sure what it is you want. You weren't very specific on the phone." He smiled again and waved her to a comfortable chair. His English had a strong accent; Dutch, she guessed.

"I'm sorry, Professor, I wanted to explain it to you in person. I'm investigating the disappearance of a young girl. She's been missing for about four months. I believe she was abducted."

Van der Meer saw the point at once. "You think she was taken by a witch doctor? For *muti*?"

Samantha nodded. "That's possible. It could also be a sex crime, but then I think we would have found her by now, though perhaps not alive."

The professor paused. "A lot of African children are taken and sold overseas as prostitutes or sex slaves. You'd never hear about what happened to them." He shrugged. "Anyway, just what do you want to know from me, Detective? I study traditional healers and why their remedies and spells are often more effective than Westerners would expect. That's what my book is about. Healers, not witch doctors."

"But you must know about them, too, if you're studying that part of our culture."

He sighed. "Yes, of course the two blur. It's the border between black magic and white magic, as a Westerner would say. What do you want to know?"

Samantha hesitated, then decided to start at the beginning. "The trail is cold now. Months have passed, and the police in Mochudi found no clues to what happened. If I'm right, the girl's been dead for a long time. I'm going to investigate the crime again, but I'll be surprised if I find anything new. I'm hoping you can help me understand the motive. If I can find out who is most likely to have benefited, perhaps I can find some connection, some insights." She hesitated, realizing that her idea was pretty tenuous. But the professor just nodded.

"What's the girl's name?"

"Lesego." She was glad he cared enough to ask.

The professor shook his head. "It's not a good name."

"It means Lucky. A nice name, I think."

Van der Meer paused. "How much do you understand about how witch doctors operate, Detective? Do you believe in some of these things yourself? And please don't be embarrassed; it may actually help if you do."

Samantha shook her head angrily. "It's nonsense. It's only for ignorant people and children!"

Van der Meer's eyebrows rose. "I've heard stories—and experienced things myself—that make me wonder whether the world *is* as rational as we like to think. May I tell you a story? When I came to Gaborone I rented an apartment near here. At first I was comfortable there, but after a while I started to develop a bad cough and allergies, like hay fever. I thought it might be dust. The apartment wasn't very clean, and I felt better when I went out. My doctor prescribed antihistamines and for a while I was okay, but then it started up again. My maid said it was a curse—that a witch doctor had put a spell on the apartment. I thought it was nonsense, but as you say, I'm interested in such things. So partly just to observe what he'd do, I contacted someone who had a reputation for detecting spells. He came to the apartment and walked around for a while, sometimes stopping as if he were hearing something in the distance. Eventually he got a kitchen chair and lifted one of the ceiling panels. He took out a packet of something wrapped in cloth. After he'd removed it, I started feeling better. Now I have no problems."

Samantha shrugged. "He could've hidden it there himself."

"Yes, of course. But the point is that I had no idea it was there. I still have no idea why anyone would put a curse on the apartment. I hadn't offended anyone. Perhaps someone else wanted to rent it, and the idea was to drive me out."

"Maybe." Samantha shrugged again. "What I want to know is how these things are supposed to work."

"Well, let me try to explain the basic principle they use. It's not all that complicated. The idea is to transfer a desired property exhibited by one organism to another through some medium. Let's say you admire the strength and courage of a lion. So you kill it and eat its heart. You believe you ingest its strength and courage with the organ. This concept of transference is widespread in a variety of cultures, especially African and Eastern. But don't think it's restricted to them. I myself take a homeopathic remedy that consists of tiny, tiny amounts of a material that *causes* the symptom I want to cure. The amounts used are far too small to have a measurable biochemical effect. Why does it work?" He shrugged. "Maybe only because I *believe* that it does."

Samantha said nothing, and the professor could see that she was completely lost.

"Let me give you a concrete example. Let's say Tau is a man who is rich and powerful, but is not successful sexually. As you know, in the culture here it's very important to a man's self-esteem to have great sexual prowess and many offspring."

Samantha nodded. "And to a woman's also."

"Yes. So Tau goes to a witch doctor for help. Tau's a rich man and goes to a powerful witch doctor. It'll cost him a lot, but he doesn't care—that just shows how successful he is and how powerful the medicine will be. The witch doctor tells him what he needs. He must take the sexual power from another man—a young virile man, maybe a boy, who hasn't spent any of his sexual power yet."

"So Tau gets that boy's sexual organs?"

"Yes. Exactly. Made into a potion in a special way, of course. That potion is very powerful *muti*."

"It's all complete nonsense!"

The professor shrugged. "Physiologically it's nonsense, of course. But think of the effect in Tau's head. He believes he's obtained great power from the medicine. What's more, power that he's caused to be taken from another man by force. That makes it even more potent. Sex is driven by the mind in any case."

Samantha disliked the story but could believe it. Men always seemed to be looking for power and sex. This was just another example.

"However, this was a young *girl*."

Van der Meer thought for a moment. "A woman who can't make milk may get *muti* made from the nipples or the breasts of a healthy young woman. If a woman can't conceive, the *muti* must be made from a womb. Someone with a weak heart needs the heart of a healthy person. Young. Fresh."

Samantha felt a bit queasy. These are my people he's talking about, she thought. I'm ashamed for them.

The professor continued, "But I think this case may be different. Sometimes there is something very unusual about the individual, which suggests strong spirit power. For example, it could be a special birthmark on the face. And albinos are thought to have enormous power. Do you see the connection with Lesego?"

Samantha shook her head. "Lesego wasn't an albino."

"But her name. Lucky. That's why I said it was a bad name. Not many children are called that. The name gives them a power that others want badly, perhaps badly enough to steal. Potions for luck usually involve animals thought of as fortunate for a special reason: the scaly anteater—safe from attack with its armor plating, the klipspringer—escapes easily by jumping between rocks on hooves that seem to hold like Velcro. But in this case . . ."

Samantha absorbed this new idea. "So it could be for fertility, young organs to fix unhealthy ones, or even just for luck." She felt more nauseous. And she was uncomfortable with this white European, who seemed to find all of this reasonable. She stood up.

"You've been a big help, Professor. I need to think about how all this fits with my case. Can I come back if I have more questions?"

"Of course, Detective." Van der Meer stared at her without smiling. "I just want you to understand something important.

Many, many, people believe in witchcraft. Not just ignorant people and children, but businesspeople, people in the government." He paused. "And many in the police also believe. That's why so few cases are solved. They're scared the witch doctor will put a spell on them if they get too close." Samantha didn't react. "Most of these people would never dream of using *muti* themselves," he continued, "but they're scared to death of it. And the few who would use it are powerful people, and they use powerful witch doctors. They've a lot to lose." He paused. "I think you should be careful with this investigation, very careful."

Samantha clenched her jaw. Another man telling her to go slowly, fit in, be careful.

"Thank you for your time, Professor," she said and left abruptly.

Part Two

FELL SWOOP

*"What all my pretty chickens and
their dam
At one fell swoop?"*

MACBETH, ACT 4, SCENE 3

SIX

She hopped and skipped over the sand alongside the road. It had been such a happy afternoon, and she had the whole weekend ahead of her. For the first time since her mother had died ten months ago, she hadn't felt pangs of grief. Playtime had been nothing but fun—she and her friends kicking a soccer ball all over the grassless playing field, shouting incessantly for a pass and screaming with excitement when someone neared the goal.

She knew her father would be angry that her school uniform was covered in sand and her shoes scuffed, but she couldn't wait to tell him that she'd scored a goal—her first—a shot from twenty yards that sped past the fingertips of the goalkeeper. Her father had played soccer when he was young, so he'd understand her excitement and be proud of her. She looked forward to that.

She heard a crunching behind her. She turned and saw a white Toyota pulling off the road onto the sand. It slowed down and stopped next to her. As the window opened slowly, she saw a man leaning over, struggling with the handle.

"Hello, Tombi."

It took a few moments for her eyes to recognize him in the dark interior.

"Oh! *Dumela*, rra. I didn't think it was you."

"My car's at the garage, Tombi. They loaned me this one while mine's being fixed."

It must be nice to have a car, she thought.

"Can I give you a lift home? You live near here, don't you?"

"Yes, rra. Not far from those shops down there."

"Jump in. I'll buy you a milk shake on the way."

A grin split Tombi's dusty face as she clambered into the car. "Oh, thank you, rra. I haven't had one for a long time."

He smiled back, put the car into gear, and moved off. There was a click as he engaged the door locks. Tombi took no notice. A milk shake would be the perfect way to end the afternoon.

Witness stirred the pot of *pap*. It would be done soon. The tomato and onion sauce was ready, simmering on the back burner.

Where was Tombi? he wondered. She should've been home more than half an hour ago. Maybe she was still playing soccer with her friends. He shook his head. Girls playing soccer! When he was in school, boys played soccer. Girls played . . . He stopped stirring. What *had* girls done after school? He couldn't remember. He wasn't interested in girls then. It was only when he met Tombi's mother when he was nineteen that he started paying attention. That was fifteen years ago. Now she was gone.

He started stirring again. Still, he was lucky. Tombi was a good girl. Naughty from time to time—she was a teenager, after all—but never anything serious. More important, she studied hard at school, had three or four close friends, and wasn't distracted by boys. So far.

He dreaded that moment. He wasn't sure how he'd cope. His friends with daughters didn't know what to do. None of them seemed to understand their kids. But he knew what he would do—he'd forbid her from having sex even though it seemed that all schoolchildren were doing it. For them, it was as natural as shaking hands. But he knew what AIDS could do to a family. He would have to talk to her soon—remind her of what had happened to her mother.

Tombi was now more than an hour late, and Witness was worried. He drove to her school in his dilapidated Volkswagen and saw a few boys kicking a ball around.

"My daughter's name is Tombi. Tombi Maleng. Do you know her?"

The one boy looked at the others. They shook their heads.

"We don't know any of their names."

"There were some girls playing soccer, but they all left a long time ago," another interjected.

"How long ago?"

"I don't know. A long time! An hour? Maybe two?"

"No," another said. "It was only half an hour."

"You're sure you don't know her?"

They all shook their heads.

Witness thanked them and walked over to the school buildings, hoping to find someone working late. His stomach began to ache. Other girls had disappeared . . .

He was in luck. A teacher was still there, grading tests. She knew Tombi but hadn't seen her that afternoon.

"She probably went home with a friend and has lost track of the time."

"She's never this late. Her best friends are Chastity, Zuni, and Asakona, but I've no idea where they live. I don't even know their last names. Do you know any of them?"

"Yes, I teach them all. It's Chastity Maboda, Zuni Tsimako, and Asakona Ramotwa."

Witness borrowed pencil and paper and wrote the names down. "Do you know where they live?"

The teacher shook her head. "You can find out at the office. But it'll only be open on Monday."

"I can't wait until then. Perhaps you have their phone numbers?" The teacher took a notebook from her desk and flipped the pages.

"I've only got the Mabodas' number." She read it out. "I'm sure Tombi's fine. Don't worry. She's probably back home by now. Check there before you get everyone upset."

Hoping she was right, Witness thanked her, walked back to his car, and drove home.

"Hello. Is that Mma Maboda? This is Witness Maleng— Tombi's father. Is Tombi there by any chance?"

Mma Maboda said she wasn't.

"Please could you ask Chastity if she saw Tombi this afternoon?"

He took his cell phone out to the veranda and looked up and down the road. Nobody.

"Rra Maleng? Chastity said they all played soccer this afternoon. Tombi scored a goal apparently."

"When did Chastity get home?"

"It must've been around five-thirty, I think."

"That's an hour and a half ago! Can you ask Chastity if she knows where Tombi was going after soccer?"

There were muffled voices on the line.

"Chastity says she was going home."

"Mma Maboda, I'm very worried. Please call me if Tombi comes to your house. Now can I speak to Chastity? I need to get hold of Asakona and Zuni."

After speaking to Chastity, Witness hung up. The pain in his stomach was worse.

The calls to the homes of Asakona and Zuni were similar. Both children had returned home about the same time as Chastity. Both said Tombi was going straight home.

Witness grabbed a photo of Tombi and drove to the little cluster of shops at the end of his road. He went into the minimart and showed the photo to the woman behind the counter.

"Have you seen her?"

The woman shook her head. "I know Tombi. But she didn't come in today."

At the gas station next door, the attendant looked at the photo and shook his head. Finally Witness spoke to a number of minibus taxi drivers who used a vacant area near the school entrance as a parking lot, but none had noticed Tombi.

It was after nine when Witness walked into the Broadhurst police station. He explained the situation to the constable on duty.

"Don't worry, rra. Kids do this all the time. She's off with a friend. Probably spending the night. It hasn't occurred to her that you'd be worried."

"She always lets me know."

"Fill out this missing-person's form." The constable handed Witness three forms and two sheets of carbon paper. "Press hard." He smiled. "Maybe she's with her boyfriend."

"She's not like that." Witness was having difficulty containing his anger. "She's a good girl. She doesn't have a boyfriend. Something's happened to her. Here's a photo. Please make copies and have your people go out and look for her."

The constable took the photo. "Nice-looking girl," he said. "I'll make copies. But you'll see. She'll be back in the morning."

Witness banged the counter with his fist. "Something's happened to her. I'm telling you." Then he lowered his voice. "Please get your people out and look," he pleaded.

"Sorry, rra," the constable replied. "I know you're worried, but it's too soon to do anything tonight. Besides I don't have the staff. Wait until tomorrow. Kids always show up."

Witness hurried home hoping desperately that Tombi would be there. But she wasn't. He didn't know what to do. He drove back to the school and slowly followed the road Tombi would have used to walk home. There was no sign of her. No sign of anything. Even though it was late, he banged on the doors of several houses. Nobody had seen her.

"Don't worry. She'll be back," they all said. "Our kids often stay out with friends."

"She's not like that," he snapped. "She's a good girl."

When Witness eventually returned home, any remaining hope was dashed. Tombi was still not back. He took a beer from the fridge and sat down at the kitchen table. What could he do? He popped open the can and drained it without taking it from his lips. He liked the cold fizzing as the liquid slipped down his throat almost as much as he liked the taste. He grabbed another.

It was too late to go and search the neighborhood. But he couldn't just sit and do nothing. What *could* he do?

He drained the second can.

I'll organize a search party in the morning, he decided. Get all my friends to help. He decided he'd better call them right away even though it was late; otherwise he might miss them in the morning.

He started with the parents of Tombi's friends.

"I'm sorry to call so late. But Tombi still isn't back. I need help looking in the fields along the road. Anywhere she may have walked. Can you meet me at the school at eight tomorrow morning? Please come and help. And bring as many other people as you can. And long sticks to poke under bushes. Please help me."

Then he called all his friends and acquaintances and even some of his colleagues at work. Most said they would come.

When he finished calling, he collapsed on the sofa with another beer. How was he going to get through the night? He'd never sleep.

He put his head in his hands. His body shook, and tears dripped from his eyes. He was desperately afraid.

SEVEN

Witness tossed and turned all night. His mind played out the worst of scenarios, and the pain in his belly intensified. When the first streaks of light crept through the torn curtains, he climbed out of bed and pulled on his clothes. It was time to renew his search for Tombi.

He had nearly two hours before meeting his helpers at the school. In the meantime he'd go out on his own. He made himself a cup of strong tea, added milk and lots of sugar, and cut himself a thick slice of bread.

He was terrified. Over the past few years, several young girls had disappeared without a trace. Some said the girls were kidnapped for sex, but most whispered that it was for *muti*. Witness shuddered. The thought of his little girl being cut up . . . He cried out in anguish. What sort of man could do that to an innocent girl?

And what would he do if he lost her? What had he done to deserve this? First his wife, and now his beautiful daughter.

"No!" he shouted. "No, no!" He wasn't going to give up. He was going to find her.

Witness walked Tombi's likely route to the school. He looked for any hint of what had happened, but to no avail. The sandy shoulder had many tire tracks and many more footprints. There was no way he could know which were Tombi's—if, in fact, she had been there. Then he walked back on the other side of the road with the same futile results.

When he reached his house, he called the police station to ask if they had any information.

"No, rra," was the reply. "But I'll send a constable over this afternoon to take a detailed statement. As we told you last night, we'll only start searching tomorrow if we have enough men. It will probably have to wait until Monday."

"But she may be dead by then!" he shouted. "You need to start looking today!"

"Sorry, rra. That's impossible. I suggest you phone the hospitals in case she's had an accident that hasn't been reported to us. Goodbye, rra." The line went dead.

Witness felt like throwing his phone at the wall.

He still had nearly an hour before the search party was going to gather at the school, so he decided to drive to the Princess Marina Hospital. The nurse at Admissions checked the records, but no one matching Tombi's description had been admitted. She suggested that he call the two private hospitals in Gaborone and gave him their numbers. He called both, but neither had any information.

With a few minutes remaining, he stopped at a shop near his

home, where he knew the owner. When he understood the situation, the owner sympathetically made a pile of copies of Tombi's photograph. Witness thanked him and scribbled his phone number on one of the copies. "If you see her, please call me."

When Witness arrived at the school, he was grateful to see about twenty people waiting. Most of the helpers had brought sticks of some sort, either broomsticks or cut from a tree. Two women came up as soon as he climbed out of the car. He recognized them as the mothers of Chastity and Asakona.

"Oh, Rra Maleng. I hope Tombi is okay. We're all praying for her." Mma Ramotwa touched him on the arm.

"She's such a lovely girl. Chastity doesn't know what could've happened. They all left for home at the same time," Mma Maboda said. "I've brought my husband and one of my neighbors to help. I also went to all the teachers' houses, and some of them have come, too."

Witness fought back his tears.

"Thank you."

A large man with a bright shirt, shorts, and sandals walked over.

"*Dumela*, Rra Maleng," he said, extending his hand. "I'm Charlton Tsimako, Zumi's father. My wife cannot be here, so I have come in her place."

They shook hands in the traditional manner.

"I'm a security guard at a bank," Charlton continued. "I've had some training in searches. Let me help you."

"Thank you," Witness responded. "I have no experience. But I have something that will help." He held out the packet containing copies of Tombi's photograph. "I was able to make these this morning."

The big man turned and shouted: *"Dumela*, everyone. Please come here so we can get started." The group walked over to him.

"Thank you for coming to help. We all know how Witness must be feeling. So let's get started." He took the copies from Witness. "We're going to break into groups. Some are going to go to every house between here and Witness's home on Dutela Crescent. Show them Tombi's photo and see if they saw her or saw anything unusual last night around five-thirty. Also ask at the tuck shops. There are several on the way. And see if any of the taxi drivers saw anything."

He made four groups of two people each and gave them each a set of roads to cover. They took their copies and set off. "We'll meet back here in an hour!" he shouted after them.

"The rest of us will search all the bush areas around here. We'll start outside the school gates and check the big vacant area along Segoditshane Way. When we get there, we'll form a line with about three or four yards between us. Use your poles to check under bushes or in long grass. We'll keep doing that until we've covered all the areas around there. Then we'll check along the railway line, even though that's in the opposite direction." He clapped his hands. "Let's go!"

"Why aren't the police here?" one of the men shouted.

"They say they'll send a constable this afternoon," Witness answered. "They don't seem interested. They say kids often disappear for a few days."

"Aaii," one woman exclaimed. "The police never do anything. They're useless. All they're interested in is their paycheck. We can do a better job than them."

They picked up their sticks and set off to start the search.

The searchers kept a ragged line as they walked in the soft sand, sharing gossip and shouting encouragement. They poked clumps of long grass or crouched to peer under bushes. Even when they used their poles to move branches aside, thorns often managed to scratch their arms. Most difficult were the *wag-'n-bietjie* (wait-a-bit) bushes, with their thorns curved toward the center.

It took about twenty sweaty minutes for the line to reach the end of the first section of bush. After a few minutes' rest, they moved to the next section and slowly worked their way back.

When they reached the school, several of the other groups had already returned and were standing in the shade of an acacia tree.

"Did you find anything?" Witness asked as he walked up.

Nobody had anything positive to report. No one had seen Tombi the previous evening, and no one had seen anyone or anything suspicious.

Big man Charlton took control again. He widened the area for the groups to go house-to-house and asked one of the men, who ran a small business, to make fifty posters with a photo of Tombi and Witness's phone number. "When you've made them, staple them to trees and lampposts in the area. Maybe somebody will recognize her or remember something."

Then he led the rest of the group to the next area where they would beat the bushes for any sign of the missing girl.

As Witness worked his way through the bushes, he became increasingly despondent. I'm never going to find her, he said to himself. She's gone. What have I done to deserve this? He lifted his pole and smashed it against the nearest bush. And again, and again.

Charlton walked over and put his arm around Witness's shoulders. "Have faith, my friend. If she's alive, we'll find her. And if she's not, she's in a better place."

For just a moment Witness buried his face against Charlton's chest. Then he pulled away.

"Let's keep looking," he said as he went back to his place in line. "Let's keep looking."

It was nearly noon when the remaining searchers assembled back at the school. There wasn't a single lead, not a scrap of information that could help Witness find Tombi. She had disappeared without a trace.

"Thank you for your help, my friends," Witness said to the group. "You did everything you could. I fear the worst. Someone has taken her. For what, I don't know. Please pray for her; pray that she's alive." He wanted to add that otherwise they should pray that her death was quick and without pain. But he knew he'd choke on the words if he tried to say that. "And take care of your own children. Look after them. Protect them."

When the others had left, Witness sat down under a tree outside the school gate and leaned against its trunk. He thought back to his wife, and the familiar feeling of sadness came over him. And anger. When had it happened? Who was it?

He thought they'd built a good marriage. They'd laughed and played together, and he'd loved watching Tombi grow from a little black ball, squirming in his hands, to a happy teenager, well on her way to becoming a woman.

Then came the shock—the night his wife told him that she was HIV positive. That he should get tested, too. He'd been devastated. And she refused to answer any questions, which made him furious. He had a right to know. She was his wife.

She was different after that night. The sparkle was gone, as were the energy and laughter. And a year later she died, a wasted shadow. He hadn't known whether to be relieved or sad.

So he transferred all his love to Tombi. She'd filled the void. And hadn't disappointed him.

But now she was gone.

He sobbed. It wasn't possible. It wasn't fair.

He continued to lean against the tree, head down, until he became aware that someone was watching him. He looked up and saw Gordon Thembe. He dropped his eyes again. Gordon was not one of his friends. He did odd jobs when he needed money, and otherwise hung around the *shebeen*s drinking and chatting with his friends and women. Witness thought him lazy and unreliable. He wished the man would go away and leave him in peace. But Gordon flopped down next to him. "Courage, my friend," he said. "Somehow she will be found."

Witness grunted.

"You must try and relax, man. Keep calm. You're no use to Tombi this way. Here, share this with me." The man pulled a plastic packet from his jacket, removed a crinkled cigarette paper, and poured out some dried plant material. Witness guessed it was *dagga*, the local name for marijuana. He wanted to be angry with Gordon, to tell him to leave. But after all, the man had risen early to help search for Tombi. He shrugged. Gordon rolled the *dagga* in the paper and neatly sealed it by licking along the edge.

When the pungent smoke started to rise, Witness took the joint and inhaled deeply a few times. He coughed a little, but after a while felt the tension ease. As Gordon babbled about nothing in particular, Witness listened quietly, taking a drag from time to time, letting his brain unwind.

"They're probably right," he said at last. "Tombi will come home. I'll be very cross with her!" That struck him as funny, and he giggled. Gordon chuckled, too, while he rolled another joint.

Suddenly Witness grabbed Gordon, almost pulling him over. "Look at that man!" He pointed toward the road, his hand shaking. "You can see he's a witch doctor!"

Gordon looked at the shabbily dressed man walking along the road, perhaps looking for work. There seemed nothing unusual about him. He started to chuckle again.

Witness turned to him angrily. "Can't you see? He's changed himself into a man but he still has hyena fur! He's a witch doctor. He has Tombi!" Witness clambered to his feet, but Gordon grabbed his arm.

"Witness, my friend, it's just a man. He has torn clothes, not fur. No one is with him. Come, sit down again."

Tense, Witness watched the man until he was out of sight. Then he collapsed back under the tree and smoked more *dagga*. He started to count the branches of the tree, but they kept moving, confusing him. He laughed aloud. He tried to explain the joke to Gordon, but he was laughing, too. Witness closed his eyes. It was much easier to count the branches that way. Gordon watched him for a few minutes while he finished the joint. Then he climbed to his feet.

"Witness will be all right here," he said to himself. "He'll sleep in the sun with good dreams." He shook his head. "But he'll wake again to his pain." He rose to his feet and shambled away.

"Are you all right, rra?" The young female voice seeped into Witness's mind.

"Tombi!" He jumped up. "Tombi, where have you . . ." He stared at the young woman, dressed in a T-shirt and jeans, and the smiling man next to her.

"You're not Tombi! You're not my daughter." His temper flared. "I've lost my daughter. How dare you pretend to be her!" He gave her a shove but was so unsteady that he nearly fell over and had to grab the tree for support. He glanced at the man and shouted, "You're old enough to be her father! Leave her alone!"

The girl looked at him in surprise. "It's a *poster*, rra," she said hesitantly. "We're putting up posters for the election. I was going to put it on the tree here. It's just a poster."

Witness shook his head vehemently. "You're too young to have sex!" he shouted at her. "You'll die of AIDS! That man could be your father!"

Still holding the poster, the young woman backed away, turned, and ran to a couple of other women taking posters out of the trunk of their car. She pointed at him. They talked for a few moments, stacked the posters back in the trunk, and drove away, shouting something he couldn't hear properly.

Witness leaned against the tree and closed his eyes, his mind swirling.

When Witness eventually pulled himself together, he decided to go home, grab some lunch, and then call the hospitals again. And the morgue. If there was no information, he'd go back to the police and make them do something.

As he drove home, he noticed that each telephone pole had a poster, but not of Tombi. One poster read FREEDOM PARTY. PUBLIC MEETING. SATURDAY. MOTSWEDI JUNIOR SECONDARY SCHOOL. 11 A.M. The next showed a picture of the handsome man who had been with the young woman. He smiled down at Witness, teeth glistening. VOTE FOR FREEDOM was splashed across the bottom.

"There's nothing to smile about!" he shouted. "My daughter's gone!"

But the man continued to smile, and Witness felt his eyes following him down the road.

EIGHT

Samantha had arranged to meet Lesego's family on Saturday around six, when they all gathered before supper. Driving to Mochudi, she recalled Kubu's advice and comments, and admitted to herself that she was a little nervous about how the meeting would go. But when she arrived at the house, her confidence returned, and she knocked firmly on the front door.

She was greeted by a man who introduced himself as Tole Tobogo. He was polite, but she disliked the appraising way he eyed her. A bitter-looking woman sat stiffly on the thread-bare couch with a teenage girl next to her. The teen must be Dikeledi Betse, the missing girl's sister, she thought. Two boys squatted on the floor. Tole introduced her to Constance Koma and told her the names of the others. He pulled up a rough-wood chair from the dining table for the detective.

Constance spoke for the first time. "So the police are interested in Lesego's disappearance now. It's a bit late. Nearly five months late."

Samantha had talked to the investigating officer and agreed with the woman's opinion. Not much investigating had, in fact, been done. The police had asked around the town and found nothing. They'd filed a missing-persons report, and then they'd lost interest. Nevertheless, she felt obliged to defend them. "The police have always been interested in the case, mma. There just hasn't been a lot to go on."

"So what makes you think you can do anything? You look very young."

Samantha bristled but kept her voice calm. "I'm reviewing the case for the CID. To see if we can find anything that was missed."

"And what do you think happened?"

"She was probably abducted and killed for *muti*." But for Constance's hostile tone, Samantha would have been more circumspect in her choice of words. The faces around the room registered shock. Only Dikeledi showed no reaction. In her heart she'd known this since Christmas.

For a moment there was dead silence. Then Constance put her hands to her face and started to cry. The expressions of surprise and disbelief on the faces of the others would have been almost comical in any other context. None of them moved; it was Samantha who went across to the couch and put her arms around the woman, but Constance pushed her away, then seemed to regain her composure.

"I'm all right," she said. "What do you want with us after all this time?"

"Can each of you please tell me everything about the day Lesego disappeared? Anything at all that was unusual. Even if you don't think it's important. Let me decide that. Please try. Otherwise we may never find out what happened."

Each member of the family described what they recalled of that day, but no one remembered anything unusual.

Then Tole spoke about the following week.

"I asked everyone I met. But no one had seen anything. At least that's what they said. I think they were scared a witch doctor was involved."

"The people you talk to only want to drink at the bar," Constance interjected.

Samantha ignored that and spoke to Tole. "Did anyone seem evasive? As though they were hiding something?" Tole shrugged and subsided.

Samantha turned to Dikeledi. "The police at the station said you were very concerned. Very loyal. That you came back several times. Did you find anything? Is there anything else you can remember that might help me?"

Dikeledi looked down at her feet. After a few moments she shook her head.

Constance stood up and put a pot of *pap* on the stove to cook. Samantha realized it was a signal for her to leave, but she had noticed Dikeledi's hesitation.

"Would you show me the route Lesego would've taken to school, Dikeledi? Would you drive with me? It won't take long, and I'll bring you right back." The girl hesitated again, but then nodded. She jumped up and left the room, reappearing a few minutes later with a jacket, despite the warm evening.

Samantha gave Tole her business card and thanked them all for their help. Constance just nodded and concentrated on the *pap*.

* * *

Dikeledi directed her down the hill to the town; there was only one way to go. Then she described how Lesego might have reached the hill from the school via the shops she needed to visit. Samantha stopped the car at the deserted school and turned to the girl.

"You were close. It must be terrible for you. I'm so sorry."

Dikeledi nodded but didn't reply. She fought back tears.

"You wanted to tell me something at the house, didn't you? But not in front of the others. Won't you tell me now? I really want to find out what happened."

Dikeledi turned away from her and stared out at the afterglow of the sunset. "Why do you care? I suppose it's your job, but no one ever listened to me. Now it's too late."

Samantha wondered how to reach the girl, knowing she couldn't take too long. Dikeledi was expected home.

"I grew up in Mochudi as well. Did you ever hear of a girl called Segametsi Mogomotsi? She also lived here in Mochudi. She disappeared, too, when she was about your age. Segametsi was one of my best friends."

"What happened to her?"

Samantha didn't want to talk about the details. She didn't even want to recall the details. "They never found the men who did it. I vowed I was going to, but I didn't, either. She was murdered for *muti*."

Suddenly Dikeledi was sobbing in her arms. All the tears held back over the past months came flooding out. Samantha just held her and let her cry.

Almost as quickly as they'd come, the tears stopped, and Dikeledi wiped her eyes and nose with her hand. She dug in a pocket of her jacket, pulled out a piece of paper, and offered it to Samantha. "I found this at the bottom of the hill. You remember where it turns into the town? Exactly there." Samantha examined it. It was a handwritten list of items, obviously a shopping list. She noticed the exaggerated loops on the *g*'s.

"It was Lesego's, wasn't it?"

Dikeledi nodded. "I'm sure. And she dropped it there when they took her. I *know* that's what happened, but the policeman didn't believe me. They didn't do anything." The tears were close again.

"I believe you."

"What are you going to do?"

"Next week I'm going to ask at every house close to the bottom of the hill. I'm going to tell them that's where Lesego was abducted. Perhaps someone will remember something. I'm going to find out what happened. And then I'll come and tell you."

Dikeledi digested this without comment. At last she said, "Can I have it back? The list? She left it for me."

Samantha hesitated but, after all this time and handling, the chance of finding any prints on the list was remote. She passed it back to the girl.

"I need to go home now, please. My aunt will be cross if I'm late."

"Of course," said Samantha, and started the car.

NINE

The hospitals had no news for Witness, nor had the morgue. Witness didn't know which way to turn, what to do. So he sat in his house and did nothing.

Late on Saturday afternoon, there was a knock at the door. Witness flung it open, hoping. But it was a police constable.

"I have come about the report of your missing daughter."

Witness waved him to a chair and sat down opposite.

"Rra," the constable began, "please start at the beginning."

For the next twenty minutes, the constable asked questions and made notes.

"Thank you, rra. We'll send your daughter's photo to all police stations and ask them to keep a lookout for her. And on Monday morning, we'll send some men to search the area around the school."

"We've already searched there!" Witness snapped. "We found nothing. You're too late. You should have been here this morning."

"The station commander had no one available this morning. And may not have anyone tomorrow, either. That's why we may have to wait until Monday."

"The police are useless," Witness growled as he showed the policeman to the door. "I'll phone the station tomorrow to see what you've done. And it better be something."

That evening, after waiting well past suppertime in some vague hope that Tombi would return, Witness walked to the BIG MAMA KNOWS ALL *shebeen*, a favorite of his friends. This local bar was named after its proprietor, accurately reflecting her size, her knowledge of local gossip, and her willingness to dispense advice. It was in a small house in the middle of a residential area of sandy streets and few trees. The front rooms had been converted into a single large one, with a few cheap tables and a counter that groaned every time someone leaned on it. On the wall was a pinup, undressed to within a hair of Botswana's laws, and a few faded posters featuring St. Louis beer. The fluorescent lights weren't designed for romance.

None of the neighbors had ever complained about the *shebeen*—there were rumors that Big Mama was a witch doctor. In fact, she was a traditional healer, whose potions were sought after from near and far.

As he walked through the door, Witness was grabbed by Big Mama and lost his breath to a huge hug. "Have courage, my friend," she whispered in his ear. Then, almost deafening him, she yelled out, "Get Witness a beer! Right away! On the house!"

As the evening passed, Witness's friends plied him with several more cartons of Chibuku Shake Shake beer, the cheap local favorite, to cheer him up. But it only made him maudlin.

"What will I do if Tombi doesn't come back? I'll be all alone. There won't be anything to live for."

His friends slapped him on the back and told him to be optimistic—that the police were probably right, and she'd be back on Sunday evening, embarrassed because she'd fallen in love or some such thing and had forgotten to let him know.

"What have I done to anger the spirits?" he wailed. "First my wife, and now my daughter."

"Have another beer," they said. And he did.

Witness had been drinking for several hours when a group of young men and women marched through the door chanting "Vote for Jacob Pitso. Vote for freedom!" They spread out and put pamphlets on every table. Witness grabbed one, angry at the smiles and happiness. He didn't recognize the one face, but where had he seen the other? He'd seen it recently. He grimaced, trying to squeeze the memory into the open. Who was it? Who was it? Then the fog of alcohol lifted for a moment. It was the man outside the school with the girl who had pretended to be Tombi! This was that man, the smiling man. Witness stood up, a little precariously, and pointed to the photo.

"He's evil!" he shouted. "I saw him with a girl this afternoon. He was in her arms. She was just a baby. Like my Tombi!"

One of the young men walked over. "Oh, shut up. You're drunk. Rra Marumo was in Lobatse today, and he'll only be back tomorrow."

"No, he wasn't! I saw him at the school this afternoon. With a girl. He was smiling as though they'd just made love.

Then I saw him on the street—still smiling. He should be flogged at the *kgotla*."

"Go home," a young woman said. "Go and sleep it off." She pushed him, and he staggered against the wall and fell to the floor.

Witness pushed himself to his knees and screamed, "He's the Devil! You are all evil!"

Two of his friends lifted him to his feet, dragged him to his car, and threw him on the backseat. One friend drove Witness's car home; another followed. When they reached the house, they lifted Witness, found his keys, and dropped him on the sofa in his living room.

"He'll be okay," the one said.

"He's not going to feel good when he wakes up," said the other. "I hope Tombi doesn't come home and find him like this."

It was six in the morning when Witness woke up. It took him a few minutes to work out where he was. He was shivering from the cold, so typical of Gaborone nights at that time of year, and felt awful all over. A furry substance lined his mouth, and his head pulsed out a monotonous rhythm of pain. Surprisingly, he was not nauseous.

After several cups of strong tea and a couple of thick slices of bread, he showered, changed, and set off for church. He wanted to be early so he could ask the pastor to say a special prayer for Tombi.

As he waited, he was approached by a man he recognized but didn't know.

"Rra Maleng? I'm Tumiso Mikopi. I live near the Motswedi school. I was in Molepolole yesterday and only heard about your daughter this morning. I'm very sorry to hear that she's missing. You must be very worried."

Witness nodded and shook the extended hand.

"Rra Maleng, I know Tombi, because she sometimes plays with my daughter, Alice. When I was driving home from work on Friday, I saw her walking—"

"Where was she?" Witness was almost shouting. "Where did you see her?"

"She was on the road next to the playing fields."

"Did she look okay? Was everything normal?"

"She looked happy—as though she was dancing."

"Did you see anything else?"

"Well, I parked my car and got my briefcase from the trunk. I looked up the road, but she wasn't there. I thought she must've gone into one of the houses. But I did notice a white car along the road going away from the school. It was too far away to see what type it was, and I've no idea if Tombi was in it. I didn't give it any thought. Then I packed a suitcase and drove to Molepolole to see my sister. Only got back late last night."

"Could you see the driver? Surely you could tell the make of the car?"

Mikopi shook his head. "It was too far. I couldn't see it very well. I didn't recognize it. They all look much the same these days. A few seconds later, and I wouldn't have seen it at all."

"Can you remember what time it was?"

"It must have been around half past five. That's usually when I get home."

"And Tombi looked fine?"

"Yes. She was skipping along the road."

Witness was very restless during the service. He wanted to race to the police station and give them this new information. He sat near the back and gazed at the dirty stained-glass window behind the altar. As the service dragged on, he fidgeted, wishing for it to end. Normally he enjoyed the hymns, but today there seemed to be more than usual. Not one. Not two. But four! And each with more verses than he remembered. He didn't hear the resonant basses and soaring sopranos. His mind was elsewhere, thinking back on the good times he and Tombi had enjoyed, and the things he'd said that he wished he could take back.

Even though he was anxious to leave, he tried to pay attention and draw comfort from the sermon. Witness didn't understand the prolonged and convoluted discussion of Exodus 21:22–25—"eye for eye, tooth for tooth"—and whether the pastor was for or against the concept. All he knew was that if he found the man who had taken Tombi, he'd chop him into little pieces.

After what seemed an eternity, the pastor ended the service by asking the Lord to give Witness strength and urging the congregation to pray for Tombi. However, it was nearly half an hour more before Witness was able to leave. Several of the parishioners wanted to talk to him, to console him, and, of course, to reassure him that Tombi would show up.

When he eventually reached the police, a peeved duty constable raised his voice. "Rra Maleng, please! We'll definitely start searching tomorrow morning. We don't have the staff today. It *is* Sunday."

"And my daughter is missing!" he yelled. "She may be dying! Don't you care?"

"Rra Maleng—"

"She was fine after school. Rra Mikopi saw her. Then she disappeared in a white car! You've got to look for a white car . . ."

The constable came from behind the counter, took Witness's arm firmly, and led him from the building. "Come back tomorrow at lunchtime, rra. We may have some information then."

"You're useless!" Witness shouted. "You do nothing while people are being murdered! Go to hell, all of you!"

Witness took the week off supposedly to look for Tombi. In reality, he spent most of each day either walking up and down the road where she was last seen or moping at home, replaying memories of incidents where he could have been a better father. In the evenings, further depressed by a total lack of progress by the police, he visited BIG MAMA KNOWS ALL and drank increasing amounts of Shake Shake beer. Sometimes he would go outside with Gordon Thembe and they would surreptitiously share a joint. Big Mama wouldn't tolerate that in her *shebeen*. On other occasions he would go on drinking until he ended up picking a fight with someone and being taken home by friends, who were now worried about his state of mind.

"He'll drink himself to death," one said as they dropped him off at home for the fourth time that week.

"If he doesn't get killed by someone at the bar first," replied a second.

On Thursday Witness was walking toward the school when a pickup truck drove slowly by, posters pasted to its side, a loudspeaker blaring.

"The government is destroying the country. It's corrupt and getting worse. What are you going to do about it? Now is the time to stand up to the government and its nepotism. Join us in the fight. Come to a rally on Saturday morning at Motswedi Junior

Secondary School. Come and hear the Freedom Party candidate, Jacob Pitso, and the leader of the Freedom Party, Bill Marumo, tell you how they can make the country strong again. How you can prosper. Believe in yourselves, and we can change the world!"

Witness turned and shouted at the truck. "Marumo seduces young girls! He's unfit for any office! He should be in jail!"

Some of the people on the truck made obscene gestures in reply.

On Saturday morning, Witness woke up with a blinding headache. A week's worth of Shake Shake and *dagga* was catching up to him. He struggled to his feet, swaying unsteadily, then stumbled toward the kitchen to make tea.

As he sat drinking it, he was overcome by sadness. Now he was sure that Tombi was gone; gone forever. His prayers hadn't been answered; the police hadn't turned up anything, and hadn't traced the white car. No one except Rra Mikopi had come forward with any information. As he drooped over his tea, he heard music outside, bright, cheerful music. Then he heard the loudspeaker again, encouraging people to the school where the rally was to start in twenty minutes.

Witness's sadness turned to anger in a flash. It was people like Marumo who were responsible. Rich, famous, with big smiles, they could attract girls like the one who'd impersonated Tombi. Marumo and his friends were responsible for how bad Botswana had become, where nobody had morals anymore, where girls could disappear without a trace for God only knew what reason.

He threw his teacup onto the floor and rushed to get dressed. Then he ran down the road toward the school. A large group of people were headed toward the playing field, which had a small platform set up at one end, surrounded by Botswana flags, alternating with posters of Pitso and Marumo. VOTE FOR FREEDOM posters were everywhere.

"I'll show him," Witness muttered as he neared the school. As he panted into the parking lot, he saw the politicians walking toward the platform.

"Rapist!" Witness shouted and sprinted toward the group. "You're the Devil!"

As he charged, several people tried to stop him, but he shoved them aside. Gordon and another of his drinking friends from Big Mama's, who'd come to see the Freedom Party rally, spotted him and called out. When they saw Witness running toward the dignitaries, they shouted at him to stop, but he didn't hear them. As he reached the front of the crowd, several young men pounced on him and brought him to the ground. He screamed and lashed out, catching one of the men with a glancing blow to the head. But they hung on, shouting for the police. At that moment, Witness's two friends dashed up.

"Don't call the police!" Gordon exclaimed. "We'll take him home. His daughter has disappeared, and he's not himself." Each took an arm. "We'll make sure he doesn't do anything silly." Reluctantly, the men pinning Witness agreed, not wanting a scene. Witness's friends hauled him away from the crowd to their car and drove him home.

They spent the next few hours inside Witness's house drinking beer. The two men tried to persuade Witness that Marumo was just another politician, that his morals were no better and no worse than anyone else's.

"Witness, my friend. You're imagining things. Marumo wouldn't pick up young girls in a public place. And he wasn't even in town that day!"

"Get this nonsense out of your head," Gordon said. "You'll only get into trouble, and that won't help matters."

Witness listened, but he didn't believe. He knew what he knew. Marumo was an evil man. A man without morals. A man who seduced young girls. But, as they spoke, he just nodded, wishing they'd leave him alone.

Eventually, when the men were sure that the rally had ended, they took their leave with a stern warning that Witness should behave. "Listen to us! Don't do anything stupid!"

As they walked to their car, Gordon shook his head. "Poor Witness," he said to his friend. "He lost his wife last year, then he lost Tombi last week. Now he's lost himself."

TEN

Sundays were family days in the Bengu household. Kubu liked to stay in bed late, Joy curled up by his side, and let his mind float in and out of sleep. Later they would drive to Mochudi for lunch with his parents, a tradition that was rarely missed. Finally, in the evening, the family would relax at home.

This Sunday, Kubu woke near seven with the sun streaming through the window. Joy was still asleep, and he could hear that Tumi and Nono were already awake and playing with Ilia in their room. They were obviously teasing the fox terrier, because every time she barked, there were loud shushes from the girls. Kubu smiled, but it faded as he thought of Nono's future.

She and Tumi played well together and enjoyed each other's company. Around Joy and Kubu, she was polite and restrained, and she seemed to regard her temporary home with acceptance rather than enthusiasm. Kubu sighed. They really needed to find her a new home as soon as possible, so she could settle into a new life. But it was very difficult. No one wanted an HIV-positive little girl.

At last Joy stirred and gave him a sleepy kiss. Kubu put his arm over her and pulled her into his embrace. He kissed her neck. "I love you, my darling. So very much." She smiled and snuggled even closer. Just as he was about to kiss her again, the door flew open, and the two young girls burst in. Tumi jumped on the bed, followed by Ilia. Nono stopped at the foot of the bed.

"Mommy, Ilia caught a rat! A big one. It's dead. In the hallway."

This news didn't exactly make Joy's day, so Kubu rolled out of bed to take care of the matter.

"Coffee in bed?" Kubu asked. Joy smiled and nodded. He walked over to Nono and lifted her onto the bed with the others. "Do you girls want cereal for breakfast? With milk and sugar?"

Tumi enthused, and Nono nodded with a shy smile. Kubu smiled back and went to start the day.

The traffic to Mochudi was unusually light, and few cows and sheep had strayed onto the road to slow progress. As soon as they turned into Kgafela Drive, Ilia jumped up and stuck her nose out the slightly open window, tail wagging furiously. She knew where they were. They drove past the Taliban Haircut & Car Wash and the dubiously named Jailbird Security Company. Nono, who had never been outside Gaborone before, looked around with wide eyes.

They arrived at Kubu's parents' house at around noon, earlier than expected. As soon as Joy opened the door, Ilia

bounded up the stairs to the veranda and jumped onto the lap
of Kubu's waiting father. Wilmon patted her for a few moments
and then struggled to his feet to greet his family. Ilia yelped as
she jumped off his lap. At the sound of the car doors, Kubu's
mother, Amantle, came out of the house and stood at the top of
the stairs beaming.

Kubu walked up the stairs and greeted his parents formally,
in the traditional Tswana way. "*Dumela*, rra. *Dumela*, mma."
He then extended his right arm to his father, touching it with
his left hand as a mark of respect.

Wilmon took Kubu's hand and responded solemnly: "*Du-mela*, my son."

"I have arrived," Kubu said. "And I apologize for being
early. The traffic was light."

"You are welcome in my house. How are you, my son?"

"I am well, Father. How are you and Mother?"

"We are also fine." Wilmon's voice was strong, but quiet.

Then Joy reached the veranda, the girls in tow. She and
Amantle embraced affectionately—Amantle had long regarded
Joy as a daughter. Then Joy hugged Wilmon—a nontraditional
greeting that always confused the old man. He obviously liked
the touch but was uncomfortable with the intimacy. Tumi
rushed around demanding to be picked up and kissed, and her
grandparents reciprocated her affection with huge smiles. Finally, Joy introduced Nono, who was hanging back, apart from
the proceedings.

"Come, Nono. This is Kubu's father, Uncle Wilmon, and
this is his mother, Aunt Amantle. Come and say hello."

The girl came forward, accepted a hug from each of them,
and then stood looking around. With her usual enthusiasm,
Tumi said, "Come, Nono, let's go to the garden. Grandfather

has plants for medicine. I know their names!" She glanced at Wilmon for permission. He nodded, and they ran off.

The women went into the kitchen carrying the provisions that Kubu and Joy had brought, leaving the men alone on the small veranda. Wilmon turned to Kubu and nodded thoughtfully.

"I am glad you have another child. It is good for a man to have many children."

Kubu looked at him with surprise. "We can't keep her, Father. We're only looking after her for a few weeks."

Wilmon frowned. "Where did she come from then?"

Kubu sighed. He had told his father the whole story by phone earlier in the week. "She isn't my child, Father. Joy knew her sister. We're just looking after her."

Wilmon shook his head. "You should have more children," he said with annoyance. "You should not look after the children of other people, because they will not look after you when you are old!"

He looked around. "Where are the girls?" He struggled to his feet, causing an irritated Ilia to fall to the ground again. He stepped off the veranda and looked toward the back of the house. "Look! They are in my herb garden." He called out angrily to the girls. "Children! Come out of there right away. Quickly now!"

The girls ran up with worried expressions. Kubu came to their defense. "Father, you told them it was okay to look at the herbs." But now Wilmon was smiling. "Tell me what you saw, girls. Tumi, what are the names of the plants?"

Kubu frowned. His father's thoughts often jumped without apparent connection these days. His mother must have noticed it, too. He would have to talk to her. It was time for his father to see a doctor, but he had no idea how they would persuade him to do that.

Joy had brought fresh tomatoes, lettuce, cucumbers, radishes, and a selection of cold meats and fruits. It wasn't traditional fare, but Kubu liked a generous cold lunch on a hot Sunday. And the older Bengus had also come to enjoy this style of meal. At home, Kubu would wash it down with a generous helping of dry white wine, suitably chilled, and retire for an afternoon nap. However, Wilmon didn't approve of wine on the Sabbath, so Kubu had brought a cooler with the makings of steelworks, his favorite nonalcoholic drink—Kola tonic, lime juice, ginger beer, bitters, and ice.

While Kubu made a pitcher of the drink, Joy and Amantle worked in the kitchen, slicing cucumbers, washing lettuce, halving radishes, and making a fruit salad.

"Nono is a sweet little girl," said Amantle. "It is a pity about the AIDS. It is so sad."

Joy paused. "She doesn't have AIDS, my mother. She's HIV positive. She's had the virus from birth. But she's perfectly healthy right now. As healthy as you and me." She went back to her vegetables.

Amantle continued. "And you must be worried about Tumi. You know how children are. Touching and kissing. I am very worried about her. She could pick it up, too." She finished washing the lettuce. "Do you want to keep Nono?"

"She's just with us for a few weeks. Till we can find her a permanent home," Joy said firmly. "Have you finished the lettuce?"

"I think you want to keep her. I do not mind—everybody needs a family, but you must fix the AIDS problem."

"Fix it? What do you mean?"

"When Kubu told me about it on the phone, I spoke to Wilmon. He knows about these matters. He makes good medicines from his herbs, but not for this. First, we must all pray." She hesitated. "And then Wilmon knows someone who handles such things. A very wise woman. She only deals with good spells and medicines. She can fix the AIDS. But Kubu will have to pay. You will need to arrange it with him."

All Joy's training and education kicked in. Nothing cured HIV. Antiretrovirals only held it at bay—if you could get them. She shook her head.

"Joy? Are you listening to me?"

"A witch doctor? It's not possible. You can't *fix* AIDS. HIV is a virus. You can't wish it away."

"This woman can. You know Funile, who lives by the school? She tested positive. She took the special medicine, and we all prayed. And the next test was negative!"

Joy muttered about false positives, then finished the salad in silence. Amantle let the matter drop. But just for the moment.

When the preparations were complete, they all sat down around the small dining room table. After Kubu poured the steelworks, they joined hands, and Wilmon said grace. Then they all tucked in.

As they ate, Kubu watched the two girls. Tumi picked out the food she liked best, while Nono, as usual, ate everything she was given. She's never had enough to eat before, Kubu thought. That should never happen in a country as rich as Botswana.

When the meal was over, Kubu turned to his mother. "Do you recall the Khama family here? There was a girl called Samantha. She's in the CID now. She works with us."

Amantle thought for a moment. "Yes, it is a good family. I remember Samantha. She was a pretty girl. Is she married now?"

Kubu realized that he didn't know the answer to this most important of questions, so he just shook his head. Amantle continued, "Well, I am not surprised she cannot find a man if she joined the police. It is not a proper job for a girl. She should already have several children." She paused. "It is interesting that you should mention her. I was thinking about her last week."

"Why was that, Mother?"

"I saw Dikeledi Betse at the café. She is the sister of Lesego Betse. You know, the girl who disappeared last Christmas?" She looked at the two children, who were staring at her wide-eyed. "Never mind. She reminded me of another girl who disappeared in Mochudi—Segametsi Mogomotsi. You remember her, of course. It is nearly twenty years since *she* disappeared. The police never solved that case, either. Samantha and Segametsi were very good friends."

Kubu said nothing. This explained a lot about Samantha's behavior.

It was Joy who responded. "The case was never solved because the police didn't care enough about it. Probably they were told not to. It's all part of the corruption in Botswana. The people who run this country are only interested in their own positions. I'm tired of it."

Amantle and Wilmon stared at her. They were not used to Joy straying outside her social role. She was usually the oil that made the family functions harmonious.

Wilmon said, "My child. You were not even alive when Botswana became independent. And you did not live through the period before independence. We had very little. We were poor. But today the country has cities and factories and employment. We can be proud." He nodded and leaned back in his chair with a satisfied look.

"The things we have, we have because of the diamonds," Joy said. "Some of that money went to useful things. But only some of it."

Amantle chipped in. "Joy is right, my husband. They never found who killed Segametsi. And now there is Lesego, and there have been others. Who knows what happens to these girls? The police do nothing or everything is kept secret."

Kubu said, "What you say isn't right, Mother. In fact, Samantha is working on exactly these issues, and I'm helping her. The police are very active in these cases. But they are hard to solve because—"

"Because they aren't seen as important, or there are high-up people involved," Joy interrupted.

The two children sat quietly and looked from one adult to the other. The talk of the murders didn't frighten them—they didn't understand that—but they sensed friction developing. Nono put her hands over her mouth.

"That's why I support the Freedom Party," said Joy. "Marumo may not have all the answers, but at least he's asking the right questions."

Kubu snorted. "I had the pleasure of meeting him last week. I'm sure you all heard about the dog's head at his door? I was sent to investigate. He wasn't interested in *that* at all. He just cared about getting as much publicity as possible for the by-election in Gaborone North. I wouldn't be surprised if he set up the whole thing himself."

"There are stories that he sleeps with many women," Wilmon began, but Amantle interrupted.

"Many people here have heard him speak and have met him. He is trying to make things better. I do not think you should talk about him like that."

Kubu was dumbfounded. On the domestic front, Amantle's word was law. But he had never heard her contradict a man on a matter of business or politics. He realized that he'd underestimated his mother after all these years. Perhaps Joy was influencing her.

"Bongani and Pleasant support him, too," Joy said. "Bongani is a professor. So he knows about these things."

Wilmon shook his head. "These people do not understand that we must preserve our culture and our history. They want everything changed. But change does not always mean that things are better. Sometimes they are only different. Sometimes they are worse." Wilmon leaned back and folded his arms.

Amantle stood up abruptly and started removing the dirty dishes. Kubu could see she was angry. He could see Joy was angry. He could see that Wilmon—stubborn as always—wouldn't budge. How had this discussion got out of hand so quickly? Why was it that women always reacted emotionally instead of weighing the points of discussion? Was this Marumo's secret weapon? That the women believed his façade?

It was Tumi who saved the situation. "Please, Grandmother," she said. "Is there any dessert?" Amantle laughed, the tension broke, and the women went to fetch the fruit salad.

ELEVEN

Thinking about Tombi consumed Witness for the rest of the weekend. And the more he thought about her, the angrier he became. He didn't deserve to lose both his women, both his loves. He felt he was about to explode.

On Monday morning, Witness phoned the police station yet again—with the same result. They had no new information. Witness screamed at the policeman on the phone. "You're all useless! You've done nothing to find my Tombi. You should all be fired!"

He slammed down the phone and, totally frustrated, headed to BIG MAMA KNOWS ALL, even though it was only nine in the morning. When he arrived, he found he was the only patron. He sat down at the counter and, after a few minutes, heard a door slam at the back of the *shebeen*. Moments later Big Mama wheezed her way behind the counter.

"Witness, my friend, it's too early to drink. You must take

hold of yourself." The counter creaked as she leaned on it, her gigantic cleavage looming in front of Witness's face. "And why aren't you at work? It's important you keep yourself busy."

"Big Mama," Witness replied, "I have to understand what's happening to me. I need to do something. I can't sit around and do nothing."

"Some things are just meant to be."

"*Aaii*, Big Mama. I don't believe that. I've always been good to my family. I've worked hard. But I've lost everything. First my wife, now my daughter." He shook his head. "Witchcraft is behind it. Someone has put a curse on me."

Big Mama looked at him, weighing her words. "It may be so. It is indeed strange."

"Who would do that? And why? I've done nothing bad to anybody."

"Perhaps you need help from someone who understands these things."

"But *you* are powerful, Big Mama. People come to you from far away. *You* can explain these things."

"No, Witness, my power is in healing. My medicine is for making people well, not for casting spells, or for removing them. I can't help you." Her upper arms and breasts wobbled as she stood upright. "There is a woman not far from here who is very powerful in such matters. People visit her from all around the country—for help in getting married, or having children, or making money. I'm told she's very successful. But she's also very expensive. You could ask if she will help you. But be prepared to pay many pula."

Witness walked up to the nondescript house surrounded by nothing but sand and a few rocks marking the path to the front door. An elderly man wearing long pants, patched at the knees, and an old sport jacket sat barefoot on a milk crate outside the door. Gray hair curled from underneath a brown fedora.

"*Dumela*, rra," Witness said, standing several yards away.

"*Dumela*," came the reply. Most of the man's teeth were missing and, when he spoke, there was a slight whistle.

Witness stood waiting.

The man looked at Witness but said nothing.

Eventually Witness broke the silence. "Rra, is this the place of Mma Gondo?"

The man pulled a handkerchief from his pocket and wiped his eyes.

"Yes."

"Rra, I'd like to consult Mma Gondo on a problem I have—a daughter who is missing."

The man gazed at Witness without saying anything.

"Rra, I don't know what I must do to see Mma Gondo. Can I make an appointment? And how much will she charge?"

"Tomorrow at ten in the morning. She will tell you how much." The man closed his eyes and leaned back against the wall.

The next morning Witness was at the witch doctor's house with plenty of time to spare. The doors and windows were shut, and the old man nowhere to be seen. Witness waited a few minutes, then walked to the end of the street and back. When he returned, nothing had changed. He wondered if the old man had remembered to tell the witch doctor of his appointment. Now agitated, he walked tentatively around the house. The curtains were drawn behind all the windows. But when he reached the front again, the door was open. Hesitantly he moved toward it, peering into the dark interior.

"Come inside, Witness Maleng." The voice was old and husky. Witness started to tremble. How did she know his name? He edged inside. To his right, through an open door, he saw an old woman with white hair and heavily wrinkled face, sitting on a pile of pillows. Around her shoulders was a heavy blanket even though the day was warm.

"Sit over there." She pointed to a low wooden stool. Witness sat down and waited.

For several minutes, the woman stared at him. He was afraid to say anything.

"You have brought the money?"

"Mma," Witness stammered, "the old man said you would tell me how much. I have brought all I have. Nearly a thousand pula. It's all I have."

The woman continued to stare at him. Witness glanced away. What would he do if it wasn't enough?

Eventually the woman pointed to the floor between them. As she did so, the old man hobbled slowly through the door and put down a wooden bowl. Then he turned and left.

"Put your money in there," she rasped.

Witness pulled a pile of dirty pula bills from his pocket and put them carefully in the bowl.

He sat back and waited.

"Your daughter is missing, and you want to know how to find her." It was a statement, not a question. Witness nodded.

"A girl like your daughter can provide very powerful *muti*. There are people who seek such *muti* to get what they want—power, money, good luck. And there are witch doctors who will help them. They do not think of the children's families." She paused. "*Muti* like that costs many pula. More than you dream about."

The old woman rocked back and forth, eyes shut.

"Your daughter is a virgin?"

"Yes, mma. I believe so. She has no boyfriend."

"Did she bleed each month?"

Witness was not used to such talk and looked at the floor. "Yes, mma. I took her to the clinic before Christmas."

"That is good, but it is also bad."

Witness frowned but said nothing. There was silence for a few moments.

The old woman sighed. "You must seek a man. A man who was nothing and is now everything. A man no one knew and now all know. A man who was weak and now is powerful. That is where you must look. That is where you will find out about her."

Witness was puzzled. He didn't understand. "But where will I find this man? Where must I look?"

"You will know the man when you see him." She turned away.

"But, mma! I don't understand." Desperation was beginning to creep into Witness's voice. He felt a hand take hold of his upper arm. It was the old man.

"Come!" The grip was strong. It led him to the door, where he was blinded by the glare. He turned to argue, but the door closed. He heard the lock turn.

"Big Mama! Mma Gondo took all my money, but she was no help. I don't understand what she told me."

Big Mama pulled a carton of Shake Shake from the fridge and shook it vigorously. "On the house," she said. "Now tell me what happened."

Witness recounted what the witch doctor had said. "She said look for a man who was nothing, and is now something!" he cried. "There are many like that. Where do I start?"

"Sit down, Witness. Listen to me. She's a very powerful witch doctor and wouldn't cheat you. Hear what she said."

"I told you what she said. Nothing that can help me."

"It's very clear to me what she told you to do."

Witness frowned.

"She said you must look for someone who was nothing, who now enjoys great success."

"But where do I start? There must be many like that."

"The man's fortune would've changed since Tombi disappeared. You must look for something that's happened in the last week."

Witness nodded slowly. "But where will I start? Gaborone is a very big city."

"Tombi was stolen from here. Here's where you must start."

"But Big Mama, I've been looking since the day she disappeared."

"Not for the right thing. You've been looking for information, for clues. You must now look for people."

"But where?"

"You paid Mma Gondo for her wisdom. Now trust she will guide you."

Witness walked out of the *shebeen* into the bright afternoon. For a moment he stood blinded by the light and blinked a few times. Then, starting to cross the street, he looked up and saw the man, the man Mma Gondo must surely have meant all along. In front of him, crooked on a lamp post, the man's face leered at him. Bill Marumo! Witness stood staring at that smiling, taunting face.

A man pushing a wheelbarrow of potatoes shouted at him to get out of the street, but Witness didn't hear him. He only moved when a car hooted loudly, the driver swearing at him.

It had to be Marumo; the man was evil. He knew that. Yet, how had Marumo benefited? He puzzled about it for a few minutes, and then he laughed aloud, attracting odd looks from passersby. How easy it was; how clear now that he'd thought it through. The man *hadn't* benefited. *Not yet.*

He turned round and walked back into BIG MAMA KNOWS ALL.

"Witness! You back already?"

"Yes, I'm back. You were right. Mma Gondo showed me." He nodded slowly. Big Mama folded her arms, using them to support her impressive breasts, and waited for him to continue. But he changed tack.

"The Freedom Party," he said. "Everyone says it is impossible for them to win. Isn't that right?"

Big Mama shrugged. "People here have always supported the BDP. A few young people support the Freedom Party, yes. It's Marumo's charisma and his empty promises. But the BDP will wipe him out."

Witness shook his head. "No!" he said. "He'll win. You'll see. Marumo will win." She started to reply, but he turned and walked out. Then he drove home. He was sure he was right, but he'd wait for the election on Friday to be absolutely certain. In the meantime, he'd plan his next move. He was calm now, satisfied in his hate.

TWELVE

Joshua Gobey was an important man but, in his own eyes and those of his wife, not as important as he deserved to be. He was short and thin and had spent much of his life looking up at taller and broader men. He didn't do that anymore. Not since he'd become the head of the key diamond division of the Botswana Police, the section tasked with preventing the theft and smuggling of diamonds from the rich Debswana mines, which formed the backbone of the country's economy. When he spoke, people listened—even his uncle, Tebogo Gobey, deputy commissioner of police.

Joshua arrived early for his appointment, but his uncle's personal assistant showed him in immediately. Tebogo was behind his desk working but rose at once and accepted and reciprocated Joshua's respectful greeting. But there was a touch of reservation in his welcome; too many favors had been requested and granted for

Tebogo to be really warm. He was fond of his late brother's ambitious son, but he was uncomfortable with their relationship within the police. At least Joshua was competent, although not brilliant. Tebogo wondered what had brought him to his office this time.

Joshua closed the office door and chose a chair while Tebogo returned to his seat behind the desk.

"How are you, Uncle?" The voice seemed to indicate real concern. Tebogo frowned. His mind went back to his last visit to the doctors and their useless advice.

"As well as can be expected. They say the emphysema is getting worse. That I must cut out smoking." He shrugged to indicate his reaction to that proposal. "I've cut down. And I have some herbal medicines from a man I know who is a great healer. I'm sure that will help."

"Are you looking forward to your retirement?"

Tebogo smiled. Of course, this was his nephew's interest. "I'm not sure. Maria says I mustn't get in her way at home!" They both laughed.

"I was wondering—" Joshua began, but Tebogo interrupted.

"If I've spoken to the commissioner about my successor?"

"Well, yes."

Tebogo nodded. "He was receptive to the idea of considering you. He has some other possibilities, of course."

"The grapevine says he favors Jacob Mabaku."

Tebogo hesitated. Joshua was well informed. Indeed, the CID director was probably the front-runner. At last Tebogo said, "He's made no decision as yet."

Joshua, too, hesitated. "It's too uncertain," he said at last. "I think we must explore other ways."

"Other ways?" Tebogo frowned, unhappy with Joshua's use of "we."

Joshua leaned back and folded his arms. "Uncle, you're a man of the world, and a very successful one." He leaned forward. "All entirely on merit of course. No fair person would suggest otherwise. But in rising so high, you must have protected yourself from other men. Men intent on bringing you down and replacing you. Men who used improper ways of advancing their own ends."

Tebogo said nothing, wondering how much his nephew knew and where this was going.

"Mabaku now. He's a decent detective, good administrator. But vision, leadership?" Joshua shook his head. "How do you think he came to the commissioner's notice? By solving a murder here or there? There has to be more to it than that."

"More to it?" Tebogo tried to sound puzzled.

"Of course. He's had help. Like you've had help with your lungs. I'm sure you'll have a long, healthy retirement, Uncle. Maria is sure of it." So that's it, Tebogo thought. He's been talking to my wife. Nothing stops the wagging of her tongue.

"What are you asking?"

"I just want to meet the person you use, Uncle. The one who gives you the 'herbal' medicine. So that I can also have some help. Help to ward off what the other candidates are doing. Just so the commissioner can see clearly that your recommendation is the best one." Joshua nodded slowly. "That I'm the best person to succeed you as deputy commissioner. On merit."

So, thought Tebogo. This is the price. In addition to all the pula these witch doctors and healers have sucked from me, I am now sending my brother's son into their clutches— the brother who would never forgive me if he knew. His skin crawled, and his heart sank.

"I'll see if it is possible. I don't know. He can be busy. Or difficult. And expensive. Very expensive."

Joshua nodded again. He had what he wanted. He thanked his uncle and rose to take his leave.

Joshua pulled his BMW 323i up on the shoulder of the dirt track and switched on his interior light to check his uncle's directions. He was in the middle of a poor area, houses little better than shacks dotted over a few acres of stony dust. It wasn't the kind of place he expected to meet a powerful witch doctor. But the hand-drawn map was quite specific, showing the shack on the corner of the track he was on and the one intersecting from the right. He reversed slightly so that his headlights picked out the building. There was no sign of life, and no car was visible. He switched off the headlights and the engine and waited. He'd been told to wait until he saw a light come on inside.

After twenty minutes he was getting irritated. Was this all a waste of time? He checked his watch. He would give it another ten minutes.

Just as he was ready to give up, a reddish light appeared in the window facing the street. It was there for about thirty seconds, then it vanished. He grunted, locked the car, and walked to the makeshift door.

As he reached for the handle he stopped. He had a strong feeling of danger, and his police experience warned him to take such premonitions seriously. He should quietly get back into his car and drive off. Leave this behind him. Never look back.

But that was silly. Then Mabaku would become the new deputy commissioner, commissioner in due course, maybe minister in the government. Just because Joshua didn't have the guts. That's what his wife would say, and she'd be right. He gritted his teeth and pulled open the door.

He found himself in the main room of the house. Its single window was now covered by a heavy blind. In one corner was a table supporting a kerosene lamp. The breeze of the door opening caused the flame to flicker, throwing moving shadows. At the side of the table, with the light somewhat behind it, sat something large. The face had sunken eyes and a baboon snout with exposed teeth. The torso was bare and strong, a leopard skin wrapped around the loins. The baboon head is a mask, Joshua thought. And what right does he have to leopard skin, the mark of royalty? He swallowed. The most powerful witch doctors were said to be shape-changers, becoming baboons or hyenas at will to do their evil work in the night. He felt an urge to run but stood his ground. This man is just dressed up to frighten me, he thought. Like a monster in a horror show for children! It's laughable. He didn't laugh, but he felt calmer.

"Close the door. Sit down." The voice was cold.

Joshua closed the door and paused, waiting for his eyes to become accustomed to the dimness. Then he moved forward to the only other chair in the room, facing the witch doctor and looking into the dancing light.

"My name is Joshua—"

"I know who you are," the baboon man interrupted in a voice that slithered like a snake. "I know what you want. You are here for me to decide if I want to help you, to decide if you are worthy."

"I am the head of the diamond division of the Botswana Police," Joshua said angrily. "I am—"

"I said I know who you are." The words were said softly, but Joshua subsided.

"How are you with women?"

The question was so unexpected that Joshua stammered. "I . . . I . . . I'm strong. With my wife. And there are others. This is not my problem."

The witch doctor seemed satisfied. He thought for a moment. "We need something very rare and very special. A *leswafe*."

Joshua sucked in his breath. "An albino?"

The witch doctor nodded. "Yes, there is great power there. We will take that power for you. Then you will be strong. Not just with women." The last was said with contempt.

"Will I become deputy commissioner?"

"For that answer, you need to find some old man squatting in the street to throw the bones for you. I offer you *real* power, not empty promises sold for a few pula. Don't waste my time."

Joshua swallowed. "When will it be ready?"

"I must find the right one. These things are difficult. When I have him, I will call you. You will come at once, and we will take the power you desire from him."

"I must be here when you do it?" Joshua was horrified.

"Not here. But, yes, you will do it with me. The power is much stronger that way."

Joshua was silent. He realized what the witch doctor was saying. He was to participate in a murder. I will leave now, he thought. I will tell no one this happened. He stood up so that he was looking down at the witch doctor. That made him feel a bit better. Then he sank back into the chair.

The witch doctor nodded, satisfied. "It will be fifty thousand pula."

"That's a fortune! How will I explain the payment of all that money?"

"You are still not understanding! You do not explain. After this you will have power. And you walk that road from this point on with me as your guide. It is very little money. I do it so cheaply as a favor to your uncle."

"I'll need to think about it."

The witch doctor shook his head. "You need to decide now. I won't waste my time with a man who cannot make up his mind. *I* will give you power, but *you* must use it."

Joshua decided to leave. He wanted to escape this evil man with his cold snake-voice. Again he got to his feet, but he realized it was too late. It had been too late once he opened the door of the shack, too late once he'd spoken to his uncle. Perhaps it had been too late after the first time he'd gained something he didn't deserve.

The witch doctor seemed to know all this. "I will tell you when I want the money."

"All right," said Joshua.

THIRTEEN

It was nearly midday on Wednesday, and Kubu was contemplating lunch. Perhaps the café at Game City would have one of its specials—generous and cheap. This pleasant contemplation was interrupted by a knock on his door, and Samantha appeared in answer to his shout. Because of their previous meeting, Kubu's reaction was mixed. Still, he waved her to a chair.

"How's it going?" he asked. Samantha seemed excited. Was it possible that she was actually getting somewhere?

"Well, I've found a few leads. Can I tell you about them? See what you think?"

Kubu grunted, and she continued.

"First, I think Lesego was abducted for *muti*, not as a sex slave. She had something special that may have made her attractive to a witch doctor." She gave Kubu a brief account of her interview with Van der Meer.

"So you think it was her name? She was killed for her name?" He was shocked. Samantha nodded. "Maybe. Then I went to see the family. There wasn't much—nothing they hadn't already told the police. But the girl's sister had something. She'd found Lesego's shopping list discarded at the bottom of the hill leading up to her house. She was sure that Lesego threw it there when she was abducted. If that's so, then we know exactly where she was taken."

"Why didn't the sister take it to the police at once when she found it?"

"She did. They weren't interested."

Kubu grunted again and waited for her to continue.

"I decided to go to each house in the immediate area and tell them that we knew Lesego was abducted there that day—to see if I could get them to remember something." She paused.

Kubu thought this over. Samantha shouldn't have told potential witnesses that the police knew something that they did not. This was hardly police procedure by the book. But Kubu wasn't exactly renowned for going by the book, either, as Mabaku was fond of pointing out. He let it go. "That's a pretty long shot," he said mildly.

"I know. But it paid off. One man I spoke to yesterday said he saw a red car stop at the bottom of the hill. He remembers because it was an odd place to stop—on the curve at the bottom of the hill—and he thought perhaps it had broken down. But when he went out to look, it started up again and headed up the hill."

"Was he sure it was that day? It was four and a half months ago!"

Samantha hesitated. "He thought so. He has a very good memory and remembered other things from before Christmas. But no, he wasn't sure."

"Did he remember seeing the girl?" Samantha slowly shook her head. "Why didn't he tell the police at the time?"

"Well, he didn't see anything suspicious. Anyway, they didn't ask him. The police didn't do much at all. They should react at once when someone goes missing, especially a child. They don't take these cases seriously."

"Maybe so." Kubu was beginning to agree with her sentiments.

"So, I think that she was abducted in a red car that evening. I'm trying to work out how to check up on red cars in Mochudi."

"You realize, of course, that there could be hundreds of other explanations for the car and everything else?" Samantha started to object, but Kubu held up his hand. "Let me finish. Suppose that your whole theory is right. Let's see where that takes us. So, if the abductor wanted her specially—for her name, as you suggest—then he must've known her and where she'd be that afternoon. Perhaps she knew him, too. That would explain why he found it so easy to get her into the car."

"Yes, I also thought of that. That's why I want to try to find red cars in Mochudi."

"Good. But if I were going to abduct a child, I wouldn't use my own car. I'd borrow one, or rent one, or—best of all—steal one. I suggest you take a look at cars reported stolen around that time that turned up a while later, probably undamaged."

"That's an excellent idea, Assistant Superintendent! I'll start with cars reported stolen in Mochudi."

Kubu shook his head. "Probably not there. I'd steal a car somewhere in Gaborone. Much less obvious. And it's only half an hour drive to Mochudi anyway."

Samantha was thinking ahead. "The trouble is the man wouldn't have to know her. Maybe he'd heard about her. Maybe someone tipped him off." She hated the idea of a gang earmarking suitable children for dismemberment, but it was a possibility.

Kubu nodded. "Of course that might be the case. But *some-one* knew her or knew of her, so that makes a personal connection. Did she have a lot of friends? Maybe she had a weekend job? Check if anyone was asking about her at the school—who she was, where she lived, and so on." Samantha was making notes, obviously excited. Kubu realized she was very likely to be disappointed. All this was speculation and would probably lead nowhere.

"Any luck with unidentified bodies?"

Samantha shook her head. "Nothing that fits a girl of that age."

Kubu hesitated. "That suggests that she was abducted to be sold. A witch doctor would have to get rid of the body once he had taken the body parts he wanted for *muti*. So maybe the name is just a coincidence after all."

Samantha bit her lip but didn't argue.

Kubu checked his watch. "Well, it's lunchtime."

Samantha was already on her feet. "No time now. I'll get something later. I want to check up on any car thefts and then start a list of Lesego's friends and acquaintances. I'll need to go back to Mochudi. Thanks, Assistant Superintendent."

Kubu watched her go and heard her hurried progress up the corridor. He'd tried to be encouraging, but her theory was based on a set of flimsy connections. Well, he thought, at least she's keen.

He decided to walk to Game City. The exercise was good

for him, and he'd work up an appetite. Not that that had ever been a problem. He chuckled as he locked his door.

It was Friday afternoon, and Kubu had his feet up on his desk. Although he had eaten a paltry lunch of salads, lovingly provided by Joy, he had managed to invite several of his colleagues for tea in his office. This, of course, enabled him to delve into his tin of mixed cookies without guilt. His eyes were closed, and he was contemplating with pleasure a weekend with his family—time alone with his wonderful wife, and playtime with the always effervescent Tumi. Even Nono was slowly coming out of her shell and was joining the games with some enthusiasm.

As a smile spread across his face, there was a banging on his door. Kubu hurriedly put his feet on the floor and opened a folder on his desk.

"Come in!" he shouted.

Samantha rushed in, obviously upset.

"Assistant Superintendent, it's completely unacceptable!"

"Detective, please sit down. Let me get you a cup of tea. I was just going for one myself. Problems have a habit of shrinking over a cup of good tea and a cookie."

Kubu walked out of his office and returned a few minutes later with two cups of strong tea.

"Here, have a cookie." Samantha took two from the offered tin, and Kubu matched her.

"So, tell me what's happened."

Samantha took a deep breath. "When I started on the Lesego case, I sent a memo to all police stations to let me know whenever someone young went missing. Well, someone from the Broadhurst police station phoned yesterday and told me that a girl had disappeared on the thirteenth. That's nearly two weeks ago!" She took a deep breath. "How will we ever stop these terrible crimes if the police do nothing?"

"Calm down, Samantha. Just because they only phoned yesterday doesn't mean they've been doing nothing. When people go missing, and this is particularly true for kids, they've often just forgotten to tell someone."

"Well, why didn't I hear of it sooner?"

"You *should've* been told right away, but the reality is that everyone is busy, things fall between the cracks. Maybe they don't like the CID interfering in their missing-persons case. Who knows? Overall the police do the best they can, but like everyone else, they're not perfect."

"Aren't you just condoning incompetence?"

"Calm down, Samantha. So, what do you want to *do* about this new case?"

Samantha leaned back in her chair, and Kubu noticed her shoulders relax a bit.

"Well, I want to interview the family. I'd like to get to it right away. I'll go and see if they are home tomorrow or Sunday. It's not far from here, so it should be quite easy. I don't mind working on the weekend."

"Good. Following up soon will improve the chances of making some progress. Please keep me informed." Kubu wriggled in his chair to find a more comfortable position.

Samantha checked her watch and rose to leave. "I must go and vote. I live in the Gaborone North constituency, and I think the Freedom Party might actually win this by-election. Maybe Rra Marumo will help make things change."

Kubu grunted. He wasn't convinced.

FOURTEEN

Witness waited with what patience he could muster for the election. He didn't vote. What would be the point? But he went to the school—Tombi's school—where the result would be announced. Although the constituency was small and less than a thousand people had voted, the count took longer than expected.

It was nearly midnight when the electoral officer led the candidates and party dignitaries onto the platform. The BDP candidate looked shocked. But Marumo had a huge smile, and the young people who'd worked for him erupted into cheering and dancing even before the result was announced. Their man had won by a handful of votes.

Witness stood silently, his fists clenched. At last, he was certain. He was looking at a man who came from nothing to become a man everyone knew. A man whose party had won an unbelievable victory. A man who said he was going to be president. And Witness was sure, too, that Tombi was dead, murdered to give that man the power for this impossible win.

He slipped away and drove home, tears running down his cheeks. But he now knew what he had to do.

It had been easy to find where Marumo lived—a house on Pela Crescent. The telephone directory listed his address. It was that simple.

Late on Saturday afternoon Witness drove across town, found Chuma Drive, and a few moments later saw Pela Crescent on his left. He turned in and followed the road as it circled to the right. And there it was. Marumo's house, surrounded by a high, concrete wall, with a heavy gate blocking the driveway. Witness looked around at the surrounding houses. This is a rich area, he thought. The properties are big, and the houses are set far apart. He was confident he would not be seen after dark if he was careful.

He turned left on the frontage road adjacent to Chuma Drive, drove past the Falcon Crest Suites, and parked a few hundred yards away under some trees alongside Julius Nyerere Drive. There he waited. The sun was setting and purple hues filled the western sky. Soon it would be dark.

Once night had fallen, Witness walked back to Pela Crescent. He had no real plan but hoped that Marumo would return home in the evening. Then he would confront him. He walked to Marumo's house and peered through the gate. There were lights on, but there was no car in the driveway. He moved a short way down the street and slid behind a large bush. Nobody would see him there.

It was less than an hour later when a car drove down the

street and turned into Marumo's driveway. Witness heard the heavy gate sliding open. He jumped up, pulled a knife from his pocket, and slid toward the car. As it went through the gate, so did Witness. The gate trundled shut behind them.

Witness waited while Marumo turned off the engine and got out of the car, briefcase in hand. The car beeped as it locked, and Marumo turned to go inside. Witness stepped forward, grabbed Marumo from behind, covering his mouth with his hand, and pressed the knife against his throat.

"I'll kill you if you call for help. Understand?"

Marumo nodded.

"I need answers. I'm going to take my hand off your mouth. Don't make a sound except to answer. Otherwise I'll kill you. Understand?"

Marumo nodded again.

"If you tell me the truth, I'll let you live. Understand?"

Another nod.

Witness pushed Marumo against the garden wall. He pressed the knife harder against Marumo's throat and took his hand off Marumo's mouth. Marumo said nothing, but he was shaking.

"Turn around slowly." Witness kept the knife at Marumo's throat.

Witness could barely see Marumo's face. Only the whites of his eyes were clearly visible. He pushed the point of the knife against Marumo's throat. Marumo flinched and stifled a cry.

"Do you know who I am?"

"No!" gasped Marumo.

"I am Witness Maleng."

Marumo said nothing, then flinched as Witness pushed the knife harder.

"You know who I am! Don't lie to me!" Witness hissed, jabbing the knife even harder. "Do you remember the girl you stole from the road near Motswedi School? She was my daughter. My lovely daughter, Tombi."

Marumo's eyes darted from side to side, but he said nothing.

"You stole her for *muti*! That's why you won the election yesterday. The witch doctor told me."

"You're wrong. You're wrong! I don't know what you are talking about. I didn't steal your daughter! It's not true!"

Witness pushed on the knife again. Marumo winced, and blood trickled down his neck. "You're lying! My daughter disappeared just before your party wins? When nobody thought it would? I understand these things! You used her for *muti*! The witch doctor told me." Witness's voice was louder now.

"He's lying! I didn't get anything from him!"

"Mma Gondo is a famous witch doctor. She doesn't lie!"

Marumo took a deep breath.

"Listen, she's wrong. I never harmed anyone. Please believe me! Please." Marumo's voice and eyes pleaded with Witness.

"You lie! Tell me the truth, or I'll kill you!" He pressed the knife even harder.

Marumo gasped and pushed at Witness.

"Help!" he shouted, flailing his arms.

Witness lunged forward, slashing at Marumo's face. Marumo screamed, and Witness plunged his knife into his throat. The scream died, and Marumo collapsed, gurgling. Witness fell on him and stabbed him repeatedly until there was no more movement.

"You killed my daughter!" he sobbed. "You killed my Tombi!"

Part Three

POWERFUL TROUBLE

"For a charm of pow'rful trouble,
Like a hell-broth boil and bubble."

MACBETH, ACT 4, SCENE 1

FIFTEEN

Kubu arrived at Marumo's house with his hastily swallowed dessert—Joy's special fried bananas with cinnamon and brown sugar—turning to indigestion. The street was again blocked by police cars, and a uniformed constable demanded identification before letting him through. There was no sign of reporters yet, but it was only a matter of time. And then all hell would break loose. Kubu was glad that Mabaku was on his way.

Kubu abandoned his Land Rover at the gate. He would probably be parked in, but he expected to be at the scene for quite a while anyway. With a sigh, he clambered out and joined the group gathered outside the taped-off area. A technician was setting up a portable floodlight, and a sergeant Kubu had known for many years was battling to write notes in the weak light of the half-moon. Apparently Zanele Dlamini and her forensics team hadn't arrived yet, but the pathologist, Ian Mac-

Gregor, had. He was standing carefully inside the tape wearing latex gloves and shoe covers and shining a flashlight over the body.

Kubu greeted him, and Ian responded with a nod, his attention focused on the spot of light moving from wound to wound. Kubu turned to the sergeant.

"What do we know about what happened?"

The man shrugged. "Marumo's girlfriend discovered the body." He consulted his notes. "Jubjub Oteng. She spotted the car in the driveway. When Marumo didn't come in, she came out to see what was holding him up. She found him here, saw the blood, and screamed her head off. A neighbor, a Dr. Jake Pilane, heard her and came over. He called us. That was about half an hour ago. He's inside the house with her now."

Kubu turned back toward Ian, who was leaning over the corpse to peer at a blood-crusted wound to the throat. The light spilled off the neck and leaked around the dead man, picking out the dried blood on the crushed leaves around him.

"Is that what killed him?" asked Kubu.

Ian shook his head. "I doubt it. Unless it went into the spine. Didn't hit the carotid artery, either, so he didn't bleed to death. Of course, the lungs could've filled with blood over time, and then he would have suffocated."

Kubu frowned. He hadn't liked the man, but the thought of him drowning in his own blood was unpleasant.

Ian was moving the light around the body. "Anyway, he's covered in wounds by the looks of it. Several of them could've been fatal. I'll know better when we've got some more light. So far I just checked that he was dead. The doctor did that also." He shrugged. "But general practitioners aren't used to this sort of thing."

At that moment the technician connected the floodlight, and the sudden glare revealed Marumo covered in blood, staring. Momentarily blinded, Ian pulled back, but then knelt and settled to a more careful examination of the body. Without looking up, he said, "He's got at least ten stab wounds. Could be more. I can't distinguish them without removing his clothes. Looks like the work of a dagger or sharp-pointed knife." He shook his head. "Whoever did this was in a frenzy." He looked at the position of one of the chest wounds. "I'd guess this one hit the heart. I'll know for sure after the autopsy."

Kubu heard a car drive up, and moments later he was joined by Mabaku. He looked without expression at the dead man being examined by the pathologist.

"Do you think he set this up himself, too, Kubu?" he growled. "You'd better hope this isn't the work of the dog killer. The newspapers will skin you like a *duiker*. And I'll help them." He shook his head. "Whatever happens we're in for a media circus. And if the killer is somehow connected to the BDP, it will be a disaster for the government and for the country." He shook his head again and, uncharacteristically, cursed.

"This looks like someone in a frenzy, Director," Kubu responded. "Hardly the work of an assassin. He could've slit Marumo's throat with the knife and been gone in seconds."

"Politicians attract madmen," Mabaku replied sourly. "Ian, how long ago did all this happen?"

McGregor stood up. "Greetings, Director. Now we've got some light, I can get to work. Give me five minutes, and I'll be able to give you an estimate. But I doubt it was more than a few hours ago."

Kubu turned to the sergeant. "Can you organize your men to go door-to-door? Try and find out if anyone noticed anything in the last couple of hours. A vehicle parked in the street, someone running off, shouting, anything."

Mabaku nodded. "Yes, do that. Right now. And keep the damn reporters away!"

A police van arrived and parked behind Kubu's vehicle. "That'll be the forensics team," Kubu said. "We'd better give them some space. I'm going to talk to the girlfriend."

Mabaku turned back to the body. Night insects had been attracted by the floodlight. Some had settled on the drying blood or buzzed around Marumo's open mouth. Mabaku grimaced. He knew he'd have little sleep and no peace until this case was nailed down and the culprit safely locked up in a high-security jail.

"I'll come with you," he said to Kubu.

Jubjub was sitting at the dining room table. She had eye shadow smeared over her face, and her eyes were red and moist; she no longer looked the young consort of an aspiring politician. A half-full cup of tea cooled on the table in front of her.

She ignored the arrival of the two men, so Kubu walked around the table, sat down directly opposite her, and pulled out his notebook. "Mma Oteng, I'm very sorry to meet you again under these awful circumstances. This is Director Mabaku, the head of the CID." Mabaku expressed his sympathies and sat to one side, out of the direct line of the questioning. "Finding Rra Marumo's killer is the CID's top priority now," Kubu continued. "We need you to help us by answering some questions."

She glanced up from the table. "What about the dog's head? You didn't find who did that."

"I know, but we had nothing to go on. This'll be different."

"What do you want to know?"

"Just tell us exactly what you saw and heard."

"I told the other policeman. I heard nothing. I came in here to set the table for supper. Billy was late, but he's often held up at meetings and so on. No one seems able to do anything without him. Anyway, I glanced out the window here and saw his car in the driveway."

"What time was that?" Kubu interrupted.

She thought for a moment. "It must've been around seven. The news program had just started on the TV."

Kubu made a note and nodded for her to continue.

"I thought he'd just arrived and would be in in a minute, so I went back to the cooking—I was making roast chicken and vegetables for him. He likes that. But he didn't come in, so I went outside to see what the matter was. And I saw him slumped against the wall. I thought he'd fallen or had a heart attack or something, so I ran up to him. But then I saw all that blood . . ." Her voice trailed off, and Kubu waited while she got control of herself. "I just started screaming and screaming, and Dr. Pilane came from next door. He called the police."

"Did you see or hear anything before you found Rra Marumo? A shout, scream, anything?"

She shook her head. "I told you I had the TV on in the kitchen. I wanted to see the news because I was sure Billy would be on after the big win. You know. But none of it matters now, does it?" She covered her face with her hands and started to cry.

Again Kubu waited a few moments. "I asked you this before, but please think about it hard again. Can you think of anyone who would want to kill Rra Marumo? Someone who would hate him enough to kill him like this?"

"Billy had lots of political enemies. After the election, the government was really scared of him. He was showing them up for the bunch of self-important fat cats they are. I think they're behind it."

Kubu grunted. Jubjub had been calm and uninterested when he'd interviewed her the day of the dog incident. She'd added nothing to what Marumo had already said, confirming all the details he'd given almost word for word. But now she was deeply shaken.

"Mma Oteng, I'm sorry to raise this issue again, but it could be very important in finding Rra Marumo's killer. Are you sure there's nothing more you can tell me about that incident with the dog's head? Anything you heard or saw when you found it? Please think about it very carefully."

Kubu kept his eyes on Jubjub's face, and eventually she looked down. "Actually *I* didn't find it," she said softly. "Billy found it. He went outside, and a few minutes later I heard him shout. He didn't want me to look, but I did. It was sickening. When I calmed down he said I should say I found it."

"Why was that?"

"He said it was aimed at him, but we'd get a more sympathetic reaction that way. He thought it would help the election campaign." Her voice was expressionless.

Kubu started to ask another question, but Mabaku interrupted. "Never mind who found it." He sighed. "Mma Oteng, does Rra Marumo have parents, brothers, sisters? We need to let them know what's happened."

She wiped her eyes with a tissue and nodded. "I'll give you their details," she said.

Mabaku took on the job of breaking the news to Marumo's parents, but he had parting words for Kubu. "Get on with it,

Kubu. Let's get this wrapped up as quickly as we can. It's obviously an amateur job; we should be able to catch the killer easily. And why pursue the dog head issue? Someone is running around out there with *human* blood all over himself."

"Well, it established that Jubjub lied to us before, so she may do it again. We can't rely on what she told us tonight. Actually, I think Marumo planted the head himself. That means that the two events are probably unrelated. I want to check his car for animal blood."

"There's no point, Kubu. If Marumo did it himself, then it's no longer an issue. And if someone else did it, we haven't been able to trace him. Drop it. Focus on the murder." He turned to leave, but he had a final comment. "Get this business sorted out, Kubu. Otherwise we're both going to have a hard time."

Kubu sighed. At least it had become "we" now rather than "you." He went back into the driveway and found the sergeant who was coordinating the house-to-house questioning.

"Anything turn up?"

The sergeant shook his head. "No one's reported back yet."

"Where's the neighbor?"

"He's in the house with Mma Oteng."

"Well, he's not with her now," said Kubu testily. His indigestion was getting worse.

"I told him to wait. Maybe he's in another room. Maybe he thought Mma Oteng was better left alone."

Kubu pouted. Was he supposed to search the damn house now? He grunted, walked back into the house, and almost collided with a man coming out. He was of middle height, fit looking, and wearing a gray tracksuit. The pant legs were stained at the knees with mud and something else that looked like dry blood.

"Dr. Pilane?"

"That's right. And who are you?"

"I'm Assistant Superintendent Bengu of the CID. I was looking for you."

"Oh. Yes. The sergeant said someone else would want to talk to me."

Kubu didn't want to go back to the dining room; he wanted Pilane on his own. Off the entrance hall there was a side room, a study, the desk cluttered with papers and newspapers. He herded the doctor there, shut the door, and took the chair behind the desk, leaving Pilane to sit on a leather couch along a side wall.

"Please tell me what happened. Everything you can recall in the order it happened."

The doctor hesitated, collecting his thoughts. "Well, I was just back from a run. That's why I'm dressed like this. So I was catching my breath outside my house on the back veranda, where it was nice and cool. Then I heard screaming coming from here. So I ran over to see what was happening."

"Brave of you."

The doctor shrugged. "I didn't think about it. A woman was screaming."

"Do you recall what time that was?"

The doctor thought for a moment. "After examining Bill, I checked my watch to establish the legal time of death. It was seven-twenty-one. I must've heard Jubjub screaming about five minutes before that."

"Did you hear or see anything before you heard her scream?"

Pilane shook his head. "I'd run farther than I meant to. It was late, and there weren't many people about."

"Go on."

"When I got here the electric gate was closed, and Jubjub was standing in the driveway screaming her head off. I got her to calm down and go inside and open the gate. Then I came in and examined Bill." He sighed. "He was stabbed all over his upper body. No pulse, no breathing. Pointless to try CPR."

Kubu thought that Ian might have underestimated this general practitioner. He seemed to know what he was doing.

"Is that how you got the stains on your clothes?"

The doctor glanced at his soiled pants. "Yes. I'd like to get changed and showered as soon as we're finished here."

"We'll want the clothes. I'll send someone with you to collect them when you change."

Pilane frowned. "Is that necessary?"

"We'll be looking for traces of the killer on Marumo's body. Forensics will find particles of material from your clothes. We'll want to eliminate those. Also we'll need your fingerprints—again for elimination purposes." Kubu didn't add that although the doctor's story sounded reasonable, there could be other explanations. A murderer would want to have a believable excuse if traces of blood were subsequently found in his house.

The doctor looked somber and nodded.

Kubu prompted him. "What happened next?"

"I took Jubjub inside and phoned the police. Then I went back to my house, washed my hands, and got her some tranquilizers. She was in a pretty bad way. The police arrived just after I got back. You know what happened after that."

Kubu nodded. "Thank you, doctor. I may need to talk to you again later, but for now let's get your fingerprints and get you cleaned up."

The doctor looked relieved. "Good," he said. "And I could use a strong drink after that."

Kubu left the doctor with one of the forensics people and went to check if Ian MacGregor had any news or if the sergeant had heard from his door-to-door team. He found the forensics team going about their business and Ian packing up his tools. Kubu looked at him inquiringly.

"Rigor mortis hasn't set in. Maybe a trace in the eyelids." He shrugged. "And his temperature has only dropped about two degrees. There's some lividity developing, though."

"And that means?"

"I'd say he died sometime after half past six. Certainly not before six."

Kubu thanked him and walked to the gate to look for the sergeant. From there he could see that a noisy crowd had gathered at the police roadblock. He felt another twinge of indigestion. The press had arrived. He tried to reach Mabaku on his cell phone, but there was no reply. He turned away. He wasn't going to face this music on his own.

SIXTEEN

When Witness eventually woke up on Sunday morning, he was curled in a ball clutching the bedclothes, eyes tight shut. One pillow was near his feet, the other on the floor. He felt totally drained, despite sleeping for more than twelve hours.

The previous night was a blur. He remembered standing in the garden, the darkness broken by slivers of light from the house windows and streetlamps, and looking at Marumo's body motionless on the ground. He remembered thinking that somebody must have killed Marumo, because there were dark stains on his shirt, a slash across his face, and a black stripe down his neck. Or had *he* killed him? He had a vague recollection of trying to stop Marumo from making a noise.

Witness pulled himself into a tighter ball. He lay still for some time, flitting in and out of sleep. Eventually he uncurled himself and opened his eyes for the first time that morning.

The sun was already high, judging by the shadows of the windowpanes. He glanced at his wristwatch. It was noon. He looked again and caught his breath, shocked. His hand was covered with a dark brown stain. So was his arm. He looked down. He was still wearing his clothes, and his shirt and trousers were covered in brown stains, too. He was still wearing his shoes!

He couldn't remember getting into bed.

He couldn't remember what had happened.

Witness lay there for another hour trying to bring the previous night into focus. He decided he must have killed Marumo and felt some satisfaction about revenging Tombi's death. The man was a murderer! But had he meant to kill him? A confession would have been enough, so he could take him to the police. Had he changed his mind? Slowly it came back to him. Marumo had pushed him and shouted for help even though he'd promised not to harm him if he kept quiet. He'd had no choice then.

It was nearly three in the afternoon, and Witness was still in bed. He was no longer curled up but was lying on his back, hands behind his head, his brain now clear. Behind his closed eyes, he recalled Marumo's terror. He was not Mr. Smiley Face when he had a knife against his throat. Oh no! He was like anyone else in that situation—terrified. Witness smiled. The man deserved to die. Tombi's spirit would be happy.

But now he had to think about what to do, and for the next hour he pondered his options. He eventually decided that nobody could possibly know that he'd killed the smiling Marumo. Nobody had seen him; of that he was sure. He had no police record, so no one would suspect him. All he needed to do was wash his clothes and polish his shoes to make sure there was no blood on them. Just in case. Then he'd take a shower and clean himself. Finally, after dark, he would wash the seat in his car in case any blood had come off his clothes.

And if someone asked him where he was on Saturday evening, he'd say he had driven over to the Broadhurst Mall and walked around. He knew it well. He would be convincing.

He had a plan! He couldn't see how it could go wrong.

Suddenly his reverie was shattered by a loud banging on the door.

"Witness! Witness! Are you there?" It was Big Mama. Witness didn't move.

"Witness! Open up! I've got to talk to you."

Witness curled up and pulled the blanket over his head.

"Witness. It's Big Mama. Let me in."

Witness lay still. A few moments later, he heard footsteps crunching on the sand outside his window. Fortunately the window was closed; otherwise Big Mama would have been able to pull the curtain aside and peer in. Then the footsteps continued around the other side of the house. Finally, he heard a car start and drive off.

Did she know? he wondered. Had she guessed it was him?

It was nearly evening before Witness dragged himself from his bed. He stripped and put his clothes in the sink full of hot water. He added soap and kneaded the pile for about five minutes. Leaving the clothes to soak, he took his shoes and wiped them carefully with old newspaper. He'd burn that later. Then he took shoe polish and gave the shoes a good coat, followed by a brisk brushing. When he'd finished, he returned to the sink and rinsed his clothes a couple of times. He wrung as much water from them as he could and hung them from various places in the bathroom. They would dry by morning in the arid Botswana air.

Finally he showered, needing extra time to scrub the brown stains from the back of his hands. Looking in the mirror, he noticed that one side of his face was also stained. He washed that vigorously, too. When darkness fell, he would take care of the car.

SEVENTEEN

Mabaku looked around the meeting room and checked his watch. Five to eight. Eleven people were already present, most with a hot drink, several chatting quietly. Ian Mac-Gregor, the pathologist, was sipping coffee with a grumpy expression; clearly he wasn't an early riser, especially on a Sunday. Zanele Dlamini, the head of the forensics team, looked fresh and attractive as usual, despite having been up most of the night. The others were detectives. He'd asked his assistant, Miriam, to phone around and call in every available CID detective. Even Samantha Khama was there. He didn't really expect much from her, but it was important that she wasn't excluded, and she'd learn from being involved in a murder investigation. She was sitting next to Zanele and chatting, obviously delighted to find a female colleague, and a senior one at that.

Mabaku had a bad feeling about this case. A pessimist by nature, his fear was that there was more behind the murder than a lone madman. And if it led back to the BDP, there was going to be trouble. He sighed. He didn't believe the government was responsible. For all his bravado, Marumo hadn't really been a danger, at least not yet. He was probably more of a threat as a martyr. And assassination simply wasn't the way things were done in conservative Botswana. But it could be the work of a hotheaded BDP supporter and, if that came out, the situation would deteriorate rapidly.

Eight o'clock. Where was Kubu? He sighed again. Having breakfast, of course. He was relying on Kubu, whose flashes of intuition illuminated his carefully pieced together cases. But he had his blind spots. And he never missed a meal. As if on cue, Kubu hurried in, carrying a mug of tea and two cookies, and squeezed himself into a chair between Ian and Samantha. Mabaku spotted crumbs on his shirt.

So here was his team: ten detectives led by Kubu, Zanele for forensics, and MacGregor, the pathologist. Thirteen counting himself. Not a lucky number.

He cleared his throat, and at once everyone was quiet.

"You all know why we're here. You've heard the news. I want it clear that this is top priority. I spoke to the press already this morning, and so far they're supportive. But I indicated that we expect to make an arrest soon. Probably this week. If we don't get them something quickly, they'll turn critical, start raking up the dog head thing and so on." He gave Kubu a dirty look.

"Jacob Pitso has declared himself leader of the Freedom Party and is calling for a massive demonstration on Parliament

Drive this afternoon to protest what he calls the assassination of Marumo and to demand the government's resignation." Detective Thibelo grinned. Mabaku glared at him. "I'm glad you think it's funny, Thibelo. These sorts of demonstrations can get out of hand very quickly and lead to all sorts of trouble." Thibelo became serious at once. "At least that's not our problem. I just hope the demonstration is handled sensibly and doesn't turn nasty.

"Let's get on with it. Kubu is in charge of this case, and he gets anything he wants. Is that clear?" Without waiting for a response, he continued: "Let's start with Ian and Zanele, and then I'll hand it over to Kubu."

Ian put down his cup and examined the notes he'd brought with him. "Time of death between six-thirty and seven-fifteen," he said in his soft Scottish accent. "I haven't done the autopsy yet, but I cut his clothes off when we got the body to the mortuary. Fifteen wounds, all in the chest and abdomen except the face slash and the stab in the throat. All from the front. From the angle of entry, it looks like a right-handed assailant and, from the look of the wounds, I'd guess it was a one-sided blade. Maybe a pointed kitchen knife or the like. I'm pretty sure one of the stabs went into the heart." He shrugged. "That's about it. I'll get to the autopsy right away, but I'll be surprised if it turns up anything dramatic." He paused, but no one had any questions.

"Zanele?"

"Yes, Director. We basically worked through the night, but we haven't got that much to show for it yet. We're not sure how the murderer got onto the property. There's a six-foot wall around it. Maybe he pulled himself over the wall, or maybe he was waiting near the gate and slipped in when Marumo drove through. Anyway, we couldn't pick up any traces from the outside of the wall.

"But we're pretty sure we know how he got out. There's a tree in the corner of the garden where the body was found, and he climbed that. We found blood on the trunk and some snagged threads of material, too. Then he jumped down from the top of the wall onto the sidewalk. And there were bloody shoe marks on the sidewalk outside the house. Probably he stepped in blood at the scene, and it was on his shoes. We got a couple of nice clear shoe prints." She consulted her notebook and, in the pause, Samantha stuck up her hand. After Mabaku's permissive nod, she asked, "What size?"

"Ten to eleven. Bigger than average."

Kubu nodded to Samantha. "Big feet. Probably a big man. Useful." Then he asked Zanele, "Did you pick up any fingerprints?"

She shook her head. "Some smudges, but nothing useful. The bark was too rough."

"All right, go on."

"Various foreign fibers were vacuumed from Marumo's clothing. We're pretty sure that some are the same as the material on the fence, and some are from the doctor's tracksuit. Some seem to match the dress that Jubjub was wearing."

Kubu interrupted. "She said she hadn't touched the body." Then he relaxed. "But maybe she kissed him goodbye that morning."

"There's lots of other stuff. Dirt from Marumo's shoes, dirt or blood under his fingernails, what could be the assailant's hair, or his own, or Jubjub's. We need some time."

"That's exactly what we haven't got," Mabaku growled. Zanele was doing her usual good job, but he was disappointed.

He'd hoped for some nice clear fingerprints to match with the database. What they had so far would help convict the killer, but wouldn't help catch him.

"Kubu?"

Kubu filled them in on the interviews with Jubjub and the doctor. "And I managed to raise someone at the Freedom Party last night, too. She confirmed that Marumo was there till nearly six-thirty p.m. He couldn't have been home much before seven p.m. So I think we can be pretty certain that he was killed around that time. That agrees with what Jubjub and the doctor told us, and with Ian's assessment. And we have a witness of a sort." He hesitated, and Mabaku leaned forward. A straw to grasp?

"The door-to-door questioning last night turned up a lady who'd heard someone running. From her front window she saw quite a large man running toward Chuma Drive. But she saw him from the back, and it was dark so she can't really describe him or his clothes. She didn't think he was dressed like a jogger, and she said he was running as if someone was chasing him. She didn't see anyone else, though. But she noted the time: seven-fifteen p.m." Mabaku scowled. The straw hadn't kept him afloat after all. "That's about it at the moment," Kubu concluded.

Mabaku thought it over, but nothing further occurred to him. "Where do we go from here?"

"Well, we'll expand the door-to-door. And also see if anyone saw anything suspicious *before* the killing. I'd guess the murderer got there earlier and was waiting for Marumo either outside the gate or in the garden. He must've parked his vehicle nearby. The *Daily News* tomorrow will carry an appeal to anyone who knows anything or saw anything to come forward;

we'll get lots of false leads that we'll still have to follow up. I want to interview the Freedom Party people and Marumo's family members about enemies and threats he may've received. Then check Marumo's house for clues. We'll need to check phone records and bank statements. There's lots to do. I'm grateful for the help."

Mabaku nodded. It didn't look as though they'd make his one-week deadline. He checked his watch. He needed to brief the commissioner.

"Well, let's get to work then," he said.

EIGHTEEN

It was mid-morning by the time Kubu returned to Marumo's house in Pela Crescent. With Mabaku's suggestion in mind, he'd asked Samantha to join him. She'd been pleased, even though it meant putting off her visit to the Malengs. But the morning had not added much to what they already knew. Marumo had political enemies—plenty of them—but they were more likely to stab him in the back than in front, as Kubu wryly told Samantha. Of course, they would follow up on those, but Kubu was not optimistic. He feared they were looking for a madman, and if he had no obvious connection to Marumo, he'd be hard to find.

They found Jubjub calm with her mother and brother in attendance. Kubu greeted them, introduced Samantha, and then explained that they wanted to look through the house. Jubjub had no problem with that and showed them around.

Kubu decided to start searching in the study, where he'd interviewed the doctor. Jubjub left them there and returned to the consolation of her family.

"What are we looking for?" Samantha asked.

Kubu rubbed his chin. "Something like a threat note, maybe bank records, large amounts of cash, anything unexpected. I don't know yet. But we'll know when we find it."

He sat at the desk and thought about Bill and about the house. The house was in a good area, and although not new, it had been extensively renovated. The furnishings were good quality. Not ostentatious, but certainly not cheap. And Bill's car was a relatively new Toyota Fortuner. Plenty of money had gone there. There was no doubt that Bill was wealthy. Where had all the money come from? Not from a member of parliament's salary. Perhaps he'd inherited it.

Samantha was looking through the bookcase. She pulled out a book by Karl Marx.

"*The Communist Manifesto*! Do you think Marumo was a communist?" She sounded shocked.

Kubu shook his head. "Certainly not a Marxist. He was far too fond of the finer things of life. It's probably from when he studied political science at university."

Relieved, she returned the book.

Kubu pulled on latex gloves and turned his attention back to the desk. There was no diary, but there was a laptop computer. He'd leave that to the experts. There were three drawers. The top one contained pens and stationery, the second old checkbooks, correspondence, and what looked like a draft speech. He skimmed it but found nothing of interest. He flipped through the check books, too. There were some large payments but nothing that caught his attention.

The third drawer was locked.

Kubu dug in his pocket for the bunch of keys that Zanele had found on Bill's body. He chose one that looked right, but it was hard to fit. Looking closer, he saw that the casing around the lock had been scratched and bent. That was interesting. He fiddled until the key slipped into the lock and turned.

At first he thought the drawer was empty, but when he reached to the back he felt a smooth, roundish object. He pulled it out and placed it on the desk. It was a yellow-brown gourd, the top of which was sealed with what looked to be an ordinary wine cork.

"Take a look at this, Samantha. I'm not sure what to make of it."

Samantha was searching under the cushions of the couch where Dr. Pilane had been sitting the night before. She dumped the cushions in a pile and walked over to the desk.

"Don't!" she said sharply as Kubu reached to uncork the gourd. "It's *muti*."

Kubu pulled his hand back. She could well be right. *Muti* would be in a natural container, something the ancestors would recognize and appreciate. Hide, wood, gourd. Not metal or plastic. His hand tingled. He wished he hadn't touched the object at all. God only knew what it contained. Suddenly he recalled Marumo's lack of concern for his safety. Perhaps he believed himself protected by magic. Then Kubu recalled Marumo's unshakable confidence in his political future. And the recent shocking election upset. The skin crawled on the back of his neck.

"What're you going to do?" Samantha asked.

"Get me an evidence bag. We'll see what Zanele's people can make of it."

Dog's heads, gourds of *muti*. Marumo was certainly mixed up with something unpleasant. But could it be connected to the murder? Had he raised some demon, either real or imaginary? Kubu shook his head to clear the fantasy. A real man with a real knife had killed Marumo for a reason that was real, at least to him. Find the reason, find the clues, find the man. It was very unlikely to have anything to do with black magic and a gourd containing an unpleasant but probably harmless mixture.

Yet he felt a chill, and was glad when the gourd was safely stowed in an evidence bag, out of sight.

NINETEEN

Witness didn't sleep well on Sunday night. The enormity of what he'd done had started to seep into his consciousness, and he wondered how he'd turned from a God-fearing man into a murderer. But *murderer* was too strong a word, he thought. Yes, he had killed the smiling Marumo, but he hadn't really intended to. If Marumo hadn't shouted for help, he wouldn't have tried to keep him quiet.

However, the realization that he *had* killed frightened him. What would happen if the police tracked him down? He couldn't imagine spending the rest of his life in jail—with real killers, and drug pushers and addicts. What would his friends think?

He tossed and turned and began to wonder whether his simple plan of cleaning all his clothes and the car was enough. What if someone had seen him, seen his car near Falcon

Crest Suites at the time of the murder? There were cameras everywhere these days. What if one of them had recorded his comings and goings from Pela Crescent? Or maybe there was a security guard at one of the fancy houses near Marumo's. That big house with metal gates with diamond-shaped centerpieces surely would have a night watchman. What if he had seen Witness running by?

Sleep continued to elude him as these thoughts swirled through his head with increasing frequency and greater ferocity.

Maybe he should get out of town for a while. Get work at one of the diamond mines. Get a long way from Gaborone until he could be sure the police had nothing on him.

What had he to lose? He probably couldn't get his job back, because he hadn't told them about taking time off. He had hoped they'd understand and be supportive of his mission to get Tombi back. But after two weeks? They'd probably hired someone to replace him by now.

And what had he left in Gaborone? A few friends, certainly.

And bad memories.

After a fitful night, Witness eventually dragged himself from bed around 7:30 a.m. During the night he had decided to pack his belongings and head off for either Orapa or Jwaneng. He'd call both mines to inquire whether there were any jobs available.

Once there, he'd ask someone to find a tenant to rent his home—probably Big Mama would be best. She knew everyone in the area. He needed to get some money quickly—the witch doctor had depleted his savings.

He made himself a cup of strong tea and cut a thick slice of bread, which he covered with jam. He sat down at the table and started to think through what he would have to do before

he left. After a few minutes, he realized there was little to do—
pack his clothes in the tattered suitcase on top of his cupboard,
fold his only sheets and two blankets and put them in plastic
bags, put his plates and cups, knives and forks, and pots and
pans in a box, take whatever was in the fridge, and leave. He'd
then stop on the way out of town and draw the final pula from
his bank account.

Witness drained his second cup of tea and walked out to his
car to fetch some plastic bags. He'd just opened the hatchback
when a Toyota Corolla stopped outside his house. It was about
ten years old, but clean. The owner looks after it, he thought.
A short, thin woman in her late twenties, maybe early thirties,
walked over and asked, "Rra Maleng?"

Witness nodded, puzzled as to who the woman could be.
She extended her hand, which he shook, surprised by its firmness.

"Rra Maleng. My name is Samantha Khama. I'm with the
Botswana Police, Criminal Investigation Department."

Witness didn't respond. He was in shock. How had they
found him so soon?

"Do you have a few minutes?" she asked, glancing at his car.
"May I come in?"

Witness looked at her. She was alone. He wondered
whether he could knock her out and get away before she regained consciousness. "Of course," he stammered.

Once inside, he pointed to a chair. "Please," he mumbled.
He wondered if she had a gun in her purse. He'd have to be
careful and try to get the purse out of her reach. He sat down,
facing her.

"Rra Maleng. I live not far from here, on Dedia Street in
Extension 33."

Witness nodded, wondering why she was taking her time.

"It seems there are a lot of bad things happening in this area at the moment." She glanced at Witness waiting for a response. He sat impassively, jaw clenched, and his foot tapping furiously.

"First your daughter—I'm so sorry that she's missing. And now Bill Marumo."

Witness had to clasp his hands together to stop them from shaking. When was she going to accuse him?

"I only heard about your daughter last Friday. The Broadhurst police let things slip. They should've reported that she was missing to me immediately. I really apologize for that."

Now Witness was puzzled. Why didn't the policewoman get to the point? He stared at her.

"Rra, are you all right?" she asked, frowning.

Witness nodded.

"Rra Maleng, please tell me about the Friday evening when Tombi went missing." Samantha took out her notebook.

She's not here about Marumo! he thought. She doesn't know! He took a deep breath and started talking.

"It was a terrible day." The words came out in a croak. He cleared his throat and continued. "I was at home cooking supper . . ."

"You were cooking supper?"

"Yes. My wife died last year . . ."

"I'm sorry. Please continue."

"As I was saying, I was at home cooking supper. . . ."

For the next half hour Witness recounted the fateful weekend when Tombi disappeared—the community coming together to help search for her, the father of one of Tombi's friends who saw a white car drive off in the distance just after he'd seen Tombi on her way home, the prayers at the church, the lack of interest by the police. But the worst was the waiting and waiting for her to come home.

Samantha didn't interrupt his story but sat quietly taking notes. When he stopped talking, she asked for clarification on a number of points, including the name of the man who had seen the car, something that hadn't appeared in the police reports. Eventually she closed her notebook.

"Rra Maleng, have you heard of Lesego Betse?"

Witness shook his head. What was this about? he wondered.

"She was a young girl who we think was killed for *muti* . . ."

Witness gasped at the mention of *muti*.

Samantha leaned forward and touched his knee. "I don't know whether that was what happened to Tombi, but it's a possibility. My job at the CID is to investigate missing children, so I want you to think whether any men were paying attention to her. Did she ever mention anything to you?"

Witness relaxed again. "I never saw anything like that, and she never mentioned anything to me. Maybe you should speak to her school friends."

Samantha opened her notebook again and took down the details.

"Rra Maleng, please let me know if you think of anything or hear anything. Anything at all. Anything you haven't told me. It could be important." She gave him her card.

She stood up and extended her hand. "Thank you for your time. My sympathies again."

Witness was so weak from stress that he was barely able to stand to walk her to her car. As the Toyota disappeared, leaving a trail of brown dust swirling above the sandy street, Witness stared after it. "Thank you, Lord," he said out loud. "You know what I did was just."

He turned and walked back into his small house to resume packing.

Fifteen minutes later, he carried his suitcase, the plastic bags, and boxes to his car. He returned to the house, closed all the windows, drew the curtains, and gave one last sad look around the house where he'd lived for the past seven years. He wondered whether he would ever see it again.

Witness locked the door and drove away. He'd call the mines when he was far from Gaborone.

TWENTY

Kubu looked around the table at the assembled CID staff. Mabaku looked worried. Not much had changed in the last thirty-six hours to give him comfort. If anything, the issue of the gourd that Kubu had discovered made things worse. It seemed likely that Marumo had been involved in something very unpleasant. That would open a gamut of new potential motives and possibilities.

Samantha looked disturbed and unhappy. Her hopes of Marumo as a hero had been dashed by his murder. And by his use of *muti*.

Mabaku turned to Zanele first. "What have you got, Zanele?"

She shrugged. "Not much more, Director. But we have two pieces of hair that don't come from Marumo or Jubjub. Black African, I'd say."

Mabaku perked up. "That's good. If we catch a suspect and can DNA-match the hair, we're home."

Zanele nodded. "Doesn't help us find the murderer, though."

Mabaku already knew that. "What about Kubu's gourd?"

For a moment Zanele said nothing. "It's not good. It's a mixture of all sorts of stuff. Some common herbs and so on. But we've looked at it under a microscope, and I'm sure that it contains animal remains. There's a reasonable chance they're human."

Kubu looked around the table again, assessing how the team was taking this news. Samantha clasped her hands tightly in front of her and avoided his glance. Ian MacGregor looked as relaxed as usual. Mabaku frowned, obviously concerned about the new complications. The others looked uncomfortable or plainly scared.

"We have to find out what it is and where it came from," Kubu said. "We already have the dog's head issue. Now we're talking *muti*. There was always something about Marumo—I admit I didn't like him—but there was a confidence that was unnatural. Definitely unnatural."

"You think it could link to motive?" Mabaku growled.

Kubu shook his head. "Once you're mixed up in this sort of stuff, it could be anything."

"You're not suggesting a demon or a *tokoloshe*?" It was the beefy Detective Thibelo who asked this in a tentative voice.

Kubu looked at him sharply. "No, of course not, we all know that's nonsense." He stopped and glanced at each of the other CID detectives in turn. He got several nods in response, but they didn't meet his eyes. "But there could be witch doctors who need to be paid, maybe relatives seeking revenge, perhaps someone wanted to steal the so-called magic. I don't know. There are lots of possibilities now."

Mabaku looked unhappy. "We keep this quiet. You all understand? We don't want to alert the culprit if there is a connection, and we certainly don't want a media field day. Marumo supporters will say it's a smear and link us to the government. This doesn't go outside this room."

Kubu nodded firmly, but he wondered about it. People had seen him bring in the gourd; people had seen Zanele working with it. He was pretty sure it was already an open secret.

"It may be the best lead we've got. Ian, can you get your friends in South Africa to help us get the DNA information quickly?"

Ian nodded. "I'll see what I can do." He paused. "As for the autopsy, nothing unexpected there. One of the stab wounds went into the heart, as I thought. He would've died very soon after that."

"What have the rest of you got for two days' work?" Mabaku's tone suggested that it had better be something.

Thibelo stuck up his hand. He's regained some courage, Kubu thought.

"We've done door-to-door." He looked at his notes. "Not much to report, but one man noticed a beaten-up blue Volkswagen parked outside the Falcon Crest Suites. There's a place there where you can pull off the road. It's a short walk from Marumo's house. He noticed it because it looked out of place. He thought perhaps it had broken down. He'd taken his dog for a walk, and when they came back the car was still there."

"What time was that?" Kubu asked.

"He thinks it was about seven when they came back."

"Any chance he remembered all or part of the registration number?"

Thibelo shook his head. "He was sure it was a local number. But that's all."

Kubu sighed. An old blue Volkswagen that might possibly be involved didn't offer much to go on. Mabaku started to say the same thing, but Samantha interrupted.

"I'm sorry, Director. It's just . . . Well, it's a really long shot, but . . ."

"What?" asked Mabaku, irritated.

Samantha hesitated. "I interviewed a man called Witness Maleng this morning. It was about the disappearance of his daughter. When I first arrived he seemed very nervous. I even had the feeling he might not talk to me. He calmed down a bit, but he was very bitter about his daughter. He felt the police hadn't done enough soon enough to find her. I think he believes she's been abducted for *muti*."

She paused, and Mabaku interjected, "You think he could be connected to Marumo because of the gourd?"

Samantha nodded. "I was thinking about what Kubu said about relatives. And his car was a battered blue Volkswagen Golf."

Suddenly there was complete silence around the table. All were focused on the first distant scent of prey.

Kubu shrugged. "Maybe he was nervous that you had bad news about his daughter. We don't even know if the Volkswagen Golf was connected to the murder, and there must be dozens of them around." Samantha started to protest, but Kubu held up his hand. "Having said that, it's definitely worth following up. I'd like to do that right away."

Mabaku nodded. "I agree. As soon as we've finished." He recalled the *Daily News* report that had run in the morning and turned to the detective who had been manning the phones. "Anything from the public on the hotline?"

"Half the callers were sure the government was behind it," the man replied. "Some just phoned to have their say. Then there were a few cranks. One confessed, but he didn't even know where Marumo lived. We'll follow up what we can."

So this is what we have, Kubu thought, a gourd of *muti*, a blue Volkswagen Golf near the scene, and a bereaved man. It was tenuous, but he had a hunch there was a connection.

TWENTY-ONE

It took Witness less than two hours to drive to Jwaneng. He turned off the Trans-Kalahari Highway and followed a sign to the Circle Filling Station. He was pleased to see that it had a Chicken Licken fast-food restaurant next to it.

He put two hundred pula of gas into the car—leaving him with less than a thousand. He asked the cashier to let him look up the number of the Jwaneng Mine in their phone directory. Then he called the mine, and the switchboard put him through to Human Resources. They said there were vacancies, and he arranged an interview for that afternoon at four o'clock. He felt his luck was about to change.

It was not yet noon, so he decided to find a cool spot and try to sleep.

* * *

Witness dozed on and off until about an hour before his appointment. He returned to the gas station and used its toilet facilities to wash and tidy up as much as possible.

Half an hour later he presented himself to the receptionist at Human Resources, filled out the usual paperwork, and waited for the interview. It was brief, and he was finished by 5 p.m. They would contact him in the next two days, he was told.

Witness was in a quandary about what to do. Should he wait in Jwaneng until he heard whether he had the job—working in the pit—or should he drive to Orapa and apply there? The problem was that Orapa was about an eight-hour drive, which would cost him a large portion of his remaining money.

He decided to wait in Jwaneng, particularly since the man who had interviewed him seemed positive. He found a liquor store and bought two cartons of Shake Shake beer. Then he went to the Chicken Licken and walked out with a large order of LekkerBig chips and a packet of Soul Fire sauce. He drove around until he found a place, a little out of the way, where he could park for the night and sleep in his car.

He hoped he would sleep better—another night of Marumo's terrified face popping into his mind would not be good.

Still, he felt his luck had turned. He'd get the job at the mine and would disappear from sight.

TWENTY-TWO

Kubu and Samantha waited until about five before they left for Witness's house; they decided to drive separately since Samantha lived close by. As Kubu followed Samantha's old Toyota, he wondered what to expect from this man who had just lost a daughter. Could Witness Maleng have turned his grief into rage and then murder? And, if so, why Marumo? Or did he somehow know that Marumo had *muti* in his desk? Did he think some witch doctor had killed his daughter for Marumo? As for the blue Volkswagen, there were many on Gaborone's streets. Was it just a coincidence that a car that looked like Witness's was parked near Marumo's house on the night of the murder? The man who reported the car hadn't seen it in the neighborhood before.

Kubu thought it unlikely that Witness was responsible for Marumo's death, but they needed to check it out. After all,

Mabaku was on a mission. If they left a single stone unturned, there'd be trouble.

Kubu pulled in behind Samantha, climbed out of his Land Rover and joined her in front of the small house. The curtains were drawn, and there was no Volkswagen in the drive.

They banged on Witness's front door, but there was no response. They circled the house but the windows were closed.

"Let's check with the neighbors. You take that one. I'll take this." Kubu walked to one of the houses and knocked on the door, but there was no reply. He glanced at his watch. It was nearly half past five. Maybe they haven't got back from work, he thought.

He looked over to see how Samantha was faring. She was talking to an elderly woman, so he walked over to join them.

"This is Mma Bule. She's been at home all day," Samantha said, closing her notebook. Kubu nodded as Samantha continued. "She saw me this morning, and says Maleng drove off after loading his car not long after I left. She doesn't know where he was going."

"*Dumela*, Mma Bule," Kubu said. "How's Witness been since his daughter disappeared?"

"Eish." She shook her head. "I think the spirits are in him. Ever since Tombi didn't come home, he's been a different person. He loved her very much, and, after his wife's death, this must be too much for him. Tombi was such a good girl. They were always happy together."

"How did his wife die?" Kubu asked.

"Of the AIDS! They were very happy together, then she told him that she had it. Witness was very angry that she wouldn't tell him how she got it. She died very quickly—just over a year."

"Did he talk to you about who may have taken Tombi?"

"No. Everyone tried to help, and we looked everywhere. It's so sad. Then he started drinking, and many times I saw his friends bring him home late at night."

"Do you know where he went to drink?"

"Everybody around here goes to BIG MAMA KNOWS ALL. It is a *shebeen* not far from here, on Letsopa Street."

Kubu glanced inquiringly at Samantha. She nodded. "I know where it is."

"*Aaii*. He was angry. Sad and angry." Big Mama wiped her brow with a dishcloth from behind the bar. "Until Tombi disappeared, he didn't come here very often. Never drank very much and was always quiet. I think he preferred being at home."

Kubu and Samantha didn't say anything.

"But after Tombi couldn't be found, he started coming here a lot. And drank too much. Sometimes he was so drunk that his friends had to take him home." She looked at Kubu. "I tried to stop him, but he wouldn't listen. He drank and drank and would sometimes cry into his beer. It was so sad. He loved Tombi so much, especially after his wife died. She was all he had."

"Did he ever suspect anyone of taking Tombi?" Kubu asked. "Did he ever mention anyone who might have done it?"

Big Mama shook her head.

"No. Eventually he thought someone must have put a curse on him. He said it was the only way to explain why a good man like him could lose everyone he loved."

"Did he suspect anyone?" Samantha asked.

"No, but I suggested he visit Mma Gondo."

"Mma Gondo?" Samantha asked quietly. "Who's she?"

Big Mama looked at her curiously. "Everyone knows Mma Gondo. She's a very powerful witch doctor."

Kubu stiffened, and Samantha inhaled sharply.

"Big Mama," Kubu said taking out his notebook, "tell me about Mma Gondo. Everything you know."

Big Mama pointed to a small table in the corner. "Sit there." She then went through the door behind the counter.

Kubu and Samantha looked at each other, then walked over to the table and sat down. A few moments later, Big Mama re-emerged with a tray on which there were three plastic glasses, a pitcher of water, and a Tupperware container of ice cubes. She filled the three glasses, pushed the Tupperware container into the middle of the table, and sat down.

"Help yourselves to ice."

She leaned back in the chair.

"About a week after Tombi disappeared, Witness came to me and said he was convinced that someone had put a spell on him. There was no other reason that made sense. He was a good man, then his wife died, and now his daughter had disappeared. It had to be a spell."

She took a deep drink.

"He wanted me to confirm this."

"Why you?" Kubu asked.

"He thought I was a witch doctor. But I'm not. I'm a traditional healer. Anyway, I told him about Mma Gondo. Now she *is* a witch doctor—a powerful one, known far and wide."

"Does she deal in *muti*?" Samantha interrupted.

Kubu raised his hand, indicating that she should be patient.

"Yes, she does. But not in human body parts, as far as I have heard. Animals, yes. Plants, yes. But not humans."

"Did Witness see Mma Gondo?"

"Yes. He told me he was very disappointed. He said he had spent nearly all his money, and all she had said was that he must look for a man who was nothing, and is now something. He was very angry, because he didn't know how to find such a man in a big city like Gaborone. He said there must be hundreds of men like that."

Big Mama shook her head.

"Sometimes men don't listen. I told him when the time was right, he would recognize the man. I didn't convince him, and he stormed out."

"Is that all? Did he say what Mma Gondo had told him about *muti*?" Samantha was getting frustrated.

"I haven't finished. Mma Gondo didn't talk about *muti*, only about who may have benefited from it. Anyway, a few minutes later, Witness came back and said he knew who Mma Gondo meant and started talking about Bill Marumo and the Freedom Party. He said that they were going to win the by-election. I told him that was impossible because the BDP always wins in this area, by a large margin. He told me to wait and see. Then he left."

She took a deep breath and looked at Kubu.

"And the Freedom Party did win—against all odds," he whispered.

Big Mama nodded.

"And Bill Marumo was murdered right after." Samantha's eyes glistened with excitement.

"Was that the last time you saw Witness?" Kubu asked.

Big Mama nodded, then hesitated. "I went to his house to look for him yesterday. I was worried after that talk about the Freedom Party and then the news about Marumo. I think Witness was in the house because his car was there, but he didn't answer when I called him. So I gave up."

The three of them sat quietly for a few moments.

"There's one other thing," Big Mama said. "A few weeks ago, just after his daughter disappeared, Witness went to a rally for the local Freedom Party candidate, Jacob Pitso. Marumo was also there. Witness tried to attack him. Luckily some of Marumo's supporters stopped him before he did any harm."

"Did he tell you why he went after Marumo?"

"No. But people I spoke to said Witness called him the Devil and accused him of being a rapist."

"A rapist?" Samantha asked. "I haven't heard anyone accuse him of that."

"It was nonsense," Big Mama replied. "He was very mixed-up."

Kubu struggled to his feet. "Thank you, Big Mama," he said, a little self-conscious at using that name. "Thank you very much."

As soon as they left the *shebeen*, Kubu phoned Mabaku and told him what Big Mama had said.

"I'm going to get a constable over to Witness's house in case he comes back," Kubu concluded.

"Good," Mabaku replied. "And I want you to come to the office now to fill out a search warrant application for his house. I'll phone Judge Lope to alert him we need the warrant signed this evening." He hung up.

That's Mabaku, Kubu thought, a bit miffed. Not long on positive reinforcement.

"How will the courts regard a revenge killing?" Samantha asked. "Especially if that *muti* you found at Marumo's came from Witness's daughter."

Kubu shrugged. "Nothing's clear when *muti* is involved. Everyone's scared that a spell will be put on them. I think you're going to see the ball passed along the line like a hot potato."

"That's why *muti* murders never stop," Samantha cried. "Nobody has the guts to stand up to the witch doctors. If the president had a daughter, and she disappeared, maybe things would change."

Before Kubu could answer, his phone rang.

"Assistant Superintendent Bengu," he answered. He listened for a while.

"Are they sure it's not at his office?" He frowned.

"And you've searched the house and his car?" He listened to the answer.

"And the garden?" He nodded.

"I'll send someone there right away to get the details. Thank you very much for calling me." He pressed the red button on his cell phone.

"That was Jubjub Oteng, Marumo's girlfriend," he told Samantha. "The new head of the Freedom Party just phoned her asking for Marumo's briefcase. It has important party documents in it. Apparently they saw Marumo take it with him when he left the office on Saturday evening. Jubjub checked in his car and around the house but can't find it. Please go and speak to her and get a detailed description. Check also whether she knows what he may have had in it. Then do the same at the Freedom Party offices. If it's still missing, let all the local police stations know and also the garbage haulers. They should all keep a sharp lookout for it."

Samantha nodded. "I'll see if anyone at the Freedom Party headquarters has a photo of him with it. That'll help."

"Good thinking." Kubu nodded. "Also, talk to the woman who saw the man running from Marumo's house. Ask her if she can remember whether he was carrying something. Call me when you've finished. I'll probably be at Witness's house if we get the warrant. Maybe the briefcase is there."

Samantha left and walked to her car. Kubu stood deep in thought. If we don't find the briefcase, maybe it was a politically motivated murder, he thought. The country doesn't need that. He shook his head.

I'd better give Joy a call, he thought. Tell her I'll be late. And to put my dinner in the oven. He grimaced. He detested dried-out meals.

TWENTY-THREE

When Zanele arrived at Witness's house, Kubu was already there. She spotted his Land Rover first, and then saw him standing at the front door. He was talking to two policemen who had just come out of the house. Obviously the assistant superintendent had obtained the needed search warrant, and they had broken into the house already. She sighed as she pulled in next to the Land Rover. She doubted that they'd been careful not to disturb things inside, but she accepted that the house had to be secured before she and her team entered.

She jumped out of her car and directed the driver to park the forensics van next to the house. Then she walked quickly to the others.

"Hi, Kubu. All clear? No one inside?"

Kubu nodded. "According to these two." He nodded toward the two constables. "I'll come in with you."

Zanele nodded. Not much harm could be done now. She liked pristine crime scenes—ready to test her skills and insights like science experiments. This house didn't look as though it would be that way. She waited while her team unpacked equipment and everyone put on latex gloves and plastic bags over their boots, and then they all entered the house.

The front door opened onto a living area that included a couch and two lounge chairs, a scarred wooden dining table with four mismatched chairs, and a small kitchenette. The room testified to a departed owner. Cupboard doors stood ajar, revealing empty shelves. Zanele pulled out a drawer and found nothing inside. Kubu carefully opened the fridge and found it empty also, and the interior light didn't come on. It had been turned off at the wall. The kitchen was stripped.

They moved on to the next room, a small bedroom off the living area. It contained a double bed with a worn mattress and a cheap two-drawer bedside table made from a wire frame and woven reeds. No bedding. There was a rickety clothes cupboard, and it too was empty. Kubu shook his head and muttered something Zanele didn't catch.

There was another bedroom, which was even smaller, hardly more than an annex off the living room. Judging by the magazine pictures stuck to the wall, it had been the daughter's room.

"He's on the run," Kubu said, looking angry. "Damn! I should've sent out an APB as soon as we'd talked to Big Mama."

Zanele wondered what he was talking about, but she wasn't really interested. She was focused on the task at hand. She was now in the small bathroom, just a washbasin, shower in one corner, and toilet. The cistern was cracked and sweated a little, but the room was clean. Their suspect was a good housekeeper, or maybe he'd cleaned the room recently. She felt a twinge of excitement. She liked bathrooms. They always revealed secrets no matter how carefully scrubbed. She called over one of her men.

"Jonas, have you got the fluorescein and the ultraviolet light? Bring it in here."

Using a swab, she collected a sample of brownish stain from around the plug hole. Then she sprayed the basin with the fluorescein mixture, and shone the lamp into the basin, carefully positioning it to pick out a hairline crack in the porcelain. It fluoresced. So did the ring where the plug hole met the sink.

"Kubu, there's blood here. Doesn't prove anything, of course. Not yet. We'll have to test the sample. Doesn't have to be human at all, or he could have cut himself shaving. Let's look around some more."

They walked back to the living room, and Zanele found more blood traces in the kitchen sink. Kubu said nothing, but his eyes roved around the room taking in the signs of the hasty departure. Jonas called out from the larger bedroom that there was a blood smear on one leg of the bed also.

"It's him," Kubu said suddenly. "There's the blue Volkswagen and what Big Mama told us, now the bloodstains, and why did he suddenly take off after talking to Samantha? He killed Marumo all right. We just have to find out why. And I'd bet that his missing daughter and that *muti* we found at Marumo's house are involved somehow." Zanele looked up, puzzled at the mention of Big Mama, but Kubu hadn't finished. "Damn! I've let him have a head start. I've got to get hold of Mabaku right away to send out an APB. Then I can finally eat my dried-out dinner if Joy hasn't given it to Ilia!"

After he'd gone, Zanele was left in peace with her team and her crime scene, checking for fingerprints, scraping up blood samples, packeting hairs, collecting soil particles and even a leaf that might be traced to the murder scene. They worked quietly, efficiently, knowing what to do, starting to build the case against Witness Maleng piece by tiny piece.

TWENTY-FOUR

It was already 9 a.m. when Kubu walked into his office. His late dinner and his inability to shut down his mind had caused a poor night's sleep. He fetched a strong cup of tea, then sat down to a stack of notes. On top was one from Samantha—*0800: Please call me when you get in, S Khama.*

The note felt formal, which made Kubu realize that he was already thinking of "S. Khama" as Samantha. He reflected for a moment. That's a good sign, he thought. If that's how I'm thinking of her, she must be doing a good job.

He phoned her and asked that she come to his office in fifteen minutes. He still needed to attend to the other notes.

"I've two things to report," Samantha said as she settled in one of the chairs in Kubu's office. "Last night I went to see Marumo's girlfriend. She says that he always had the briefcase with him.

He never even left it in the car if he went into a restaurant or meeting. She swears he would've had it when he arrived home."

"And you checked with the woman down the road, who saw the man running?"

"Yes. She thought he might've been carrying something, but she wasn't sure. I don't think we learned anything from her."

"And the police who responded to the call?"

"I spoke to them, too. None of them remember seeing it."

"I didn't see it, either," Kubu said, "but I arrived a bit later. What about the doctor?"

"He says the same thing. He didn't see it. He says whoever murdered Marumo must have taken it."

"Did you check with the Freedom Party?"

"Yes, I went there last night. There were still people working. They confirmed that he always had the briefcase and wouldn't have left without it. They gave me several photos with him holding it. It's nothing special and didn't have any distinctive markings. I circulated one of the photos to all the police stations and rubbish disposal people."

"Did the Freedom Party people say what was in the briefcase?"

"They said the most important was the party's plan for the next election. If someone in another party got hold of it, it could really hurt their efforts. They claimed that the murder and theft of the briefcase were both politically motivated, probably by the BDP."

"Why would the BDP do such a thing?"

"They say the BDP is running scared after the by-election and will do anything to stop the Freedom Party."

Kubu felt depressed. "And I suppose Zanele and her crew found nothing, either?"

"Well, they didn't find the briefcase," Samantha said, glancing at Kubu, who leaned back in his chair. "It's starting to sound like a politically motivated murder."

"That's the last thing we need," Kubu groaned, shaking his head.

"I also checked that the APB went out last night," Samantha continued. "The *Daily News* will have a short article in today's paper, but there won't be a photo. And some of the TV stations will broadcast a request this morning for the public to keep their eyes open for a Witness Maleng. I sent them all a copy of the picture on his driver's license. Not very good, but better than nothing."

"Excellent," Kubu responded. "We'll go and see if we can find the witch doctor he consulted, but I've no idea whether she'll be there. We'll just have to take our chances."

"I wouldn't know how to contact a witch doctor." Samantha frowned. "Would you?"

"No. But I'm sure if you wanted one, all you'd have to do is put out the word and you'd get several phone calls."

"It's weird, isn't it? They're all phonies, yet they're such a big part of our culture. People actually believe in them. In this day and age." She shook her head. "I would've thought we knew better today."

"As long as people believe in them, they'll be around—whether we think of them as charlatans or not." Kubu stood up. "Let's go and meet one."

Following Big Mama's scribbled directions, Kubu negotiated his Land Rover through the dusty streets until they found the witch doctor's house.

"She can't be doing very well," Kubu said wryly, as he looked at the nondescript structure. "I wonder if that's her receptionist." He pointed at an old man who was sitting outside the house on a milk crate.

"*Dumela*, rra," Kubu said. "We are looking for Mma Gondo."

The old man slowly stood up. Kubu thought he could hear the man's knees creaking.

"She is not available now. Only by appointment. Who wants to consult her? And for what purpose?"

Kubu pulled out his police badge. "If she's here, I need to see her now."

The old man squinted at the badge.

"She is very busy, but I will see what I can do."

A few minutes later, the old man gestured that Kubu and Samantha could enter the house. Once they were in, he pointed to the side room. "There."

As their eyes slowly adjusted to the darkness, they saw an old woman wrapped in a blanket. She had white hair and a heavily wrinkled face.

"Sit over there." She pointed to two low wooden stools.

Kubu and Samantha sat down and waited.

The old woman stared at them. Eventually she spoke in a husky voice.

"You want to know about Witness Maleng." It was a statement, not a question.

Samantha gasped. "How did you know that?"

The old woman ignored her.

Kubu nodded. "Yes, mma. We *are* here about Witness Maleng."

After a short silence, she spoke. "He came to see me after his daughter disappeared." She paused again. Kubu and Samantha said nothing.

"His spirit was disturbed and angry. He said he had lost all he had. He wanted to know what had happened to his daughter and whether someone had put a spell on him." Another pause.

"I told him to look for someone who had recently been nothing and was now something."

"Why did you say that?" Samantha asked eagerly.

Mma Gondo turned her head slowly and stared at Samantha. "*Muti* from a young girl is very powerful. It is used to bring success and power."

"And you believe that nonsense?" Samantha's voice was tinged with anger.

"Samantha. Please listen to Mma Gondo."

"Your friend does not believe in the spirits." Mma Gondo nodded. "But she will learn."

"Mma Gondo," Kubu said quietly. "Did you suggest that Rra Marumo was responsible for Witness's daughter's disappearance?"

"Why would I do that?"

"Big Mama told me that he came to her *shebeen* thinking that Marumo was going to win the election even though no one thought he could."

"You think he killed Rra Marumo?" The old woman looked into Kubu's eyes.

"Yes, mma. He is a suspect, but we don't have final proof yet."

"You asked if I mentioned Marumo's name. No, I didn't mention *anybody's* name. I told him to look for someone whose luck had changed. That is the way of powerful *muti*."

"Do you make *muti*?" Samantha blurted out.

Again, the old woman stared at Samantha.

"Of course."

"From children?"

"My child. You know so little. It is not allowed to make *muti* from humans. And it is not proper."

"But you said you made *muti*!" Samantha's exasperation showed in her voice.

"*Muti* does not have to use human parts. Most witch doctors do not do that. They think it angers the spirits—harming one person to benefit another. Our *muti* uses herbs and barks and flowers. And sometimes we use parts of an animal if we can get them—from a cow or a lion. But never human body parts."

"But some witch doctors do?"

The woman nodded slowly.

"Mma Gondo," Kubu said quietly. "We need your help. Do you know anyone who would use human body parts to make *muti*?"

"You understand what you are asking?" She looked into his eyes. "If I say anything, a *tokoloshe* may kill me when I sleep. Or I may get very sick. Or my children may disappear. Witch doctors who make *muti* using humans are very powerful. The most powerful."

Samantha took a deep breath and was about to speak, when Kubu touched her on her shoulder and shook his head. He could sense the anger in her.

"Mma Gondo. You said yourself that killing people for *muti* is a bad thing."

Gondo nodded.

"But you know it happens. And unless we stop it, unless we find the few witch doctors who commit such terrible deeds, it will never stop."

Mma Gondo nodded slowly.

"I am told," she started hesitantly, "that there is such a powerful witch doctor here in Gaborone. He is much feared. But he is invisible. No one has seen him. All are scared of his powers, so they don't speak of him or seek him out."

"So how do people get *muti* from him?" Samantha looked puzzled.

"Perhaps he has the power to know when someone wants such *muti*," Mma Gondo answered.

"This is nonsense!" Samantha was losing patience. "People pay for *muti* like this. A lot of money, I believe. How do they pay someone who is invisible? It's nonsense."

"My child. You are young and keen to stop people harming others. That is good. But you do not yet understand the power of witch doctors. But you will learn."

"Mma Gondo. We need to know who this powerful person is. We need you to tell us." Kubu too was getting exasperated.

"I do not know who it is, and even if I knew, I would not tell you. It would be known immediately, and I would suffer from many bad spells. But I hope this thing stops. It is bad for all of us."

"Mma Gondo. You must tell us! This is a murder investigation. I don't want to have to take you in for questioning."

"You can take me in, Rra Bengu, but I have told you all I know. If I knew who it was and I pointed in his direction, my life would be at an end. I do not want that."

Kubu saw he was getting nowhere. "Do you know of any other witch doctors who also make such *muti*?"

The old woman shook her head and pointed to the door.

As they were walking back to the car, Kubu's phone rang. He listened to the caller for a few moments, then hung up.

"That was Zanele. Marumo's gourd definitely had human tissue in it. As far as they can tell from a preliminary DNA test they did on hairs they found at his house, it wasn't Witness's daughter's, though. At least that is their initial finding. A more thorough analysis will be available next week."

"Was it from the girl in Mochudi?"

"They haven't checked that yet. They'll have to get a DNA sample from her sister. It was more important to try and tie it to Witness's daughter."

"What did you make of Mma Gondo?" Samantha asked as she climbed in the Land Rover.

"I believed her when she said she didn't know who the witch doctor is. But it's useful to learn that there's at least one witch doctor here who uses human body parts. And she did give us one small clue. She said it was a man. I don't think she would have said that by accident." He turned and looked back at the house.

"All we can hope for is that he will make a mistake some time. They always do. We just have to recognize it."

Again Kubu's phone rang.

"Mr. Director. You have? Where?"

He listened for a short time.

"Jwaneng. He's applied for a job?"

Again he listened.

"Here's what I suggest. Ask the mine to call him and tell him they want to give him a job. They should ask him to come to the mine in a couple of hours to finish the paperwork. Please contact the Jwaneng police and tell them to be at the office at that time. They should be discreet. We don't want him to get wind of what is happening. We should have no difficulty arresting him there. He won't be expecting us."

Samantha looked at Kubu.

"Ah, yes," he responded to some comments from Mabaku.

"If he sees that, he'll try to get away. We should put road blocks on the A2 on either side of Jwaneng. There are no other roads he's likely to use. Of course, all this assumes he stayed in Jwaneng to hear whether the mine wanted him. But I suspect he did."

After a few minutes, Kubu hung up.

"As you gathered, Witness Maleng has applied for a job in Jwaneng. Someone in HR read the article in the newspaper and recognized his name. We're lucky someone is awake. We're going to try and arrest him there this afternoon."

He smiled. "Progress at last!"

TWENTY-FIVE

When he woke up, Witness was ravenous. The previous night's beer and chips just weren't enough. He hadn't slept well, and he had a very stiff neck. Optimistic about the job in the mine, he decided to splurge and have a decent breakfast. He drove back to town and found a small eating place that served *pap* with a palatable sauce. He washed it down with a large glass of Coca-Cola.

He wondered how to kill a day or two in this little town in which he knew no one. *I'll walk around to see what it's like. It's not that big.* So after breakfast he started walking.

About an hour later, about 10 a.m., his phone rang.

"Rra Maleng?"

"Yes?"

"This is Jessica from Jwaneng Human Resources. I'm pleased to tell you that we want to offer you a job. Can you come into the office at noon?"

Witness's heart jumped. His premonition had been right.

"Of course. Thank you so much. The same place as yesterday?"

"Yes."

"Will I start work today?"

"No. You can start tomorrow or the next day."

"Thank you. Thank you. I'll see you at noon."

He hung up, elated.

He started walking again, a spring in his step.

With plenty of time left before the meeting, Witness strolled around the shopping center, which had the usual assortment of stores. After window-shopping for nearly an hour, he wandered over to an outdoor kiosk for a cold drink. He picked up a copy of the *Daily News* to see if there was anything about Marumo. He gasped. There on the front page was a headline, SUSPECT SOUGHT IN MARUMO MURDER CASE. Flustered, he pulled out some coins and paid for the drink and newspaper. He walked away to read the article.

The Botswana CID is looking for Witness Maleng, who is a suspect in the murder of the Freedom Party's Bill Marumo last Saturday. A police spokesman told reporters that Maleng had apparently fled his house on Monday morning, taking all his possessions. The public is asked to keep an eye open for him and to report to the police immediately if he is seen. He is regarded as very dangerous.

Unfortunately a photograph of Maleng was not available at the time of going to press.

Witness's hands started to shake. He had to get out of

Jwaneng immediately. What if the mine had seen the article? They'd arrest him on the spot.

He walked as fast as he could, face down, to where he'd parked his car.

He wasn't sure what to do. Should he go back to Gaborone, where there were lots of people? Or should he try to make a dash for South Africa? It was easy to walk over the border between Makopong and Bray. He decided to wait outside town until dusk, then head south to the border.

"Miriam, I've got to see the director immediately." Kubu was breathless after hurrying from his office.

"Sit down, Kubu," Mabaku's personal assistant responded. "Or you'll have a heart attack. The director's on the phone with the commissioner. I don't think he'll be long."

Kubu sat down and fidgeted. Then he stood up and stared out the window at Kgale Hill. "Come on, come on," he muttered to himself. "I've got important news."

He sat down again and picked up a copy of the latest *Police News*. But before he could start reading it, Miriam told him to go in.

"Director," Kubu blurted as he came through the door. "Bad news! I just had a call from Jwaneng. Maleng didn't show up for his appointment at the mine. He should've been there over an hour ago. He must've picked up a newspaper and seen the report."

"Sit down, Kubu. And calm down."

Kubu settled in one of the armchairs. He was about to speak, when Mabaku continued.

"That's too bad, but it isn't the end of the world. The road-blocks are in place around Jwaneng?"

Kubu nodded.

"He's probably waiting for dark. Or he may have tried some back roads. But where's he going to go? Back to Gaborone? Unlikely. To Namibia? We've got roadblocks on the Trans-Kalahari Highway. The only real possibility is South Africa, and that's a long way south."

"He could walk across the border. He doesn't have to go through an official border crossing."

"Alert all border crossings to be on the lookout for him. Also, as far as I know, there are only two ways out of Jwaneng other than the A2. One goes south, and the other loops around back toward Kanye. Have roadblocks set up on both of those, but quite far away from Jwaneng. If we're lucky, we'll get him."

"Yes, Director," Kubu said glumly. When the initial call had come in from the mine, he'd thought the manhunt was nearly over. He heaved himself to his feet. "All we can do is wait."

Witness sat in the car on a sandy back street with a hat pulled over his face in case someone walked by. He thought it was still two or three hours to when he could slip unnoticed across the border. At about 6 p.m., as the sky darkened quickly, he decided to leave.

As he turned onto the Trans-Kalahari Highway toward Sekoma, worries crowded his thoughts: What if the police caught him? How could he explain what had happened? What if he couldn't? How would he survive in jail? He'd heard terrible stories of what happened there.

Still, he thought, Marumo had got what he deserved—raping young women, using *muti*, and who knows what else. Bastard.

It was now dark, and he was driving quite slowly because

his headlights were bad. Suddenly he noticed a police road-block ahead. He knew these were common—usually checking driver's licenses and the roadworthiness of the many older vehicles that populated Botswana's streets. Part of him cautioned him to stop and let the police do their job; another part wanted to make a run for it. The police were obviously searching for him and would arrest him at once—if they recognized him. He pulled his hat lower over his face. He dithered as he slowed down. Should he take his chances and stop?

Just as he was approaching the policeman who was flagging him off the road, he panicked. He pushed the gas pedal to the floor, and the old Volkswagen picked up speed, scattering orange traffic cones. He could see policemen waving at him, and he was sure they were shouting, too.

He looked in his rearview mirror. People were dashing for their vehicles. In seconds they would be after him. The Volkswagen continued to pick up speed. There were rattles everywhere, and at 60 miles per hour the steering wheel developed a severe shake. He held on, continuing to gain speed. At 75 miles per hour, the shaking stopped.

Now he was going too fast for his dim headlights to give him warning of something in the road. He peered forward. Faster, faster he went. Now the speedometer was showing 85 mph.

The road swept to the left. He pulled on the steering wheel, and the car shuddered. He glanced in the mirror. Nobody in sight yet. Maybe he could pull off the road and turn his lights off. They would drive right past. Or if he could get to Sekoma before they caught up with him, he could just disappear. But that was hopeless, Sekoma was almost an hour away.

Suddenly his feeble lights picked out something in the

road. A cow! Witness pulled to the left, but it was too late. The Volkswagen hit the animal and skidded sideways. Witness screamed as the car rolled over. It tumbled four or five times in a cloud of dust before coming to rest on its side next to the fence, whose purpose was to keep livestock off the road. The only sound was a hissing from the engine and a repeating squeak as one of the wheels rotated slowly.

Constables Ngema and Sesupo approached the car cautiously, flashlights probing.

"Oh God, can you smell that?" Sesupo shouted. "Petrol is leaking. It's all over the place."

"He's still in there!" Ngema said, pointing the beam of light at a bleeding head. "Help me push the car over."

"What if it catches fire? We'll be fried."

"We can't just leave him there. Give me a hand."

The two men rocked the car a few times, then gave it a big push. It rolled back onto its wheels. Sesupo tried to open the driver's door, but it was jammed. He ran around to the other side, but the passenger's door was stuck also.

"Call an ambulance!" he shouted to Ngema. "I'll knock out all the glass. Maybe we can pull him out through the windscreen." He started banging on the shattered glass with his nightstick. When it was all gone, he climbed on the hood and stretched into the car, just managing to reach Witness's wrist.

"He's still alive," he said to Ngema, who had just returned.

"The ambulance is on its way. Should be here soon. It only has to come from Jwaneng."

"Let's see if we can get him out."

It took only a few attempts for the men to see that Witness was jammed by the steering wheel.

"I'll get a crowbar from the car." Ngema ran into the darkness. He returned a few moments later, crowbar in hand. "Let's see if we can open his door."

"Be careful! We don't want any sparks." Sesupo's voice was tinged with fear.

They pushed and pulled, but the door didn't budge. A second police car arrived, and Ngema called to them to bring their crowbar.

Soon four men were working at the door. Suddenly it popped open.

"Careful now." Sesupo leaned in and tried to extricate Witness but couldn't move him. "He's stuck. What do we do now?"

"We should wait for the medics. I can hear the siren already."

In the distance they could see flashing lights. A few minutes later the ambulance pulled up and two men jumped out. They ran over to the car, and Ngema explained the situation. One of the men then examined Witness.

"No seat belt. He's got chest and head injuries. Bad. We'll have to cut him out."

"But there's petrol everywhere. We'll all go up in flames."

"Cover the area with foam," one of the medics said. "There's an extinguisher in the ambulance. Let's hope that works."

Fifteen minutes later, they lifted the unconscious Witness onto a gurney and into the ambulance. Lights flashing, they headed for the mine hospital. The police followed right behind; Ngema and Sesupo had checked the license plate number of the Volkswagen and the description of the man the Gaborone police sought. They were convinced that the person in the ambulance was Witness Maleng—wanted in connection with the murder of the high-profile politician Bill Marumo. They would remain with him until a constable arrived at the hospital to guard him.

Ngema and Sesupo followed the medics up to the door of the surgery. Then they went to find coffee while they waited for their replacement to arrive.

"I wonder if he'll survive," Sesupo commented. "He looked pretty bad to me."

Ngema shrugged. "Serves him right if he doesn't. He nearly ran me over at the roadblock."

Sesupo nodded in agreement.

Part Four

BAD BEGINNING

*"Things bad begun make strong
themselves by ill."*

MACBETH, ACT 3 SCENE 2

TWENTY-SIX

Deputy Commissioner Tebogo Gobey was not looking forward to another meeting with his nephew. What does he want this time? It's never enough. Probably he wants to boast about his new powers from the witch doctor, and persuade me to put pressure on the commissioner about giving him my job. I'm not going to do it. I'm not going to interfere any further.

Yet when he arrived, Joshua seemed reticent, almost respectful. The bluster and innuendo were gone. He asked after his uncle's health and listened as if he cared.

He's seen the witch doctor, Gobey thought. And something went wrong. Eventually the small talk bored him, and he jumped to what he knew was the point.

"Did you see the man I suggested?"

Joshua hesitated. "Yes, he seems very good."

Gobey wondered how anyone could know that. "But?"

"I'm having second thoughts. He's very expensive. And what he wants to do . . ."

Gobey coughed and then couldn't catch his breath. "What does he want to do?" he wheezed at last.

"It's about power. And, of course, I need that."

"Isn't that why you wanted to see him?"

Joshua hesitated and glanced at the door as though he regretted coming. "It's the *muti*," he said.

Gobey nodded, irritated. "He wants to use some animal for power. That's what they do. That's how it works."

"Yes, that's it."

But Gobey wasn't satisfied. Suddenly he had a horrible insight. "What type of animal would that be?"

Joshua wouldn't meet his eyes. "I don't know; he said it was very rare."

"It's human, isn't it? He wants to take the power from a human. My God, Joshua, you're talking about murder! Probably the murder of a child!" Gobey was shocked to the core. It had never crossed his mind that the witch doctor would consider such a thing. He had thought the man a healer! But then he thought, perhaps all this time I have lied to myself.

Joshua denied it at once, flustered and tongue-tied, and then Gobey was sure. A wave of anger and disappointment broke over him.

"Get out. Don't come near me unless I send for you, and never see that man again. Do you hear me? Or I'll have you up for murder."

"Yes, Uncle."

"Yes, Deputy Commissioner!"

"Yes, Deputy Commissioner." Without another word, Joshua got up and left.

Gobey started to cough again. The medicine that the witch doctor had given him helped. But then he thought about what might be in it, and he felt his gorge rise. He gasped for breath. What had Joshua come to ask him, or to tell him? He didn't care anymore.

Suddenly he thought about the money. The witch doctor would want a lot of money. Had Joshua come for a loan? But Joshua and his wife lived well, too well. Suspicion overwhelmed him. He knew a senior man at Joshua's bank, someone who would help him without waiting for all the formalities. Someone he could trust.

By the time he reached home, Gobey had come to a decision. Partly it was based on self-disgust, a desire to divorce himself from unsavory aspects of his past while he still had time. Partly it was based on anger at Joshua, the nephew he had treated like a son and spoiled, and who now had let him down so badly. He hadn't become deputy commissioner of police by prevarication; once he came to a decision he would see it through. It was in this mood that he accepted a generous hug from his wife.

"Tebogo, something's wrong. You look upset."

He nodded. "It was a tough day. I'll tell you about it after dinner."

She smiled. "We're having one of your favorites. Beef *seswaa*."

Gobey tried to be enthusiastic. He loved the slow-cooked beef stew, and Maria made it for him with extra chili, exactly the way he liked it. "I'll have a beer with it," he said. "But I'm going to shower first. It's really hot outside."

It had been a sticky day, but he needed the shower to feel clean after a day wallowing in muck.

Once in the bathroom, he pulled the large bottle the witch doctor had given him from the back of the cupboard. He'd believed it contained herbal remedies, things to make him better. Or he'd persuaded himself of that. And he had to admit that it worked. It relaxed him, eased his chest, stopped the coughing. He wanted a swig right now. It contains some sort of opiate, he thought. Maybe morphine. It may make me feel better, but it does me no good. And what else might it contain? Only God and the witch doctor knew. Again he felt the twinge of self-doubt. He'd never asked the witch doctor what was in the potion. No one did that! He shuddered and emptied the contents of the bottle down the toilet.

"Hurry, dear!" Maria called through the door. "It's nearly ready!"

"I'll just be a minute." He discarded his clothes in a heap and let the hot water spray over him. He used plenty of soap from head to toe. Then he dried himself vigorously, wheezing slightly from the exertion. He looked at his naked body in the mirror. Still pretty good. He'd lost fat, which was good, but also lost muscle, which wasn't. Once he retired, he would exercise again. Long walks. Then he would feel better. That was what he needed, fresh air and exercise, not drugs and potions. He was sure of it.

The dinner was delicious, and he ate well while he heard about Maria's day and her friends' activities. She was patient and didn't ask him again what was on his mind. And after a token second helping, he was ready to tell her.

"I have to face it," he began, not looking at her. "Joshua's corrupt."

Maria drew in her breath sharply and started to say something, but Gobey went on. "Since his father died in that shoot-out, Joshua's been like a son to us. But somehow it's never been enough for him. He's made the wrong choices, married the wrong woman, always wanted more and got it. And I've been blind to it. Until now."

"What do you mean?" Maria asked, shocked.

"I've been looking at his bank records for the last few years. Looking very carefully."

She waited.

"I found nothing. No big payments, no big deposits."

"There you are then."

Tebogo shook his head. "He's too clever for something obvious. But where's the payment for his car? I phoned the dealer. Turns out he bought it for cash. A 3-series BMW! I mean *cash*. The dealer took stacks of pula."

"Perhaps it was from his mother's estate. She left some money."

Tebogo shook his head again. "They used that for the deposit on their house. That big expensive house in Phakalane. That doesn't have a single cent owing on it anymore, by the way."

"But where would he have got the money?"

"God, Maria, he's head of the diamond division! Where do you think the money came from?"

She shook her head, unwilling to accept it.

"There's more. He's got a witch doctor helping him now. I think he's one of the really bad ones, killing people for *muti*." He didn't say what had led him to guess that. "He wants my job when I retire."

"What are you going to do?" Her voice was very quiet now.

"I'm going to stop him. And the witch doctor. No child

is going to die to make a corrupt man deputy commissioner. And then I'm going to force him out of the police. But I'm not going to push the corruption charges—for his late parents' sake, and for our sake, too. He won't go to jail. I probably couldn't get enough evidence for a conviction anyway, but he doesn't know that."

Maria was silent for a few moments. "The witch doctor? Is it that man you go to? For the medicine? And those times before?"

Gobey hesitated, anguished. "Yes, but I didn't know . . . I threw the medicine out. I'm going to arrest him. He'll pay for his crimes!"

Maria's shock was replaced by nervousness.

"Tebogo, leave this thing. Please. You're retiring. The past is past. The future belongs to others. Forget about Joshua. The people who gave him all that money—they'll be dangerous. They won't want it to come out." She hesitated. "And forget about the witch doctor." Now there was fear in her voice.

Tebogo thought about it, tempted. But then he shook his head.

"I have to stop them," he said. "I don't have much time left anyway."

TWENTY-SEVEN

By Thursday Witness was conscious and out of danger, so Kubu drove to Jwaneng to interview him. He hoped that Witness would confess and offer the missing motive for Bill Marumo's murder. Then they could put this case behind them.

The receptionist called the doctor who had been keeping the police up to date. When he arrived, he looked harried and busy.

"Dr. Baku, I'm Assistant Superintendent Bengu from the CID. I spoke to you on the phone about Witness Maleng. I need to interview him as soon as possible about a very serious case."

"Oh, *dumela*, Assistant Superintendent. You want to see Maleng? He's conscious now, but very confused. Half the time he doesn't know where he is, and he has no recollection of the accident at all."

"Will he get back to normal?"

The doctor hesitated. "It depends what you mean by *normal*. Will he be able to function properly physically? I think there's a good chance, despite the severity of the head wounds. Will he recall what happened to him? Remember all his past? I'm doubtful."

"You mean he has amnesia?"

"He needs psychiatric help. We've just been trying to keep the physical stuff going so far."

"May I talk to him?"

"I don't see why not, but I doubt you'll get much sense out of him at the moment. Now I must get on with my patients. Good luck." He nodded and hurried off.

Kubu found his way to the intensive care unit. A police constable sat at the door with his elbows on his knees and his head in his hands. Kubu thought he might be asleep, but he glanced up as Kubu approached and jumped to his feet, blocking the door. Kubu showed him identification, and he immediately became respectful and apologized. Kubu smiled, told him he'd done exactly the right thing, and then went in. He greeted the duty nurse, and she pointed out Witness Maleng.

Witness was lying in bed connected to the paraphernalia of intensive care, drips running to his arms, cables running to monitors, screens blinking and chirping. He was awake, eyes open, staring at the ceiling, apparently lost in his thoughts. There was nowhere to sit, so Kubu dispossessed the constable of his chair and pulled it into the room.

"Rra Maleng, I am Assistant Superintendent Bengu of the Botswana CID. I would like to ask you some questions.

I warn you that you are a suspect in a serious crime and that anything you say will be noted and may be used as evidence."

Witness looked around and frowned. "You're from the police?" He tried to sit up, but the connections stopped him. "Have you found Tombi? Is that why you're here?" The heart monitor raced, but then he shook his head and relaxed and things returned to normal. "No, no . . . I'm sorry. What is it that you want?"

"I want to ask you some questions about the murder of Bill Marumo."

"Marumo is dead?" Witness's face was a mask of surprise. "Well, I can't say I'm sorry. He was not a good man. He was an evil man."

Kubu was rather nonplussed by this reaction. "Rra Maleng, I think you know very well that Rra Marumo is dead. I think you know, because you killed him!"

Witness appeared to think about this but then shook his head. "No," he said calmly. "I only saw him once. He was with Tombi in the park by the school. It was quite wrong for him to be alone with such a young girl. I told him off, and he ran away. Then I drove home with Tombi."

Kubu was interested at once.

"How long was this before your daughter disappeared?"

"Disappeared? What do you mean? She's at home. She'll be here to visit me soon."

Kubu sighed. "What day did you see Marumo with your daughter?"

"It was about three weeks ago. Saturday. I was at the school looking for someone . . ." He seemed to lose the train of his thoughts, and the sentence petered out.

"Rra Maleng, where were you on the evening of the twenty-eighth of April? Last Saturday night?"

"Last Saturday?" Witness thought hard. "Why?"

"Please just answer the question."

"I was at home. Tombi wasn't there. Maybe she was staying over with a friend. So I stayed at home, had some supper. Maybe I had a beer. I don't like to drink in front of my daughter."

"Where was your car?"

"In front of my house. Where else would it be?"

Kubu hesitated. All his instincts told him this man was telling the truth, but the truth as he believed it to be. Everything else seemed to have been wiped away.

"I think you are having trouble remembering things. Do you remember that Tombi went missing three weeks ago? She did. You phoned lots of people. You went to the police, the church, all the neighbors. Do you remember?"

Witness frowned and was silent for almost a minute. "I remember we were looking for someone. I helped. Then I went home with Tombi."

Kubu tried a more circuitous tack.

"Rra Maleng, did you have a briefcase when you drove here? Perhaps you found it somewhere? Or someone gave it to you? I'm very keen to take a look at it. May I do that?"

Witness looked at him blankly. He seemed to have absolutely no idea what the detective was talking about.

"A briefcase? Where would I get a briefcase? I'm not a rich man who carries around a briefcase. What would I do with it? If I need to carry something, I put it in a cardboard box." He shook his head.

A young nurse bustled in with a cup of soup and sat on the corner of Witness's bed.

"Here, Rra Maleng, drink this. You'll feel better." She shared her smile between Kubu and Witness.

"Ah, Tombi! You look after me so nicely." Witness took a sip. "This man is from the police. He tells me Rra Marumo is dead." He shook his head. "I'm not surprised. A man like that. But we must pray for his soul." He concentrated on the soup while the nurse helped him.

"Is your name Tombi?" Kubu asked her.

She shook her head, pointed at her name badge, and gave the charming smile again.

"*Aaii,* he calls all the young nurses that! Tombi is his daughter, but she never comes to see him. I don't know why. Maybe she's far away. But there's no harm in it, and it makes him happy."

"Does he have a wife?"

"He says she left him long ago, but that it doesn't matter because he has Tombi."

Witness finished the soup and coughed a little. The nurse squeezed his shoulder, smiled again, and returned to her station.

Witness turned back to Kubu. "Was that all, Rra Bengu?"

Kubu decided to try shock tactics. "No, Rra Maleng, that is definitely not all. You know very well that your daughter, Tombi, was abducted and murdered. You decided that the culprit was Marumo. You drove to his house on Saturday night and stabbed him to death. We are quite sure of this. Your car was seen nearby. Then you went home, cleaned up, and fled. We found human blood in your house and lots of other clues. And you tried to run a roadblock. You must stop this nonsense now and tell the truth."

For a moment Witness's face expressed surprise and shock, and Kubu thought he had broken through. But suddenly Witness laughed with delight and pointed at the ceiling. Patterns spread out around the neon light. Witness tried to follow the shapes with his hands, and knocked over his water glass, which rolled to the floor with a clatter. Witness laughed again.

The nurse hurried over and retrieved it. "I think he'd better rest now," she told Kubu. He wanted to argue but gave up. There was no point in continuing until Witness regained his senses, and interviewing him now might do more harm than good. He climbed to his feet.

Witness ignored him but said to the nurse, "Now, Tombi, you mustn't neglect your schoolwork. It's very important. I'll be fine. I can look after myself." Then he smiled and closed his eyes.

TWENTY-EIGHT

As soon as Kubu returned from Jwaneng, Mabaku summoned him, Samantha, and Zanele to his office. Mabaku sat at his desk with his hands behind his head, seemingly relaxed, but the stiffness of his body indicated tension.

"Okay, Kubu. What have you got?"

Kubu drained the tea he'd grabbed on the way. "Well, in a nutshell, Witness Maleng is insane, at least for the moment. He denies killing Marumo but says that Marumo was with his daughter, Tombi, on April the fourteenth, and he was upset about it. He says he chased Marumo away. But that's all nonsense. Samantha checked. Marumo was in Lobatse that day addressing a meeting. There's no way he could have been in the area where Witness Maleng said he saw him. He's obviously making it up. He's confused about his daughter as well. He thinks she's still alive and comes to visit him. He calls every young nurse in the ward Tombi and treats each as though they're his daughter."

Mabaku frowned. This wasn't what he wanted to hear. "No confession?"

Kubu shook his head. "He expressed surprise that Marumo had been murdered but seemed to think he deserved it."

"Do you think this madness is genuine, or is he just pretending?"

Kubu thought for a moment before he answered. "If he was acting, he's better at it than most actors. He missed his calling if he was faking it."

Mabaku turned to Zanele. "What have you come up with on the forensics side?"

"Director, I think we'll have him on the forensic evidence." She counted off on her fingers. "One, the blood in his house is probably Marumo's. It's the same type. We're waiting for the DNA tests to confirm it. Maleng's blood type is different. I got it from the hospital. Kubu also brought back all his clothes, and we'll check those for blood later today. Two, some of the hairs we found on Marumo's clothes match ones we found at Maleng's house. We'll confirm that they are Maleng's. And three, his foot size matches the prints we found in the driveway. Now we have his shoes and boots, we'll test those too for soil and blood."

Kubu nodded. "Add to that the circumstantial evidence. From what he told his friends and Big Mama at the *shebeen*, he hated Marumo. He tried to attack him at a public meeting. Then a blue Volkswagen Golf was seen near the murder scene, and Maleng owns a blue Golf. Finally, for no obvious reason, two days after the murder he abandons his house, he moves to

Jwaneng, and he runs a roadblock—nearly knocking over an officer—before racing at a mad speed into a cow."

"Well, we'll get him with the forensic evidence," Mabaku said. "Zanele, we need to exploit that and make it absolutely iron-clad."

Kubu looked pensive. "But—" he began, but Mabaku cut in.

"We'll charge Maleng with the murder but, from the sounds of it, he isn't fit to stand trial. It may be months before the psychiatric reports are in. And our problem is motive. If we can't show a clear motive, Freedom Party troublemakers will say it's all a setup. Find a madman with a grudge against politicians, fake some forensic evidence, and pin the murder on him. Or, worse, a government agent exploited him and egged him on, telling him where Marumo lived, telling him he had *muti* made from the daughter." Mabaku shook his head. "And he did have *muti*. We mustn't forget that."

Kubu sighed. "They'll say government agents planted it. To discredit him and to persuade Maleng to commit the crime."

"It doesn't add up—" Samantha began, but Mabaku interrupted again. "No, of course it doesn't add up. They didn't need to actually plant the *muti* if they told Maleng that Marumo had it. But that's how conspiracy theories work."

"How would they get to him? Why would he believe them?" Samantha asked. Then she had another thought. "Oh, no, they could be working through that awful witch doctor he consulted, that Gondo woman." She looked shocked.

"I think Gondo just made the sort of general statement that can be interpreted in different ways, and Maleng twisted it to mean what he wanted it to mean," Kubu said.

Mabaku looked as though he had just tasted something extremely disagreeable. Why was life always so complicated? He needed a nice clean solution to the murder to get the press off his back, calm down the antigovernment hotheads, and make the commissioner happy. Right now, it was very important for him to make the commissioner happy, if he wanted to be the next deputy commissioner.

Kubu shifted in his seat. "Let's take a step back and think this through. None of us have doubts as to whether Maleng murdered Marumo. The problem we have is to find out why. If he was persuaded by someone else, we have to find who that was even if he was working for the government or the BDP. That would be our worst case from a political point of view. The country would erupt in turmoil. Personally, I don't think that's a likely scenario, but we can't dismiss it." He paused. "The only other possibility is that he did it of his own accord and, as the director says, that could provide the Freedom Party or someone else an opportunity to exploit the situation for their own gain. So how do we prevent that?"

The others waited and let Kubu think.

"The answer is the *muti*."

"Marumo's *muti*?" Samantha asked with astonishment.

"Yes, Marumo's *muti*. It's the only way to prevent the situation being exploited. We can't do that by just announcing that we found *muti* in his desk. We'll be accused of planting it—that it's also part of the conspiracy. We'll have to follow the trail of Marumo's *muti*. Find out who was the unfortunate person who died to make it. Find out who Marumo got it from and bring that person to trial. And have that person tell the court and the people of Botswana that Marumo ordered it, paid for it, and used it. That's the only way to keep the conspiracy theory people quiet."

For a few moments nobody said a word. They all looked at Mabaku.

"You're right," he said finally. "If we can't find a clear motive for Maleng's actions, we'll have to show that Marumo wasn't as clean as he presented himself. He may, in fact, have been an accessory to a *muti* murder. That will stop the Freedom Party critics in their tracks." He paused. "Let's do it. We've got to wrap up the Maleng case properly, but let's see if we can trace this *muti* back to the witch doctor who made it."

He turned to Samantha. "Samantha, we may well be able to tie the murders you are looking into with Marumo's *muti* even if neither of the missing girls was used for this *muti*. It's not unlikely that the same witch doctor is involved in all of them. This is no longer a cold case. It's scorching hot. I'm putting Kubu in charge of it. We need his experience."

"But—"

"This has nothing to do with you or your competence, Samantha. You'll work closely with Kubu—he'll need lots of help. Understood?"

Samantha didn't look enthusiastic, but nodded her assent.

"Okay. Now tell me what we've got on these missing-girl cases."

Kubu and Samantha filled Mabaku in on the backgrounds of the two girls and what little they had discovered about their abductions—Lesego in Mochudi and Tombi in Gaborone.

"We think the girls knew the person who abducted them," Kubu said. "But that may not have been the witch doctor. In each case—according to the people who caught glimpses of the cars—it was very quick, which suggests that the girl got in willingly."

"Why don't you think the witch doctor would do it himself?" Mabaku asked.

"I think it's too risky. If someone else is caught, there may be no ties to the witch doctor, and if there are ties, the witch doctor would put a spell on the abductor, which would effectively shut him up." Samantha shook her head in disgust.

"Also it seems unlikely that the abductor used his own car, so Samantha's been trying to come up with other possibilities," Kubu added.

"I checked the files of stolen cars but nothing seemed to match," Samantha said. "I decided to take a look at rental cars, too, so I spoke to all the rental companies in the area. That was over a week ago. They've all promised me lists of cars rented on the days of the abductions and the day before with the names of who rented them. I'll push them again to get them."

"Tell them if we don't have them by Monday morning, I'll find all sorts of reasons to make life difficult!" Mabaku was getting impatient. "And how do we link all this to Marumo in any case?"

"Zanele has confirmed that the DNA found in Marumo's *muti* is not from Tombi," Kubu said. "She's going to Mochudi tomorrow to get some DNA from Lesego's sister to check whether it's from Lesego."

"And if it is?" Mabaku asked.

"If it is, we at least have some sort of timeline for when Marumo got it. We can then go back through his records to see if there's a suspicious payment or a strange meeting. We'll push hard on his girlfriend to see if she can remember anything. If it's not from Lesego, we're no worse off than we are now."

Mabaku thought about that for a moment and then nodded. "And no bodies have turned up?"

Kubu shook his head. "No, and that's very odd. Usually they're buried in shallow graves or just dumped once the witch doctors have the parts they want. But there's been nothing."

Mabaku frowned. "Well, what clues do you have to the witch doctor himself?"

"When we interviewed the Gondo woman, she denied any involvement but said there was a witch doctor in town who deals with body parts. She refused to identify him because she said she was scared. But she did say it was a male. That may help a little."

There was a pause. "That's all you've got at the moment?" Mabaku asked.

Kubu and Samantha nodded.

Mabaku frowned. "Not much to go on! Still we've got something."

He sighed and turned to Zanele. "Zanele, please wrap up the forensics as quickly as possible. In the meantime, I must inform the commissioner, and I'll call a press conference for five o'clock to announce we have Marumo's killer."

He waved at his three subordinates, dismissing them.

As they walked out, Mabaku said under his breath, "Let's pray this doesn't stir up a nest of puff adders."

TWENTY-NINE

Mabulo Owido sat alone at a table outside the BIG MAMA KNOWS ALL *shebeen*, a cold St. Louis beer in hand. He didn't feel like going inside, where most of the action was. The stares made him feel uncomfortable, even after all these years. Of course, he wanted to make small talk to the Batswana girls who leaned provocatively against the counter, but he knew he would be brushed off. He wouldn't like that.

As if by magic, Big Mama walked out just as he drained the bottle.

"Another one?" she asked in English. He nodded.

A few minutes later, she walked out with two bottles in her hand. "Here, have one on me." She put them down in front of him.

"You don't have to feel sorry for me!"

"That's not the reason. I want everyone to enjoy being here. The regulars aren't very friendly tonight." She smiled broadly. "And I want you to come back."

"Thanks," he said, returning her smile.

"Do you live around here?"

"Yes, near Broadhurst Mall. Been there for about four months."

"Where are you from?"

"Tanzania. Left there just after New Year. There's been too much trouble for people like me."

"*Aaii.*" Big Mama rolled her eyes. She'd heard about the awful problems for people like Owido in east Africa and knew that prejudice might follow him wherever he went.

Owido looked down. "People hate us," he whispered. "And yet we're just the same as them. Except for this." He held up a pinkish arm.

Big Mama shook her head. "You don't have to worry. Botswana is very tolerant. Our first president married a white woman, and some of the elders were very upset, but they got used to it and got to love her like they loved him."

"I like it here. Some of the people I work with are very kind."

Big Mama leaned over and whispered in his ear, "We'll find you a nice girl. It's bad to be far from home and have no company."

Owido didn't respond immediately as he was distracted by the huge cleavage just in front of his face.

"Um. Yes. That would be nice," he stammered eventually.

"Next time you come, I'll introduce you to someone. I know just the girl. You'll see." She winked at him, flashed her infectious smile, and returned to the patrons inside.

He leaned back in his chair, put a bottle to his lips, and enjoyed the cold fizz as the beer slid down his throat. Not bad beer, he thought. Not as good as a Serengeti or a Ndovu. But pretty good.

Two men walked into the *shebeen*, glanced at him, and sat at a nearby table.

"Hi!" Owido said as they passed, but they ignored him.

It'll never change, he thought. He sighed and took another deep swig.

For the next hour, Owido sipped more beers and chatted to Big Mama when she delivered them. She was interested in all sorts of things: what it was like in Tanzania, what he thought of Gaborone, where he worked, and how he liked it there. Also, she seemed intent on matchmaking, and kept mentioning a girl called Lemme. Someone she thought he would like. He was nervous of possible embarrassment, but Big Mama assured him that the young woman was not prejudiced, and promised to tell her in advance that Owido was an albino.

Eventually he decided it was time to leave. He had about a twenty-minute walk home. He said goodbye to Big Mama, grateful for her attention, and promised that he would return the following Saturday to meet Lemme. By then the beer had given him the courage. He even accepted her farewell hug, but couldn't completely ignore the disapproving looks of some of the other patrons.

Once he was in the open, he shivered. He wasn't used to how quickly Gaborone's temperature dropped now that winter was approaching. Where he came from, on the equator, the seasons hardly fluctuated.

He turned into a narrow path that would take him to Sego-ditshane Way. He'd found the shortcut earlier in the evening, when he saw several people turn off the main sidewalk. It saved at least five minutes. Suddenly he had the impression that he was being followed. He glanced back and saw two men some way off. He picked up his pace, trying to distance himself from the men. At the same time he felt a little guilty of suspecting them—after all, he was in Botswana now.

Then he heard running footsteps. As he turned to look, a body crashed into him, sending him sprawling. Winded, he gasped for air. "Take my wallet," he croaked. "There's a little money in it."

One of the men pulled a knife, the other a heavy stick.

"Take my watch, too." Owido started to feel desperate.

The man with the stick clubbed him on the side of the head. Owido could feel blood dripping down his face.

"Please . . . ," he pleaded. "Take everything."

Another blow on the head. The pain was terrible.

"Careful! We don't get paid, if he's dead."

"Shit! All albinos should be dead."

A third blow. And Owido lost consciousness.

"Quick. Let's get him to the car."

The two men dragged Owido back along the path.

"Makes me nervous; touching someone like this."

"He's just a man like you and me. He just looks different."

"I'm told they have powerful spirits. I'm sure that's why they want us to find one."

"Come on get on with it."

"Why do they want him alive?"

"Shut up. You ask too many questions. Here, tie his hands and feet, and tape this rag in his mouth. I'll fetch the car and bring it over there." He pointed to the road running parallel to the path and just visible through the bushes. "Get him off the path and out of sight, then wait for me. Think you can manage that? I'll only be a few minutes."

Ten minutes later they dragged Owido to the road, waited

until no one was around, then lifted him into the trunk and slammed it shut. The leader of the two pulled out his cell phone and sent a text message.

"I said we'd drop him off in half an hour."

When Owido came to his senses, he was being dragged behind the trunk of a large tree.

"Aaah. Aaah." Owido tried to shout for help. He thrashed around, pulling at the ties that bound him, causing them to cut into his skin.

"Shut up, *leswafe!*" one of the men hissed and kicked him in the head.

Owido winced and lay still. The rag in his mouth kept making him gag.

This can't be just a mugging, he thought. They would've left me where they attacked me. Did they take my wallet and watch? he wondered. The way he was tied, he couldn't tell. Then he had a thought that frightened him. The men hadn't worn masks; they weren't worried about being seen. Did that mean they were careless, or did they know that it wasn't important? He shivered, his mind going back to the atrocities that had happened at home in Tanzania.

Owido was desperate. He was convinced that it hadn't been a simple robbery. But why dump him in the middle of nowhere? Maybe it was just a bad joke—leave him and let him suffer until somebody found him. That calmed him a little since no other explanation made sense.

He lay there, wrists hurting from the struggles against the sharp plastic ties. Every now and again, he'd try to push himself closer to the road so he could be seen, but a steep bank prevented him. The problem was that he couldn't align himself to go straight up. With his feet tied, he was able to go forward, but not change direction.

After what seemed like a couple of hours, he heard a car driving slowly down the road. Maybe the men had returned to end the joke. He tried to shout again, but all that resulted was a muffled sound that would not be heard more than a few yards away.

The car came closer, and he could see a torch beam shining in the ditch where he lay. As the car passed, the beam shone on him, passed, then returned. The car stopped. He heard a door open, but not shut. A few seconds later a man walked over to him, like a shadow in the night. He could barely see him, it was so dark. A beam of light shone in his face, blinding him.

The figure leaned over and felt his neck. Then he pulled something from his pocket. The man grabbed Owido's head and slid a bag over it. Owido could feel a drawstring being tightened at his neck. He struggled again, to no avail. All he succeeded in doing was adding to the pain in his wrists. He felt himself being dragged by the feet up the bank, lifted, and dumped in what he thought was the trunk of a car. There was a loud bang as the trunk was closed. Moments later the car drove off.

It wasn't long before the car stopped, then continued slowly. By the bumpiness, Owido thought they must be on a dirt road. A short while later, the car stopped again, and the engine was switched off. Again Owido heard a door open and close, followed by what he assumed was the lid of the trunk. Someone grabbed him under the arms and lifted him.

He was carried and dragged for a few seconds. Then he was dumped on the floor.

The drawstring around his neck was loosened and the bag pulled off. He glanced fearfully at the person above him, but there wasn't enough light to see the face clearly.

The figure stood up and walked out of sight. Seconds later a door closed and was locked, and Owido was left alone.

The room smelled as though it had just been cleaned with an antiseptic cleaner. Owido lay on his side for several hours wondering what was going on. Lying on his back was extremely uncomfortable due to his tethered wrists. Every now and again he'd push himself around the room to see if he could discover something about it. All he found was that it had some furniture in it—a couple of pieces against a wall and another in the center of the room.

Then he heard a key turn in the lock. The door opened and a man walked in without turning on the light.

"Get up! You can go to the toilet."

The man pulled him to his feet.

Suddenly his arms were free.

"Don't try anything. Your feet are still tied."

Owido massaged his wrists. He felt the deep cuts from his struggles.

"Take off your shoes and socks."

Owido bent over and undid his laces, but he fell over when he tried to lift one leg to take off the shoes. The man pulled off the shoes and socks.

"Now your shirt." Owido complied quickly, difficult as it was on the floor.

"Stick your hands out. Put them together"

The man put another tether on and pulled it tight. Then he bent over and cut the ties around Owido's ankles. He unzipped the trousers and pulled them off, followed by the underpants.

"Stand up!"

Owido contorted his way to his feet.

"The toilet's down the hall. First door on the right."

Owido walked down a dark passage, looking for some way to escape. The door at the other end was closed. And locked, Owido thought.

He turned into a small bathroom.

"Do it!"

Owido sat down while the man watched.

When Owido was finished the man led him back to the room.

"Lie down on that."

In the gloom Owido saw the man pointing at what looked like a table in the middle of the room. Owido first sat down and swiveled his legs onto the table. Then he lay down, feeling very vulnerable in his nakedness.

He felt his legs being strapped to the table. Then his hands were free again, but immediately one was tied to something under the table. The same happened to the other arm. Owido couldn't move. Finally he felt something across his throat. It was pulled quite tightly—but not enough to make him choke.

The man left the room without saying another word and locked the door.

Owido lay like that for another interminable length of time. Every now and again, a muscle in his left arm would cramp. There was nothing he could do but try to relax it. That didn't work, and he tried to call for help. All that came out was a muffled "Aaah."

Then he heard another car drive up.

What was going on? he wondered.

Again he heard the key in the door. He turned his head and saw two figures. He gasped. One had a baboon mask on his head and a leopard skin round his waist. Owido screamed—he knew it was a witch doctor.

The other man was shorter, nervous. "You are about to receive power you have not even dreamed about," the witch doctor said to him as he opened a small suitcase.

"I can't do it." The short man stammered. He was sweating and continually mopped his brow.

"It's too late. You can't go back now."

The short man took a deep breath. He looked very frightened. He nodded his head.

"I'll do it," he croaked.

The witch doctor closed the suitcase and stood next to Owido.

"Here," he said, handing something to the short man. Owido strained to see what it was. It flashed in the light. He screamed as he saw it was a scalpel. He shook his head from side to side, trying to shout, "No!" All that came out was a muffled sound. He pulled and pushed as hard as he could against his restraints, to no avail.

"Please!" he tried to scream. Again only a muffled call. "Help. Please."

THIRTY

On Monday afternoon Kubu returned from lunch in a good mood only slightly tarnished by the fact he had a meeting with the director and Deputy Commissioner Gobey. He'd received a terse call from the director in the morning, telling him to be there at 2 p.m. As he headed to Mabaku's office, he wondered if further political fallout from Marumo's death had settled on the director's desk after Friday's press conference.

It had apparently started smoothly, with the reporters excited about the arrest and wanting to know everything about Witness Maleng. It was when they questioned Mabaku about the motive that things became tense. The director told them that Witness had some idea of a connection between Marumo and the disappearance of his daughter, but Mabaku had to admit that the police had no evidence of such a connection and were unsure how Witness came up with that idea. This led to a flurry of questions that Mabaku wanted to avoid, and he closed the meeting with the journalists dissatisfied. Kubu thought it was this that had led to the deputy commissioner's surprise visit. But he was wrong.

When Kubu reached the director's office, Deputy Commissioner Gobey was already there, standing in front of Mabaku's desk. Kubu was disturbed to see that he'd lost weight; his clothes seemed to hang on his body rather than dress it. Obviously the rumors that the deputy commissioner was retiring because of ill health were correct.

"Come in, Kubu. You know the deputy commissioner, of course." Mabaku dispensed with the pleasantries as quickly as possible. Nothing unusual there. Gobey sat down, and Kubu took the more solid, but less comfortable, chair in front of Mabaku's desk.

"The deputy commissioner wants to talk to you about the Marumo case. Well, not exactly about the case. Maybe you'd better explain it yourself, Deputy Commissioner."

Gobey looked uncomfortable, clearly uncertain where to begin. Kubu became uneasy. Something was very wrong here.

"Assistant Superintendent, I understand from Director Mabaku that you are investigating the disappearance of a number of children, and a potion discovered in Bill Marumo's house, which you believe may contain human body parts. Is that correct?"

Kubu realized he must tread carefully. There was no way of telling where this was heading. "That's correct, rra."

"I may be in a position to help you, Bengu, but I'm going to need your assurance—an assurance from both of you—that this will go no further than this room without my explicit approval. Is that agreed?"

Kubu hesitated, very unhappy with this turn of events. He glanced at Mabaku and saw that the director shared his concern. Mabaku leaned forward and summed up their discomfort.

"Deputy Commissioner, your knowledge of law is much better than ours. But I have to point out that if you tell us something important connected with a crime, then it may be our duty to report that to the prosecutor, who may then take it further and call you as a witness. We can't handle it any other way, nor would you would wish us to."

Gobey nodded. "You're perfectly correct, Mabaku, but what I'm about to tell you is something I've heard from a third person. So it's hearsay and not admissible in evidence. I don't want to be directly involved, nor do I want the other person involved." Kubu opened his mouth to interrupt, but Gobey stopped him. "Hear me out, Bengu. I understand you don't have much in the way of leads at the moment. I think I can help with that. I believe I can lead you to a witch doctor who may be the man you're looking for. Once you get him, I think you'll find that my informant will be willing to give evidence. Or perhaps you can extract a confession."

Mabaku tensed. "Can you tell us who this man is?"

Gobey shook his head. "I've met him. I don't want to go into the details. But he always wears a baboon mask and leopard skin loincloth. From his body, I'd say he's no older than mid-forties and strong, and about my height—five foot eight, I'd guess. He has big hands but always wears black gloves. Not at all the stereotyped wrinkled old man, squatting over thrown bones."

"Who sees him come and go? He can't walk around the streets like that, and nobody notices him!" Kubu was uncomfortable with the story.

Gobey shook his head again. "No one ever sees him. I've been told he makes himself invisible." Gobey looked down at the floor. "But that's impossible, of course."

Kubu leaned back in his chair, flabbergasted. The deputy commissioner was right, they were stymied. He'd even wondered if the "invisible" witch doctor Mma Gondo had told them of really existed, or if he was just an invention of other witch doctors wanting to divert attention from themselves. Now, the deputy commissioner, of all people, walks into the CID and offers to lead them to just such a man.

Mabaku stroked his chin. "Maybe not," he said. "If everyone who sees him as a witch doctor sees a baboon mask and leopard skin, maybe all he has to do is dress normally to become 'invisible.' As long as he keeps the two personas strictly separate, he can't be recognized."

Kubu said, "Rra, the *muti* investigations were initiated by Detective Samantha Khama. She's battled with them and persuaded us to pursue even the cold cases. I think she should join us to hear what you have to say."

Gobey shook his head firmly and started to cough. When he was able to catch his breath, he said, "No one else. What I say is between the three of us. No one else. Do I have your word on that?" He looked from the one to the other, his resolve still firm despite his failing health.

Reluctantly, Kubu and Mabaku agreed. "But," Kubu added, "if keeping this secret means we are breaking the law, then our promises fall away." This time it was Gobey who was reluctantly forced to agree.

"Well then," said Mabaku. "Tell us what it is that you know."

After Gobey left, Kubu returned to his chair. He wasn't satisfied. "He knows more than he's telling us. I don't believe him, do you?"

Mabaku clasped his hands and thought for so long that Kubu thought he wasn't going to answer. At last he replied, "Yes, I do."

Kubu shook his head. "This witch doctor was recommended to him long ago—he won't say who by—and he's used him occasionally over the years. Nothing serious. But the man is always masked, he's never seen the face, and he has no idea of his identity. But now, suddenly, he suspects him of black magic involving organs ripped from living children!" Kubu couldn't contain himself. "And he deduces this from what he hears last week from some other unnamed party! Isn't it possible that he knows about these things because he's the one who's been involved?"

Mabaku nodded. "But you don't know him as I do, Kubu. He's personally transformed much of the police force. His example has become our example. I hear a lot of stuff, Kubu. Lots of rumors about senior people. Some of them are just malicious, others are plausible but impossible to prove at the time, and I keep my eyes open. But I've never heard anything bad about Deputy Commissioner Gobey. Nothing."

"Until today."

"Yes, but remember, he's about to retire. He could've walked away and said nothing. No one would have been any the wiser."

"Maybe he's being blackmailed."

"Because of a few good-luck charms? And now some cough medicine? Half of Botswana's done something like that."

"We don't know what those charms and potions were for or what they were made from."

"No, and neither did he at the time."

Kubu mulled it over. His intuition told him that Gobey was deeper in the mire than he'd admitted. But he couldn't refute Mabaku's point: Gobey had come forward of his own free will. There was no reason for him to put himself at risk by revealing what he knew.

"What should we do?"

"Exactly what he proposed. You let him set up a meeting with the witch doctor. Get a team together, follow him without telling the team who they're following, and put a steel noose around that house. Arrest the witch doctor and sweat him. They're all cowards; he'll break."

"What if he doesn't?"

"Then we have another talk with the deputy commissioner."

Kubu nodded. They had nothing to lose. "What do I tell Samantha? She'll be convinced we're simply protecting another senior *man*."

Mabaku smiled tightly. "Well, we are, aren't we? Tell her you're the superior officer."

You don't know Samantha very well, Director, Kubu thought. That's going to be an interesting meeting.

"Very well, I'll set it up." Kubu wondered why this potential breakthrough had such a bitter taste.

Mabaku nodded, went to the window, and gazed out at Kgale Hill, highlighted by the rich afternoon light.

THIRTY-ONE

"It's amazing!" Kubu said to Samantha. They were sitting in Kubu's office, each with a cup of tea.

"It's amazing. Just a few years ago, getting the results of a DNA test could take months. Now Zanele is using a mobile tester that takes only four hours. The South Africans have brought it to show us. It's from the UK, apparently. She's already run the tests from Marumo's *muti* and compared the results with samples taken from Lesego's sister. The sad thing is that based on the closeness of the results, she's confident that the *muti* involved material from Lesego."

"So Marumo had *muti* with Lesego's body parts in his house!" Samantha had a look of sheer disgust on her face. Then it turned to anger. "Another girl killed to promote a man!"

"It looks like that. But we can't jump to conclusions yet."

"Why not?" Samantha exclaimed. "You found the gourd in a locked drawer! In his house! With bits of Lesego in it!"

"True, but we don't know whether it was there for a while or possibly put there to incriminate him. We have to assume that the conspiracy theory we talked about could actually be true."

He took a sip of tea. "It's possible that someone planted the *muti* before or after the murder. Remember the scuff marks around the desk drawer lock? It's unlikely, but possible. We have to keep that in mind."

"Even if that's so, Lesego was still murdered for *muti*."

Kubu sighed. "Unfortunately, that's true." He thought for a moment about his beautiful Tumi and her friend Nono. How could anybody even think about hurting someone like them? He shook his head. "We're going to do everything possible to solve these cases. We have to put a stop to this terrible practice."

Samantha took a deep breath. "All right. Let's get to work."

Kubu stood up to refill the cups. When he returned, he sat down and asked, "What did you find out about the rental cars?"

"I just received the final lists this morning. There are a lot of rental cars that are white and fewer that are red. It took so long because there's a lot of manual stuff for the companies to do. They can easily print out the make of car and model, the license plate numbers, and who rented it, but not the color. So they have to write in those details by hand. They all say it took too much of their time. But they did it."

"Anything interesting from what you've got so far?"

"There were only two people who appeared on both lists. One was a South African salesman from Cape Town. He flew in via Johannesburg the day before Lesego was abducted and flew back the day she was abducted. I don't think he could have been in Mochudi when Lesego disappeared and still make his flight. I spoke to him and got a list of his appointments. I'll check those out, but I don't think it will go anywhere. The other was the BMW dealership in Gaborone. They have a deal with Avis. If they don't have a spare loaner, they sometimes rent a car as a courtesy for their customers when their car is being serviced."

"That's not promising. Have you had a chance to look at the people who were only on one list?"

"Yes, but it will take time to speak to each of them. I've asked Detective Pho to help me with that."

"Good work. Now I have something to tell you." Kubu was not looking forward to this.

"An informant has come forward and says he can lead us to a witch doctor who deals with human body parts."

Samantha leaned forward expectantly.

"We'll know today or tomorrow when that is going to happen."

"When can we speak to the informant? Who is it?" Kubu thought Samantha was going to start vibrating, she was so eager.

"Unfortunately there's a problem. The informant wants to remain anonymous for reasons I can't disclose."

Kubu could see the anger welling up inside Samantha. "I know who he is!" she snapped. "It's a man, and high up in government. He can't be named because it would be embarrassing to him and his friends." She jumped up. "Here we go again. And you said you wanted to solve these *muti* murders. You're the same as the rest of them!" Samantha turned and stormed out of the room.

An hour later, Kubu picked up his phone and dialed Samantha's extension.

"Please come to my office. We need to talk."

A few minutes later, she knocked and walked in. Kubu waved at a chair.

"I'm sorry I walked out on you," Samantha said quietly. "I get so angry when I see the same old ways being repeated. We'll never get any of these people if that continues." She sat down.

"I understand how you feel," Kubu said. "But you will have to trust me on this one. If it makes a difference in getting a witch doctor convicted, we *will* reveal the informant's name, and he's agreed to testify. But it would be better if it didn't come to that."

He looked at Samantha, who sat without saying a word.

"Samantha, you're crucial to our investigations. You have the drive and will to succeed. I want you to continue what you're doing. I want you to come with me when we try to apprehend the witch doctor. But in this instance, I'm in charge. That's not negotiable."

Again, he looked directly at her. "Is that clear?"

He could see her fighting to control her emotions. Eventually she stood up and nodded. Then she turned and left.

Kubu sat for a while wondering whether Samantha would have the resilience to stay and work in the inhospitable environment that was the CID.

She will, he thought. She's tough and very determined to make a difference.

He smiled.

She's going to be a good detective.

THIRTY-TWO

Kubu was not happy. He was cramped in the passenger seat of Samantha's Corolla with a tub of KFC chicken on his lap, and Samantha was barely on speaking terms with him. But the main source of his concern was their location. It was a poor area, a warren of dirt roads without street lighting. He was convinced there were ways in and out that he didn't know about. And they were much closer to the witch doctor's "safe house" than he would have liked, but he was concerned about getting to it quickly in the dark on the rough streets. Gobey had said he could look after himself—he was, after all, a policeman—but Kubu knew he was weakened by his illness. He wanted to be able to come to the deputy commissioner's aid quickly, if necessary.

Samantha knew none of this and was angry about being kept in the dark, untrusted. He offered her a piece of chicken, but she just shook her head. Kubu shrugged and went on eating. It was their camouflage in case anyone suspected them of being watchers. They'd simply pulled off the road to eat. That had been Kubu's idea. Two armed constables in plain clothes sat in the back, working through their own tub.

"What happens if your informant gives us the slip?" Samantha asked. "We'd lose him in a minute in this." She waved at the dusty tracks wandering between the tiny houses and shacks.

"I told you. He's wired. I'm in constant contact with him through this." He indicated the headset he was wearing. "And anyway he volunteered for this. He's not some informer that I bought." Kubu tried to keep the defensive tone out of his voice. "All we have to do is wait. When he gets the signal from the house, he'll go in and keep the witch doctor occupied while we get there, and our second car comes from the other main road. Then we surround the house and go in. He'll have to really make himself invisible to get away. And we're covering the two main roads into the township; what can go wrong?"

"We'll see just now," Samantha grumbled.

Kubu frowned and helped himself to another drumstick. He knew Joy wouldn't be impressed, but with Samantha not eating, he had to keep up their cover.

"Bengu. Come in." Gobey's voice suddenly came through the earpiece, startling Kubu. He switched on his mike and responded.

"Yes," said Gobey. "I'm outside the house. All quiet and dark. But that's how he operates. Always makes you wait, makes sure you know he's the important one. We may have to hang on half an hour. Just be patient." He sounded nervous.

"No problem. I'll keep monitoring you." Kubu muted his

mike and radioed the driver of the other car to relay the message. Kubu was worried about Gobey. He was alone and sick, bait for a man who might well be a psychopathic killer as well as a witch doctor. He felt new respect for the deputy commissioner. Whatever he'd done in the past, he was carrying through on his promise.

As time passed, Kubu could feel tension building up in his belly—unless that was the tub of KFC he'd eaten. Samantha was still monosyllabic. Couldn't she see they were on the same side? Yet he had some sympathy for her attitude. How would *he* feel if Mabaku came up with an informant on one of his cases and refused to share that information with him? He kept his temper.

Time dragged, and Kubu brooded. What if they did catch this man? It wouldn't end the foul trade in human flesh. But if this was the man Mma Gondo had talked about—the invisible killer, feared even by other witch doctors—and if he could be brought down and sent to the gallows, then all of them would feel vulnerable. The killing wouldn't stop, but maybe it would be forced outside the borders of Botswana. That would be something.

Kubu checked his watch. Patience had never been his strongest suit; the lack of it had got him into big trouble in the Kalahari. At last Gobey's voice came again.

"There's no sign of him, Bengu. He's never kept me waiting this long—over an hour now. I think he's spooked. Did you see anything?"

"Nothing suspicious. A few people walking down the road. We sat here pretending to be eating chicken." Samantha snorted at the word *pretending*.

"Did the same person come past more than once?"

"Not as far as we could tell. But it's dark, and we didn't want to be too obviously nosy."

"Where are the others?"

"They're waiting at the turnoff on the main road."

Gobey sighed. "Somehow he realized you were police. That's the only possibility." He hesitated, and then burst out, "Of course! That's why he always comes late. He watches the routes in. Stupid of us not to realize that. I thought it was all part of his act." He started to cough.

"Let's go home," he said when he'd caught his breath. "We won't find him tonight. He was too smart for us. This time."

Kubu turned to Samantha. "My informant thinks the suspect caught on that we were watching. Maybe that's why he always keeps his clients waiting."

"So what now?"

"We call it off. We'll have to come up with a Plan B." He called the other car and told them to head back to the police station at once. He wanted them out of the way before the deputy commissioner's car headed down the road.

Suddenly Samantha turned to him and indicated he should switch off his mike. When he'd done so, she said, "Kubu, it's all a ploy. You won't tell me what you've got on this guy, but I bet he never set up a meeting at all! It's just a hoax to get you off his back. I say we pull him in. Right now. And see what he knows that he's not telling you."

Kubu thought about it. Was Gobey leading them up the garden path? Wasting their time? Even *covering* for the witch doctor? But for what reason? *He* approached *us*. We have *nothing* on him. He shook his head.

"Let's get back to the police station, Samantha, drop off

these guys, and pick up my car. There's nothing more we can do tonight. That's final."

Samantha started the car, slammed it into gear, put her foot down, and did a screeching U-turn. Kubu hastily fastened his seat belt.

THIRTY-THREE

The next morning Mabaku, Kubu, and Gobey met again in the director's office. Gobey wanted to avoid meeting in his own office. Mabaku asked Miriam to bring them tea and coffee, and cookies for Kubu, and they didn't talk until she had served and closed the door behind her.

"What now?" Mabaku asked.

"The deputy commissioner and I think that the witch doctor smelled a rat," said Kubu. "I think we should follow up on the leads the deputy commissioner has given us. We'll keep a watch on the house, but I doubt the witch doctor will go back there now. We'll also trace its owner—it's not going to be the witch doctor, I'm sure—and check for fingerprints and other forensics stuff. We'll do that discreetly. We'll also make some inquiries around the area, see if anyone's seen a man who doesn't live around there but visits from time to time."

Gobey nodded. "That sounds right. I'll contact the witch doctor again. Ask why he didn't appear. Play dumb."

"How do you make that contact?" Mabaku asked quietly.

Gobey hesitated.

"Deputy Commissioner, you're going to have to tell us anything that might help."

Gobey nodded and sighed. "I send an e-mail to what appears to be a secure address. Here it is." He pulled a small sheet of paper from his pocket and handed it to Mabaku. "He doesn't respond to it, but he phones me a day or so later. Usually he just tells me the time to come to the house."

"We can trace the calls to your cell phone," said Kubu.

Gobey shook his head. "I've done that; they come from public phones all over the place. One even from Mochudi."

Kubu sat forward, thinking of Lesego. "Even so, we need that information. We might be able to detect a pattern from the location of the calls. And we'll need to arrange a twenty-four-hour monitor on the calls you receive. With your permission, of course."

Gobey nodded. He was beginning to regret his decision to tell Mabaku his story, but he was in too deep to back out now. "I'll get you all that information," he said.

Kubu decided to push his luck. "And we're going to have to bring Detective Khama in on this. She's working on the case and can't be kept in the dark."

Gobey turned to him angrily. "No! We agreed no one else. And especially not a woman."

Kubu didn't like that, but he was forced to accept it.

As soon as the deputy commissioner had left, Mabaku and Kubu discussed Gobey's reluctance to allow anyone else to be involved.

"I know you're skeptical," Mabaku said, "but you're going to have to trust me that he's honest. He's put himself in a very vulnerable spot and is scared of losing his reputation before he retires."

"Okay," Kubu replied, standing up to leave. "Let me check on that e-mail address he gave you. That could be very helpful indeed. I'll call the IT guys in Forensics right away to find out more about it. I'll let you know."

Kubu took the piece of paper from Mabaku and headed to his office.

He immediately phoned Forensics and asked to be put through to Helenka Koslov, a young Russian woman who had emigrated to Africa both for its wildness and its warmth. Forensics immediately saw the benefits of having an outstanding IT person on its staff and hired her right away. Her skills had already been used to convict several people on identity-theft charges, as well as one potential bank robber, who had left an electronic trail as obvious as a herd of elephants.

"Yes?" Helenka said as she answered the phone.

"Helenka," Kubu replied, "this is Assistant Superintendent Bengu."

"Ah, yes. What can I do for you?"

"What can you tell me about Hushmail?"

"You have lover you want to talk to privately, no?"

Kubu laughed. "I'm afraid not. This Hushmail may be a clue in a case we're working on."

"Okay." She paused, gathering her thoughts. "You use Hushmail if you don't want others to know about your e-mails. It is very easy to read most people's ordinary e-mails without difficulty. Hushmail encrypts e-mail and attachments using PGP encryption, so if e-mail is intercepted, it cannot be read unless reader also has access to sender's private password. This type of service is very popular in countries, like Russia, where government scans many e-mails. Companies also use Hushmail to exchange trade secrets."

"The e-mails must be stored somewhere. Couldn't we get access to them there?"

"It is possible, but difficult. If I remember, the company is in Vancouver, Canada. You would have to get court order from there to make company to release information. That might be difficult and take long time."

"And would they know the real identity of the owner of the e-mail address?"

"No. Not that even. But could tell you IP addresses of computers sending and receiving messages. IP address is, well, it's sort of like serial number that computer tells them."

Kubu wasn't a computer expert, but he thought he understood how this worked.

"If I *had* a lover with a Hushmail address, would I send her an e-mail from *my* computer or would I have to sign into Hushmail or would I go to an Internet café?"

"Ah. Good question. You can send e-mail from your computer. But dangerous because wife could find e-mail in Sent folder. But if you delete it from Sent folder, wife find nothing. But police can find it from ISP if you use their e-mail, even if you delete it. But need search warrant. You know what is ISP?"

"Yes, Internet service provider," Kubu answered, trying to keep track of all the alternatives.

"But, if you use Hotmail or Gmail, more difficult," Helenka continued. "Police can find e-mail but have to get court order to go to Microsoft or Google. In USA. Take time."

"And can someone find out if I have a Hushmail account?"

"Of course. Local ISP will know you access Hushmail. But won't know contents of e-mail."

"What about if I use an Internet café?"

"Same as home, except have to know you went there. You still use local or overseas e-mail account. Or Hushmail."

Kubu thought for a few minutes. "So, if someone sends an e-mail to a Hushmail address, we have to get a court order in Canada to get any details of who reads it. Right?"

"Yes. Any more questions?" Helenka was obviously eager to hang up.

"No more questions, Helenka," Kubu replied. "But please talk to Detective Khama and prepare an application for a court order in Canada, in case we need it. I'll e-mail you the Hushmail address."

"Okay."

"Thanks for your help. I may have more questions later."

"Okay," she said again and hung up.

Kubu pondered what he had heard and wondered whether he should send an e-mail to the witch doctor from his private e-mail asking for a consultation. After a few minutes' thought, he decided against it, because it would likely alert the witch doctor that his e-mail scheme had been found out.

The call came at precisely 4 p.m. Deputy Commissioner Gobey hadn't expected that. He'd expected the ring in the dark hours of the morning when, perhaps, he'd finally drifted into sleep. He picked up the cell phone, noted the number as private, and answered.

"Gobey."

"Yes. Why, Gobey? Why did you do it?" The voice was cool, almost a whisper, appearing just vaguely interested in the answer.

Gobey recognized the voice at once. Adrenaline flowed, but he kept his voice calm as he quickly walked through to his PA's office.

"Do what? I came to the meeting as arranged. But you weren't there."

He picked up the PA's pen and scribbled on her blotter: "Trace."

"Don't play games with me, Gobey. You knew you were followed. By the police."

"Followed? The police?" Gobey tried to sound surprised. He had to keep the witch doctor talking. Soon they would know where the call originated, and a police vehicle would be on the way.

"You think I don't know?" There was a laugh. It started like a deep chuckle but finished as something that should never come from a human throat. Gobey's skin crawled.

"I know everything," the voice continued. "I know where you are, what you're doing. Everything. Perhaps one of your own people is watching you for me. Or, maybe, it isn't a *person* at all." The laugh came again.

"What are you talking about? I came to the meeting. Waited as always. But you didn't appear, so eventually I came home. That's what happened." He had to keep the conversation going, had to give them time.

There was a moment's pause, and the response when it came was almost sad. "You're waiting for them to trace this call, aren't you, Gobey? You're pathetic. Now listen carefully." There was another pause, and then the voice said, much more loudly, "I don't need you anymore, Gobey. Do you understand? *I don't need you anymore.*"

Gobey felt that the phone had become a live thing, writhing in his hand. He nearly dropped it. He wanted to disconnect the call, but he knew he shouldn't. And the voice came again, *"I don't need you anymore."* Then the connection was broken.

Gobey dropped the phone and rushed to his secretary.

"Did they get it?"

She was speaking to someone on the phone but covered the mouthpiece and turned to him.

"The call came from a public phone in Africa Mall. A police car is nearly there." She turned her attention back to the phone.

Africa Mall! Right downtown! So close. Gobey collapsed into the visitor's chair and waited. But he knew the witch doctor wouldn't be there. Knew he would vanish. He wouldn't be walking around dressed in an animal skin and a mask. He would fade into the shopping crowds. No one would know where to look. Gobey waited a few minutes that seemed endless. At last she turned back to him.

"They grabbed a man at the phone, but he was the next caller. But he remembered the man who was there before him. They're getting a description. And checking for other witnesses."

Gobey nodded. He knew the value of casual eyewitnesses. They would get more from his own description of the man, even dressed in his witch doctor camouflage.

"Get onto Assistant Superintendent Bengu and tell him what happened. He should talk to the witness and check if there are any CCTVs around." Then he walked back to his office and collapsed into his desk chair. His breathing, never easy, became labored. He reached for his inhaler, took a couple of puffs, and tried to calm down. He looked around his office, recalling the witch doctor's words. He coughed and spotted his cell phone discarded on the desk. He doesn't need me anymore, he thought. I'll change the number, but he won't call again. He doesn't need me anymore.

He gathered some papers and shoved them into his briefcase, closed down his computer, and grabbed his jacket.

"Lori, I'm going home. I don't feel too well. I'll see you on Monday."

The PA looked at him with concern. "Yes, of course, rra. I'll arrange everything. I hope you feel better for the weekend."

Gobey nodded, tried to smile, and left.

He had just turned into the main road when his phone rang again. He checked the number and switched the call to his hands-free car kit.

"Hello, Bengu."

"*Dumela*, Deputy Commissioner. I'm following up on the call from the witch doctor. Can I ask you a few questions?"

"Go ahead."

"Would you tell me exactly what he said? It'll take a while to get the recording."

Gobey told him.

"What did he mean by 'I don't need you anymore'?"

Gobey shook his head. "I've no idea." But a cold wave ran up his spine. "Have you traced the owner of that house?"

"The registered owner thinks it's empty. He was pretty upset that someone was using it."

"Was he telling the truth?"

"I think so."

"Where could he have been? He obviously watched and saw that I was being followed. That's why he always comes after you've been waiting for a while. He—or some helper—is checking. We should've been more careful."

"We didn't realize he was that clever. But we'll get him. He had to walk to the shack; you said there was no car there the other times. Someone will have noticed him."

"It won't do me any good." Why did I say that? Gobey asked himself. Suddenly he had an overwhelming feeling that *something* was watching him from the backseat. The feeling was so strong that he turned at once and was surprised to see the seat empty. When he turned back to the road, a truck had cut in front of him, and he had to slam on the brakes. His tires screeched.

"Bengu, I'm in traffic. I need to concentrate. Call me later if there's anything else." He cut the connection.

He was sweating and wheezing. The shock of the truck, he thought. And the thing in the back . . . He shook his head. *Nothing* was in the back. But his skin crawled.

He dug in his pocket for the inhaler.

THIRTY-FOUR

"The witch doctor had to get to the house, which means he either drove or walked. Somebody had to see him." Kubu wrestled with the wheel of the Land Rover as one of the front wheels hit a deep pothole.

"You still believe your informant?" Samantha asked. "I think his story was just a setup to deflect attention from himself. Have you checked him out?"

"Yes, we've checked him out and believe he's telling the truth."

"And you still can't tell me who he is?"

"Unfortunately I can't. I tried to include you but wasn't able to. He made it absolutely clear that if anyone else knew about his involvement, he'd refuse to provide us with any information. Director Mabaku reluctantly agreed to that."

"A high-up *man*, that's what's clear to me."

Kubu didn't reply. He'd spotted the house he was looking for and was happy to change the subject.

"There's the house we're told the witch doctor uses. We'll park around the corner and walk to it. I picked up the key from the owner earlier this morning. Zanele should be here soon. I suggested that she come alone, not with the whole team." He paused. "Not that it makes much difference after Wednesday night."

He parked, and they walked the few hundred yards to the house. Next to the front door was a light with a naked bulb. Kubu looked at it carefully.

"The bulb is okay," he said. "Maybe that's what he uses to signal his clients to come in."

When Kubu tried to unlock the door, the key didn't work.

"He's changed the lock," he said. "Damn!"

"What are we going to do?"

"Let's take a look." Kubu walked slowly around the small house, carefully avoiding a footprint in the sand near the back door. He pulled out a small camera and photographed it. There were also tire tracks nearby. Kubu photographed those, too. Then he tried the key in the back door, but it didn't work. All the windows were shut and apparently covered with heavy blinds. It was impossible to see in.

"I'm going to call the owner." Kubu pulled out his notebook and flipped through it until he found what he wanted. Then he took his cell phone from his pocket and dialed a number.

"Rra Mogwe? This is Assistant Superintendent Bengu again. I'm at the house, but I think the locks have been changed." He paused to listen. "Are you sure? Thank you. I'll let you know what I find."

He hung up and walked once again to the back door. "He

says the back door has always had a suspect strike plate. He says a good kick will dislodge it and not damage the door any more than it is. Of course, if the witch doctor fixed it, we'll be in trouble."

He positioned himself in front of the door, steadied himself by holding Samantha's shoulder, and gave the door a solid kick next to the handle. The door crashed open. Kubu nodded to Samantha. "Let's take a look."

When they realized that there was no power, and no light coming in the windows, Kubu walked back to the Land Rover and fetched a flashlight. After putting on their boot covers and gloves, they walked in, closing the back door behind them. Then they searched the house, avoiding touching anything. Other than two chairs and a small table, all they found were a few candles and a kerosene lamp.

"Zanele isn't going to find much here," Samantha commented.

"We'll see," Kubu responded. "She finds stuff that no one else can see. Let's go and walk around the area and see what we can learn."

An hour later, they met in the Welcome Bar No. 2, which was only a few blocks from the house. Both Samantha and Kubu ordered Coca-Colas, two for him and one for her. They sat down at a corner table to compare notes.

"I didn't learn anything," Samantha said. "No one said that they'd seen anything or anyone out of the ordinary. And nobody had ever seen anyone go in or out of the house. It's really bizarre."

"Did you get any sense of whether they were afraid when you spoke to them?"

"No, I didn't. They all seemed to be relaxed."

"Only one of the people I spoke to had anything to report. He goes for a walk every day, past the house. He happened to notice fresh footprints at the front door about two weeks ago. But he says he's never seen anyone go in or out. He also didn't seem scared at all."

"The witch doctor is obviously a real person," Samantha said, "but he certainly tries hard to be invisible. I'm beginning to understand why Mma Gondo said he was."

Kubu glanced around. There were two large rooms. The one they were in had a dozen or so tables and a bar counter with a couple of men leaning against it; the other was a game room. There were a few pinball machines, one of which was being used by a teenage boy, who kept shaking it and banging on its side. A couple of his friends looked on. There was a foosball table, which was not being used, and a small pool table on which a quiet game was in progress between two well-dressed men, probably taking a break from work. And in the corner was a computer with a handwritten sign above—"InterNet cafee—10 pula 4 15 mins." What was a little odd was that whoever used the computer had their back to the wall so that the screen couldn't be seen by passersby.

"I'll be right back," Kubu said, standing up. He wandered into the game room and watched the pinball game for a few moments. Then he spun the handles of the foosball machine as though he were an expert player. Finally he walked over to the man using the computer. The man was so engrossed in what he was doing that he didn't notice Kubu until he was right next to him. With a start, he closed the window he was watching, but not before Kubu saw a couple of naked women entwined on a bed.

"*Dumela*, rra," Kubu said with a smile.

The man was flustered. "Yes. *Dumela.*"

"Can you tell me a bit about this computer?"

"Um, I just use it every now and again. To do e-mail."

Kubu nodded. "So, it's connected to the Internet?"

The man nodded, still embarrassed.

"Is it used a lot?"

The man nodded. "Yes, it's the only Internet café nearby."

"Anyway, sorry to disturb you. Please get back to your e-mail." Kubu gave the man a big smile and winked. He walked back to the table where Samantha was still sitting.

"*Shebeen*s have certainly changed since I used to go to them." Kubu smiled. "And that was a long time ago and not very often. Then they were just rooms where you could buy beer and a few spirits. Now they look like entertainment centers."

"Should we talk to the owner?"

"Of course, but after I've finished my drink."

It turned out that the owner rarely visited the premises, but the establishment was run by a manager, who was behind the counter, chatting to customers. When Kubu and Samantha asked to talk to him privately, he took them into a back room that served as an office.

"We have a very mixed crowd here. On the one hand, we have businessmen, and a few doctors and nurses because there's a clinic nearby, and we also have construction workers and people who only work occasionally. They're the ones who seem to spend most of what they earn on beer."

"Over the past month or two, have you noticed anyone unusual? Someone who seems nervous or keeps checking his watch as though expecting an appointment?"

The man shook his head. "The most unusual thing around here is how many of the professional guys use the computer to access porn sites or Facebook. They must be chatting to someone they don't want their wives to know about." Kubu nodded knowingly.

Kubu thought about what Gobey had said about leaving a message on a website. It would certainly be easy for the witch doctor in normal dress to check any website in complete privacy right here in the *shebeen*.

"Do you have a pay phone anywhere?"

The man shook his head. "No, but there's one a block down the road on the corner."

Kubu turned to Samantha. "Samantha, please could you go and get the number of the phone and check that it's working." Samantha nodded and left.

"And do you have a landline?"

The man nodded.

"Can I get its number, please? Do you ever let customers use it?"

"Occasionally, but I charge them five pula for a local call."

"That's a lot," Kubu exclaimed.

"I know, but I don't want to encourage it."

The manager gave Kubu the *shebeen*'s number. Kubu wrote it down and handed the man his card.

"Please call me if you hear or see anyone who you think is suspicious. Unfortunately that's all I can tell you."

"What's this all about?" the man asked with a frown.

"We're trying to find a murderer."

"A murderer!" the manager gasped. "In here?"

"No, no," Kubu replied. "We don't know if he's ever been here, but he was seen a few weeks ago *near* here. So we're just trying to see if something will turn up."

"What does he look like?"

Kubu shook his head. "We don't know that, either. All we know is that he's probably in his forties and of medium height. Not much to go on, unfortunately."

"Well, that's not much help, but I'll keep my eyes open."

"Thank you, rra." Kubu shook the man's hand and walked out.

THIRTY-FIVE

Kubu had set up one of the meeting rooms for the coordination of the *muti* cases. Two walls had whiteboards displaying mind maps. Two outlined the hypothetical connections between Lesego and Tombi and their abductors; another dealt with Bill Marumo; and in the center was the witch doctor with tentative connections to the others.

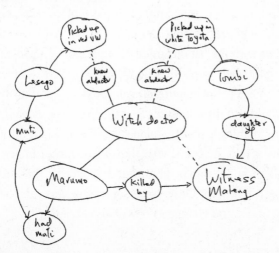

Half an hour after Kubu and Samantha returned to the CID headquarters, they met Mabaku in the meeting room.

"I need to remind you of our promise, Kubu," he said, nodding at Samantha.

"There's nothing that I'm going to say that will breach that promise, Director." Mabaku scowled and sat down. Kubu went to the whiteboard and drew.

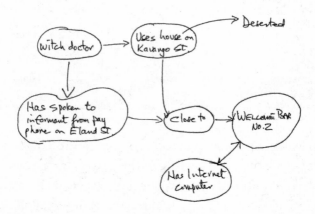

"This morning we visited a *shebeen* only a couple of blocks from the house the witch doctor used. We learned a few very interesting things. The most important piece of information is that there's a pay phone nearby—on Eland Street. We cross-checked its number with the list our informant gave us. The witch doctor phoned him once from it. Second, the *shebeen* doubles as an Internet café. I'm speculating, but it looks to me that the witch doctor could use the computer to pick up messages, and the pay phone for making calls. It's plausible. Then, when an appointment was set up, he could visit the *shebeen* in ordinary clothes and walk around the neighborhood to check that his client hadn't been followed. Only when satisfied it was safe, he would go to the house and change into his baboon outfit."

Mabaku took in this information. "Does the barman have any suspicions as to who it could be?" Mabaku asked.

"No, but I'd like to have the IT people in Forensics take a look at the computer. I'm told there's so much information on every computer that they can tell the color of the underwear users had on."

Samantha rolled her eyes.

"I'd like to leave a computer in the *shebeen* while we look at the one there," Kubu continued. "That'll make the manager more likely to let us take a look without formalities. Also, if the witch doctor does return, which I think is unlikely, it won't be so obvious we're snooping around."

"What do you expect to find?" Mabaku asked.

Samantha couldn't contain her excitement. "We'll be able to see if the website we were told about has been accessed and, if so, when," she said. "We'll also then be able to see what other websites and webmail sites were accessed around the same time. That may give us additional clues. I really think there's a chance we'll find something."

Mabaku sat quietly for a few moments. "Very well. Follow up on the computer, but don't do anything without checking with me." He stood up and headed for the door. He opened it, then turned. "Tomorrow is Marumo's funeral, Kubu. You need to be there." Then he was gone.

"He's given us the go-ahead!" Samantha exclaimed.

Kubu smiled weakly. He was pleased to have Mabaku's support but concerned about what the witch doctor would do as they closed in on him.

Then he groaned. The last thing he wanted was to spend an afternoon at the funeral of a politician he didn't respect.

THIRTY-SIX

Looking around the crowd packing the cemetery, Kubu wondered if every supporter of the Freedom Party had turned up. It was more like a political rally than a funeral. Whether they'd come to bid farewell to their old leader or to offer support to Jacob Pitso, the new one, he couldn't say. The only reason he could see and hear what was going on at all was that a platform had been erected at the graveside and a portable public address system had been installed. The coffin, draped in a Botswana flag, rested at the front of the platform in silent witness to the dignitaries' speeches.

Marumo's brother gave a dignified eulogy on Bill's life, but the speech given by Pitso was, in Kubu's opinion, more of a political diatribe than a tribute, and he found it in poor taste. Kubu suspected that Marumo's brother felt the same way, because when Pitso called for all to cry out against the injustice of the government and its tardiness in bringing Bill's murderer to justice, he remained unmoved in his seat with his arms folded. But the crowd erupted into angry cries and waved fists. Pitso waited for several moments with obvious satisfaction before he raised both arms to quiet the mourners so that he could continue.

Kubu wondered why he'd bothered to come. It was thought important for the police to attend a victim's funeral to show their concern to the family, but also to keep an eye open for unexpected mourners or peculiar behavior. However, Kubu had been unable to speak to Jubjub or any of Marumo's relatives. Their sorrow was out of reach—on display only from the platform.

Several hours had passed, and afternoon was turning to evening. Kubu was exhausted. He was hot, his feet were killing him from standing all afternoon, and he was irritated by the crush of sweaty people around him. The last words had been spoken, and people were starting to drift away. Although he was tempted to join them, he decided he'd better try to have a few words with the family. As the crowd thinned, he made his way forward.

Pitso and the relatives were still surrounded by well-wishers and friends. Also, Kubu noticed, they were attended by a small contingent of uniformed police. Pitso complained about the undemocratic government and questioned its handling of the murder, Kubu mused, but at the same time expected its protection.

Eventually Kubu was close enough to see Jubjub. She was sobbing on the shoulder of Dr. Pilane. Obviously the stress of the funeral, the heat, and the crowd had proved too much for her guarded composure. It was interesting that it was her neighbor to whom she'd turned. Perhaps her relationship with Bill's family hadn't been particularly close.

Kubu stepped back, not wanting to intrude, and walked around the group to the grave itself and looked around. He realized he was being watched by the undertaker and, not wanting to appear rude, walked over and greeted the man.

"*Dumela*, Rra Rampa, a very ornate affair today."

The man nodded. "Indeed, Assistant Superintendent Bengu. Very different from the last occasion when we met."

Both men smiled, each surprised that the other had remembered his name from their meeting at Nono's sister's funeral a month before.

"Obviously you manage a wide variety of funerals."

"Indeed. As I told you then, I direct funerals of distinction. But not all people can afford them. Then I do what I can to provide an appropriate farewell on a limited budget—sometimes on my own with volunteers from the deceased's family." Kubu was not altogether convinced about the altruism; these days, funerals seemed to be a growth industry in Botswana.

At that moment Pitso called to the undertaker, who made his apologies and hurried away. Jubjub also seemed to be in a better state, and Kubu offered condolences.

"Detective Bengu. Thank you. I read that you've caught Bill's murderer. You said you would."

"We have a suspect in custody."

"But not much has been said about why he killed Bill. Rra Pitso isn't convinced you've got to the bottom of this."

"Mma, we have good evidence, and we're confident that the man in custody is guilty. But I can't say more than that at the moment."

"I see," she said and abruptly turned away.

There seemed little point in staying longer, but as Kubu turned to go, he saw Jacob Pitso moving purposefully toward him.

"Detective? I understand from Mma Jubjub Oteng that you're the person in charge of the Bill Marumo murder case."

"That is correct, Rra Pitso. I am Assistant Superintendent Bengu of the CID." He offered his hand, but Pitso ignored it.

"I demand that the police make a full disclosure of the case. Not here to me, but publicly to the people of Botswana. You saw for yourself this afternoon how angry the people are. It was only with great difficulty that I restrained them."

"I saw how hard you tried."

Pitso nodded, missing the irony. "I must warn you, Detective, we don't buy the story of some madman taking it into his head to murder Bill. That's simply not good enough."

"Rra Pitso, I'm not sure where you got that information. We've arrested a suspect. We haven't established his motivation at the moment. We're still building the case. Everything will be out in the open when he comes to trial."

"*If* he comes to trial. I've heard that he may be declared unfit to stand trial. How convenient for the government."

Kubu sighed. The man wasn't as stupid as he appeared, and he had more information than had been given to the press. It seemed as though Mabaku's fears might be realized.

"I think it would be improper to speculate on the case, Rra Pitso. We'll just have to wait and see."

"I'm warning you, Detective, we won't wait too long." Pitso turned on his heel and stalked away.

Kubu sighed again. The whole afternoon had been wasted,

and now he was also late for supper. He'd achieved nothing except upsetting Jubjub and being upset by Pitso.

He took a last look at the remaining group. Pitso was talking animatedly to Jubjub and Marumo's family—no doubt telling them of the police's incompetence or worse. Workmen were dismantling the platform, taking down the loudspeakers, and packing up. And off to one side, Dr. Pilane was talking to the undertaker.

Kubu checked his watch. If he hurried, he could still spend some time with Tumi and Nono before they went to bed. He smiled, and his feet felt better as he started walking away.

THIRTY-SEVEN

It was Sunday morning, and Kubu was looking forward to seeing his parents. They hadn't visited the previous week because his parents' church in Mochudi had hosted an all-day retreat that they'd attended. When Kubu spoke to his mother during the week, she said that she'd found the day very uplifting, but that his father had behaved strangely. Wilmon had become quite agitated and had argued with the pastor about a variety of issues. It had started with Wilmon being upset by two young women who arrived in shorts and T-shirts, and he'd harangued the pastor to eject them, saying that they were being disrespectful. When the pastor replied that he was pleased to see young people taking their religion seriously, Wilmon had shouted at him for ignoring the traditions of respect and for encouraging disrespect. It was only when Amantle led Wilmon from the room and scolded him that he settled down.

As they drove to Mochudi, Kubu and Joy ignored the squeals and shouts of Tumi and Nono playing in the back of the Land Rover and discussed Wilmon's uncharacteristic behavior.

"I'm worried that he's getting dementia or Alzheimer's," Kubu said, as he negotiated a small herd of cows that had wandered onto the road. "I can't remember ever seeing him shout at anyone, except that time he got so angry with the kids for being in his garden. I think he needs to see a doctor."

"Good luck!" Joy replied. "I'd be amazed if Amantle can make that happen."

"Perhaps you can talk to her, my dear," Kubu said. "She loves and respects you. I think you've a better chance."

Joy thought for a few moments. "I'll try, but I'm not optimistic."

"Now let's have some fun," Kubu said with a smile. "Tumi. Nono. Get ready. We're going to sing."

The two girls squealed with delight.

"What do you want to sing?"

"The hippo song! The hippo song!"

Kubu sighed. Ever since the girls had heard the song—which Kubu had translated into Setswana for them—they always wanted it. He needn't have bothered to ask.

"Okay, let's go." They all joined in.

Mud, mud, glorious mud.
Nothing quite like it for cooling the blood.
So follow me, follow, down to the hollow,
And there let us wallow in glorious mud!

When they finished the rousing Flanders and Swann song,

the kids clamored for a reprise. And so Kubu and his family sang all the way to Mochudi.

The Land Rover pulled up in front of the senior Bengu's home just before eleven-thirty. As soon as they opened the doors, Ilia bounded up the stairs and jumped onto Wilmon's lap. He scratched her nose and tickled her ears, and she started to pant contentedly.

Tumi followed closely behind Ilia and was enveloped in a big hug from Amantle. Even the reserved Wilmon smiled as Tumi threw her arms around the old man's neck. Nono was more hesitant but obviously enjoyed Amantle's attention. However, Wilmon's frown kept her from embracing him.

"My son," Wilmon said as Kubu reached the veranda. "Why did you not tell me you had another child? What is her name?"

"Father, she's not our daughter. Her name is Nono, and she's Tumi's friend. We are looking after her at the moment. She was with us two weeks ago when we visited you. Remember?"

Wilmon looked puzzled for a few moments, then extended his hand and greeted Kubu in the traditional manner. As was her wont, Joy was much less formal and embraced both of them with much affection.

Wilmon gave the two children permission to explore his vegetable garden, and the adults sat down to enjoy a cup of tea and catch up on the previous two weeks' news.

"And how is Pleasant?" Amantle asked Joy. "Is she pregnant yet? Bongani takes so much time to make decisions that soon she'll be too old to have children. I've never met a man who is so slow."

Joy smiled. "I'm hoping that there will be good news soon.

Pleasant told me that they had decided it was time to have a child soon."

"*Aaii*. I don't understand people anymore." Amantle shook her head. "When you get married, you should have children right away. People think too much now. They should just do what God intended them to do."

"You are right, my mother," Joy said. "But Bongani wants to be a good father and have the time to spend with his child."

"I hope Pleasant will stop working. She's lucky to have found someone who would marry a woman who worked. A woman's place is at home."

"I'm sure she'll be a wonderful mother."

While this exchange was taking place, Kubu watched his father. The old man looked the same as ever, quietly watching the others talking.

"Father, let us leave the women and take a walk before lunch. I always like seeing your friends."

Wilmon struggled to his feet, and the two men walked down the steps to the sandy road.

Preparing the cold meat and salads was an excellent time for the two women to talk about topics they would not discuss in front of the men.

"Joy dear, how are things with Nono? What are you going to do about her?"

Joy stopped what she was doing. "I don't know. She is such a lovely girl when you break through her shyness."

"Do you want to adopt her?" Amantle cut to the core of the matter.

"At first we thought we'd look after her until we found a

good home. We never thought we'd start to love her as though she were our own."

"What does Kubu think about the idea?"

"Well, we haven't actually talked about it directly, but I can see how much he enjoys having her around. And Tumi would be very upset if Nono left. She's like a sister now. I'll have to speak to Kubu soon about it all."

"And what about her AIDS?"

Joy controlled herself. "She doesn't have AIDS, my mother. She has the HIV virus, but it is under control with retrovirals."

"I think you should speak—"

"Wilmon can't help her, nor can any of his healer friends."

"But . . ."

"I always listen to you, my mother, but this is one thing you are wrong about. I work with kids the whole time, and I know all about it."

Amantle took another tack. "Has she seen a doctor?"

"Yes. We've taken her to see Dr. Patel—he's our doctor— and she also sees the doctor who comes each week to where I work. They both say she's fine and quite safe to be with Tumi."

"Do they know what they are doing?"

"Yes, my mother. They both work at a lot of schools and know all about HIV."

"Well, my dear, I can see you want to adopt Nono. Even though I am afraid for Tumi and you, I will treat her as my own granddaughter. She is very quiet, but I like her."

Joy gave Amantle a huge smile, relieved that she'd come round. It would be easy to persuade Kubu with Amantle on her side.

"Thank you, my mother. Thank you."

Wilmon and Kubu walked down the street and were greeted by

numerous passersby. Wilmon smiled and proudly told everyone that his son was an important man in the police—a comment he'd made for at least ten years on their frequent walks around the neighborhood. After walking around the block, they were nearly home when Wilmon's neighbor Edwin came up to them.

"Hello, Wilmon. Hello, Kubu," he said jovially.

Wilmon took his extended hand and shook it, respectfully touching his right arm with his left hand. "How did you know my name?" he asked.

Edwin burst out laughing. "Your father is becoming a joker in his old age," he said to Kubu.

"Who are you, rra?" Wilmon was quite serious. Kubu and Edwin exchanged glances.

"Father," Kubu said. "This is your neighbor, Edwin Ngombe. You've known him for many years."

Wilmon frowned, staring at Edwin. Then he smiled. "I know you, but I can't remember your name."

"It's Edwin Ngombe, Wilmon. I live next door."

"I am pleased to meet you, rra. Please come and visit my wife, Amantle, and me for tea. I will ask Amantle to make arrangements with your wife."

"Okay, Wilmon. I will do that." Edwin looked at Kubu and shrugged.

"Come on, Father. It's lunchtime. We must go. Goodbye, Edwin." As he turned to leave, he continued in a whisper. "Have you noticed this before?"

Edwin nodded. "It's so sad to see this happening to such a wonderful old man."

"My mother, there is one other thing I want to talk to you about."

Amantle frowned. "Is there a problem?"

"You mentioned on the phone that Wilmon behaved strangely last Sunday at the retreat. We've also noticed some changes in his behavior. Is it getting bad?"

Amantle leaned against the counter. "My dear, I am so scared. He cannot remember things I tell him just a few minutes before. He sometimes does not remember people he has known for many years."

"I think you should take him to a doctor."

"I can't do that, my dear. He won't go."

"Have you tried?"

"Joy, when you have known Wilmon for as long as I have, you will know that you can't force him to do anything."

Joy sighed. "But he must see someone," she said.

Amantle just shook her head.

"I have an idea," Joy said. "Let me speak to Kubu."

"My dear, please don't force him to do anything. I have to live with him."

"I promise, my mother. We won't do anything without talking to you."

On the way home, Joy broached her idea with Kubu.

"Your mother's also worried about Wilmon. She says he's deteriorating quickly. Mentally, that is."

"I know. He didn't even remember Edwin Ngombe. He's only known him for thirty years."

"He needs to see a doctor but refuses to go."

"Can we sing some more?" Tumi shouted from the backseat.

"Your mother and I are talking. We'll sing in a few minutes," Kubu said.

"Next Sunday, let's have them to our house for lunch. We

can ask Dr. Patel if he'll come to the house when they're there."

"That's a good idea. I'll speak to him tomorrow."

Kubu and Joy sat in silence, each wondering about the implications for the family if Wilmon continued to deteriorate so quickly.

"Can we sing now, Daddy?" Tumi asked.

Although not in the mood, Kubu nodded.

"It's Sunday. Let's sing a hymn," he suggested, hoping to avoid the hippo song.

"'Jingle Bells.' I want 'Jingle Bells'!" Nono called out.

Kubu glanced at Joy and smiled.

Part Five

A DEED WITHOUT A NAME

*"How now, you secret, black, and
midnight Hags? What is't you do?"
"A deed without a name."*

MACBETH, ACT 4, SCENE 1

THIRTY-EIGHT

Mabaku and Kubu weren't sure if they'd be welcome at the deputy commissioner's home. Or what they would find, if they were. All the deputy commissioner's PA had told them was that Gobey was ill, and she was canceling all his appointments for the week.

Mabaku rang the bell, and Maria opened the door.

"I'm Jacob Mabaku, Mma Gobey. I'm a colleague of your husband. And this is Assistant Superintendent Bengu. We're from the CID. We need to see the deputy commissioner. I'm sorry he's not well, but I'm afraid it's quite urgent."

Maria looked at the two men; she was unsure what to do. But Kubu smiled and held out his hand so that she had no option but to take it. "You'd better come in. I'll see if he'll talk to you." She had meant them to stay in the hall while she found out, but they followed her up the stairs.

"He likes to sleep alone when he's not well," she said almost apologetically. "He thinks his coughing will disturb me. I don't mind, of course, but he insists . . ."

Kubu nodded sympathetically. "It's very natural that he'd be concerned." He hoped Joy wouldn't decide to solve his snoring problem that way.

She brought them to the closed door of the guest room and stopped. "When he came home on Friday, he wouldn't tell me what had happened. Just that he wasn't well. He looked terrible. I gave him supper, but he just fiddled with it. Hardly ate a thing. Just drank some water. He usually enjoys a beer on a Friday. Then he went to bed. He hasn't been up the whole weekend. And he hardly eats or drinks. Just a little water."

Kubu could see that she was close to tears.

"Can't you call family?"

"Our son phoned from Francistown. Tebogo talked to him, but he sounded so flat. They're usually so close." Her eyes filled with tears. "He won't see anyone. I know he won't want to talk to you, but I thought maybe work colleagues—"

"We'll try to help," Mabaku said. "The deputy commissioner is a good man. He has helped make the BPF a first-rate police force. He needs to know that."

Maria nodded and opened the door. "Tebogo, these men are from the CID. They need your input very urgently. Please help them." She sounded desperate.

Gobey was lying on his side wearing long pajama bottoms, with just his feet under the covers. His head was turned away from them, facing the wall. His back gleamed with sweat.

Kubu was shocked at how ill he looked. He'd never visualized the deputy commissioner as other than a leader, appropriately dressed.

"Go away," Gobey said without turning to them. "I'm sick. It's the weekend. I'll see you in my office on Monday."

"Tebogo, it is Monday," Maria said nervously.

Gobey rolled over and tried to sit up. But it seemed too much effort. Maria propped him up with some pillows. He started to cough, and she had to find his inhaler. It had fallen onto the floor and rolled under the bed.

After a few minutes Gobey was a little better and more alert. He focused on the two men.

"Mabaku, Bengu, what do you want?"

Kubu leaned forward. "We need you, Deputy Commissioner. You have to help us catch this evil man. He'll kill again. You're our only link. Our one hope of getting to him before he murders another child." Maria gasped but didn't interrupt.

Gobey looked from Kubu to Mabaku and back. "I've told you what I know. I tried to help you. I can't do anything now. *He doesn't need me anymore.* Don't you understand?" Suddenly he jerked up and peered over the end of the bed. Then he relaxed back onto the cushions and started to cough. When he could talk again, he said to Maria, "Why did you bring them here? I said I didn't want to see anybody." He turned his back and faced the wall again. He started to shiver, and Maria pulled the covers over him.

"You'd better go," Maria said. She sounded defeated. They left the room, and she closed the door.

Mabaku took her hand. "Mma Gobey, he needs a doctor."

She shook her head. "He won't see anyone."

"I've seen this before, mma. He believes the witch doctor has cursed him. It's in his head somehow. You will need a real doctor, but maybe also a witch doctor to lift the curse."

"We don't believe in that sort of stuff," Maria whispered, but she didn't meet his eyes. "We go to church. We trust in God."

"Well, get your minister then. The church also believes in demons, in exorcism. You must do this at once before it's too late."

Kubu wondered if Mabaku was serious. He was talking about a deputy commissioner of police! An educated man, respected throughout southern Africa. Then he thought of the man in the room next to them, scared and sweating and shivering. He'd probably absorbed his belief in witch doctors with his mother's milk. "I think the director is right, mma. Phone your son. Tell him to come at once. This is a crisis."

The woman appeared helpless. She just stared at them and nodded, but without conviction. Then the tears started to flow silently, and she turned away.

They saw themselves out.

THIRTY-NINE

Kubu was depressed when he returned to his office. He didn't know the deputy commissioner well—Mabaku had more inter-action at that level—but he'd grown to respect the man. Now Gobey needed help, but his wife and family seemed too weak to shoulder the load. Kubu badly wanted to get his hands on the witch doctor behind all this, but they had so little to go on. He calmed himself down by having two cups of tea and several cookies.

He was in a better mood when the door opened and one of the detectives handed him a phone message.

"For you. She rang about an hour ago."

Kubu looked at the paper. Please call Helenka, it read. ASAP.

He picked up the phone and dialed the number for Helenka Koslov, the forensic IT specialist.

"I look at computer from *shebeen*," she said, after a short greeting. "Only two times computer used for Hushmail. First one in December last year. Last one, one week ago. Monday, May seventh, at sixteen-forty-five, for three minutes. Don't know who used it. Same person also looked at Yahoo and Johannesburg Stock Exchange. Does *shebeen* have CCTV? Easy to check then."

"No, it doesn't, unfortunately. And there are none in the streets around the *shebeen*. But I'll ask if anyone remembers who was using the computer at that time."

"Maybe we put program on computer before return it to catch keystrokes. May find how to sign onto Hushmail and what is on e-mails."

"You can do that?"

"Old program. Been round many years. Easy to do. Hard to find."

"If we get the owner's permission, would it be legal?"

"Maybe legal to see what sites people use. Not legal, I think, to read people's e-mails. You should check."

Kubu thought for a moment. "Put it on. I'll get permission from the manager. He doesn't want murderers hanging out there."

"Okay. Bye." Helenka hung up before Kubu could thank her.

It's a long shot, Kubu thought. Only twice in the last five months. And he's likely to be much more careful now.

He shook his head. With computer programs like the one Helenka had described, it was impossible to have privacy online. For the police maybe that was good. For law-abiding people, maybe not.

Just as he started to work his tedious way through all the paperwork he'd been ignoring, the phone rang.

"Bengu."

"*Dumela*, rra. It's Big Mama here. Big Mama from the *shebeen*."

Kubu was immediately interested. Did the bar owner have more information about Maleng and the Marumo killing? "*Dumela*, mma. How can I help you this morning? Did you remember something else?"

"No, I want to talk to you about another matter. It's about Mabulo Owido. He's disappeared."

Kubu sighed. He hoped that Big Mama wasn't the sort of busybody who would be calling him with all her hunches and everyone's domestic problems. Still, he needed to hear her out. "Go on."

"He was here Saturday a week ago. And we chatted a bit. He was alone, you know. Didn't know anyone. He's not from these parts. So I said I'd find him a nice girl. He was pleased about that, so I arranged for Lemme to come on Saturday and dress up nicely. She's a sweet girl, not pretty but nice, and not too fussy." So perhaps Owido wasn't very attractive, Kubu thought. Odd name, too. Sounded foreign.

"He said he would come, but he didn't. Lemme was very upset."

"Maybe he went somewhere else." Some men would run a mile to avoid Big Mama's matchmaking, Kubu thought.

Big Mama swept this aside. "He also told me where he worked. I phoned them this morning. He hasn't been there all week. I'm worried. He's a foreigner. And a *leswafe*."

Suddenly Kubu was interested again. "An albino?"

"Yes, that's why I'm so worried. I think he came here from Tanzania to escape the witch doctors there. You know how they want albinos for *muti*. They'll pay a fortune. I read about the trouble for those poor people in the newspapers. It's terrible."

"And you think that may be what's happened here?"

"Yes. Maybe. It's so sad. He seemed a nice man. Will you look for him?"

Kubu promised to do that, noted the man's details and work number, thanked her, and hung up. It would probably lead nowhere, but he knew witch doctors sought albinos for making their most powerful potions. He couldn't afford to ignore this.

It took Kubu only a few minutes to get through to the owner of the small furniture factory where Owido worked. At first the owner pretended he'd never heard of Owido, but when Kubu pushed him and pointed out that Big Mama had spoken to him, he became more helpful.

"Look, superintendent, the man was hungry and wanted to work. I said he could clean up in the packing room. Maybe he helped with the packaging. He wasn't really an employee, more like casual help."

Kubu knew what this was all about. Owido was a foreigner, not entitled to work in Botswana, maybe living illegally in Botswana, and the factory owner could get into trouble for giving him any sort of job. No doubt Owido was paid half the going rate and glad to get it.

"I'm not interested in whether he was legal or not," Kubu said. "I just want to get in touch with him. When did you last see him?"

"He didn't come in at all last week. I guess he decided to move on. Maybe he went back to wherever he came from."

"He had a week's wages coming. Did you pay him?"

The man hesitated. "No, as a matter of fact we pay at the end of the month."

"So he walked away from the money?"

"Well, I wasn't really surprised. There'd been some trouble. Some of the other workers didn't like having him around. Being an albino, you know? And a foreigner. A couple of them pushed him around. I shouldn't have been so kindhearted and given him a chance."

At half wages, Kubu thought. "Do you have an address for him? Cell number?" He wrote down the information and thanked the man curtly.

He tried Owido's cell phone, but it went straight to voice mail, so it was probably off. Next he contacted the number Owido had given the factory for where he lived. The phone was answered by a woman who explained that he'd called a boardinghouse near Broadhurst Mall, and that she was the landlady. Kubu asked her about Mabulo Owido.

"Owido? Haven't seen him for a week. Luckily I get the rent in advance. I did him a favor renting him a room at all. He upsets the other tenants, but he made a good offer so I let him stay."

Yes, Kubu thought. Half wages and double rent. This town's generous to albinos.

"Do you remember exactly when you last saw him?"

"Saturday afternoon a week ago. He said he was going out in the evening, but he didn't come back."

"How do you know?"

"I lock up at night. I don't think he was in. And this is a bed-and-breakfast," the woman added with pride. "They all get *pap* in the morning. He wasn't there for breakfast on Sunday."

Kubu thought about it. "If I come over, can you let me into his room?"

"Why would you want to do that?"

"Just to look around. Maybe he's moved out."

"You don't have to bother. All his stuff's still there. I already looked. But please yourself."

"Was he behind with the rent?"

"No one gets behind with the rent here. In advance, first of the month, or they're out."

Kubu believed it. "Thank you, mma. I'll contact you if I need anything else. In the meanwhile, keep his room locked."

"All very well, but what about next month? I need to rent that room. I can't afford to have it empty. His stuff's not worth much."

Kubu sighed and promised to be in touch. Then he sat back and thought about it. Wages abandoned, possessions abandoned with the rent paid for the month, a foreigner no one would miss, an albino whose body parts were prized for *muti*. He started to feel excited. This might be a new lead to the witch doctor they sought, or at least to someone close to him. Then again, there might be a simple explanation. Owido might have been scared off, or even arrested as an illegal immigrant.

Kubu called Samantha and filled her in. "This could be nothing, but it could be important. See what you can find out about this Owido. Did he enter the country legally? See if Immigration knows anything about him. Then get over to BIG MAMA KNOWS ALL and try to find out what you can about that Saturday night. Who was there? When did Owido leave? Did anyone follow him?" Samantha said she'd get onto it right away.

Kubu thought it through. This wasn't a young girl being offered a lift on the road. This was a grown man who was used to being taunted and used to danger because of his unfortunate lack of skin pigment. If he had been abducted for *muti*, it would have taken at least two people. The witch doctor would have needed help. And that help wouldn't be invisible, even if the witch doctor was. This was a potential breakthrough.

Then Kubu's excitement faded and was replaced by sadness. The albino had come to Botswana, probably in search of a haven, and had found only discrimination and exploitation and, perhaps, a horrible death. Disgust overwhelmed him.

And he became very angry.

FORTY

Samantha was pleased, and a little surprised, to find a help-ful man at the Department of Immigration and Citizenship, who was able to retrieve information on Owido quite quickly. Apparently he'd entered the country legally about five months before, indicating that he was a tourist. He'd given a motel in Gaborone as his address. There was, however, no record of him leaving Botswana, and he was still within the time allowed him at entry. He was, of course, not entitled to work in the country.

Samantha thought it likely that Owido's plan was to stay in the country illegally, but at the moment there was no reason for him to be on the run from the police or anyone else, as far as she could tell.

She checked her notes and then headed for the factory where Owido had worked. The owner was a little nervous about a follow-up visit after the call from Kubu, but he was polite and tried to answer her questions. However, she learned nothing more than what Kubu had discovered. At her request, he pointed out the people with whom Owido had worked. Most had little time for her—or, it appeared, for Owido—but one man was more helpful. He had a broad, open face and his ready smile made Samantha smile also.

"Mabulo? He was a good guy. Willing to do the jobs other people didn't want, like cleaning up at the end of the day. I had a beer with him once, and we had a nice chat. But people looked at us strangely. You know?"

Samantha nodded, although she couldn't see why people didn't mind their own business.

"When did you last see him?"

"On Friday afternoon a week ago. He wanted to know where he could go for a nice evening that Saturday, and I suggested a place. You won't believe it, but it's called BIG MAMA KNOWS ALL. But he said he didn't know anyone and didn't want to go alone, so I said I might join him there. He was pleased about that." He looked down at his feet. "But I got tied up with something else."

"Was he unhappy here? Any reason for him to leave suddenly?"

He shook his head. "Look, people aren't always fair, you know? And sometimes if you're different . . . and a foreigner . . . they're sometimes unkind. But it was okay, you know? I hope you find him. I hope he's all right."

Samantha nodded and thanked him.

She thought through what Kubu had told her and what she had learned subsequently. There was no apparent reason for the albino's sudden disappearance, and she had a bad feeling about what may have happened to him. She decided that a visit to BIG MAMA KNOWS ALL should be next on the agenda.

Samantha greeted Big Mama and received a big hug in exchange, as though she were an old friend. "Come and sit, my dear, and have some tea." The large woman led her to a side table. Samantha hardly expected tea at a *shebeen*, but she'd begun to realize that things were not always as expected at BIG MAMA KNOWS ALL.

The two women sipped their tea and chatted for a few minutes about mutual acquaintances before Samantha got around to her questions.

"Do you remember exactly when Owido left that Saturday night?"

Big Mama thought it was around nine o'clock, but she didn't actually see him go.

"Can you remember who else was here that night? Were there any strangers? And particularly any who came by car?" If Owido had been abducted, then it must have been in some sort of vehicle.

It was now more than a week later, but Big Mama had a good recollection of most of her customers of that Saturday night. She pointed to each table in turn, visualizing who had sat at it. Samantha noted all the names. Big Mama also remembered that there was a number of customers that she hadn't seen before. She said her waitress might know them, but she only worked in the evenings.

"As to vehicles, there's Lome, the butcher. He came in his van. He sat there." Big Mama pointed to a seat at the bar.

Samantha made a note. A butcher's delivery van sounded quite promising, although the thought of what might have happened at the butchery made her feel sick. "Do you remember when he left?"

"He kept looking at the door as though he was expecting someone. Eventually another guy turned up, and they left together."

"What time was that?"

Big Mama shrugged. "I remember it was getting really busy. Maybe it was around nine." About the same time as Owido. Samantha put a star next to Lome on her list.

She looked farther down the list for people with vehicles. "What about this Sunday Molefe and his friend?"

"Sun has an old Volkswagen Jetta. I don't know who the friend was, but I think they came in together. They sat outside. A few tables down from Owido." Samantha realized it would be a good place to keep an eye on the albino.

"When did they leave?" she asked.

Big Mama thought about it. "When I noticed Owido had gone, they were gone, too."

"Was anyone else sitting outside?"

Big Mama thought again. "Just two girls I didn't know." She took a sip of tea. "They were sharing one beer," she added with a hint of disapproval.

"Do you know much about Molefe?"

Big Mama shook her head firmly, causing a ripple through her fat. "He calls himself a businessman but never specifies what business that is." She drained her tea and chuckled. "Not really my 'cup of tea,' as they say in English." Samantha thought it an odd phrase, but she realized Big Mama didn't care for Molefe. That alone was enough to put a star next to his name.

By the time Big Mama had finished her analysis of each person, Samantha had two starred names to follow up. Then there were the two men Big Mama didn't know. Samantha decided to start with Sunday Molefe. He and the butcher seemed the most promising.

Samantha drove slowly down the street on which Molefe lived, and tried to make out the house numbers. Eventually she spotted a battered Volkswagen Jetta parked at the side of the road, outside the house she sought. It was lunchtime on a Monday, but it looked as though Molefe was home.

She banged on the door and waited. Eventually, it was opened by a youngish man wearing only khaki shorts and sandals. He was well-built and quite good-looking, but his teeth had been neglected.

"Who're you?"

"Are you Sunday Molefe?" Samantha showed him her police identification.

He studied it carefully, then nodded. "What do you want?"

"I want to ask you a few questions. Can I come in?"

"I suppose so." He stood aside enough so that she could enter by brushing past him. She got a whiff of bad breath and grimaced. He led her to the main room of the house and sat down at a wooden dining table in front of a half-eaten plate of *pap* with fatty sausages. He didn't invite her to sit, but looked her over, starting at her face and working down. His expression made it clear that he'd seen better, and he resumed his lunch.

Samantha ignored his rudeness and helped herself to a chair. "We're trying to trace a man who's gone missing."

"Why are you asking me?"

"We think you may have seen him. Where were you on the evening of Saturday, the fifth of May?"

"Saturday a week ago?" He appeared to think about it. "I went to a *shebeen* with my friend Wilson. We had a few drinks, and then went to the Gaborone Sun and gambled."

"Which *shebeen* was that?"

"It's called BIG MAMA KNOWS ALL." He laughed. "Actually she knows nothing, but that's what it's called."

"Did you notice anyone there in particular? Maybe someone who looked out of place?"

Molefe shrugged. "Look, it was more than a week ago. I don't know. I picked up Wilson; we cruised around a bit and went for a drink." He used the sausage to shovel up *pap*. He chewed with his mouth open, exposing the bad teeth.

"When did you get there and when did you leave?"

"I don't remember exactly. Okay?" It wasn't okay, but Samantha had to accept it for the time being.

"When did you get to the casino?"

"That was about nine o'clock. We gambled for a few hours. Lost. We had a couple of drinks and split. Look, what's this all about anyway?"

Samantha ignored that. "Did you speak to anyone at the Sun?"

"Yes, some girls later on. And the bartender. He'll remember us. Bastard stole a hundred pula from me."

"How's that?"

"I gave him a two-hundred pula note, and he said we'd only given him a one hundred. I even gave him our names so he could check later and call us. But he never did, the bastard."

How convenient, Samantha thought. I bet you asked for his name, as well as giving him yours. "Did you get his name?"

Molefe took out his wallet from the back pocket of his

shorts and scratched around till he found a scrap of paper. He gave it to her, smiling.

Samantha read it, then looked up at him. "What about the albino?" she asked casually.

Molefe frowned, then he deliberately put the rest of the sausage in his mouth and chewed it carefully. After he'd swallowed, he asked, "What albino?"

"The albino who was sitting near you at BIG MAMA KNOWS ALL. You must remember him."

Molefe shook his head. "You think I remember everyone I see in a bar? Maybe a girl—a good-looking girl. But there's no shortage of them, either." He shrugged.

Very relaxed, casual, not worried at all, Samantha thought. He's very pleased with himself, but that doesn't mean he's guilty of anything. She asked him for Wilson's full name and contact details, which he gave her without hesitation.

With nothing more to ask, she was glad to leave Molefe to his lunch.

The Always Best Meat butchery was in Broadhurst Mall. Lome worked there with an assistant and a woman who ran the cash register. The shop was busy at lunchtime, and Lome was doing a brisk trade in delicacies like tripe, sweetbreads, and game meat as well as more usual fare. Samantha had a good look around and watched Lome efficiently dealing with the meat. He was a hefty man; she could visualize him overpowering the albino and bringing him here. The screech of bone being sawed set her teeth on edge.

At last the shop emptied, and she was able to talk to Lome. She showed her identification, and he took her to a tiny room at the back, leaving the butchery in the hands of his assistant. He appeared nervous and kept looking out into the shop.

"I hope this will be quick," Lome said. "My apprentice is only learning."

"I just need to ask you a few questions. We're trying to trace a man who's missing. We think you may be able to help us."

Lome shrugged. "I will if I can."

"Where were you on Saturday night, the fifth of May?"

Lome jerked round, surprised. "Saturday before last? I had a few drinks at a bar. After that I went home and watched TV."

"Which bar?"

"It's called BIG MAMA KNOWS ALL. Fun place."

"Did you go alone?"

"That's right."

"Did you meet up with someone there?"

"No. I said I was alone. Just chatted to the people sitting nearby."

"And when did you leave?"

Lome glanced at his watch as though it would remind him, and then looked out to the shop again. His assistant was cutting T-bone steaks. "Around nine, I think it was. Something like that."

Samantha made notes slowly, letting Lome worry about the steaks. Then she looked up and asked, "Did you see an albino man at the *shebeen*?"

Lome returned his attention to her, and hesitated. "Maybe. I think there was an albino sitting outside. So what? I don't know him."

"And you left there alone?"

"That's what I keep telling you."

* * *

Driving back to the CID, Samantha reviewed the two interviews, deciding how she would summarize them to Kubu.

Molefe was relaxed and self-confident with a conveniently constructed alibi for later that Saturday night. But he'd reacted to the question about the albino, and had given himself time to prepare his answer. Lome, on the other hand, was clearly nervous about something, and had lied about not meeting anyone at the *shebeen*. Yet his response to the albino question was completely natural. He'd seemed surprised by it, but not at all concerned.

Could he react that way with bits of Owido in his cold room? Samantha shuddered. She didn't think so, but men occasionally surprised her. She wished Kubu had been with her, but she wasn't going to admit that to him.

FORTY-ONE

When Samantha reported back, Kubu encouraged her to follow up by returning to BIG MAMA KNOWS ALL that evening and talking to the waitress.

She tidied up her office, closed down her computer, and went to the Wimpy at Game City for a quick hamburger. Then she returned to the *shebeen*, finding it crowded despite it being a Monday night.

Big Mama was very busy keeping the customers supplied with drinks, but she waved to Samantha when she came in, and as soon as she could she bustled over with a Coke.

"Have you discovered something?" she asked, puffing a bit after all the running around.

Samantha shook her head. "I'd like to speak to that waitress you said is here in the evenings—perhaps she noticed something about Owido and the people you didn't know."

Big Mama nodded. "Her name's Nuru, but one of her children is sick, so she'll only be in later. That's why I'm so busy. We'll chat as soon as I have a chance." Then she was off again.

Samantha sat at a small table out of the way and nursed the Coke, hoping Nuru wouldn't take too long to appear. About fifteen minutes later, a rather plain girl wearing an apron approached. "I'm Nuru," she announced, pulling up a chair. "Now, how can I help you? Big Mama is already upset I'm so late, so it better be quick."

Samantha explained what she wanted, and the woman thought about it. "I don't know the two girls that sat outside. One beer between them and no tip. There were also two guys that hadn't been here before, but they joined up with some regulars and left late."

That was a dead end, Samantha thought, but perhaps the girl knew something about Owido.

"Do you remember the albino who was here that night?"

"Oh, yes. He was sitting outside."

"Did you notice exactly when he left?"

"It was just before nine. I was going to have a cigarette break at nine, and it was just before that."

"Did you see anyone else leave at about that time?"

Nuru nodded. "When I went to pick up the empty glass, I saw Sunday Molefe and his friend swallow the rest of their beers and leave as well. None of them left a tip."

Samantha leaned forward. "You mean Molefe and the other man followed the albino?"

Nuru shrugged. "I didn't watch them. Maybe they went another way. But they seemed in a hurry to leave as soon as he did."

Samantha asked several more questions, but Nuru couldn't help her with anything else. So she thanked the woman and headed for home, getting to bed later than usual.

The next morning she slept through the alarm and rushed to interview Molefe's friend, Wilson Demene, before he went to work. Although it was after eight by the time she found the house, he was still there. He responded to her third knock, unshaven and with a hint of alcohol on his breath.

"What do you want?"

Samantha showed him her police identification.

His face fell. "Oh, police." He hesitated, avoiding her eyes. "Look, I'm busy. Could you come back later?"

"It's very urgent, Rra Demene. It won't take long."

"Just a minute." He closed the door, and she heard him talking and a woman replying. He said "police" loudly, and a moment later the back door slammed and footsteps hurried away. Then Demene let Samantha in.

The front door opened onto the living room, bachelor-furnished with a wooden table, a few mismatched chairs, and a large television. He offered Samantha a seat.

"Rra Demene, I want to ask you about Saturday night a week ago." Demene nodded, looking down at the table.

"Where were you that night?"

"I was with my friend, Sunday Molefe. We drove around a bit, had a few drinks at a *shebeen*, and then went to the Gaborone Sun and gambled."

"Which *shebeen* was that? When did you get there?"

"Around seven. A place called BIG MAMA KNOWS ALL." He shrugged.

"Did you see an albino at the *shebeen*?"

Demene became agitated. "No! Why would I? I avoid them anyway. They bring bad luck. We just had a few drinks, that's all."

"There was an albino sitting opposite you. You must've noticed him."

"I ignored him. I mean I would've ignored him if I'd seen him. I told you I don't like them."

"When did you leave?"

"About nine."

"Did you follow the albino?"

"No. We went to the Sun. You can check with the bartender." He hesitated. "I told you I didn't see any albino. How could I follow him?"

Samantha didn't bother to pursue that. She would just hear Demene mouthing Molefe's story again.

She tried a few more questions, but Demene stuck to his story despite his nervousness. Eventually she thanked him for his time and left.

Next she went to the Gaborone Sun. The bartender who had served Molefe wasn't in yet, but the restaurant manager phoned him for her. She spoke to him for several minutes and discovered that he had seen Molefe and Demene, although his version of the money story was different. Then she drove to the CID, headed straight to Kubu's office, knocked, and went in. She found Kubu in a pensive mood behind his desk, nibbling cookies. He looked up and nodded toward a seat. She accepted an offered cookie; breakfast had been rushed.

"I've been thinking about the butcher, Lome," Kubu said. "Why would he deny meeting someone at Big Mama's? It happened in front of everyone there. He would know that we could check up on that. And I can't believe the witch doctor would display himself in such a public place if he meant to abduct and kill someone there. It doesn't make sense."

Samantha thought about it. "Maybe Lome met someone else he doesn't want the police to know about. Nothing to do with Owido."

Kubu smiled. "Exactly what I was thinking. We'll still need to check it, but I think if we let him know we're investigating a possible murder, he'll tell us the truth." He finished the cookie and casually reached for another. "What did you find out last night?"

Samantha could hardly contain her excitement. "The server I spoke to at BIG MAMA KNOWS ALL said that when Owido left, she saw Molefe and Demene drain their glasses and leave, too. She said it was just before nine. They may have been the last people to see him!"

Kubu put down the cookie he was about to pop into his mouth. "Samantha, that makes a huge difference. It's still circumstantial, but if Molefe and Demene were following him, they may be the culprits."

Samantha nodded. "I followed up this morning with Demene. I didn't learn much more, but he was really nervous."

"Nervous?"

"Yes. Not meeting my eyes, glancing away, hesitating over answers. Anyway, he denied he'd seen an albino at the *shebeen* even though he kept getting confused about that. He said that he wouldn't go near one anyway because he didn't like them and they bring bad luck. Apart from that he repeated exactly what Molefe said. Obviously Molefe had told him about my visit." She sighed. "I should have gone straight to Demene from Molefe yesterday."

"Maybe not. It may have been a good idea to let him stew. Anyway, Molefe would have called him the moment you left."

Samantha nodded. "And their alibi checks out as far as it goes. I spoke to that bartender at the Gaborone Sun. He remembered them all right. Molefe definitely only gave him a hundred-pula note, and then made a big fuss. However, it happened some time after he came on duty, and that was at ten p.m. So it only proves that Molefe and Demene were at the Gaborone Sun more than an hour after Owido left the *shebeen*."

"You've achieved a lot, Samantha. We've narrowed the possibilities down, and I think our best bet at the moment is Molefe and Demene. I've got an idea about how to handle Rra Demene. I think I'll pay him a visit."

"Should I come with you?"

Kubu thought about it, then shook his head. "I think this might work better if I'm on my own. You have a go at getting the truth out of Lome."

Samantha had to be satisfied with that.

FORTY-TWO

Wilson Demene was not at home, but a neighbor suggested Kubu try a small bar nearby, where Wilson was known to hang out. Kubu followed her advice, and the barman pointed out Demene, sitting with a couple of other men, deep in conversation, drinking Shake Shake beer. Kubu went to their table and sat down.

"Who're you?" one of the men asked. Kubu ignored him and focused on Demene.

"Are you Wilson Demene?" he asked the man who'd been pointed out.

Demene glared at him. "So what? We're busy. And this is private."

Kubu passed him his identification. Demene glanced at it, then scrutinized it properly. "You're from the police, the CID? I already told that woman you sent everything I know. Why are you hounding me? I've done nothing."

The other two men took their beers and moved off. Demene's eyes followed them to two stools at the far end of the bar.

"I just want to go over a few points with you. It's important," Kubu said.

"I haven't done anything. Why do you people keep asking me questions? I've told you everything."

"What sort of work do you do, Rra Demene?"

"Well, I buy and sell stuff. A middleman, if you like."

"So you fill orders for people?"

"Not so much for people. More for shops and so on."

"What sort of orders?"

"Whatever they want. I find it for them, get a good price."

Kubu nodded, as if he were satisfied. "Does that include finding people?"

"What do you mean by that?"

"Tell me about the albino, Mabulo Owido."

"The man at BIG MAMA KNOWS ALL? I told your detective. I didn't notice him. I would have avoided him anyway. I don't like them." Demene grabbed his beer and took a gulp, but his hand was unsteady.

"You see," said Kubu quietly, "my information is different. My information is that you were watching him and, when he left, you and your friend Sunday Molefe followed him."

"It's not true!" Demene cried. "Where did you get that information from? We went to the Gaborone Sun to gamble. You can ask the bartender there."

"Oh, we've done that. But you see our information is very specific. There's no doubt about it. Now, what we don't know is exactly what happened after that. And that's as important for you as it is for me. What happened to Owido after he left the *shebeen*? Where was he taken? What was done to him after that?"

Demene jumped to his feet. "You're just trying to pin it on us with no evidence at all. I'm leaving right now."

Kubu stood up, too. "I haven't accused you of anything, Rra Demene. You seem to know something we don't. What are we trying to pin on you?" He paused. "That you were involved in Owido's disappearance, perhaps?"

For several seconds the two men stood looking at each other. Kubu knew that this was the critical moment. If Demene left now, he'd pull himself together and would be much harder to break.

At last Demene collapsed back into his chair and stared into his beer; Kubu breathed a silent sigh of relief and settled himself in his seat again.

"I shouldn't be telling you this, but one of the reasons we know so much about that night is that a man came to us with information. I'm not going to say who he is, but he's never wrong. He helps lots of powerful people in the government." Kubu's voice dropped to a whisper. "He communicates with spirits."

Demene shrank into his chair. "A witch doctor? Witch doctors don't work with the police."

"Actually, we get a lot of information from them. Especially when there's a murder involved."

"Murder! Who said anything about a murder?" Demene tried to meet Kubu's eyes but failed.

"This man said he'd had a communication from Owido's spirit. That he was looking for the people who'd attacked him. I wasn't sure I believed him at first, but the man was so sure. And there was a strange feeling in the room."

As the silence lengthened, Demene said, "What sort of feeling?"

Kubu dropped his voice again. "Hard to describe. As though someone was watching us, but there was no one else there."

Demene swallowed. "Why are you telling me this? It's got nothing to do with me."

Kubu stared at him. "I think you should tell the truth, Rra Demene. I wouldn't want to be in your shoes."

Kubu waited for Demene to react, but he just shook his head and clasped his hands together. Kubu continued, "You see, the witch doctor explained to me that albinos have *very* powerful spirits. The spirit has sucked up everything from the body—even the color of the skin. It's very bad to free one of those spirits by force. It's very powerful *muti* for a witch doctor, but *extremely* dangerous."

"I don't want to talk about this anymore. I had nothing to do with this Owido man. I want to leave now." Demene looked to where his mates had been at the bar, but their seats were empty. They'd finished their beers and gone. He got to his feet.

Kubu stood up, too, and blocked his way. "I need you to come with me for questioning."

"Questioning? What about? I've done nothing. I've told you all I know."

Kubu shrugged. "I need to get an official statement from you. I can only do that at my office."

"I'm busy. I can't come now."

"You have a choice. You can come with me now with no fuss—we just walk out of here like old friends and go to my office—or I can arrest you for obstructing a police investigation, handcuff you, and drag you out like a dog."

For a few moments, Demene didn't say anything, his

mouth opening and shutting. He looks like a guppy, Kubu thought.

"All right," Demene said eventually, but his eyes flicked from side to side looking for an escape route. Kubu took his arm firmly and led him to the door.

Kubu drove to Millenium Park and left Demene in an interrogation room alone for more than half an hour. Eventually he returned and pretended to turn on a tape recorder.

"This is Assistant Superintendent David Bengu. It is two-thirty on May the fifteenth, 2012. I'm with Wilson Demene, who has volunteered to come in to provide information about the disappearance of Mabulo Owido, an albino." He turned to Demene. "Please could you state your full name."

"You said this would be quick. Where's the statement I have to sign?"

"Please state your full name."

"You know my name! I'm Wilson Demene."

"Some new information has just come to light. I need to ask you some more questions."

Kubu made a show of pulling out his notebook and flipping through the pages.

"Ah, here it is," he said, nodding. "Someone at BIG MAMA KNOWS ALL says you were sitting at the next table to the albino. Is that right?"

Demene nodded. "I suppose so."

"So you *did* see the albino?"

Demene hesitated. "Yes. I saw one sitting at a table outside."

"Why did you lie about it before?"

"I forgot about it! I have nothing to do with those people. I suppose there was nowhere else to sit."

"And when did the albino leave?"

"I don't know! I told you I wasn't taking any notice."

"So the fact that you left at the same time was just coincidence?"

"Yes. I mean I don't know. I mean we went to the Gaborone Sun. I don't know where the albino went." Demene was completely flustered.

"You told me that you didn't like albinos. Why is that?"

"They look disgusting."

"Is that all?"

"Yes!"

"I don't think so. I think you know they have powerful spirits, and witch doctors use them for their most powerful *muti*. You know that."

Kubu noticed that Demene couldn't keep his hands still.

"Come on, Rra Demene. You knew albinos make strong *muti*, didn't you?"

Demene swallowed.

"Yes, I've heard that."

"Rra Demene. Do you know why witch doctors never catch albinos themselves? Why they always ask someone else to do it?"

"No!" The word sounded strangled as it came out.

"The witch doctor protects himself very carefully. Hides himself from the albino's spirit. So the albino's spirit comes back and haunts the men who caught him. He blames them. And eventually he drags them off. No one knows where, but no one sees them ever again." Kubu waited for about thirty seconds, but Demene said nothing. He just sat staring.

Kubu stood up. "I'll be back in a while. I have things to do.

Just remember that there's nowhere to hide from such a powerful, angry, spirit. Nowhere at all."

He turned and walked out.

Twenty minutes later, Kubu received a phone call. "The man in the interrogation room wants to see you."

Kubu smiled. He picked up the phone again and called Samantha. "Meet me at the interrogation room in five minutes," he said.

Before they entered the room, Kubu told Samantha to watch and listen, but not to interrupt.

"Okay," she said, puzzled.

Kubu brought a third chair into the room, and he and Samantha sat down opposite Demene, who now looked terrified.

"Now, Rra Demene, are you ready to tell us what happened?"

Demene looked at Samantha but didn't recognize her. "I didn't do it. It was Molefe. I just helped him. I didn't know what he was going to do. You have to believe me."

"Does it matter if I believe you? It's Owido you have to convince."

"You've got to help me," Demene cried. "I don't want to die."

Samantha looked at Kubu, amazed.

Kubu stared at Demene. "There's only one thing you can do, and even that may not work."

"I'll do anything," Demene begged. "What do you want me to do?"

"You have to confess the whole truth and then ask the albino for forgiveness."

Kubu leaned over and turned on the tape recorder.

"This is Assistant Superintendent David Bengu. It's three-thirty on May the fifteenth, 2012. I'm with Wilson Demene, who has volunteered to come in to provide information about the disappearance of Mabulo Owido, a citizen of Tanzania, an albino. Detective Samantha Khama is also in the room." He turned to Demene. "Please could you state your full name."

"Wilson Demene."

"Now," said Kubu. "If I'm going to help you, you must tell me exactly what happened and particularly anything about the witch doctor. Do you understand that what you say may be used in evidence later if you're charged with a crime? We are recording this."

"Yes, yes." Demene couldn't sit still. Then he settled down a bit and told them how he and Molefe had spotted Owido, and followed him to BIG MAMA KNOWS ALL. Then they waited and followed Owido when he left. As soon as they had him alone, they knocked him out and bundled him into the trunk of the car.

"We drove out of town and dumped him by a tree at the edge of the road." He described exactly where they had left him. "I've no idea what happened after that."

"Oh, yes, you have! You can guess." Samantha could no longer contain herself.

Demene looked at her blankly for a moment but then turned back to Kubu. "That's everything. You have to help me now."

Kubu met his eyes. "No, that's not everything at all. Who told you to abduct an albino? How did you know where to leave him? How did you get paid and how much and by whom?"

"I don't know! Molefe handled all of that. He told me we

had to catch an albino, and we'd be well paid. I didn't ask why or who would pay. I hate those people, so I was willing to help. He gave me a thousand pula and said there would be more later if his client was satisfied. And maybe we could get more work like that. I was okay with that."

"Who did Molefe speak to? How did he make contact?"

"I don't know! When we caught the albino, Molefe sent a text message to someone, but I don't know who that was. It's the truth. I swear it. I wish I'd never gotten mixed up in this."

Kubu stood up and leaned over the table, his face close to Demene's. "Are you sure that's all you know?" he hissed.

"I promise. I promise."

"That is the end of the interview." Kubu turned the tape recorder off. "Now you'd better apologize to Owido."

Samantha's face was a study in astonishment as Demene fell to his knees, tears streaming from his eyes.

"Forgive me, Rra Owido, sir. Please forgive me. I didn't know what I was doing. I didn't mean to harm you. Please don't make me die! Please!"

Kubu signaled to Samantha to come with him, leaving Demene sniveling on the floor. As he left the room, Kubu looked back and said, "I'm going to charge you with being an accessory to assault and kidnapping and perhaps murder. You'll be okay. But Owido will be in your head for the rest of your life."

He was breathing heavily as he left, slamming the door on Wilson Demene.

Kubu had to calm down before he could tell Samantha what he'd done to make Demene confess. She was delighted, but Kubu shook his head.

"It was risky. We needed a breakthrough quickly, and you'd established that he was the weak link. But it wasn't good police work. He could have laughed in my face and my credibility would have been gone."

"But it worked!"

"Yes, it worked." Kubu allowed himself a wry smile. "But we were lucky. There were many other possibilities. But we trusted your instincts, and this time we were lucky." He paused. "Did you get to the bottom of the butcher's story?"

Samantha nodded. "I also wasn't exactly honest with him, either. I told him he was the main suspect in a murder investigation. After that he was only too happy to tell me about the man he met at the *shebeen*. Seems he was buying game meat through the back door—not supposed to be sold commercially. I don't think he'll try that again."

Kubu chuckled. "Good! Now we need to start behaving like detectives again. First, we'll arrest Molefe on suspicion of assault and kidnapping, and get Zanele's people to go through his car, particularly the trunk. Get his cell phone and Internet records. Then we must check the spot where Demene said they attacked Owido and the place where he said they dumped him, and especially look for vehicle tracks there. Also get formal statements from Big Mama and the people at the *shebeen*—they'll be used to doing that by now. When we've got him cold, we offer Molefe a deal. He's not going to fall for the sort of mumbo jumbo that worked with Demene, but he'll know that it's often the middlemen in *muti* murders who end up in jail, because no one will finger the witch doctor. But it's the witch doctor we want."

"Yes, Kubu," Samantha exclaimed. "And we will get him!"

FORTY-THREE

When Kubu and Samantha arrived at Molefe's house, there was no sign of his battered Volkswagen. They'd brought a constable with them; Samantha's description of Sunday Molefe had suggested that he may be dangerous and that backup might be required. Kubu sent the constable around the back of the house to check escape routes, while they approached the house from the front. However, banging on the door produced no response.

On the third try a neighbor came out and informed them that Molefe was out, and that she was trying to have an afternoon nap. Kubu was worried and wondered whether Molefe had discovered that the police had grabbed Demene, but that seemed unlikely. There was nothing to do but wait.

Half an hour later Samantha spotted his Jetta coming down the street toward them. They let him pull over and get out of the car before all three of them approached him in a line so that he was trapped between them and the vehicle. He stood with his back to it and watched them.

"What do you want?"

Kubu stepped forward. "Are you Sunday Molefe?"

The man nodded slowly.

"I am Assistant Superintendent Bengu of the CID." Kubu held up his identification but didn't get too close to Molefe. "I believe that you can help us with our investigation into the disappearance of a man called Mabulo Owido. I have to ask you to accompany us to the police station."

"Right now? I've got important things to do today! Are you arresting me?" Molefe looked angry, and his fists clenched reflexively.

"If necessary."

Molefe considered the matter. "All right, I'll come with you." He turned and carefully locked his car. "I need to go to the toilet first." He started toward the house, but Kubu blocked his way. "You can go at the CID. It's not far." Molefe took a moment to assess Kubu's bulk, Samantha's slight build, and the burly constable. Then he shrugged and allowed them to herd him into the backseat of Kubu's Land Rover. The constable climbed in next to him. Kubu locked the doors, and they drove to the CID in silence.

Once they were settled in an interrogation room, and Molefe had been warned that his answers would be recorded and could be used as evidence, Kubu asked him about Saturday, the fifth of May. Molefe was calm and told the same story he'd spun to Samantha, starting with the drinks at BIG MAMA KNOWS ALL and finishing with when he and Demene had left the Gaborone Sun. Kubu took notes, nodding from time to time. When Molefe was finished, the detective sat for several moments as though digesting the man's evidence. Then he sighed.

"Rra Molefe, much of what you've told us is lies. We know this because your friend Wilson Demene has given us a full statement. So we know that you were paid to abduct an albino—any albino, but Owido was unlucky that you found him. We know that you followed him, attacked him, and abducted him. According to Demene, you abandoned him where a witch doctor was going to pick him up. Of course, that's his story. Maybe you actually murdered him for money or some other reason. So we already know that you are guilty of assault and kidnapping. We may later charge you with murder, conspiracy to commit murder, or being an accessory to a murder."

Kubu rubbed his cheeks, feeling the scratch of late afternoon beard.

"Your best bet is to tell us exactly what really happened that night and who you were working for. You and Demene are just the hired help; we know that. We want the man behind this crime. If you help us get him, we can consider a deal for you. You know perfectly well what the witch doctor was going to do to the albino, but you can say that you didn't. That way you won't find yourself hanging at the end of a rope." He glared at Molefe, but the man held his stare. Half a minute passed before he replied.

"What I've said is true. Demene has told you lies! Why has he said these terrible things about me?" Then another thought struck him. "Maybe he's said nothing. Maybe you're only telling me this to try to confuse me. Maybe you're telling Demene that *I* said *he* attacked this albino. You're just fishing. What evidence have you got? Nothing. Because there isn't any." He folded his arms. "I've nothing else to say."

And that was that. Kubu tried threatening, cajoling, leaving him to stew for half an hour, letting Samantha try on her own. Nothing worked. Molefe was a very different character from Demene. When Kubu mentioned the awful things that could happen to persons who injured albinos, Molefe laughed. Eventually he demanded to speak to a lawyer.

At that point Kubu gave up, thoroughly frustrated. "Very well, Molefe. You've had your chance, and you won't get another one. I'm charging you with aggravated assault and kidnapping. And you're wrong about evidence. You can't imagine what we can find with modern forensics. We'll find plenty of evidence—in your car, on your clothes, through your cell phone. You'll have your lawyer, but that's not going to help you one little bit."

He walked out and slammed the door.

FORTY-FOUR

The morning after Molefe's arrest, Kubu went to report developments to Mabaku. "We may have a breakthrough, Director," Kubu started, after settling in the most comfortable chair in front of Mabaku's desk. "Do you remember Big Mama from the BIG MAMA KNOWS ALL *shebeen*?"

Mabaku nodded.

"On Monday afternoon, she phoned me to report a missing person. He was to meet some people on Saturday night at the *shebeen*, but didn't turn up. Big Mama tried to contact him at his place of work to find out what had happened but was told he hadn't been at work for a week."

Mabaku frowned. "You've got better things to do than run around trying to find someone who has probably taken an unauthorized vacation with a woman he's just met."

"That's true, Director. Normally, I wouldn't pay attention to such a call. But when Big Mama told me that the missing person was an albino, I paid attention."

"Shit!" exclaimed Mabaku uncharacteristically. "An albino missing?"

"Yes," Kubu said. "That's what I thought. There's too much talk of *muti* to ignore it."

"So, what have you done about it?"

For the next twenty minutes Kubu recounted the events of the previous day—the confession of Demene, the refusal of Molefe to answer any questions, and his subsequent arrest.

"On what charges?"

"Kidnapping and aggravated assault."

"If Molefe hires a decent lawyer, he'll be out in no time at all. You've nothing except what one person says. Who knows why he said it. Maybe he can't stand Molefe and is trying to get him put away. Has anyone received a ransom note or some sort of demand?"

Kubu shook his head. "He's not a Motswana. He's from Tanzania."

Mabaku groaned. "This gets worse and worse."

"I've applied for a search warrant to go through Molefe's car. Demene says they used that car to take the albino to a remote place outside town, where they left him on the side of the road. Demene also told me that he and Molefe had been hired to abduct an albino—any albino. That sounded like a witch doctor wanting an albino for strong *muti* to me."

Kubu was about to try to link this with Gobey's witch doctor, when Mabaku's telephone rang.

"Miriam, I told you I didn't want to be disturbed!" Mabaku listened to the response. "Okay. Please put him through."

He waited several seconds before the caller was on the line, a worried frown on his face. "Commissioner, *dumela*, rra. What can I do for you?"

Again he listened, this time for longer.

"That's terrible news, Commissioner. He brought so much to the force. He'll be sorely missed. Thank you for letting me know." He replaced the receiver, stood up, and went to the window. Kubu said nothing, but he was sure he knew what the news was about.

Eventually, Mabaku sat down. "Deputy Commissioner Gobey died this morning. Of emphysema."

They both sat lost in their thoughts: Mabaku wondering how this would affect his bid for the deputy commissioner job, Kubu thinking of the witch doctor's curse.

It was Mabaku who broke the silence. "Emphysema is, of course, the *official* cause of death. I think we both know what the real cause was." Kubu nodded.

Mabaku leaned back in his chair and tapped the desk. Again Kubu said nothing, waiting to see what his boss was going to do.

Then Mabaku picked up the phone again. "Miriam, please get an appointment for me with the commissioner. This afternoon, if possible. I have a very important matter to discuss. It's imperative I see him."

He hung up and turned to Kubu. "I have to tell the commissioner about what Gobey told us. I want his permission to dig into Gobey's records and so on to see if we can identify his informant."

"But, Director, can't that wait until Gobey's position is filled? You have to be the favorite for the position. You don't want to muddy the waters with an investigation into witchcraft.

You know how unsuccessful those have been in the past, and it could damage your reputation. We all want you to get the promotion you deserve."

"I don't think we can wait. Who knows how long it will take for the commissioner to make the appointment. And it seems we have some leads now that may be useful. I'm going to have to take my chances."

Kubu stood up and extended his hand. "Jacob, it's an honor to work for you."

Before Mabaku could shake Kubu's hand, the phone rang.

"Yes? Four o'clock? Thank you."

He leaned back. "For better or for worse, I'm committed."

Kubu came out of Mabaku's office and headed directly down the corridor to where Samantha had a desk. It was in a tiny alcove off an interrogation room—Mabaku had found it for her to give her a little privacy. Kubu knocked, went straight in, and settled in the bare wooden chair in front of her desk. Samantha looked very surprised to see him there. "Hello, Kubu."

He nodded in greeting. "Deputy Commissioner Gobey passed away this morning at his home."

"Oh . . . I didn't know. I met him once, and he was nice to me. I'm sorry. Was it cancer?"

Kubu shook his head. "He was cursed by a witch doctor. Not *a* witch doctor, *the* witch doctor."

"The witch doctor? But how do you know? Oh . . ." Samantha caught on quickly.

Kubu nodded. "He was the informant. That's why I couldn't tell you. He insisted that no one else was to know unless he gave permission. It's too late for that now, it doesn't really matter anymore, and you have a right to know. But keep it to yourself."

Samantha thought about it. "I thought he was ill; that's why he was retiring."

Kubu nodded. "Yes, he had emphysema, but had years to go. It was the witch doctor's curse that killed him."

Samantha hesitated. "Actually, he did it to himself. Because he believed he would die, he did. It was all in his head."

Kubu shrugged. "You're always looking for a rational explanation, Samantha. And maybe you're right. But either way, I think it's murder like all the others."

Samantha let it go. "What do we do now?"

"Now," he said, "we find out who this witch doctor really is, and then we make him pay for his crimes. We're going to start with Molefe."

Even though he'd known the commissioner for years, Mabaku still felt intimidated going into his office. After all, the man was the most powerful person in the police force.

After the usual pleasantries, Mabaku cleared his throat.

"Commissioner, I have a very delicate issue to raise. I can't tell you how awkward I feel, particularly at this sad time. But I believe I could not wait, now that the deputy commissioner is dead."

The commissioner treated Mabaku with a taste of Mabaku's own medicine. He glared and said nothing.

For the next thirty minutes Mabaku outlined the various *muti* murders and the discovery in Marumo's house of *muti* made with human remains. Mabaku ended with a detailed recounting of what the deputy commissioner had told him and their failed attempt to catch the witch doctor.

"One other thing, Commissioner. Two days ago we received a credible report of the disappearance of an albino. Through a bit of luck and good detective work, we have a confession from a man who says he and another man abducted the albino and left him on the side of the road out of town. We checked the spot, and it looks likely that the marks in the sand are consistent with what the man claimed. We are in the process of checking phone records and have a warrant to search the second man's car. That's the vehicle that the first man says was used to transport the albino." Mabaku paused and let the commissioner think it through.

"Why are you telling me this now? It could have waited at least until after the deputy commissioner's funeral."

"Commissioner, we think the albino's life is in danger, if he's still alive. So we need to move as quickly as possible. What I want is your permission to examine the phone and appointment records of the deputy commissioner and to interview his staff, in an attempt to find out who his informant was. That may be the quickest way to identify the witch doctor."

The commissioner stood up and walked to a side table and poured himself a glass of water. He gestured toward Mabaku, asking whether he'd like one. Mabaku shook his head.

After the commissioner had sat down again, he spoke in a quiet voice. "Jacob, you and I have known each other for nearly twenty-five years. I think we respect each other."

Mabaku nodded.

"I think also that we both held Deputy Commissioner Gobey in the highest esteem."

Mabaku nodded again.

"What you are asking me to do—even the *appearance* of an investigation into his affairs—will sully his reputation. I can't do that to him or his family."

Mabaku's shoulder slumped. He'd tried but lost.

"But . . ."

Mabaku looked up.

"But, if you can guarantee that this investigation can be done extremely discreetly, that no one will be suspicious, then you should go ahead. We need to deal with these despicable murders. However, if it comes out that you are investigating the deputy commissioner, I will deny any knowledge of what you are doing."

He paused.

"Understand?"

Mabaku nodded firmly. "Thank you, Commissioner. I won't let you down, I promise. Thank you."

FORTY-FIVE

Kubu and Samantha sat in the meeting room with the sketches of connections in the *muti* cases on the whiteboards around them. Zanele had just brought in her report on the forensics examination of Molefe's possessions, and it was disappointingly thin.

"Well," said Kubu after he'd scanned it, "the best news is the piece of albino hair. That will be hard to explain away."

Zanele nodded. "Microscopic examination is enough to prove it's a black-race human albino hair, but the trouble is it's just a fragment. It doesn't include the follicle. I'm not sure if we'll be able to do a DNA test against the samples I collected from Owido's room at the boardinghouse."

"Nothing else in the car trunk? Owido was supposed to have been in there for a while."

Zanele looked pained. "Molefe did a good job. It was vacuumed and the carpets recently washed. Nothing we could pick up on his clothes, either. Of course, we might be able to link something else to the scene where they attacked him, or to where they left him. I've taken some soil samples and so on. But it's a long shot."

Samantha held up the photographs they'd taken of tire treads at the place where Owido had supposedly been dumped. "The treads match those of Molefe's car."

"Yes, and probably several thousand other cars," Kubu grumbled. "It's going to be hard to hold Molefe on what we have now. His lawyer is making a big production about the whole thing being a setup."

"But how does he explain Demene's confession?" Samantha asked.

"He claims that Demene was badgered into making it, and it won't stand up in court if he changes his mind. And if Demene sticks to his story, then he'll just say Demene is making it up to protect the witch doctor—probably out of fear. And he's implicating Molefe just because they were together at the *shebeen*. It's Demene's word against Molefe's. And probably a judge will find Molefe the more credible of the two. Our whole case hangs on one albino hair. Now, if we can match that to Owido, it's a different story."

"I'll get to it right away," said Zanele, already on her feet.

Kubu turned his attention to Molefe's phone records. "Anything in this lot?" he asked Samantha.

"There are dozens of numbers, and it will take time to check them all. But I concentrated on those around the fifth of May. There are several to Demene—calls and text messages—but nothing that would shake Molefe's story." She became more enthusiastic. "But he *did* send a text message at nine-twenty-one p.m. on the fifth. That seems to be the best lead. It reads 'Next half hour.'"

Kubu nodded. "That would fit with the timing of when they dropped off the albino. Who was the message to?"

Samantha checked her note. "It's to a man called Kopano Rampa. It's his personal phone number."

"Kopano Rampa?" Kubu looked at Samantha with his mouth open.

"Yes. Do you know who he is?"

Kubu nodded slowly. "I certainly do. He's an undertaker." He thought for a moment, then slapped his forehead. "Samantha, the missing bodies! Who would be in a better position to make bodies disappear than an undertaker? He would have access to the cemetery to dig an extra grave. Or even bury them at the bottom of a grave he's dug for someone else. That could be why we've found no traces of any of the missing girls."

Samantha checked her notes. "He doesn't live far from the *shebeen* with the computer. Kubu, it could be him. And he'd have access to plenty of other body parts, too. He'd only have to abduct people when he wanted them alive." She felt a little sick at the thought of it all.

Kubu recalled Gobey's description and tried to visualize the undertaker wearing the witch doctor outfit. His physique, age, and voice might just fit. Kubu was sure the late deputy commissioner would have been able to tell at once, but they'd have to do the best they could without him.

"Let's get his business address. I think we should pay Rra Rampa a visit."

Rampa Undertakers—Funerals of Distinction, was a large showroom just off the Broadhurst Mall. The inside was in somber grays, with a selection of "Caskets of Distinction" displayed on low pedestals. Polished quality wood, elegant carving, silver handles. Kubu shuddered to think what they would cost. But few of Rra Rampa's clients would be lowered into the earth in one of these; the rough pinewood coffin in which he'd buried Nono's sister would be the norm. Kubu had heard that the carpenters couldn't keep up with the demand for those.

A young man in a charcoal suit came to greet them, his face as somber as the surroundings. The fact that they'd come to see his boss and had no one to bury seemed to cheer him not at all. He led them to a comfortable office off the main showroom. There they found Rampa at his desk.

"Assistant Superintendent! I trust it's not a close family member who has passed on? Of course I will help in every way. And we'll certainly be able to come to a satisfactory arrangement as far as the cost is concerned. Please sit down, please sit down."

"Rra Rampa, I'm glad to tell you that this is a police visit, not the result of bereavement. This is Detective Khama, also of the CID. We're hoping you'll be able to help us with a case we're investigating." Both detectives passed Rampa their identification. He glanced at them and handed them back.

"I don't quite understand," he said.

Kubu opened his notebook. "Rra Rampa, do you know a man called Sunday Molefe?"

The undertaker looked around the room as though he expected to find Molefe hiding somewhere. "Molefe? I don't think so. But we have so many clients these days—too many really—that it's possible I've forgotten." If Kubu had hoped for shock to be displayed on Rampa's face, he was disappointed. But he plowed on.

"Well, it seems that he knows you."

"Does he say so? In what context?"

"He contacted you about ten days ago. Perhaps you recall that? It was on Saturday, the fifth of May, at around half past nine."

The undertaker shook his head firmly. "I don't give clients my private cell phone number. And I'm an early riser; I don't take calls that late."

Kubu thought for a moment. Then he said, "This was a text message."

Rampa shook his head again.

"Would you mind if I looked at your phone?"

"You won't take it away?" Rampa looked uncomfortable, but after a few moments' hesitation, he dug in his pants pocket and handed Kubu a phone. He passed it to Samantha.

Turning back to the undertaker, Kubu said, "The text message read: 'Next half hour.' Does that ring a bell?"

Rampa shook his head again. "Someone was trying to set up an appointment at ten on a Saturday night? It makes no sense. Are you sure you have the correct phone number?"

Kubu took out his own phone and typed in the number he'd written in his notebook. After a few seconds Rampa's phone started to play "Amazing Grace." Kubu gave a wry smile and cut off the call. Samantha passed Rampa's phone back to him.

"Look, Assistant Superintendent, we all get spam messages or messages sent to the wrong number from time to time. It happens. Now, how does Rra Molefe claim to know me? If you give me some context, maybe I can help you."

Kubu stared at Rampa, trying to strip off the formal dark suit and tie and replace them with a leopard skin and baboon mask. Somehow it seemed comical. But if Rampa was indeed the "invisible" witch doctor, then Kubu was looking at an extremely dangerous and vicious man.

"Do you mind telling us where you were on the night of Saturday, the fifth of May?"

Rampa thought for a few moments. "I was at home. I had supper, watched some television. Then I went to bed at around ten."

"Do you live alone?"

"I do. My wife died about three and a half years ago. And yes, I arranged the funeral. People always ask. What is supposed to have happened on that night?"

"An albino man was abducted and, we believe, delivered to a witch doctor to be used for *muti*."

"And you think I was involved?" Rampa sounded angry now, and somehow the image of the baboon mask seemed a better fit.

"I didn't suggest that. But the text message was probably connected to it."

Rampa hesitated. "It's possible I got the message. If I don't recognize the sender, I often delete the message without reading it. That must've been what happened."

Kubu nodded. "Probably," he said. He rose, thanked the undertaker for his time, and left with Samantha.

On the way out, Kubu thanked the receptionist and picked up a couple of copies of a flyer advertising Rampa Undertakers and containing a head-and-shoulders picture of Rampa in a jacket and tie. He handed one to Samantha, and when they got to the street he asked her what she'd made of the interview.

"There was no text message on Rampa's phone, and I quickly checked his contacts for Molefe's number, but it wasn't there, either. Still, I don't think he's telling the truth. He seemed uncomfortable when you mentioned Molefe, although he hid it pretty well."

Kubu nodded. "I agree with you. And he immediately thought the call was to his cell phone at nine-thirty at night—I didn't say that—when a business call at nine-thirty in the morning was more likely."

"Of course!" Samantha had missed that. "Another thing, if Molefe did send the text message to the wrong person, why isn't Owido still at the place where they left him?"

Kubu nodded again. "Of course, it's possible Owido got free eventually and was so scared that he fled, leaving all his possessions behind. That's credible, and I hope for his sake that's what happened. But I don't believe it. I think he's buried somewhere in an unmarked grave or maybe in someone else's grave. Certainly *not* a funeral of distinction."

FORTY-SIX

On her way home, Samantha paid another visit to the Welcome Bar No. 2. This time the place was buzzing with people having an after-work drink. A noisy group seemed to be set on breaking the foosball machine with their excessively enthusiastic playing and, from time to time, there was a yell of triumph or disgust. The manager was busy helping the bartender, but he recognized her as she reached the bar and brought her a Coke.

"Everyone's happy with the machine you loaned us," he said, indicating the group around the computer. "I've told them the other one is in for repair. One guy was worried about some stuff he'd stored on it. I told him he was an idiot to leave anything on a public machine, but his data would probably be okay. Is that right?"

Samantha nodded, but the man had already rushed off to

pour more beers. She'd almost finished the Coke by the time he returned.

"Sorry, busy here this evening. But that's good, isn't it? Did you have some more questions?"

Samantha showed him one of the flyers Kubu had picked up at Rampa's funeral parlor. She'd carefully folded the paper so that only the picture of Rampa in his formal suit was visible. "Does this man ever come in here for a drink?"

The manager looked at the picture carefully, then shook his head. "Ron! Come over here a minute."

The bartender finished taking money for two cane spirits, then hurried over, looking harassed. "What?"

Samantha showed him the picture, and he nodded. "Yes, he comes in occasionally. He's that undertaker chap. I think he visits the clinic up the road sometimes to collect bodies, you know? Stops for a drink on the way."

"Do you remember when he last came in?"

The man shook his head. "He only comes very occasionally. Maybe a couple of weeks ago?" Someone thumped his empty glass on the bar and waved. "Do you think I remember who comes in and when with this lot?"

"Does he ever use the computer?"

"Can't recall. Is that all?" Samantha nodded, and the man hurried off to refill the thirsty glasses.

Samantha finished her Coke, thanked the manager, and left. So Rampa had the opportunity to pick up the Hushmail messages that had been sent to the witch doctor. And the pay phone the witch doctor had used was just down the road. Samantha felt they might be getting close to tying up the case.

* * *

On his way home, Kubu stopped at Debonairs Pizza and collected two large *quattro stagioni*s. He would polish off one by himself, and Joy and the girls would eat the other. No doubt Ilia would get a few crusts also. Joy was making a salad to go with it, and Kubu decided they would wash the food down with an inexpensive but acceptable dry red he'd discovered. The aromas of herbs and warm cheese filled his Land Rover, making his mouth water as he drove home.

I always think of them as Joy and the girls now, he mused. My family. What happens if they find Nono a permanent home? We'll all miss her, and Tumi will be devastated. My mother already loves Nono, and my father thinks she's our daughter. I must speak to Joy about her.

When he opened the gate, Kubu managed to finesse Ilia's overenthusiastic welcome at the same time as keeping her away from the pizzas. But at the house, with both girls demanding his attention and the fox terrier jumping up at him, he nearly dropped the boxes. Joy grabbed them, laughing as Kubu collapsed into an easy chair under a pile of children and dog.

"I'll put the pizzas on a plate and get the wine," Joy said. "The salad is ready. Come to the table as soon as you can before the pizzas get cold. And you girls must wash your hands nicely first. Especially with Ilia licking everything." Tumi and Nono nodded and then returned their attention to Kubu.

"Daddy," said Tumi. "I found a chameleon today. My friend said it was unlucky, but mommy says it's very lucky. Mommy put him in a box so I could show you. She says then we must let him go so he can get food." A thought struck her. "Maybe he'll eat pizza?"

While he took them to the bathroom to wash, Kubu explained how chameleons catch live insects and wouldn't like pizza. Tumi was uncomfortable with the idea of eating flies, but Nono said she'd eaten moths a few times, and they weren't too bad. Kubu decided they should have dinner while he still felt like eating and promised to admire the chameleon later.

After all the food had been polished off, and the children had climbed into bed, Kubu read them a story while Joy cleaned up. Later, Joy came in to kiss them good night and rescue Kubu from further encores. Then the two adults could settle for a few hours of peace, and drink another glass or two of the wine.

"Nono really loves you, Kubu," Joy said. "Do you see the way she looks at you? As though the sun comes out of all that bulk." They both laughed.

"I've been thinking about Nono," Kubu said. "Tumi is very fond of her, and it will be awful to separate them. And where will she go? With the HIV and everything? Perhaps we should think about adopting her?"

"You don't have to ask me, Kubu," Joy said quietly. "It's what I want, but I waited for you to come round. It was only fair." She gave Kubu a big hug, and they sat close together for a few minutes. Then she moved away, looked at him sternly, and said, "But we're not keeping the chameleon!"

Kubu laughed, but then his face turned somber as he thought of Nono as he'd first seen her, tiny with not an ounce of fat. Hungry enough to catch moths.

"Seloi would be so grateful," Joy said quietly. A few tears trickled from her eyes, but she wiped them away.

Kubu remembered Nono, big-eyed at her sister's funeral, not knowing what to make of it. That was the first time he'd met Rampa. Funerals of Distinction. At the time he'd thought the title laughable—a one-man show arriving late in a *bakkie* with the coffin bouncing on the back. But he'd been wrong about that. It turned out Rampa was very successful. So why had he come by himself? Did he work alone in the hot sun to save a few pula? And why was he late? The mourners had been forced to wait for quite a while.

He realized Joy had said something.

"I'm sorry, my darling."

"I asked if you wanted coffee."

"Coffee? Yes, please."

Joy smiled, recognizing Kubu in think-mode, and left him to it while she made the hot drinks.

Kubu went over the funeral again in his mind. He remembered the undertaker, hot and sweating, calling for a few strong men to help him. And the strong men struggling with the pinewood coffin of a girl wasted away by AIDS.

Rampa had come late. What if he'd done something along the way that delayed him? What if he'd opened the coffin and added another corpse? Then he would have had to be alone. And the coffin would indeed be heavy if it contained two bodies instead of one. But the timing was wrong. It couldn't realistically be either of the two girls they knew had been abducted. Maybe there were others?

Joy put the coffee down next to him. It came with two shortbread cookies on the side. He smiled his thanks.

"Joy, do you remember Seloi's funeral? Do you know who organized it?"

Joy nodded. "It was the relatives Nono was staying with before she came to us. They said that Rra Rampa—the undertaker—occasionally helped very poor people to have a proper funeral when they couldn't afford it. They approached him, and he agreed to do it for very little money. We all chipped in to cover the cost, and to have some cake and tea for the mourners at the house."

Kubu put a shortbread in his mouth and chewed slowly, savoring it along with a new idea.

"Was that why he came alone with the coffin on the back of a *bakkie*?"

"Yes, he said the men there would have to help him bury the coffin; he couldn't afford to pay for workers. I suppose his hearse was being used for another funeral. There are so many nowadays . . ."

"Yes," said Kubu, sipping his coffee. "Only this time maybe there was one too few." Joy looked at him, puzzled.

He smiled at her. "Let's talk about something else. Tomorrow, let's tell Nono we want her to stay with us and see what she says. Maybe we should ask Tumi first? But they're sisters already, aren't they?"

Joy laughed, delighted. "Oh, yes, they're sisters already!"

FORTY-SEVEN

The next morning Mabaku, Kubu, and Samantha gathered in the meeting room. Kubu reported on his meeting with the undertaker and his subsequent thoughts about the rather odd funeral of Nono's sister. Samantha chipped in with the news that Rampa had occasionally visited the Welcome Bar No. 2. In turn, Mabaku informed them that he'd obtained the commissioner's grudging approval to probe the late deputy commissioner's records for leads to the witch doctor.

Kubu and Samantha split up the tasks ahead. Kubu said he would follow up on phone calls and text messages to and from Gobey's phones, particularly during the week prior to his meeting with Mabaku. He also would check with Helenka in Forensics to see if she'd prepared the necessary paperwork to send to Canada to get information from Hushmail. Samantha would interview Gobey's personal assistant to see if she had any useful information.

Kubu and Samantha agreed to meet back at CID headquarters after lunch.

"My meeting with Lori, Gobey's PA, wasn't particularly helpful," Samantha told Kubu. "She said that nothing out of the ordinary had happened during the week Gobey told you he'd spoken to his informant. He was his normal self, except when he received the call from the witch doctor and another time after he'd talked to his nephew, Joshua."

"Joshua Gobey? That's his nephew? He's head of the diamond division. I wonder what he was talking to his uncle about."

"Lori said he visited Gobey twice. Once"—she pulled out her notebook—"on the twenty-fourth of April, and then on the second of May. It was after the second meeting Lori thought Gobey was upset."

"I wonder if he's also after his uncle's job," Kubu mused. "Perhaps he was trying to persuade Gobey to pull some strings."

"That's the job the director wants. Right?" Samantha asked.

Kubu nodded. "Gobey wouldn't try to influence the commissioner, from what I know of him. He might have advised his nephew, but he would never have used his position to push him just because he was his nephew."

"Maybe that's why Gobey was upset. His nephew was angry that his uncle wasn't going to oil the process. Lori also said that Gobey was like a father to Joshua—ever since Joshua's father died."

"I think I'll have a talk to him. Perhaps he knows something about the witch doctor, although I'd be surprised. I should also speak to Gobey's wife, although I doubt she'll say anything."

He stood up. "I'd better speak to the director about this first."

Mabaku's reaction to Kubu's request to speak to both Joshua Gobey and the late deputy commissioner's wife was not what Kubu expected. He'd thought that Mabaku would have sent him to Joshua and visited Gobey's wife himself.

"Kubu, I'll try for an appointment to speak to Joshua Gobey tomorrow. I'm told he also aspires to the position of deputy commissioner. I don't want him or anyone else to think I'm undermining his position by having one of my staff question him. You've met Mma Gobey, so it's fine for you to talk to her. Don't push too hard if she doesn't want to share what they talked about in private. She may not want to talk to you at all, and that's fine just at the moment—at least until after the funeral."

It seemed like a long shot, but Samantha took it anyway. Something had happened to Owido on the night of the fifth of May, and Molefe had sent Rampa a message that night at about the right time. If Rampa had been involved in some way, she thought, it was possible Owido had been brought to the funeral parlor, or perhaps even to Rampa's home. If so, someone might have noticed something. The area around the undertaker's premises would be pretty dead on a Saturday night, so her best chance was if something had happened at Rampa's house.

Rampa lived on Tshwaana Road in a newer middle-class area not too far from his Broadhurst premises. His house was well set back from the road, and from the outside it looked comfortable, but not ostentatious. A narrow driveway led down one side of the property to a single garage. Samantha spent a few minutes looking at the house from the street to fix the layout in her mind. She checked her watch. It was 6 p.m., a good time to find people at home after work.

There were seven houses on each side of the street, and Samantha chose to start at the one opposite Rampa's home. She worked her way up the street, asking the residents if they could recall any activity late that night. Most just shook their heads, puzzled by the question. One or two had grouses about noisy neighbors and their even noisier pets, but no one had anything remotely useful until she reached the house on the right of the undertaker's.

When she knocked, the door was opened by a large woman wearing a loud dress printed with bright red roses. Samantha stated her business, and the woman looked blank.

"We're about to go out," she said. "Let me call my husband. I don't remember anything special about last Saturday night. But he sometimes stays up late."

Samantha called after her that it was the Saturday *before* last, but the woman had already disappeared into the house. She was replaced by a tall man, conservatively dressed with no floral extras, who proved to be more chatty than his wife. He listened carefully to Samantha, and then slowly shook his head.

"No disturbance or anything like that. I remember we were watching television. A very long movie about a war somewhere and building a bridge. Kefilwe—that's my wife—gave it up and went to bed. I went to the kitchen to get a snack and heard Rra Rampa driving out. Our kitchen faces his driveway. It was very late for a visit. I thought maybe someone had died, and he was going to fetch the body. Depressing how busy he is. It's the

AIDS, you know. Well, he has to make a living, too, I suppose. I don't remember anything else happening that night. This is a quiet part of town. Nothing much ever happens around here. Which is not a bad thing."

Samantha controlled her excitement. "Are you sure Rra Rampa went out on Saturday, the fifth of May?"

The man nodded. "Oh, yes. Because of the movie. The Bridge on the River something."

"And are you sure it was Rra Rampa's car?"

"Oh, yes. He has to back out from his garage, you see, and his car is a bit loud. Perhaps there is a hole developing in the exhaust?" He looked at her as though she might know the answer to this.

"But you didn't actually see it?"

He shook his head.

"What time was that?"

This caused a thoughtful pause. "I think it was after ten. That's why I thought it was so odd."

"Did you hear him return later on?"

He shook his head. "I must've gone to bed by then."

"Did you ask Rra Rampa about it?"

He shook his head again. "None of my business, and we're neighbors rather than friends. He comes and goes quite a bit with his job. But he doesn't often go out in the middle of the night."

His wife called from inside the house, and he added, "Kefilwe's always in a rush. Is there anything else?"

Samantha thanked him and added silent thanks to heaven for nosy neighbors. Kubu would be very interested to learn that after receiving the text message, the undertaker had gone for a drive somewhere.

FORTY-EIGHT

The next morning, Mabaku drove the few miles to Joshua Gobey's office in downtown Gaborone. The PA showed him into Gobey's comfortably large office.

"*Dumela*, Director Mabaku. Please sit down. This is an unexpected pleasure."

Mabaku didn't think that Joshua Gobey's face mirrored the words of welcome. It was unsmiling, and the man looked tense.

"Thank you, rra. I know this visit comes at an awkward time. First, your uncle's untimely death. My wife and I extend our deepest sympathies. And second because I understand that we are both interested in his position. I assure you that my visit has nothing to do with that."

Joshua Gobey nodded but said nothing.

"In fact," Mabaku continued, "it is only *because* your uncle has passed away that I am able to be here."

Joshua frowned.

"About a week before he died, he visited me with a strange story. He said an informant, whom he refused to name, had told him of a witch doctor who was going to make *muti*, using human body parts. The witch doctor was someone whom he himself had visited for traditional medicines. Your uncle was very upset with what this witch doctor was planning to do and wanted to help us apprehend him."

Joshua didn't respond.

"So I wonder . . ." Mabaku continued. "I wonder if your uncle mentioned anything like this to you? I am told you were very close to him and saw him a couple of days before he passed away."

For several moments Joshua didn't say anything, but just sat staring at Mabaku. Then he shook himself out of his thoughts.

"No. My uncle did not mention such a thing to me. We spoke of my father and of his illness."

"If I may ask, what did he say about his illness?"

Again Joshua paused before answering, as though weighing each word before delivering it.

"He was worried by his health. He was having trouble breathing—emphysema, I think. But he was optimistic that his medicine would help him."

"Were you surprised that he passed away so soon after you saw him?"

"What's that supposed to mean?" There was a hint of aggression in Joshua's voice. Mabaku wondered why.

"Let me put it another way. When you saw him last were you worried that his death was imminent?"

"No." Mabaku thought Joshua was beginning to look agitated.

"Do you have any idea what caused the rapid decline?"

Joshua shook his head. "No, I don't."

"Rra Gobey, do you have any idea who the witch doctor was that your uncle consulted?"

"No!" Joshua almost spat out the word. He stood up and hissed, "I don't know what you are trying to do. Why are you trying to smear my uncle's memory? Or are you trying to implicate *me* in some *muti* scandal? Is that why you're attacking me? You know you'll never become deputy commissioner unless you can discredit me! Just wait until I'm in my uncle's office. Now get out of mine!"

Mabaku stood up slowly, wondering whether to respond. He decided against it. "Thank you for your time, Rra Gobey. You are reading too much into this visit." He turned and left.

Joshua thumped his fist on his desk, causing an empty teacup to rattle in its saucer. He was worried. What does he really know? he wondered. Does he know about my visits to the witch doctor?

He sat for a few minutes trying to regain his composure. Then he pulled his laptop toward him and opened his browser.

I need to speak to the witch doctor about this, he thought. And soon.

At much the same time, Kubu arrived at the home of the late deputy commissioner. He'd called ahead to ensure he would be welcome to visit. At the ring of the doorbell, Maria Gobey answered the door.

"Please come in, Assistant Superintendent," she said.

After they had settled in the living room, each with a cup of tea, and had completed the mandatory pleasantries, Kubu broached the subject at hand.

"I know this is very difficult for you, mma, but I wonder if you can shed light on a problem we have." He paused. "A few weeks ago, on the seventh of May to be exact, your late husband visited my boss, Director Mabaku, and told a story of a witch doctor. He said that an informant, whom he wouldn't name, had provided information that this witch doctor was going to kill someone for *muti*. We have reason to believe that the witch doctor has now abducted an albino to do just that."

Mma Gobey sat motionless, with a vacant look on her face.

"Mma, did he ever tell you who the witch doctor was or where he could be found? Or did he perhaps relate all of this to you and tell you who his source of information was?"

Tears welled up in Maria Gobey's eyes. She shook her head. "I cannot tell you these things. Tebogo obviously wanted to keep this information confidential. Otherwise he would have told you." She took a deep breath. "I'm sure he asked you to be very discreet, so why are you now breaking your promise?"

"Mma Gobey," Kubu said quietly, "your husband was one of Botswana's finest policemen. He wanted the witch doctor caught—to prevent further murders. And he could have kept silent. He was about to retire. No one would have faulted him for that. Yet he came forward in an effort to catch this murderer. We can't let him down now."

Mma Gobey let out a big sob and buried her head in her hands. "I can't say anything. I promised Tebogo."

Kubu sat quietly, hoping that Mma Gobey would regain her composure. After several minutes, Kubu stood up. "Mma Gobey, I'm very sorry to have intruded at this very sad and difficult time for you." He walked toward the door. Before he left, he turned. "Last Christmas, a young girl called Lesego disappeared in Mochudi. We are convinced she was killed for *muti*.

Just a few months ago, another young girl, Tombi, disappeared on her way home after school, not far from here. We think she was also taken for *muti*. There have been others." He paused. "And about a week ago, a visitor to our country, an albino from Tanzania, disappeared. From what your husband said, he too was to be killed so some politician or businessman would find new strength or good fortune. We think all of these people were killed by the same man. How many more are there going to be?"

He walked out the door. Before he closed it, he added, "If you know anything that could help us, you should say so. I truly believe your husband would want you to do that."

He closed the door and left.

Back at the CID, Kubu briefed the director. "Gobey's wife knows something but won't tell us. She thinks that she would be breaking his trust if she says anything."

"And his nephew wasn't happy to see me," Mabaku responded. "He told me to leave because I was trying to tarnish the Gobey name so I'd get the deputy commissioner position. I couldn't persuade him that the purpose of the visit was strictly police work."

"We didn't learn much, did we?"

Mabaku shook his head. "No, we didn't."

There was a knock on the door, and Miriam let Samantha in. She'd asked the director's PA to let her know when Kubu and the director returned, so that she could tell them about the undertaker's neighbor. When she finished her story, there was a moment of silence as the men digested the implications.

"Rampa could be the 'invisible' witch doctor," Kubu said at last. "From an opportunity point of view, he's very well placed to get body parts and dispose of bodies afterward." He reminded them of Seloi's funeral and his suspicions about the contents of her coffin. "The only real connection we have, though, is his use of the Welcome Bar No. 2's computer, the text message from Molefe, and now the evidence of the neighbor that he went out somewhere after he received it."

"It would never stand up in court," said Mabaku.

"Can't we trace his movements around the abductions? Maybe through his cell phone?" Samantha asked.

Mabaku shrugged. "Suppose—best case—we discover he was more or less in the right area on each occasion. He got a text message from Molefe, which he says was a wrong number, the neighbor heard a car that night, and he used a public computer. Then Kubu is suspicious of undertakers because they can get and dispose of bodies. That's not a case. It's not even close to a case."

"Is there some way we can connect him with Marumo? He did do the funeral."

"Yes, he did," Mabaku said sarcastically. "He's an *undertaker*, Samantha."

"Well, we can go door-to-door and show his picture," Samantha responded, chastened.

This time it was Kubu who shook his head. "He works near where Tombi was abducted, so it wouldn't be surprising if people recognized him there. We could ask around in Mochudi. Maybe that's worth a try. But the director's right. It won't be anything like enough. We have to find out what's in that grave."

Mabaku sighed. "Good luck with that. I'd like to see you explaining to the authorities why that's necessary. And to the family. Anyway, the timing doesn't work for either of the two missing girls."

Samantha shook her head, frustrated. "This man may have a dozen unreported victims for all we know. There are children who stay with foster parents who don't care if they go missing. And other kids who don't stay with anyone and get food from charities. And what about the albino? It's just by chance that we know he's missing."

Kubu had been thinking while this exchange took place. "What if the family asked for the grave to be opened? What if they had a suspicion that the wrong person had been buried?"

Mabaku looked surprised. "You could convince them of that?"

"I could try. Seloi didn't have much family left. Her sister lives with us now. But Joy worked with a few distant relatives and helped them arrange the funeral with Rampa."

"Even so, you'd need more than we've got right now. You can't dig up a grave just because someone's unhappy!"

Kubu nodded. Mabaku was right.

"Suppose he kills someone else while we're trying to decide what to do next?" Samantha asked.

"I'll question him again," Kubu said. "I may be able to shake something more out of him. At worst, he'll know we're close and watching. That should keep him away from any more victims. For the time being."

"Won't he try to stop us if we get too close?" Suddenly Samantha sounded less confident than before.

Kubu looked at her in astonishment. "Are you beginning to believe in the powers of witch doctors, Samantha?"

"No, of course not," she said quickly. But Kubu could detect a note of uncertainty in her voice.

"Well, that's a real possibility," said Mabaku. "He may try intimidation, too, like the dog's head or casting spells." He paused. "I think we must all be more alert from now on. If we're right about him, he's a dangerous man."

On that somber note, the meeting broke up, and Kubu went to visit the man they now thought might help people into their coffins as well as bury them.

FORTY-NINE

Once more Kubu found Rampa seated at his desk, involved with paperwork. He looked up as the detective was shown in, but his face expressed none of the welcome it had displayed on the previous visit. He waved Kubu to a chair.

"How can I help you now, Assistant Superintendent?"

"I just have a few more questions, Rra Rampa. A few points that I want to check about that Saturday night. May the fifth, if you remember?"

Rampa nodded and waited impatiently, but Kubu wasn't in a hurry to get to the point.

"I understand that you sometimes do charity funerals, Rra Rampa. Low cost so that poor people can have a proper burial. That's very good of you."

"Well, yes. If I know the people, and they have no one who can pay, I try to help."

"My wife tells me you kindly did that for one of the people at her child-care place. You remember the funeral? That was where we met."

"I remember." Rampa looked wary.

"You did everything by yourself. I'm sure the family was very grateful."

Rampa shrugged. "I'm a Christian. We must all do that we can to help people."

"Have you done any of these charity funerals recently?"

"As a matter of fact, I had one this week. But what has this got to do with the matter you want to discuss?"

Kubu hesitated, and wrote something in his notebook. When he looked up, he asked, "Do you know the Welcome Bar No. 2 on Eland Street?"

Rampa hesitated. "I've been there once or twice. Foosball is fun, and I have a drink and chat. You never know who your next client is going to be." Kubu didn't smile. Obviously the man realized that he'd be known at the *shebeen*, so he wouldn't lie, Kubu thought. He leaned forward.

"Do you ever use the computer there? It's an Internet café, too."

Rampa shifted in his chair. "Once. There was no one to play foosball or interesting to talk to, so I took my drink and caught up with personal stuff. Why are you interested in this *shebeen*?"

"Have you heard of Hushmail, Rra Rampa?"

The undertaker looked down at the scatter of papers on his desk. "Hushmail? What on earth is that?"

"It's a type of e-mail that you use if you don't want any-one to know who you are. You give no personal information. There's no way to trace what messages you send or who you send them to." Kubu deliberately overstated the security and waited for the man's reaction.

Rampa shook his head. "Never heard of it. I have a Gmail account. Why would I need something secret?"

"I only asked if you'd heard of it, not if you had an account."

"What has this got to do with that Saturday night?"

"I'm coming to that." Kubu made a production of checking his notebook. "Last time we spoke, you told us that you didn't go out that night. Is that correct?"

The undertaker nodded.

Kubu decided to stretch the truth a bit. "In that case, how would you explain that your car was seen late that night?"

Rampa shook his head. "I didn't go out."

"Not even a short trip? Perhaps to buy some milk or something?"

"No, I was at home. I told you. Who says they saw my car?"

"I'm afraid I can't tell you that."

"Well, they made a mistake. There are lots of cars like mine."

"What sort of car is it?"

"A Toyota Corolla."

"What color?"

"Red. Look, Detective, you're wasting my time. I didn't go out. Someone saw another car and thought it was mine."

Kubu took his time before he posed his next question. "Have you had any dealings with witch doctors, Rra Rampa? I'm not talking about the albino now. Other occasions."

"Certainly not! I don't believe in that sort of stuff. I told you I'm a Christian."

"Have you ever had a case where the deceased died *because* of a witch doctor?"

"Detective, we do everything by the book here." He gestured at the papers on his desk. "In every case we require authorization from the city. There's no question of anything improper."

"I didn't suggest there was," Kubu said quietly. "Have you ever been approached about a burial where the paperwork wasn't completely in order? You would have refused, of course. But have you had such a case?"

The undertaker shook his head firmly. "Is that all? I have work to do, Detective."

Kubu nodded slowly. "That's all, Rra Rampa," he said, getting to his feet. "For the moment."

Kubu crossed the road and turned to look back at the imposing premises of Rampa Undertakers. Why would someone who had a good business—a very good business—want to risk it by witchcraft and murder? An unpleasant thought occurred to him: was it possible that the business was built on evil magic? Was that how Rampa had become successful, or at least how Rampa *believed* he'd become successful? Suddenly the elegant and formal outside of the premises struck him as a mere façade disguising something unsavory behind it.

He turned away, climbed into his car, and headed to the CID at Millenium Park.

Part Six

THE WAY TO DUSTY DEATH

"And all our yesterdays have lighted
fools
The way to dusty death. Out, out,
brief candle!"

MACBETH, ACT 5, SCENE 5

FIFTY

"Daddy. Daddy. Please take us to the mall today. I want to ride the ponies." Tumi was always energetic in the morning.

Kubu grunted and rolled over. He wasn't awake enough to start planning the day. He put his arm over Joy and pulled her closer. After a long week, he'd decided to sleep in a little this Saturday morning.

He felt one of the girls sit on him as if he were a horse. He did nothing, wishing that they would go and lie down for another half hour. Then there were two riders. Next thing they'll tell me to giddyup, he groaned. Sure enough, the two started to bounce up and down as if they were galloping. He sighed. His thoughts of a slow morning were rapidly fading.

The final straw was Ilia barking and jumping up on the two girls.

He rolled onto his stomach, causing the girls to fall onto Joy. They giggled and tried to snuggle between the adults. "Move over, Daddy!" Tumi shouted into Kubu's ear. "Nono also wants to cuddle you."

Kubu pulled a pillow over his head, but that encouraged the girls to climb all over him. Eventually he rolled over once again and sat up. He gave both girls a big hug and a kiss. "Can't you girls sleep later on weekends?" he asked rhetorically, trying to look stern.

"We want to play, Daddy." Tumi grabbed Kubu's arm and tried to pull him to his feet.

"Girls, girls!" Joy was now awake. She also sat up and put an arm over Kubu's shoulders. "Morning, darling," she said and kissed him on his cheek.

"That was nice." He turned and gave her a lingering kiss on her neck. She snuggled closer.

"Don't start what you can't finish," she said with a smile.

"This hasn't been a good month for Saturdays," Kubu said between bites of toast. "First Marumo's funeral, and this afternoon, Deputy Commissioner Gobey's. I have to go."

"You liked him, didn't you?" Joy asked.

Kubu nodded.

"What's a funeral, Daddy?" Tumi asked, forever inquisitive.

"Remember when we said goodbye to Seloi?" Joy asked.

"When they put her in the ground to see Jesus."

"Yes. We call that a funeral." She glanced at Nono to see how she was reacting to the mention of her sister. Nono seemed far away.

"This afternoon, I have to go to the funeral of a very good policeman. He died suddenly last week."

"How did he die, Daddy?"

"He was quite sick. He couldn't breathe properly."

"Will he be able to breathe properly after he's in the ground?"

"No, my darling," Joy said, leaning over and taking Tumi's hand. "He's dead and won't breathe again."

Tumi frowned but didn't say anything.

"My darling, can you drop me off at the cemetery and then pick me up afterward?"

"What time?" Joy asked.

"The service is at two, and it will probably be six by the time everything wraps up."

"I can do that, but you'll owe me. The traffic will be bad—it will be a huge funeral."

Kubu smiled. "I can think of some fine ways to repay the debt."

"Daddy, come outside and play!" Tumi's shout prevented Joy from answering.

It was indeed a huge funeral. The church the Gobeys attended was overflowing, and even more people arrived at the cemetery. All the top brass from the police were there in their ironed uniforms and medals, and wives in attendance, as were dozens of police from different divisions. There were many Defense Force higher-ups—a testament to the cooperation between the two organizations—as well as representatives from other government departments as diverse as Labour and Home Affairs, and Environment, Wildlife and Tourism. There were also several cabinet ministers.

As the crowd worked its way toward the grave, Kubu held back to observe. Gobey's family had seats under an awning to protect them from the sun. Maria Gobey was trying hard to be stoical, but would break down and sob every few minutes. She was being consoled by a man and woman with similar features. Kubu assumed they must be Gobey's children, now in their late thirties or early forties. Their spouses and children were also seated out of the sun, in the second row. Also in the first row was the commissioner of police and his wife. Finally, at the end of the first row, Kubu saw Joshua Gobey, and presumably his mother and family. Joshua was in close conversation with the commissioner. No doubt buttering him up for the deputy commissioner position, Kubu thought uncharitably.

Next to the grave, the choir from Gobey's church was in full voice with both hymns and traditional songs. Many members of the crowd joined in with gusto. Kubu thought the scene had the air more of a celebration than a funeral. But that was how it went, sometimes, when a beloved man died.

Then suddenly the crowd parted, and an impressive hearse inched its way toward the grave, FUNERALS OF DISTINCTION painted on its side. As the hearse came to a stop, a suited Kopano Rampa stepped out of the driver's seat, face solemn, and walked over to Mma Gobey. He extended his arm to shake hands, touching it with his left hand in the traditional manner. Kubu watched closely. Was he the witch doctor? he wondered. He certainly had opportunity and a perfect way of being invisible.

Rampa then walked over to Joshua and shook his hand. They chatted for a few moments, then Rampa leaned forward and said something in Joshua's ear. Kubu frowned. What was that about? Payment for the funeral? Or something more sinister? Rampa returned to the hearse, where he talked to six uniformed policemen, who were obviously going to carry the coffin to the grave. Probably instructions on how to carry the casket without dropping it, Kubu thought.

"A lot more dignified than the last funeral we were at." A voice came from over his shoulder, startling him. Kubu turned to see Dr. Pilane behind him. "At least there are no political protests at this one."

"What brings you here, doctor? Did you know the deputy commissioner?"

"Oh yes. I've been his doctor for many years."

"Did you treat him for his emphysema?"

"Oh, no. I referred him to a specialist, a Dr. Mapunda. I'm just a family doctor."

"I spoke to him on police business about a week before he died. He was quite sick, but I didn't think his life was in danger. It seemed very sudden. When did you last see him?"

"Oh, it was several months ago," Dr. Pilane replied. "A minor unrelated ailment."

"How's his wife doing?"

"She's struggling. She's taking it quite badly, as you can see." Pilane pointed to Mma Gobey under the awning. "I paid her a visit last night. Gave her a sedative."

"Do you know his nephew, Joshua?"

"I've met him a few times, but he lives out of town, in Phakalane, I believe. He'll have his own doctor out there, I'm sure."

"Yes, he's done well for himself," Kubu commented sourly.

"Well, I must go and check on Mma Gobey. I said I'd stop in and see her. I hope this is the end of the funerals."

"Me, too, doctor. Goodbye."

Kubu watched Dr. Pilane walk over to Mma Gobey and talk to her. After a while he patted her on the shoulder and turned to Joshua. The two men shook hands and spoke. Words of condolence, Kubu presumed. He looked around to see whom else he knew. He saw Mabaku in the distance talking to Ian MacGregor and a few other police colleagues. But overall, most were strangers.

A hush settled on the crowd, and Kubu saw the cortege move solemnly to the grave. The bearers lowered the coffin next to the open hole onto the ropes that would be used to lower it into its last resting place. They covered the casket with a Botswana flag, the blue standing out against the red of the earth and the black of the mourners.

A few minutes later, as the priest blessed the deputy commissioner's passage into the afterlife, and the casket was lowered into the ground, haunting ululations so common at African ceremonies filled the air. Kubu felt goose bumps all over. They certainly get into one's soul, he thought.

As the crowd slowly dispersed, he made his way to the area of the awning to pay his respects to Mma Gobey. As he passed Joshua Gobey, he offered his condolences, and then went to wait in the line.

"Mma Gobey," Kubu said when he reached the front, "once again I want to say how much we will miss your husband. He did a great deal of good for the police force and for the country. He set a very high standard for all of us by always choosing the right course of action rather than the expedient one."

Maria Gobey looked at him sharply, then lowered her eyes. "Thank you, Assistant Superintendent. I will miss him more than anyone can know. He was a wonderful husband."

"God bless his soul," Kubu said quietly. "And may He look after you, too."

He turned and walked toward the entrance to the cemetery, where he was to meet Joy.

"That was very moving." Dr. Pilane was again at his side. Kubu nodded.

"I hear you've caught the man who murdered Bill Marumo."

"I think so. The evidence is very strong."

"Has he said why he did it?"

"No," replied Kubu. "He's in hospital. He had a car accident as he tried to evade the police."

"From what they were saying the other day, the Freedom Party thinks you are covering things up."

Kubu bristled. "They can think what they like," he said sharply. "We don't take political sides in murder investigations."

At that moment he saw Joy ahead, holding her girls by the hand. She let them go and they came running over to Kubu. "Daddy, Daddy!" they cried. They flung themselves at him and each hugged a large thigh.

He patted them on the head as Joy kissed him and took him by the arm.

"*Dumela*, Dr. Pilane," she said.

"*Dumela*, Joy," he replied.

Before Kubu could say anything, the doctor waved. "Well, I must be off. Good afternoon to you all." He turned and headed toward the parking lot.

"You know him?" Kubu asked as soon as he was out of earshot.

"Of course, darling. He's a pediatrician and is involved in the fight against AIDS. He gives Nono her antiretrovirals."

Kubu shook his head. Gaborone was certainly a small town.

FIFTY-ONE

The following night Kubu sat in his garden and gazed up at the stars. The Milky Way was bright, as were Orion and the Southern Cross. There were the Seven Sisters—the Rainy Pleiades—and Orion's Belt, and Canis Major, the Dog, with its bright eye, Sirius—in fact the brightest star in the sky.

The kids were in bed, and Joy had offered to wash the dishes. The stars offered some balm to Kubu's churning mind.

Earlier in the day, Kubu and Joy had changed the direction of the normal Sunday visit by fetching his parents from Mochudi to have lunch in Gaborone. This had been carefully planned by Joy and Amantle, because they wanted Wilmon to be assessed by a doctor—something he had vigorously resisted. He was unaware that Kubu's additional guest was their family doctor, Dr. Patel, who had agreed, after some persuasion, to have Sunday lunch with the family so he could assess Wilmon's failing mind.

"I can only be sure after the appropriate tests, but I'm pretty sure it's Alzheimer's, not dementia," he told Joy and Kubu in the kitchen after lunch. Then he went on to explain the difference to them. "It's worse than dementia, because he is likely to lose his temper and become intolerant. He'll remember less and less as time passes. You are going to have to look after Amantle—it's extremely hard to have a husband who declines the way he's likely to. She'll feel guilty and angry, as well as lonely."

Kubu had felt a great sadness when he heard this. His memories of his father were all good—a loving man, born poor, but with a vision of what he wanted for his only son, namely the best education he could afford; a man who was revered for his kindness and ability with traditional medicines; a loving husband.

As Kubu gazed upward, a satellite moved slowly across the sky, growing bright then fading into nothing. Even now, Kubu felt he was losing part of himself as his father lost his memory. They had shared so much, just the two of them. Now the only person with whom he shared so many memories was fading away. Less and less the laughter of mutual reminiscences.

What would that leave for him? Kubu wondered. Would those memories be as sparkling without his father's participation? Or would they wane in his head, too, shriveling for lack of stimulation.

As Kubu gazed into the heavens, he felt a great emptiness.

Slowly he pulled himself back to the present. He had a family to look after, a job to do. And he would do those things in a way that would make his father proud.

He looked around. Joy hadn't joined him, had left him to his thoughts. What a wonderful woman she is, he thought.

He leaned back and gazed up to the night sky again, his mind beginning to engage.

Was Rampa actually the witch doctor? They had circumstantial evidence, but nothing really incriminating. And Rampa had access to bodies, which he could use for *muti*. But which bodies? Where were they? The cemeteries were large, with many new occupants. They couldn't dig them all up, even if they received permission from the minister, which was unlikely with the little evidence they currently had.

Rampa also could hide bodies in the coffins of others. Kubu had a hunch that was why Seloi's coffin seemed so heavy—two bodies not one. Again, the minister would never give permission to exhume based on Kubu's intuition.

And that was all they had. Very little indeed.

Kubu lifted his arm and ran his finger along the Milky Way. He tried to remember the bright star in the middle. Canopus? He couldn't remember. Then he traced the outline of Orion's big dog, Canis Major, and the little dog, Canis Minor. He was surprised he could remember any of the constellations—it was nearly twenty years since he had attended the Astronomy Club at high school.

Was there an Undertaker constellation? he wondered. Probably not. If there was, would it have Coffin Major and Coffin Minor as appendages? He smiled. Coffin Major and Coffin Minor! That was funny. Stupid, but funny.

Suddenly a thought crystallized in his mind. Coffin Major! If Rampa needed to bury Owido, he would never be able to double up in someone else's coffin. He was an adult—too big. The others were kids. He would have to bury Owido in a coffin by himself.

Kubu sat upright, his mind in high gear.

How could he do that and get away with it? There had to be a part of a cemetery where unclaimed bodies were laid to rest; where people were buried whose families had no money. Surely the undertaker could bury the body there without questions being asked?

He stood up, an idea forming in his head.

He started to hum—a melody from *Pirates of Penzance*, he thought. It was the first time in several weeks that he felt encouraged.

He walked inside. Where was Joy? He looked at his watch. It was nearly midnight. He'd been outside for four hours. He walked into the bedroom. Joy was snoring quietly. He wanted to give her a big hug, kiss her, hold her, caress her. He stood, undecided.

Eventually, he undressed, climbed into bed, and fell asleep.

"Do you have today's newspaper?" Kubu asked the receptionist at CID headquarters as he arrived on Monday morning. The man nodded and pulled it from under the counter. Kubu went to his office and opened it to the classifieds section. Funerals. He ran his finger down the list until he found one by Funerals of Distinction. Eleven o'clock at the Gaborone Cemetery. Perfect! Rampa's assistant was about to have a visitor while his boss was supervising a burial.

Robert Tibone was sitting behind his neat desk when Kubu walked in.

"Good morning, rra," he said. "Rra Rampa is not in at the moment. I expect him back about one."

"Oh, that's okay," Kubu replied. "I'm sure you can help me."

"Please sit down." Tibone jumped up and dragged a chair in front of his desk. "What can I do?"

"I'd like some information about how you organize your records. For example, how would I know how to find the grave of a particular person you had buried?"

"That's easy. You would go to the right cemetery and ask. They'd give you the location of the grave—which row and plot, etc."

"If my father died, what documentation would you need in order to bury him?"

"Also easy. We'd need a letter from the city that all the formalities had been completed."

"And how about, if I wanted to know who was buried on a certain day?"

Tibone frowned. "Why would you want to know that?"

"It's just hypothetical. I'm trying to understand how everything works."

"Why's that?"

"We're trying to trace someone who may have died recently. We don't know if he had any family and we don't know his name."

"Ah, so you would be interested in indigents and unknowns buried on a certain day?"

"Yes. Or perhaps between two dates. Say between the seventh and tenth of May."

"Hold on a second." Tibone tapped away on his computer. A few seconds later he continued, "I can tell you only who we dealt with. There are several other funeral services. So you may be better off going to all the cemeteries. They could tell you about everyone who'd been buried. Amongst our clients, we had three funerals on the seventh, but they were all regular people. On the eighth there was a man from the Broadhurst area and one unknown male. On the ninth there were two brothers who were hit by a train two weeks earlier. And on the tenth a female, Agnes Taung, who died from AIDS."

"And where was the male of the eighth buried?"

"I can tell you which cemetery, but you'll have to go there to find out which plot."

"May I see the documentation that came from the city?"

Tibone stood up and went into a side room. Kubu could hear filing cabinet drawers being opened and shut. A few minutes later, Tibone returned with paper in hand. Kubu glanced at it. It seemed genuine.

"Do you remember how the body got here?"

Tibone shook his head. "When I came to work on the eighth, the body was already here. Rra Rampa said it had been dropped off the evening before, after I left."

"Did he say where it came from?"

"I assume it came from the morgue. That's where a body like that would end up before being buried."

"Rra Tibone, you've been very helpful. Thank you. Could you make a copy of this document, and then I'll be off."

Kubu climbed into his car and slumped in the seat. He'd hoped that his insight the previous evening would have yielded some dramatic results, but that hadn't happened. He felt like returning to his office.

If I've come this far, I'd better follow up, he thought without enthusiasm. So he headed for the city offices. When he arrived, he explained that he was trying to find more information about the man whose documentation he had. The receptionist was obviously displeased with the interruption, but disappeared, clutching the copy. Kubu sat down and waited.

About ten minutes later, the woman returned with an elderly man, who walked over and introduced himself.

"I'm manager here. May I ask where you got this document?"

"Why do you want to know that?" Kubu asked. "Is there a problem?"

"Well, it's not genuine. We have no record of such a person."

Kubu jumped to his feet and snatched the document. "Are you sure?"

The man nodded. "No doubt about it. We send out duplicates of records we keep here. There's no original for that one."

"Is it possible that it's been misplaced?"

The manager shook his head. "Of course, mistakes are possible. But the number on the document isn't in the right sequence. It doesn't match with the date. That document's forged!" The man was offended, as though it were a personal insult. On the other hand, Kubu was ecstatic.

"That's wonderful news! Thank you. Thank you. I'll see you later."

With that, Kubu almost ran from the building, leaving the manager staring after him, open-mouthed.

Kubu had phoned ahead, asking that Mabaku and Samantha meet him on his return. So when he burst into the meeting room, they were already there.

"This had better be good," Mabaku grumbled. "I've got five reports to write today."

"It's better than good," Kubu exclaimed. "I think we may have him." He sat down, then jumped up again and told them about Coffin Major and Coffin Minor and his realization that the albino had to have been buried alone in a coffin. He explained how he'd obtained a copy of the burial documentation from Rampa's funeral parlor for an unknown person buried just after the albino died. He finished by saying that the city told him that the certificate was not genuine. It was a fake; a forgery; they had no record of such a person.

"Now we have reason to exhume the body! The state needs to know who it is! In the meantime, I'm going to interview Rampa." Samantha had never seen Kubu so revved up. It was quite endearing.

Rampa was busy preparing for a funeral the next day, but Kubu insisted that they talk in private. Once they were in Rampa's office, he passed him the copy of the document he'd been given by Rampa's assistant.

"What do you make of this, Rra Rampa?"

"It's a burial document from the city. Where did you get it?"

"It's a copy of the certificate for one of your clients. He was buried on the eighth of May."

Rampa looked at the certificate again more carefully. He was quiet for a few moments. "Oh, yes. Identity unknown." He shrugged.

"How was he brought here?"

"By ambulance. I accepted the body and the paperwork."

"Did anyone help you with this?"

"The ambulance man brought the body in."

"Rra Rampa, that document is a forgery. What do you say to that?"

"It's a forgery? I'm very surprised."

"Didn't you check that everything was in order? You told me last time that you do everything by the book."

"An ambulance delivers a body with what appears to be genuine documentation. What am I to do?" Rampa was clearly agitated. "I can't go to the city every time and check. That's plain nonsense. I've a business to run."

"Did you recognize the ambulance or the driver?"

"No. I don't pay attention to those things. All I'm interested in is the body and the documentation."

"Where do you think the body and the ambulance came from? They had to come from somewhere."

"From the state mortuary! Where do you think they came from?" Rampa was beginning to raise his voice.

"I don't think there was an ambulance. And I think you know very well where the body came from."

"What are you saying? That I killed the man? You're crazy."

"Rra Rampa, we have a report of an albino who's missing. And we have a man who says he helped abduct an albino. During the abduction, his partner sent a text message to your phone. We know that's true. You say it wasn't meant for you. How convenient! A couple of days after the albino was last seen, a mysterious ambulance delivers a body to you, and you claim you obtained a burial document. Yet there's no such record at the city. What do you want me to think? That all of these things are unrelated? I don't believe in coincidences, Rra Rampa. I think you are using your business to make *muti* from human body parts. Sometimes you take them from the people you are burying, sometimes you kill people for them."

"You're crazy! Get out of my office."

"Rra Rampa, we are going to exhume the body that you so conveniently buried. I expect a positive response tomorrow. In the meantime, I have a constable stationed at the grave to make sure you don't disturb it overnight. And I have two others patrolling the cemetery to ensure nobody does anything else to disturb our case."

"Get out!" Rampa screamed.

Kubu got to his feet and leaned toward Rampa.

"Your spells aren't going to help you now, Rra Rampa. You're not an invisible witch doctor anymore. I see you very clearly!"

With that, Kubu turned on his heel and walked out.

FIFTY-TWO

It was 6:30 a.m. on Wednesday, and the sun was still below the horizon. Although the air temperature wasn't really cold, an unpleasant wind was coming from the west, and the three men standing around the grave were wearing sweaters.

"Reminds me of Scotland," said Ian MacGregor, the pathologist. He wasn't keen on early rising or cold weather, and wasn't used to either in Botswana. Kubu grunted and returned his attention to the two cemetery workmen who were digging open the grave in front of them. They had used a backhoe to dig down the first three feet, but now couldn't use it, for fear of disturbing the remains. At least the burial was recent so the ground was relatively soft. Screens had been erected around the grave for privacy and to prevent any inadvertent disturbance to the neighboring graves.

"I hope this is necessary," the cemetery officer said. "I don't like this sort of thing in my cemetery." Kubu didn't think it was worth responding.

The digging continued, and the only sound was of the spades going into the ground and the earth being added to the pile at the head of the grave. Slowly the pit deepened until the workers were in it up to their chests. Then came a different sound.

"We've hit the coffin," one of the diggers said. "We'll have to dig around it so that we can get the ropes underneath to winch it up."

Kubu felt a twinge of excitement. Detective Thibelo had the undertaker under surveillance. If the body in the coffin was the albino, he would arrest Rampa at once. The witch doctor would be in custody, Mma Gobey would be spared the embarrassment of further questioning, and the news of the arrest would even overshadow the Marumo case, especially if Rampa could be made to confess to being the source of Marumo's *muti* and the murderer of the missing children. And, no doubt, Mabaku would get the deputy commissioner position he deserved. Kubu brooded about that. We'll miss him, he thought.

After some effort, the workers in the grave had hooked up the coffin, and one was guiding it as the other winched it to the surface. The rough pine exterior was stained, and the box wasn't sealed well enough to stifle the smell. Kubu was glad of his mask. Ian didn't seem to notice; he watched the coffin rise with interest.

At last it was brought to rest on the dolly, which would be used to wheel it to the waiting vehicle for transportation to Ian's mortuary.

"Can we look into it here?" Kubu asked.

"Certainly not!" the cemetery officer responded. "We'll be

opening to the public soon. There'll be dreadful disturbance if you lift the lid of this coffin now. You have your body; get it out of here."

"He's right, Kubu," said Ian. "I think we should do this at the mortuary. Whoever's in this coffin, I'm going to need to do an autopsy. We may as well deal with everything there."

Kubu had no option but to be patient a little longer.

It was an hour later by the time they wheeled the coffin into the pathology laboratory at the Princess Marina Hospital. Kubu wanted to be present when the coffin was opened, but as the lid was removed and the stench of putrefaction filled the room, he regretted it. Ian looked into the box. "Certainly not an albino," he said. "Look at the hair."

Kubu looked for himself and saw black curly hair and dark skin broken up by decay.

He pulled back. "I was so sure," he said.

Ian glanced up at him, then immediately back at the body as though he resented being distracted from his new interest. "Well," he said. "Your undertaker's still in deep water. Very deep, I'd say. This is a normally pigmented black male, and he looks pretty well fed to me—even overweight. I doubt he's an indigent or unknown person. What was he doing in a pauper's grave? Well, we'll know more when I've done the autopsy." He glanced up at Kubu again. "Do you want to stay?"

Kubu shook his head. He thanked Ian for his help and left to find fresh air.

Who was the man in the coffin? A well-fed individual, who was secretly buried in a pauper's grave? Was this another murder, and if so, for what motive? Or was a body indeed delivered to the funeral parlor in an ambulance as Rampa insisted?

They needed to search for an appropriate missing person. He started to call Samantha on his cell phone to do that, when he realized how he'd been had.

"He switched the bodies, Samantha," he told her. "He knew there was a chance the extra grave would be discovered, so he swapped the murder victim with one of his clients. Of course, after a few years it wouldn't matter anyway; there'd be no evidence of the murder left."

Samantha asked what they should do next, and Kubu took a few moments to think about it.

"He won't have kept an extra body for long. We should check all the burials Rampa did around that time. I'm going to ask his assistant, Robert Tibone."

Kubu found Tibone much less cooperative than he'd been on the Monday before.

"Rra Rampa is not in, Assistant Superintendent. He may be some time. I don't think you should wait."

"That's okay, Rra Tibone. I think you can help me."

Tibone shook his head. "Rra Rampa was very angry about the help I gave you before. I thought I was going to be fired. He shouted and screamed at me. And his orders were quite explicit. If you have a search warrant, we cooperate; otherwise nothing." He folded his arms.

Kubu pulled up a chair and sat down. He wasn't going to be brushed off that easily.

"Rra Tibone, when I took that photocopy from you, I thought I was getting a copy of the city documentation for the burial of an unknown man. Did Rra Rampa tell you that the document turned out to be a fake? The city has no record whatsoever of that person. The document was forged."

Tibone's mouth hung open as he digested the implications. "That's impossible." He paused, and then added, "He didn't tell me that."

"So, you see, your boss is in very big trouble indeed. Now the question is whether you want to be associated with that trouble—when you're looking for another job, for example—or whether you want to be the person who helped the police get to the bottom of the matter."

Tibone swallowed. "I can't help you. He'll kill me if he finds out."

Kubu shook his head. "I just want some information. You don't have to give me anything, just answer a few questions. And it's information I could find out by other means anyway, so no one can trace it back to you."

"What do you want to know?"

"I just need the names of other men whose funerals you handled on the seventh, eighth, and ninth of May. You told me about them on Monday anyway."

Tibone hesitated, then turned to his computer and read out the names and the dates of the funerals. If he was curious about why Kubu wanted the information, he gave no sign of it. He breathed a sigh of relief when Kubu had what he wanted and left.

Back at his office, Kubu phoned the appropriate department at the city and asked for the manager who'd helped him before. Soon he had the information he wanted—the ages and causes of death of the five men whose funerals Rampa had handled over the key three days. All he needed now was information from Ian. As if on cue, the pathologist phoned.

"I've just finished the autopsy, Kubu. I thought you'd want my preliminary findings."

"Very much!"

"Natural causes." Ian sounded almost disappointed. "He died of a massive heart attack. It'll take longer to check for drugs and whatnot, but I'm pretty sure there was no foul play. He was overweight and smoked. Heavily by the looks of his lungs."

"How old was he?"

Ian had to think about that. "I'd say mid to late fifties. Early sixties at the latest."

"Fifty-nine?"

"That would fit."

"Well, Ian, our friend is Aka Ndode, late of Broadhurst. Died of a heart attack on the twenty-fifth of April, 2012, buried by Funerals of Distinction on the eighth of May, 2012." Kubu quickly explained Rampa's deception. "One of the other deceased men died of heart failure, but he was seventy-eight."

"Get me Ndode's dental records, and we'll be sure."

Kubu thanked him and mused about the protocol of what he should do next. In his own mind he was certain that Owido was buried in Aka Ndode's elegant coffin with, no doubt, a fine headstone on order. So he was within his rights to open Ndode's grave without reference to the family. But he felt that was the wrong thing to do. The wife's grief was still fresh. What if she came to the grave to be near her departed loved one and discovered an open hole with her husband gone? It was out of the question. His next visit would have to be to the widow.

The Ndode residence was a middle-class house on Kgame Street. The garden was neat, the house recently painted. Kubu knew that his visit, so soon after the funeral, would be a most unwelcome intrusion.

A neatly dressed woman answered his knock.

"Mma Ndode? I'm Assistant Superintendent Bengu of the Botswana Police. I phoned earlier and asked for a few minutes of your time." He showed her his identification.

"Oh, yes, rra. Please come in." She led him to a sitting room where the furniture was carefully positioned, the cushions plumped, the side tables clean and polished. *Neat*, thought Kubu, is what seemed to characterize this couple. Even the funeral would have fitted with that. Until now.

Once they were seated, and he'd refused refreshment, Kubu started to explain the matter as best he could.

"Mma, I'm very sorry to disturb you when you are in mourning for your husband." The woman nodded, idly playing with the black-cloth mourning strings she was wearing round her neck. "It's in connection with your husband's funeral that I wish to speak to you," Kubu continued. He hesitated, trying unsuccessfully to find a gentle way of breaking the news. "I'm sorry to tell you that a terrible mistake occurred at the undertaker's premises. Two bodies were switched and buried in the wrong graves. Your husband was one of them."

The woman sat for several seconds trying to digest this. "You mean I didn't bury Aka? How can that be? That very morning I saw him in the coffin that Rra Rampa helped us choose. How could there be a mistake?" He could hear the growing tension in her voice.

"It's very regrettable, mma," Kubu said. "A very strange story indeed. But all is well. Your husband's remains are absolutely safe, and as soon as the whole matter has been cleared up, he'll be placed in the correct coffin and restored to his proper resting place. If you and your family would wish to be involved with that, it can be arranged, of course."

Mma Ndode thought about that. "Why are the police involved? Why haven't I heard from Rra Rampa? He was so helpful before . . ." She was close to tears.

"Mma, you can appreciate that when such a serious event occurs, the police have to be brought in. To ensure that the remains are safe and properly treated." He thought it tactful not to mention Ian's activities of that morning. "I'm sure Rra Rampa will speak to you in person. He's very busy trying to discover exactly what happened, and he'll want to tell you himself when he finds out."

"Who . . . who is in Aka's grave?" Tears filled her eyes and started to run down her cheeks.

"We're not sure at the moment. We'll know soon."

"And you're sure he's safe? I've heard terrible things. Things about witch doctors . . ."

"Yes, mma. His remains are absolutely safe."

She hesitated, then nodded. "I'm sorry. This has brought it all back to me. Would you leave now?"

Kubu nodded and rose. "There is just one more thing, mma. Could you tell me who your husband's dentist was?"

"Why do you want to know that?"

"We'll be able to get an absolutely definite identification from his dental records."

"I could identify him."

Kubu shook his head. "I don't think that would be wise."

She understood and gave him the details of the dentist. Then she showed him out.

Before he drove off, Kubu phoned Samantha and asked her to contact the dentist and get the records to the pathologist right away. He also asked her to contact Broadhurst cemetery and arrange another exhumation for the next morning. That would be definite as soon as Ian confirmed the identity of the body in his laboratory.

At 8:30 a.m. on Thursday, a much more imposing coffin rested on the table in the pathologist's mortuary. When the lid was levered off, Owido's sightless eyes stared up at Ian and Kubu. Even before the autopsy, there was no doubt about the unpleasant and violent nature of his death. Even Ian's face registered shock.

Although Kubu had kept the second exhumation quiet, Rampa had got wind of it somehow or had simply realized that Kubu would quickly see through his ruse. Detective Thibelo, who'd been keeping a careful eye on him, followed him to Tlokweng and arrested him as he tried to cross into South Africa. Thibelo treated Rampa with nervous respect, and carefully handcuffed him to the passenger-seat armrest. He'd heard a rumor that Rampa could make himself invisible.

FIFTY-THREE

Kubu wasn't entirely comfortable when he opened the door to the interrogation room just after lunch. Intellectually, he didn't believe that witch doctors had any real powers, only that they relied on the power of suggestion to influence their clients' lives. But, he had to admit, he had a niggle of concern about confronting Rampa.

"So, Rra Rampa, we meet again. This time I hope you'll tell the truth."

Rampa didn't respond, but Kubu noticed how he was clasping and unclasping his hands. Kubu pressed the button to start the recorder and completed the necessary formalities.

"Kopano Rampa, you are under arrest for the murder of Mabulo Owido, a Tanzanian citizen. You are also under suspicion for the murder of Lesego Betse and Tombi Maleng, two schoolgirls who disappeared from near their schools."

"I haven't killed anyone!"

"You have the right to have a lawyer present. Do you want one?"

"No. I haven't done anything."

"Okay. That's your choice."

Kubu flipped through his notebook until he reached the page he wanted.

"Rra Rampa, this morning we exhumed another body that you buried recently. Your documentation and that of the cemetery indicates that it was the grave of one Aka Ndode. The problem is that the body in the coffin was not Aka Ndode, who was a black male. We believe it was the body of the Tanzanian I mentioned, Mabulo Owido, who was an albino."

Rampa just stared at Kubu.

"In addition, we've now verified that the body we exhumed yesterday, which should have been the unknown person you claim was delivered by ambulance from the morgue, was in fact Rra Ndode. Moreover, Mma Ndode tells me that before the funeral she saw her husband in the coffin the albino was buried in, not the cheap pine one in which we actually found him."

Rampa wiped his brow with the back of his hand.

"Finally, the documentation for the unidentified man you buried was a forgery. So the evidence for a willful switching of the bodies is overwhelming. I'm sure the Ministry of Trade and Industry will agree, revoke your license, and probably press charges.

"But that's the least of your worries," Kubu continued. "The person whose corpse we exhumed this morning—the albino—did not die of natural causes. He had been murdered and several organs had been removed, almost certainly for *muti*."

Rampa jumped up. "I didn't murder anybody!" he shouted.

Kubu ignored the outburst and continued. "We also have a signed confession from a man, Wilson Demene, who claims he helped another man, Sunday Molefe, kidnap Owido. We have a record of the fact that Molefe sent a text message to your phone shortly after Owido disappeared. We also have a witness who says you left your house about that time. No doubt to pick up the albino, so you could kill him for body parts."

"I haven't killed anyone! You've got to believe me!" Rampa screamed.

"How can I believe you? All the evidence points to you. What can you tell me to change my mind?"

Rampa shook his head, his face looking as though he were in great pain.

"All right, let's take this one step at a time. Tell me how the two bodies were switched. Who did it? Who murdered the albino?"

"I swear I didn't kill anyone."

"But did you switch the bodies?"

Rampa covered his eyes with his hands, but said nothing.

"Did you bury the bodies?"

Rampa was now shaking.

"Let me tell you something, Rra Rampa," Kubu continued. "I'm sure you know that Botswana has the death penalty. If you confess to the murders and help find the bodies of other people who have disappeared, we may be able to persuade the court to offer some leniency."

Rampa looked down, his face twisted in anguish.

"If you're not going to cooperate, it's only going to get worse. Give it some thought," Kubu said, struggling to his feet. He turned off the recorder.

"I'll speak to you tomorrow."

"I want a lawyer," Rampa croaked.

"I'll arrange for you to contact yours. You're going to need one!"

Kubu had just settled in his office when his cell phone chirped. He read the text message.

"At Rampa's house. May have found Marumo briefcase. Samantha."

Kubu shook his head. Marumo's briefcase? Was Rampa involved in Marumo's death also? Was he the source of the *muti* they'd found in Marumo's desk? Were he and Witness Maleng working together?

He immediately dialed Samantha.

"Why do you think you have Marumo's briefcase?"

"It looks just like the one in the photos the Freedom Party gave us, and the initials next to the handle have been scraped off," Samantha replied excitedly.

"Good work. Have forensics test for prints and other evidence." Kubu thought it was unlikely that there would be anything useful this long after Marumo's death, but it was worth trying.

"Is there a computer there?" Kubu asked.

"Yes. Forensics has already packed it up. Some Russian woman took it."

"Excellent. I can't wait to hear the results."

Kubu hung up and wondered about the ramifications if it was in fact Marumo's briefcase. The thought jogged Kubu's memory of Marumo's *muti*, and he went immediately to Mabaku's office. Fortunately the director was available.

"Has Rampa confessed yet?" Mabaku asked as Kubu entered.

"No," Kubu replied. "But as the evidence mounts, I think he will." He sat down and continued in response to Mabaku's raised eyebrows. "Two things: First, Samantha thinks she's found Marumo's missing briefcase at Rampa's house. That puzzles me—it means that Rampa was involved in Marumo's death. I can see him supplying Marumo with *muti*, but I never thought he'd be implicated in his death. And I can't figure out how he's connected to Witness Maleng. Second, I'm going to need permission to exhume another grave."

That caught Mabaku's attention. He groaned. "Another grave? Soon you'll have dug up everyone in the country. Whose and what for?"

Kubu reminded Mabaku of his suspicions that an additional body was buried with Nono's sister. "That's the coffin I want to look at."

"Well, it's a long shot, but your man has already switched bodies once, so I think we can justify a look. If there's any problem, have them call me."

Kubu wasn't looking forward to the third coffin being opened. It was already more than a month since Seloi had been buried, and the contents of the coffin were sure to be disgusting. Kubu didn't even go to the cemetery, partly because there wasn't much excitement seeing another coffin lifted from the ground, and partly because three very early mornings in a row didn't suit his sleep patterns. He'd asked Ian to phone him when the coffin was on its way to the morgue so that he could meet him there.

"Here we go!" Ian said as he started to pry open the lid of the cheap coffin.

A few minutes later he lifted it off and peered inside.

"You're right, Kubu! There *are* two bodies in here." He gently lifted one shrouded body out. "I'll order DNA tests on both—I think I can expedite them because of the circumstances. And now I'll try to find out how they died. I'll call you later."

"Thanks, Ian. Please do—as soon as you know anything." With that Kubu made a dash for the door and a breath of fresh air.

FIFTY-FOUR

Kubu slammed the door behind him, sat down, and turned to the lawyer, who was sitting at the table.

"Who're you?"

"I'm Rra Rampa's attorney."

"I know that," Kubu snapped. "What's your name?"

"Martin Westbrook of Westbrook, Levi, and Mpape."

Kubu leaned over, turned the recorder on, and completed the introductory requirements. Then he turned to Rampa.

"We've added charges for the murder and mutilation of another girl, whose identity we don't know. I just wish they could hang you once for each person you killed. I don't like the death penalty, but it's perfect for scum like you." Kubu slammed his fist on the table.

Westbrook jumped up. "You can't talk to my client like that. If you continue, I'll advise him not to say anything."

Kubu leaned toward Rampa. "Who is this new body we've found? When did you kill her?"

"I swear I never killed anyone. I was made to do it. Made to bury those bodies. Please believe me. I'd never hurt a child." Rampa, unkempt after a night in a cell, banged his handcuffed hands against his chest. "Please believe me!"

Westbrook leaned over and whispered in Rampa's ear.

"So, who made you bury those bodies?" Kubu continued. "Who gave you those bodies?"

Rampa's eyes were terrified.

"He'll kill me if I tell you!"

"We'll hang you if you don't!"

"Assistant Superintendent Bengu, I must protest. You can't intimidate my client like this."

Rampa buried his head in his hands.

"Do you promise not to tell anyone?" Rampa pleaded, ignoring his attorney.

"I can't do that. You'll have to take your chances."

Rampa started sobbing. "He's going to kill me!"

"Who's going to kill you?"

Rampa said nothing, still sobbing.

Kubu waited.

Eventually Rampa lifted his head and said, "The witch doctor!"

For a moment Kubu was stunned. Then he burst out laughing. "The witch doctor? You must be joking. *You're* the witch doctor. Not someone else. I suppose next you'll tell me he's invisible!"

"He is, I promise. I've never seen him."

"Have you looked in a mirror? Good try, Rampa, but I'm not buying it. You're the person we're looking for, and you're going to pay for what you've done."

Kubu stood up and turned off the recorder. He nodded toward the lawyer and left, slamming the door again.

The next morning Kubu invited Samantha to join him in questioning Rampa.

"I have to say I'm a little confused," Kubu said as they walked to the interrogation room. "Zanele found a partial thumbprint of Marumo's on the clasp holding the dividers in the briefcase. So the briefcase you found is certainly Marumo's."

"How did Rampa get hold of it?" Samantha asked.

"Exactly. I can't figure it out. Maybe we'll learn something from Rampa. I'll lead the questioning, but feel free to ask anything you like."

A few minutes later they were both seated in front of a slouched and haggard Rampa, unshaven, with the unpleasant odor of someone who hasn't washed in a few days. He looked exhausted. Westbrook was again seated next to him.

"Rra Rampa," Kubu began, "we're going to continue questioning you until you tell the truth, which you haven't yet done. You claim to have been forced by an invisible witch doctor to bury all these mutilated bodies—bodies that had been murdered for body parts. That's hard for me to believe. If you expect me to believe that, you're going to have to give me some real evidence that this witch doctor exists."

Rampa, chin on chest, shook his head. "He'll kill me if I do. He said I'd die a terrible death if I said anything."

"You're quite safe in your cell. He can't get to you there."

"Oh yes, he can. His spells go through walls. It doesn't matter where you are if he puts a spell on you. I'll die a terrible death."

Kubu thought for a moment. I'll call his bluff, he decided.

"All right, I'm going to ask you some questions. If you give me truthful answers, I won't ask who the witch doctor is. If I think you're lying, I will hold a press conference this afternoon to announce how you've helped us with information about all the unsolved murders, and we'll let you go. I'm sure the witch doctor will be waiting for you to thank you for your help."

"You have to believe me!" Rampa cried. "I'm telling you the truth!"

"You can't threaten my client like that!" Westbrook said aggressively.

"Mr. Westbrook, I didn't threaten your client. I said I'd let him go. The witch doctor is his idea, not mine. He has to live with that."

Westbrook crossed his arms and leaned back in the chair. Passive-aggressive, Kubu thought.

"Rra Rampa, when we searched your house yesterday, we found a briefcase. We can prove that it belonged to the late Bill Marumo, the Freedom Party politician. How did you get it?"

Rampa squirmed in his chair. "The witch doctor gave it to me," he said quietly, as though the witch doctor might hear.

"Why would he do that?"

"He was delivering some stuff."

"What was that?"

"I don't know," Rampa said. "It was in a packet."

"And who was the packet for?"

Rampa hesitated. "I don't know. I had to leave it on a gravestone one evening. The next morning it was gone."

"And whose gravestone was it?"

Rampa shook his head. "I don't remember. It was nobody I had heard of."

Kubu brought his fist down on the table so hard that everyone jumped. "Another useless answer. What do you think was in the packet?"

Rampa drew back as far as he could in the chair. "I don't know."

"What do you *think* it was?" Kubu was shouting now.

Rampa just looked down and shook his head.

While Kubu took a few deep breaths to calm himself, Samantha jumped in. "How did this witch doctor give you instructions? Did he send spirits to talk to you?"

"Of course not. He left me a voice mail when he wanted me to pick up a body."

"So we can find the number on your phone then?"

Rampa shook his head. "I checked my phone. The numbers were always different. I think he used public phones. You have my phone. You can check it."

"Don't worry, we will," Kubu interjected. "So he told you to do this more than once?"

Rampa nodded.

"You have to answer the question."

"Yes," Rampa mumbled.

"How many times?"

Rampa looked stricken. "Several, I don't know . . ."

"How many times, Rra Rampa?"

At first it seemed he wouldn't answer, but then he blurted, "Five, no six."

Kubu, Samantha, and Westbrook all stared at him.

"Where did you pick the bodies up?" Kubu asked quietly.

Rampa sank lower in his chair. He shook his head. "I can't," he groaned.

"Of course you can," Samantha said. "The witch doctor can't hear you in here."

"He can hear me anywhere, everywhere," Rampa moaned.

Kubu turned to Samantha, "Please go and arrange for a press conference at three this afternoon. Tell them it's about a breakthrough in the Marumo case." Samantha stood up to leave.

"Noooo . . ." Rampa let out a long wail. "I'll tell you. I'll tell you."

"No, you won't," Kubu replied. "You're going to take us there."

An hour later Rampa guided Kubu to a dirt road south of the city. It was a rutted bush track, obviously rarely used. Samantha and Westbrook were also in Kubu's Land Rover, and Zanele and her team followed in their forensics vehicle.

"Those bushes on the left," Rampa said. "That's where the bodies were."

The small convoy pulled up a hundred yards from the bushes, and Zanele and her team moved slowly toward the site, looking for any signs of activity. As they neared the bushes, Zanele called Kubu over and pointed to the ground. "Tire tracks. Two sets."

Kubu could see the difference in the tread marks.

A few minutes later, Zanele again called. "It certainly looks as though something heavy was dragged on the ground here." She pointed to a drag mark from near the road to behind the bushes.

"We'll sample the soil to see if we can pick up any hairs or traces of blood. We may get lucky," she said.

"Good work," Kubu told her. "Let me know as soon as possible."

He walked back to the Land Rover, where Rampa was

handcuffed to the door, watched by Samantha. Westbrook paced up and down outside the vehicle.

"So what does that prove, Rra Rampa?" Kubu asked as he climbed into the vehicle. "It doesn't prove that you're not the witch doctor. It was a good try, but you can't fool me. *You're* the invisible person we've been looking for. You thought you were clever, but criminals like you always make a mistake. You're going to hang from your neck until you're dead. And I hope the spirits of all the people you've killed are there to watch you go to hell."

"Detective Bengu . . . ," Westbrook started to say.

"I'll tell you everything," Rampa wailed.

"I need to speak to my client," Westbrook interjected.

"Fine," said Kubu. "Call us when you're ready."

A few minutes later, Westbrook walked over. "My client wants to make a confession," he said. "Can we go back now?"

Kubu glanced at Samantha and shrugged. "That's fine, only make sure he's telling the truth."

FIFTY-FIVE

When they left the interrogation room after listening to Rampa's confession, Kubu was thoughtful. "We must bring in Sunday Molefe again. Rampa's confession contradicts his story."

Samantha nodded. "I'll do it."

Kubu walked a bit farther, then stopped. "Rampa certainly wants us to believe he's not a killer."

"That was all bullshit," Samantha exploded. Kubu looked at her askance—it was the first time he'd heard her swear.

"All he admitted to was picking up and burying bodies," she continued. "That's a clever way to avoid a murder charge. I want to do to him what he did to them! Show him the knife, cut off his balls, and then work up from there. Hanging is too good for him! We should . . . we should . . ." Words failed her.

"But are we sure he's guilty of the murders?" Kubu asked mildly.

"Of course he's guilty! He buried a butchered child with your little girl's sister, and put the albino in Ndode's grave. And there'll be lots of others, if we can find them without digging up every graveyard!" She was so angry that she slapped the wall.

"He's admitted burying the bodies."

"You can't believe his pathetic story about doing it because he's terrified of some witch doctor? He *is* the witch doctor!"

Kubu sighed. He very much wanted Samantha to be right. And yet there were things that worried him. Rampa worried him. In the face of all the evidence they'd produced, the man stuck to his unlikely story.

He had another thought.

"Is it possible that he has a split personality? He really believes there's another person because there's another *personality*?" Even to him it sounded unconvincing, and Samantha gave a derisive laugh.

"He's so good at lying, he's even getting to you," Samantha spluttered. "He lied to his funeral parlor clients as he cut bits out of their dead loved ones and then buried them in the wrong graves. He lied to his witch doctor clients about what he could do for them. And he lied to those poor little girls when he gave them lifts in his car." To Kubu's embarrassment, she started to cry. "I'm sorry," she said. "I'm fine. Just give me a few minutes." She walked away quickly toward her office.

"What was all that about?" Kubu discovered that Mabaku had walked up behind him during Samantha's explosion. We don't need a meeting room, Kubu thought. Everyone's in the corridor anyway.

"Samantha's furious about Rampa. She wants him to confess, grovel, and beg for mercy while she personally tightens the noose around his neck. And she really wants to do something much worse to him than that."

"And you don't think he deserves it? I'm inclined to agree with her."

Kubu turned to look at his boss. For someone discussing a mass murderer, he thought, Mabaku sounds in a remarkably good mood.

Mabaku caught his inquiring expression. "I've just been to see the commissioner. He's very pleased with our work on this case. He wants it all neatly wrapped up, implicating Marumo as much as possible, and the late deputy commissioner not at all. I said I thought we could manage that. He spoke very warmly about us." He raised his eyebrows. "About *both* of us."

The commissioner was another person who would like Rampa hung, drawn, and quartered, Kubu thought. I disliked the undertaker from the first day I laid eyes on him, but they all seem to be missing one point: we haven't established that he's guilty of the killings.

Mabaku gave him an encouraging slap on the back. "Let's get it all tied up, Kubu." Then he strode off to his office with a cheerful wave.

Joy had invited Pleasant and Bongani to join them for supper that evening. Joy cooked a big pot of chicken curry—hot the way the adults liked it—and a small pot of curry-flavored stew for the girls. Tumi pronounced the adult version "burny" and wouldn't eat it. Nono was less fussy, but she also preferred the milder variety.

Pleasant smiled as she watched the children dig in. Her interest suggested that she was picking up tips for the not-too-distant future.

As usual, Nono finished her food while Tumi was still fiddling with hers. "Aunt Pleasant," she said, "Tumi and I are *real* sisters now."

Pleasant laughed. "Of course you are!" She knew all about Kubu and Joy's plans to adopt her. Nono smiled her beautiful smile.

Bongani finished crunching a poppadum. "I see you're a big hero again, Kubu. Not only did you catch Bill Marumo's killer, but you've arrested a *muti* murderer. The undertaker thing is headlines in all the newspapers."

"The trouble with the press is that today's hero is tomorrow's nobody at best, and tomorrow's villain at worst," Kubu replied. He spooned desiccated coconut and banana slices onto his second helping of curry, and then mixed in several tablespoons of Mrs. Ball's chutney. He wished he had a spicy gewürztraminer to go with it, but had to make do with a chenin blanc.

"Where does the case go from here?"

Kubu shrugged. "We still have to establish just what Rampa actually did and did not do. It'll be a while yet."

"The *Daily News* is speculating that Witness Maleng is also linked to Rampa." Bongani hesitated. "The piece reads as though that tidbit came from a police source," he added shrewdly.

"There's a lot we don't know yet. I think some people may be getting ahead of themselves." Kubu felt uncomfortable about the whole issue and changed the subject. "Tell us about your big project." Bongani got the message and enthusiastically launched into the plans for his upcoming research study in the Okavango Delta.

After the guests had left, the girls were asleep, and the cleaning up had been done, Kubu and Joy snuggled into bed. Both were relaxed but tired, and a cuddle seemed in order, but Joy sensed that Kubu was distracted.

"You're not happy about this case, are you, Kubu? I could tell by the way you cut off the discussion at dinner. Something's worrying you."

"It's just that everyone has declared the case solved—a nice, satisfying outcome with no embarrassment to important people. The evil witch doctor doing unspeakable things in a funeral parlor. Great for the *Daily News.*"

"But maybe that's how it was?"

"Maybe."

Joy dropped it and soon drifted to sleep. But Kubu lay awake, turning over in his mind the various issues that bothered him.

The worst of them was the briefcase. Rampa claimed the witch doctor had given it to him, claimed it contained something important. He'd refused to say what, and Samantha had contemptuously dismissed his story as another of his web of lies.

But how *had* he obtained the briefcase?

Kubu rolled over, wishing he could put it out of his mind and fall sleep. Instead, he tried to track the briefcase from Marumo to Rampa. Marumo's assistant had seen him leave with it, and he'd had no time to take it anywhere on his way home. So it was with him when he was murdered. Although Rampa had no alibi for that night, all the forensic and circumstantial evidence pointed to Witness Maleng, none to the undertaker.

So who could have taken the briefcase? Jubjub? There was a thought. Perhaps she, not Marumo, was in league with the witch doctor? Perhaps the *muti* was for her, to help snare the politician. Maybe the dog's head was also involved somehow. Yet she didn't strike Kubu as smart enough to set up that misdirection. He shook his head and pulled up the blankets to better cover his substantial girth. Joy grunted and snuggled closer to him.

Of course, there was the sergeant in charge of the crime scene. But Kubu knew him. He was old-school and as straight as they come. Even if that were not the case, why would he take the briefcase? No one had suggested anything in it was valuable.

The only other person at the scene was the neighbor, Dr. Pilane. What possible use could he have for Marumo's political papers?

Kubu's musings were disturbed by a scratching noise in the ceiling. Could it be the wind? It sounded more like a creature—maybe a rat or a mongoose. He sighed. That would be bad news. He didn't like poison and traps with Ilia and the girls around. He lay still and concentrated, but the noise didn't come again.

None of it made sense. Maleng must have taken the briefcase, and somehow the witch doctor—Rampa or whoever it was—got it from him. Had Maleng made another visit to Mma Gondo? A visit that she hadn't mentioned? Another loose end.

He rolled over again and wondered if there was any more of Joy's excellent *melktert* that they'd had for dessert. Perhaps a mouthful or two would settle him down. He climbed out of bed, careful not to disturb Joy, and decided to check on the girls on his way to the kitchen.

Tumi and Nono were fast asleep in their room, breathing softly; two little angels. Kubu stood and watched them, smiling. Then they triggered a thought and his face fell. The two children murdered for *muti* had known their abductor. Why would they know the undertaker? Were funerals *that* common? He shook his head. He felt that somewhere during the case Nono had given him a clue. Was it that Nono knew Rampa because of Seloi's funeral? He shook his head. It was something else . . .

Suddenly he heard the scrabbling sound in the ceiling again. Almost certainly a rat. Maybe a nest of rats. He sighed. There was nothing he could do about it tonight.

He found one piece of *melktert* left and polished it off. I'm missing something, he thought. With the rats and the girls and the *melktert*, I'm missing something. I must put it aside and let my subconscious work on it.

After that he went back to bed and was soon asleep.

The next morning he woke with no new insights. After the disturbed night, he was grateful that it was Sunday, so he didn't need to rush. It took him a while to get going, but a shower woke him up. At breakfast he told Joy about the noises in the ceiling and promised to look into it, adding that it was probably the tasteless unsweetened muesli she was making him eat that attracted the vermin. Joy replied that he should stop talking nonsense and finish his coffee or else they'd be late for their visit to his parents.

Nevertheless, they were there in good time and, as usual, the girls were the center of attention and spoiled by everyone. It was a relaxed day, and Kubu found that he was beginning to accept his father's inevitable decline, and that he could still enjoy his company. He was glad of the pleasure Wilmon clearly took in both girls, and no longer corrected him when he referred to Nono as "your daughter."

And he managed to keep the mystery of the *muti* murders in the back of his mind.

FIFTY-SIX

Joshua Gobey sat in the study of his elegant home in Phakalane and sweated. The air-conditioning isn't set low enough, he thought. But he knew that wasn't the real problem. The real problem was the witch doctor sitting in jail being grilled by Mabaku and his men. How long would it take before he broke? If he couldn't save himself with his powers, he wasn't going to save Joshua.

He'd practiced his response to the inevitable questions. He'd deny everything. He'd claim that the CID was trying to discredit him in order to smooth its director's path to the deputy commissionership. He'd be scandalized by the suggestions of his involvement and go straight to the commissioner with his grievances.

After all, nothing linked him to Owido or to the witch doctor. He'd been so careful about that. But he worried about what surprises Forensics might have in store. In fact, he was sure Mabaku would find incriminating evidence whether it was there or not. It was certainly what *he* would do if their roles were reversed. He cursed under his breath and wiped at the dampness on his brow.

So when his cell phone rang, and he didn't recognize the number, he was curt.

"Yes, what is it?"

"Joshua, it's me. Listen very carefully."

Joshua felt the blood drain from his face as he recognized the witch doctor's voice.

"Where are you? Why're you calling me? Did they let you go?" His voice was a croak. Suppose the man was calling from the CID, and the call was being recorded? His hand shook so badly that he nearly dropped the phone.

The response was laughter, the witch doctor's unpleasant laugh that was all sarcasm and no humor.

"Let me go? Do you think I would allow the police to catch me? Do you think my powers are worth *nothing*?"

"But I read . . ."

"You read about a man who's my servant. He does what I say. He knows nothing about me—as little as you do. He disposed of bodies when I'd finished with them, that's all."

Joshua felt a wave of relief mixed with something else. Elation? Yes. His faith in the witch doctor's promises and powers was restored.

"That's fantastic!"

"Joshua, you seem to forget. I'm invisible unless I choose to take human form."

"Yes. Yes, of course."

"Now we want the police to tie up this case and move on to something else. So that we can get back to what's important."

"What if they discover that this undertaker—what's his name—isn't you?"

"Then we could have a problem. I don't want any more interference, any more delay. You must make sure that doesn't happen."

"Me? What can I do? That isn't my department! The CID is under a man called Mabaku." Joshua paused and closed the door in case his wife walked past. "Can't you get rid of him? That would solve all our problems."

"I'm not going to do everything by myself. You're senior in the police and have the ear of the commissioner. Make sure Rampa is charged with the killings."

"How can I do that? I know nothing about it."

"Here's something that should help you. The police either know already or soon will: Rampa has Marumo's briefcase. The one that disappeared the night he was murdered. So he's implicated there, too."

"Marumo? The politician?"

The witch doctor sighed. "Remember you're headed for the top, Joshua, just as long as you do precisely what I tell you." The line went dead.

Joshua leaned back in his chair and swallowed. For the first time he consciously realized what he'd done. He'd put himself in the witch doctor's power. A deal with the Devil, he thought. I made a deal with the Devil. Those stories always end badly. The Devil always wins. He felt the dampness on his forehead again. This time it was cold.

Part Seven

POISONED CHALICE

"Commends th' ingredience of our
poison'd chalice
To our own lips."

MACBETH, ACT 1, SCENE 7

FIFTY-SEVEN

On Monday morning Jacob Mabaku was at the CID early, as was his habit. He liked to be on top of his work, not let it pile up on him. He checked e-mail, but not much had come in over the weekend, so he sat back in his chair and gazed out at Kgale Hill.

I'll miss it, he thought. The view of the hill; working with Kubu, despite all his foibles; the satisfaction of solving a hard case and bringing the felons to justice. And in many ways I have more freedom here than I'll have in the administration and management role of deputy commissioner. He sighed. But I'm not getting any younger, and I've been in this position for ten years. It's time to move ahead if I can.

There was a knock on the door, and Miriam came in.

"Director, Mma Maria Gobey is here. She says it's a personal matter, and can you spare her a few minutes." Miriam looked uncertain. She liked the director's office to run like clockwork, and Mma Gobey's visit was unexpected.

"Of course," Mabaku said, rising. He went into the outer office to welcome Mma Gobey personally. He persuaded her to have tea and asked for coffee for himself. While they waited for the refreshments, he asked her about her family and how they were all coping with the loss of her husband. She was polite, but not very forthcoming. Her mind was obviously elsewhere.

At last the refreshments had been served, and the office door was closed.

"Director Mabaku, I'm sorry to take your time. But a certain matter has been weighing on my mind. I keep asking myself what Tebogo would've wanted me to do. I relied on him so much. I never had to make a decision on my own in all the time we were together. But that's past now."

Mabaku nodded but said nothing, allowing her to take the time she needed to get to the point.

"Your assistant superintendent said that Tebogo would have wanted me to do what I can to help you. I've thought about it, and I believe that's true. So I want to tell you what Tebogo said to me; then perhaps I can forget about it."

Still Mabaku waited. He had a feeling that what she wanted to tell him was important, but that she might change her mind if pushed. In the end, she blurted it out.

"It's Joshua. My nephew. Tebogo found evidence that he's corrupt. And somehow he knew that Joshua was seeing a witch doctor. One of the really bad ones, he said. I think it may well be this man Rampa you have in custody."

"Did he tell you anything else? How he knew about your nephew seeing a witch doctor? Why he thought he was corrupt?"

"Not about the witch doctor, no. But Tebogo said Joshua had bought expensive things—the house and the car—and paid cash for them. Cash he shouldn't have had."

She told Mabaku what details she could remember, but there was little more to add. Finally she said, "I think you're an honest man, Director Mabaku. Tebogo wanted an honest man to succeed him."

When she'd left with his thanks, Mabaku returned to the contemplation of Kgale Hill. Mma Gobey had offered him a powerful weapon against her nephew. Any evidence of impropriety would sink Joshua's chances of the deputy commissioner job. But it would be a challenge to find that evidence: Joshua certainly wasn't stupid. As for the witch doctor, Mabaku didn't want to pursue that aspect at all. He wanted to avoid anything that would link the witch doctor to Tebogo Gobey. And, anyway, Rampa was safely in his cell.

The Joshua Gobey who walked into the commissioner's office on Monday morning was a different man from the one who'd sweated through Sunday. He'd pulled himself together, realizing that his interests and those of the witch doctor were irrevocably aligned. His confidence restored, he felt able to deal with whatever was thrown at him. He shook the commissioner's hand firmly and accepted his offer of coffee.

The commissioner asked about his aunt, and Joshua assured him that she was doing well under the circumstances. He had no idea if that was true, but he sounded convincing. When the coffee came, they turned to business.

"Commissioner, I'm the last person to criticize how things are done in another man's department. You know that I like to delegate authority, give people room to develop." He paused and was pleased to receive an encouraging nod.

"I just think the Rampa case should move a little faster. There's a lot of anger out there."

"I think Mabaku and his people have done a pretty impressive job," the commissioner retorted, "grabbing that undertaker and spotting the swapped bodies."

"Absolutely. But now we must get it tied up. Rampa has been murdering little girls and using their body parts for *muti*! People out there are very angry and suspicious. There must be no hint of a cover-up. You remember the Mogomotsi case."

The commissioner nodded. Many senior people had been embarrassed over that one.

"A quick indictment, no suggestion of uncertainty. That's what we need." Joshua paused. "Perhaps a little pressure could be applied to get a confession."

The commissioner frowned. "What do you mean by *pressure*?"

"I was thinking of offering a deal if he confesses—maybe an insanity plea. Otherwise we let him go."

"Let him go?" The commissioner's jaw dropped.

"He wouldn't last five minutes on the street. He knows that. I think he's very grateful to be in custody at the moment." Joshua paused again, as the commissioner nodded slowly.

Joshua changed tack. "You know about the briefcase, of course?"

"Certainly. How do you know about it?"

"From a friend in Forensics. Anyway, it seems Rampa was involved in Marumo's murder, too. I'd charge him with that as well—that he and Maleng did it together. It probably won't stick in court, but so what? By that time the focus will be on the murdered kids. Maleng can hang on his own for Marumo."

In spite of himself, the commissioner was impressed. While he was a solid policeman first and foremost, he appreciated the political skills needed to handle tricky cases like this one. Perhaps he'd been a bit premature in leaning toward Mabaku for his deputy. Mabaku understood politics but would always follow the book. He'd see how Mabaku reacted to this less conventional approach.

"You certainly have some good points, Joshua. I'll have a word with Mabaku and the prosecutor." He nodded, thoughtful.

Then they turned to other matters until the commissioner had to move on to his next meeting.

Kubu poured himself a cup of tea and then settled down in his office. He wanted to review all the evidence in the cases from scratch, but, instead, he stared out of the window and thought.

A memory of Nono. His subconscious was trying to tell him something, but the message was getting lost in translation. Perhaps he should drop it, he thought, frustrated. In any case he was the only person in the CID who wasn't convinced that Rampa was the killer.

Suddenly a memory popped into his mind. For a moment it seemed to make sense, but then he shook his head. The idea was completely ridiculous. But he couldn't push it back to the oblivion from which it had emerged. It niggled at him, offering some answers but raising new questions.

He picked up the phone and asked Samantha to bring all the case materials for the *muti* murder investigations and join him in the meeting room.

She arrived with her arms full of files, and he helped her set them down on the table. After a distracted greeting, Kubu started sorting through the files, but he couldn't find the one he wanted.

"The rental cars," Kubu said. "Did you check the rental cars again?"

Samantha shook her head. "Rampa has a white Toyota, so that would fit the Tombi abduction. He was running a funeral at the time Lesego disappeared, so couldn't have been in Mochudi. Probably Molefe kidnapped her." She paused. "I was just going to come to tell you about him when you phoned. I brought him in yesterday and told him that now both Rampa and Demene had implicated him. He eventually confessed to abducting Owido, but insisted he knew nothing about the reason. He thought it was a bad joke."

"Good work. That's three confessions. But none to the murders."

Samantha was a bit disappointed with his reaction; Kubu was clearly distracted. She could only guess at what was bothering him.

"Can you get the Marumo stuff? I want to—" Kubu was interrupted by his cell phone. He glanced at the caller ID, frowned, and answered it. After listening for a few moments, he said, "I'll be right there." He disconnected, then turned to Samantha.

"Rampa's been screaming in his cell. They went to look, and his body's covered with wheals as though he's been lashed. We'd better go and check what's going on."

When Kubu and Samantha arrived, a doctor was examining Rampa.

"What happened?" Kubu asked. "Did someone attack him?"

The doctor shook his head. "It looks more like a rash. I've treated it with a cortisone cream and something to soothe the pain. I think he'll be okay."

"Any idea what caused it?"

"He won't talk to me, but it could be an allergic reaction to something he ate."

Kubu turned his attention to the undertaker. He was lying on his bed at the angle that caused the least of his body to be in contact with the mattress. Angry red streaks, slightly raised, crisscrossed his body. He was moaning softly.

"Rra Rampa, do you want to tell me what happened? Did someone do this to you?"

Rampa looked up and nodded. "I told you. His spells and curses aren't stopped by walls. He knows I helped you. I'm finished now. I'm finished."

"Rra Rampa, this is all in your head! He can't do anything to you here. You're doing this to yourself."

The undertaker rolled to face Kubu, ignoring the pain.

"Policeman, you know nothing. You're like someone who doesn't believe in TV because he's never seen a set. Ask your boss how he got to be at the top. Ask his boss. That's how it works. That's how it is." He groaned and lay back. Samantha looked at him in horror.

"My boss got his job because he's excellent at it, that's how," Kubu said angrily. But he had a sudden uncomfortable thought about Tebogo Gobey.

Rampa sneered at him. "Go away," he said. "Leave me alone." Then he refused to say anything more.

Walking back to his office, Kubu said to Samantha, "Are you still so sure he's the witch doctor? Do you think he'd do that to himself?"

She looked unhappy. "He's mad. He believes in evil magic and spirits and devils. Who can say what his mind does to him?"

If it *is* his mind, Kubu thought uncomfortably. But he said, "It may be an idea to have a psychiatrist take a look at him."

Then his cell phone rang again. Miriam this time.

"Samantha, the director wants to see me right away. And it's nearly lunchtime. Will you get those files, and I'll meet with you as soon as I'm free?"

Mabaku started talking almost before Kubu was settled in his chair. Although he was going by the book, he couldn't disguise his enthusiasm for tripping up Joshua. First he filled in Kubu on his meeting with Mma Gobey, and his subsequent thoughts on investigating Joshua's finances. He brushed aside the witch doctor connection, adding, "I just had a call from the commissioner. He's keen to move rapidly on Rampa. He's worried about public reaction if it looks as though we're marking time. Apparently Joshua's been sticking his nose into that also. He thinks we should charge Rampa in the Marumo case."

Kubu shook his head. "We can't charge him in the Marumo case. There's no evidence he was anywhere near the scene, and absolutely no motive. Even if Marumo was one of his clients, what reason would he have to kill him?"

"Maybe they fell out. There was the dog's head, remember."

Kubu sighed. "I don't think Rampa even *is* the witch doctor." That got Mabaku's attention, and Kubu told him about Rampa suffering a psychic lashing.

Mabaku frowned. "He could be doing it to himself to put us off. No, I think our strategy is clear. We go after Joshua on the corruption issues, and we try the commissioner's approach on Rampa." He told Kubu about the choice to be offered to the undertaker: cooperate and avoid the death penalty, or be released to the anger of the people.

Kubu shook his head. "Rampa is more scared of the real witch doctor than he is of us, or the people on the street. And forget about trapping Joshua; he's too smart for that."

"He can't hide all that money!"

"Why not? A few big wins at the casino, taxes all paid. How are you going to prove differently? Maybe we'll get him eventually, but by then he'll be nicely installed as deputy commissioner with you reporting to him, and the commissioner will be obliged to support him not to lose face."

Mabaku grimaced. He realized that Kubu could well be right. "If Joshua's corrupt we have to stop him. We can't allow him to get to be deputy commissioner."

"It's the witch doctor, Jacob. We've got to get the witch doctor. That will let us tie in Marumo and discredit Joshua at the same time. To say nothing of destroying an evil monster."

"I still think it's Rampa, wheals or not. He's a psychopath."

Kubu sat and thought it through, trying to find holes in his reasoning. At last he shook his head. "Jacob, I'm sure Rampa is telling the truth. He isn't the witch doctor; he's just been doing his dirty work. If he were the witch doctor, and Joshua has been involved with him, why is Joshua pushing so hard to get him convicted? If he takes the commissioner's deal, he'd be exposing people like Joshua. It makes no sense. The evidence doesn't add up." He told Mabaku about the briefcase and the other issues that had been bothering him. He hesitated, and then added, "Actually, I have an idea who it might be, but it's far-fetched, and I haven't had a chance to follow up. But even if that turns out to be wrong, I think there's a way we can discover who the witch doctor really is." Then he outlined the plan that had been forming in his mind while they'd been talking.

Mabaku listened the whole way through, his face expressionless, and when Kubu had finished he sat and thought for more than a minute.

At last he said, "You realize that if Joshua is corrupt and involved with people like this witch doctor, you're putting more on the line than our careers? If he gets the deputy commissioner job, he'll make it his business to destroy both of us. With what we know, he won't want us around. Not in the police force. Not anywhere."

Kubu nodded slowly. Mabaku stared at him, thinking about the times over the years when Kubu had been right and the times when he'd been wrong. At last Mabaku nodded. "Okay, we'll give it a try. Let me know what you need. If we're wrong, I just hope we live to regret it."

FIFTY-EIGHT

Joshua was daydreaming. He was certain, after his earlier meeting with the commissioner, that he would soon be appointed as his deputy. Then it would be only a few years before he would find a way to move up again. The commissioner was getting on in years, and Joshua was sure that he could be encouraged to retire if the right pressures were brought to bear.

He smiled at the thought of what he would be able to do from that position. A new house *on* the golf course, not just one nearby; a new car—an upgrade to his already three-year-old BMW; and exotic vacations around the world, tacked on to his state-funded official trips.

He was pleased he had fought back the fear that had initially gripped him at the witch doctor's place out of town. He now had the power to succeed.

He leaned back and closed his eyes.

The intercom on his phone brought him back to the present.

"The commissioner for you, rra," the tinny voice said.

Joshua pushed the blinking button.

"Gobey," he said with authority.

"Joshua." The commissioner's voice sounded hesitant. "Joshua, I spoke to Director Mabaku and urged him to do what you recommended."

Joshua smiled—his ploy was going to work.

"However, there's a problem."

Joshua sat upright. "A problem, Commissioner?" he asked.

"Yes. Mabaku just called me back. It seems that he and Assistant Superintendent Bengu no longer think that the undertaker is the witch doctor."

"Of course he's the witch doctor!" Joshua almost snapped at the commissioner.

"I have to say that they were quite convincing. There's lots of circumstantial evidence, but very little that would stick in a courtroom. And the man has suddenly been covered with welts. He says that the witch doctor has put a spell on him, and he's going to die."

"He's just doing that to himself. He doesn't want to be tried and hanged. He's trying to divert attention by using his powers." Joshua felt his stomach tighten.

"Well, that may be the case, Joshua, but at this point they're only going to charge him with offenses with respect to the burials. If they find better evidence, they'll charge him with the murders also. But in the meanwhile, they're looking for somebody else."

Joshua didn't reply as he started to weigh the consequences of what he'd just heard.

"I'll let you know if they find anything significant," the commissioner concluded and hung up.

Joshua sat for several minutes before he replaced the handset. And when he did, it rattled against its cradle.

In a matter of moments, his life had changed. Before the commissioner's call, he was contemplating the benefits of being promoted. Now he was terrified that everything he had could be ripped from him, that all his dreams could be shredded. If they found the real witch doctor and made him confess, it would be the end for him.

He needed to find the witch doctor before that happened; needed to use the powers the witch doctor had given him.

Joshua jumped up and rushed out of the office. "I'll be back in half an hour," he called to his assistant. He almost ran to his car, then drove to Broadhurst Mall. Minutes later he was seated at a computer amid a number of tourists also using the Internet café.

He clicked on the icon for the browser. The short time it took to open seemed interminable. As soon as he could, he opened his webmail, typed in a Hushmail address, and sent an e-mail: "Need to talk. SOON!! Please."

By the time he returned home that evening, Joshua hadn't heard from the witch doctor, so he went straight to his office to check his e-mail just in case the witch doctor had replied that way. But there was nothing.

Maybe they've caught him, he thought. Maybe it's already too late. He wiped his brow with his hand, feeling the dampness. What if they forced him to name his clients and what they'd done? He'd be ruined. He started fantasizing that he would be saved by the witch doctor committing suicide as the police burst into his place or by the witch doctor being shot by the police as he tried to escape. But he realized that this was all wishful thinking.

He was very distant during dinner with his wife. "I'm sorry, my dear," he said. "I've something on my mind from the office. I'm going to have to work this evening."

As soon as he finished dinner, he returned to his study. He kept his cell phone close by and checked his e-mail frequently for something to do, even though he knew it would be of no avail.

He nearly sent a second e-mail but pulled himself together and decided not to. The witch doctor normally took two days to reply. He had to try to be patient.

Joshua checked his e-mail before and after breakfast, and frequently at the office. Still no reply. Several times he used his office phone to call his cell phone to check if it was working.

By lunch, he couldn't stand it any longer and returned to the Internet café.

"Must talk to you. Urgent!" It took all of two minutes to send the e-mail, and he snapped at the attendant for charging him the minimum of half an hour.

"Can I carry forward the minutes that are left?" he asked.

The attendant shook his head. "No, rra."

"You're cheating everyone," Joshua snarled. "I'll never use you again."

He stormed out onto the sidewalk and looked around. A man leaning on the side of a white car on the other side of the street caught his eye. Wasn't that the same man he'd seen outside police headquarters when he left there twenty minutes ago? He walked briskly to his car and drove off. In his rear-view mirror, he saw the Toyota do a U-turn and pull in several cars behind him. He was being followed.

Joshua canceled the three appointments on his calendar that afternoon, spending the time closeted in his office. When his assistant opened his office door to tell him that one of his appointments hadn't received the cancellation and was waiting outside, he shouted at her to leave him alone. She scuttled back to her desk, wondering what was going on. Her boss had never behaved in such a bizarre fashion before.

The moment Joshua arrived home, his wife realized that she would have a more pleasant evening with friends. So she told Joshua to order a pizza and headed out as quickly as she could.

As soon as his wife left, Joshua found a flashlight and went to the garage. He crawled around, shining the beam on all the underparts of his BMW. When he looked under the front left wheel well, he saw it. He reached in and plucked it off the metal.

It was a police bug, used for tracking vehicles remotely. Why were the police following him? he wondered. Had they captured the witch doctor? Had he confessed? He almost dropped the device on the concrete floor to crush it with his shoe, but he stopped. If it stopped transmitting, they would know he'd found it. He opened the passenger door and put it on the seat. Maybe he could use it to throw the police off his tracks.

Joshua went inside and prowled around the house with a gnawing pain in his stomach.

He tried watching the Botswana soccer team, the Zebras,

play a friendly against South Africa's Bafana Bafana, but he couldn't concentrate.

Eventually, at about 9:30 p.m., he couldn't contain himself anymore, so he sent another e-mail to the Hushmail address.

"PLEASE call me. Need to talk URGENTLY."

He was frantic with the fear of being found out.

The phone call came just before 10:30 p.m.

"The place we last met. In an hour. Stay in your car."

Joshua heard a click as the phone was hung up. He had no chance to respond.

FIFTY-NINE

Joshua slowly put down the cell phone, his heart racing, the witch doctor's voice still echoing in his head. He jumped up. He only had an hour! He needed to hurry.

Then he told himself to be calm and sank back into his chair. I have the power, he thought. Let me use it. Let me think. He took a deep breath. Could this be a police trap? He shook his head. He'd recognized the witch doctor's voice immediately. Always cold, sibilant, reminding him of a snake.

He left a note for his wife saying that he'd been called to a breaking case, and she should expect him when she saw him. Then he went into the garage, opened the door of his BMW, and immediately saw the tracking device he'd left on the passenger seat. So why were the police watching him? he wondered, also remembering the man who had followed him outside the Internet café. It's Mabaku. He's trying to find some lever to blackball me. Or perhaps my stupid uncle told them I was interested in witchcraft, and now they're trying to use me to get to the witch doctor. He ground his teeth.

His first thought was to leave the tracking device in the garage, but he took time to think it through. If he were Mabaku, he would have someone watching the house. That man would report his comings and goings and, if he left the device behind, they'd assume he'd found it and tail him by car. It would be hard to lose them on the empty late-night streets of Gaborone. No, he'd need to be cleverer than that.

He evaluated a couple of plans, then, after a few minutes, went back into the house, took his service pistol from the gun safe, and checked and loaded it. He put on a shoulder holster and a jacket. Then he returned to the car and confidently drove out into the night.

Kubu had just fallen into a contented sleep when the phone jarred him awake. It took him a few seconds to orient himself. When he realized what had woken him, he grabbed the phone.

"Bengu."

"Assistant Superintendent, this is Edison. Edison Banda. Our man outside Suspect A's house phoned and said he'd just driven out. I've alerted the director, the rapid-response team, and Detective Khama."

"And you've got the suspect's car on your screen?"

"Yes. He's heading toward the A1."

"And what about Suspect B?"

"Nothing happening there."

"Good. I'll be there in fifteen minutes."

Kubu checked his watch. It was 10:45 p.m. A very unlikely time for Joshua to leave his house and start driving around Gaborone. This may be it, he thought.

Joshua drove to the A1, then turned south. When he came to the Game City shopping center, he pulled into the parking lot and turned off the engine. Right next to CID headquarters. Just the place to make Mabaku look stupid!

When Kubu arrived at the assembly point, six armed policemen were milling around under the floodlights. Kubu saw Edison and walked over.

"Welcome back, Edison. Did you have a good vacation?"

"Yes. It was wonderful."

"Well, you returned to a hornet's nest. You've been briefed on what's happening?"

"A little bit. Nobody seems to know what's really going on or who the suspects are."

"I'll fill you in on the details after this is over. We're trying to catch a witch doctor who, we're sure, has been responsible for a number of *muti* murders. Obviously we didn't want to tell our men that. They think it's a diamond heist."

Kubu could see the hesitation in Edison's eyes. "It's okay, Edison. Nothing's going to happen to you. He's just a criminal."

Kubu didn't think that Edison was convinced.

Just then a man ran over. "Suspect B has just started moving. It looks as though he's heading west towards the A1."

"Thanks," Kubu said. "Edison, get the men together. I want to brief them."

As Edison was gathering the team, Mabaku and Samantha arrived. Kubu quickly filled them in.

"Director, both our vehicles have backup communication systems. Each will acknowledge every one of your communications. If you don't hear an acknowledgment, check immediately with that vehicle. If you can't make contact, switch to the backup system. Each vehicle also has a cell phone. Edison has those numbers."

Kubu turned to Samantha. "If the team moves in, you are *not* to go with them. You must stay in the vehicle until cleared to move. Understood?"

Samantha stiffened and didn't reply.

"Samantha. It's not because you're a woman. It's because it's dangerous, and you don't have the appropriate training or experience. I won't be going with my team, either."

Samantha nodded reluctantly.

"The men are ready, Kubu," Edison said as he ran up.

Kubu turned to the men. "Listen carefully. The men we are following are very dangerous. We think one of them has killed several times. However, you must do everything possible to capture them alive. No shooting unless absolutely necessary. They're very careful and may lay traps for anyone following. Fortunately, both their vehicles have tracking devices on them. Director Mabaku will be in charge of letting us all know what they are doing. He will also give us the order to go in, if that's appropriate. It's essential that we work together and don't jump the gun. Wait for orders. Don't do anything unless ordered to do so. Each vehicle must acknowledge every communication from the director in order. Who is in charge of Vehicle One?"

A stocky man raised his hand.

"When the director has finished a communication, you must acknowledge by saying 'Vehicle One, roger.' Vehicle Two must acknowledge only after Vehicle One has acknowledged.

If either vehicle fails to acknowledge, switch radios, and the director will ask you all to acknowledge again. We can't afford to make a mistake. This may be the only opportunity we have to catch these two. Understood?"

The men nodded.

"As a final backup, you all have cell phones. On speed dial the number one will ring in the control room. Use it only as a last resort."

Kubu turned to Mabaku. "Would you like to say anything, director?"

"We've been tracking Suspect A for the last fifteen minutes. He has stopped in the parking lot of Game City. Suspect B has just started moving toward the A1. Good luck, men."

Kubu frowned. Why had Joshua stopped at Game City? he wondered. Surely not for a late-night snack.

"Samantha," he said. "You go in Vehicle Two. I'll be in Vehicle One."

He turned back to the men. "Okay. Let's go."

Joshua assessed his options. It was already after eleven on a weekday night, and Game City was nearly empty. There were only a few people who'd been to the movies, chatting and drinking coffee at the Wimpy. Then he spotted a taxi parked outside the fast-food restaurant. The driver had just come out of the Wimpy and was heading back to his car. Immediately Joshua saw his opportunity. He got out of the BMW and sauntered over to the taxi, timing his arrival so that the man was already seated when he reached him.

"*Dumela*, rra," he said. "I'm afraid I'm a bit lost. Can you help me? I'm looking for the Broadhurst shopping mall. I'm from Lobatse."

The driver gave him detailed directions, illustrated with pointing and hand movements.

Joshua was effusively grateful, leaning into the cab to pat the man on the shoulder and shake his hand.

"You are a Good Samaritan, rra. Where are you going from here?"

"I won't get more fares after eleven on a Thursday. I'm off home to Mogoditshane."

Joshua wished him a good sleep and walked back to his car smiling. The tracking device was now lying on the floor behind the taxi driver's seat.

He slid into his car and looked around. He waited a few minutes to see if anyone followed the taxi. Then he drove out a back exit and doubled back. Satisfied that no one was following, he drove back to the A1 and turned south toward Lobatse. After a few miles, he turned left onto a narrow road that had a sign to the Opera House. He drove cautiously down the road, then turned left onto a disused track. After a few more minutes, a cabin near the dam came into sight. He stopped a hundred yards away, switched off the engine and lights, and settled down to wait. If it was like the last time, it would be at least half an hour.

The radio crackled as Mabaku came on the air. Kubu could hear concern in his voice. "Suspect A is backtracking, now heading *north* on the A1. Suspect B is headed *south* on the A1 and is nearing the Molepolole turnoff. They will pass each other in a minute or two."

The driver of Kubu's vehicle responded: "Vehicle One, roger." The second vehicle followed suit.

That's strange, Kubu thought. Why is Joshua going north? Are they going to have a conversation on the highway?

A few minutes later, Mabaku radioed again. "Suspect A has passed Suspect B and is still headed north. Suspect B has stopped just south of Millenium Park. All units move to Old Lobatse Road and stop short of the circle just north of Game City."

"He's checking that no one is following," Kubu said, after the acknowledgments. "I bet he'll stay there for ten minutes or so."

Shortly after the two vehicles had pulled onto the verge of Old Lobatse Road, Mabaku came on the air again. "Suspect A still headed north on the A1. Suspect B still stopped on the A1."

Kubu leaned over and spoke to the driver. "Give me the radio, please. There's something wrong here."

He took the handset and pressed the transmit button. "Vehicle One to Home."

Mabaku answered immediately. "Go ahead, Vehicle One."

"Something's up, Director. Suspects A and B should be converging, not diverging. Please dispatch a car to check that Suspect A is driving a black, 3-series BMW."

"Will do."

A couple of minutes later: "Suspect B now going south on the A1 and has turned left on the side road towards the Opera House. Suspect A still heading north."

A few minutes later, Mabaku came on the air again. "You were right, Vehicle One. Location device is in a taxi. The driver says a man in a black BMW came over and asked directions to Broadhurst Mall. He must have found the device on his car and dropped it in the taxi. He's on to us, which is bad, and we don't know where he is now, which is worse."

Kubu took the handset again. "We'll have to follow Suspect B then. We'll have to be very careful. He'll expect to be followed." I'd better be right that he's the witch doctor, Kubu thought. Otherwise Joshua's on his way to meet someone else.

"Suspect B has stopped about half a mile from the A1. All units move south down the A1. Stop five hundred yards short of the turnoff to the Opera House. Two men from Vehicle Two make a wide swing south of the Opera House road and see if you can locate Suspect B if he's left his car. But don't let him see you."

As the two men climbed out of the other vehicle with their night-vision goggles and automatic rifles, Kubu's heart rate picked up. "We're going to get you!" he blurted out.

After what seemed an interminable wait, the radios came to life. "This is Scout One. Suspect B has pulled his car behind some bushes and is looking back along the road."

"He's being very careful," the driver of Kubu's vehicle whispered.

Kubu got out of the car and walked around. Everyone else did the same. "We could be here for an hour," Kubu said to Samantha. "May as well keep the circulation going."

Twenty minutes passed before Mabaku called again. "Suspect B now moving very slowly. Move ahead slowly without lights."

Everyone jumped into their vehicles.

"Suspect B has stopped again. Be prepared to stop and deploy."

The convoy moved slowly forward until they were five hundred yards from Suspect B.

"Stop and deploy. Acknowledge on portable radios." The leaders of each vehicle and both scouts acknowledged.

Good, Kubu thought. All is going well.

* * *

Joshua was beginning to fidget. He'd been waiting for more than half an hour. Was the witch doctor just being cautious? he wondered. Or had something happened to him?

I'll give him another fifteen minutes, then I'll leave.

"I'll go ahead," the leader of Kubu's group said to the remaining men. "Follow me in two minutes." He pulled on night-vision goggles and walked forward, automatic rifle at the ready.

Two minutes later the rest of the team fanned out and moved warily forward. Kubu wished he could follow them. Samantha climbed into the vehicle and sat down next to Kubu.

The earpieces crackled as one of the scouts reported. "This is Scout One. I can see Suspect B's car. He's standing about thirty yards to the side, behind a tree. There is another car about five hundred yards farther on. It looks as though there is one occupant."

"That has to be Joshua in the car," Kubu said to Samantha. "The witch doctor is making sure nobody's following."

"Everyone stop," Mabaku ordered. The team leader acknowledged and raised his hand to signal the others.

A few minutes later the scout reported again. "This is Scout Two. Suspect B is circling behind Suspect A's vehicle. Am following at a distance."

"Move forward another hundred yards," Mabaku ordered. The teams fanned out even farther and crept forward.

"Suspect B is now circling back."

"Get down," came Mabaku's order. The men dropped quietly to the ground, looking around anxiously.

"If Suspect B sees any of you, capture him alive and take Suspect A as well." As he heard Mabaku's words, Kubu said to Samantha, "I hope that doesn't happen. We won't have anything to charge either man with."

A few minutes later: "Suspect B has entered a small building about one hundred yards from Suspect A's vehicle."

"Close in another hundred yards," Mabaku ordered.

The men crept closer. Then nothing happened for interminable minutes.

He's getting ready for Joshua, thought Kubu.

"A light has come on outside the building. Suspect A has left his car and is proceeding toward the building."

"Move forward until building is in sight, then stop."

"Suspect A now in building."

"Yes!" Kubu exclaimed. "We've got them."

When the light in the house flashed, Joshua knew it was time. He took a deep breath. I'm afraid of him, he admitted. I'm afraid of what he'll make me do.

He pulled himself together, closed the car door quietly, and headed to the house. But before he reached the front door, he stopped. Something bothered him. A sound not really heard, or a movement not really seen? He stood still and carefully scanned the area, then he silently turned around and peered into the brush behind him. The half-moon was now low in the sky, and what illumination it offered was disguised by tree shadows. He waited for more than a minute. The light in the house signaled again. He felt his confidence build again, as it had when he'd held the albino's still-warm heart in his hands. He entered the house, gently closing the door behind him, letting the Yale lock click into place.

The witch doctor was waiting for him, dressed as always in baboon mask and leopard skin. Joshua felt awe, but he also felt power pumping in his veins. It was I who killed the albino, he thought. Not you.

The room had two wooden chairs set apart, and the witch doctor waved Joshua to one and took the other.

"Why did you call me?" the witch doctor asked. "What's so urgent?"

"They don't believe Rampa is the witch doctor. I had the commissioner convinced, but the CID people don't believe it." Somehow the issue didn't seem as critical here in the witch doctor's den. "It was a mistake hurting him. The welts on his body convinced them that he couldn't be the real witch doctor."

The baboon head turned to face him, but Joshua couldn't see eyes behind the holes in the mask. "It doesn't work like that, Joshua. Rampa betrayed me. He said things no one should speak. For that he was punished. He will die as he deserves."

"Nevertheless, they now believe there was someone else behind it all."

"It was your job to convince them that no one else is involved!"

"They're looking for someone else. They're looking for you. They've been watching me, too."

The witch doctor leaned forward, suddenly tense. "Watching you? Why would they suspect you?"

"I think my rival for the deputy commissioner job is trying to trip me up. But I've been careful."

"What if they followed you here?" The witch doctor's voice rose in anger.

"I gave them the slip. They're following their tracking device to Mogoditshane. And no other cars came down this road."

The witch doctor nodded. "That's true." He paused. "What did you expect me to do about all this?" he asked calmly.

"I thought it was important for you to know what was happening. Can't you put them off the track somehow?"

The witch doctor thought for a few moments. "There is no track. No one can see me unless I want them to. And I will be away for a while. There are people in Zimbabwe I can work with to get what we need. Much more cheaply, too. I'll set up new contact procedures with my clients. Maybe you will come there to see me. Maybe I will come back here." He leaned toward Joshua. "Anyway, you have what you need for now, don't you?"

Joshua felt a bit dizzy. The background seemed to fade, leaving nothing but the witch doctor. He could now see deep black eyes, staring out at him from the baboon face. The eyes were from very far away. Maybe from another world. But the thought didn't upset him. He felt relaxed.

"Yes," he said. "I have what I need."

"You have the power."

"Yes," Joshua repeated. "I have the power."

"So there is no problem."

"No, there is no problem." His voice was without intonation.

"Good. Then we have finished."

Joshua nodded. "Yes, we have finished." He knew it was true and felt relief.

"You can go now. I'll contact you when it's time."

"Yes, I can go now. I have what I need." Joshua rose to his feet, feeling groggy. At that moment, there was a sound of a snapping twig. "What was that?" The effects of the spell vanished, and he was instantly alert again.

The witch doctor had heard it, too. "Someone's out there! You said you weren't followed!"

"Quiet." Joshua tried to look through the window into the night, but there was only blackness. Then he heard a scuffing sound, the sound of shoes moving closer, faint, but he was sure.

"There are people out there. We have to get out of here."

A voice from outside shouted, "Police! Open the door at once!"

"Keep them here!" the witch doctor cried and headed to the back of the house.

Suddenly everything was clear to Joshua. It was the witch doctor who had let himself be followed. No longer invisible. No longer powerful. He couldn't allow him to leave the house. If he was caught, Joshua was finished. He pulled the pistol from under his jacket. But at that moment the witch doctor turned and gave an unearthly screech. Joshua fired, but his hand shook, and the bullet went wide.

There was a crash behind him as the door burst open. Before he could turn, he was knocked to the floor, and the pistol wrestled away. He felt a heavy foot on his neck, and his arms were pulled roughly behind his back and his wrists handcuffed.

He twisted his head to look for the witch doctor, but he was gone.

For the man guarding the back of the house, the night became a nightmare. He was expecting an escaping robber, perhaps coming out, guns blazing. He almost hoped for that. Instead he saw a creature not human—half man, half baboon. He knew at once what it was, and his heart froze. It screeched like something from the pits of hell and, before he could recover, it was on him. He pulled the trigger, but it was too late; bullets smashed harmlessly into the back of the building. The force of the witch doctor's attack, added to the recoil, knocked him over backward. The last thing he felt was the scalpel going through his throat from ear to ear.

Kubu heard the gunshot, a cacophony on the radio, and then a burst of automatic rifle fire. Forgetting his own orders to Samantha, he shouted, "Something's wrong! He's getting away. Monitor the radio and keep Mabaku informed." Ignoring Samantha's protests, he clambered out of the vehicle and lumbered up the road toward the house. He wanted to spot the witch doctor's car. That's where he'll go, he thought. If I'm wrong, and they've got him, no harm done. If I'm right, I've got to stop him.

Luckily the moon glinted off the metal of the car or Kubu might have missed it. As it was, he caught the reflection and moved off the road toward it, trying to catch his breath. He could hear the men at the house shouting and crashing around in the bushes. His decision to get involved didn't seem like a good idea anymore—he wasn't even armed. But surely the witch doctor wouldn't get through the cordon?

Kubu suddenly realized he could be mistaken for one of the suspects. He took some comfort in the fact that the scouts had night goggles, and they would recognize him by his bulk. But to be on the safe side, he moved to the side of the car away from the house.

The witch doctor came at him out of the bushes screeching as he rushed forward, something in his hand glinting.

For Kubu, time seemed to stop. Before him was a creature of nightmares, hands out like claws of a predatory beast, awful baboon face, body splattered with the blood of its kill. For a fraction of a second Kubu felt the hopelessness of opposing this evil. Then his right arm flew out, not to ward off the attacker, but to destroy it. His mind boiled with fury; his arm powered by the anger of murdered children. And he screamed back.

The edge of his right hand caught the witch doctor below the left ear, by good luck just below the wooden mask. He felt something give, and his hand exploded in agony. The scalpel cut into his arm, but then was released, and the witch doctor collapsed to the ground.

Suddenly Samantha was there. "Kubu, are you okay?"

For a moment he couldn't speak, his eyes watering from the waves of pain in his hand. "Yes, I'm fine. Handcuff the witch doctor. I think I knocked him out. Be careful! He has a knife, and he may be faking." He tried to move the fingers of his hand, but the pain was excruciating, and he stopped.

Samantha bent over the witch doctor, and Kubu heard the handcuffs close. After what seemed a long time, Samantha spoke. "He's dead, Kubu. I think you broke his neck."

She turned her attention back to him, seeing the blood staining his jacket. "Oh God. You're hurt. We must get you to a hospital. Where are the others?" She jumped up. "Over here!" she yelled. The assault team called back and moved up.

"Can you take off the mask?" Kubu asked, nursing his broken hand.

Samantha pulled loose the Velcro straps of the mask and lifted it off. Now they could see the strange angle of the head on the neck.

"Yes, it is him," said Samantha.

Kubu looked down at the face of Dr. Jake Pilane and nodded.

SIXTY

Samantha rushed Kubu to Princess Marina Hospital, but once she was convinced that he wasn't seriously injured, she left for home, exhausted. Edison Banda waited and drove Kubu home after the hospital had finished with him. They didn't talk much. Edison was also tired after the long night, and Kubu was in a haze of shock and painkillers, his mind on the events leading up to the witch doctor's death.

It was after three when Edison dropped Kubu off and headed home to his bed. Kubu knew Joy would be waiting for him; he'd phoned her from the hospital to let her know that he'd been hurt, but was okay. Nevertheless, when he came in, he could see the worry on her face. I look a mess, he thought, as he tossed his bloodied and ruined sweater over a chair. His forearm was half covered by the dressing over the stitches, and his hand tightly bound with bandages.

"Oh, Kubu!" Joy cried, running to him.

"I'm fine, my darling." He hugged her with his left arm, pulling her close.

"What did he do to you?"

He could tell she was close to tears. "The arm is just a flesh wound. And you know I have plenty of that! They put in a few stitches and bandaged it up. As for my hand, I broke one of the bones hitting the witch doctor. But it's not serious, either. A 'greenstick' fracture, the doctor called it. It will bind up by itself. They gave me antibiotics and painkillers. I'll be fine."

He decided not to mention the antiretroviral they'd given him, concerned about the blood from the dead policeman on the scalpel. They wouldn't know about the man's HIV status until later in the morning.

Kubu steered her to the couch, and they sat close together, Joy on the left so that he could have his good arm over her shoulder. For a few minutes, it was enough for them to sit together and be still. Then Joy asked, "What happened to him? The witch doctor?"

Kubu hesitated. "I killed him. I didn't mean to. He was rushing at me with a scalpel in his hand. I was scared and just lashed out and hit him as hard as I could." His hand twinged as if recalling the blow.

"I'm glad," Joy said. "I'm glad he's dead. He was an awful, evil man."

Kubu shook his head. "We needed him alive. We need to know who his clients were, who his victims were. We needed to show people that he was just a psychopath, to be reviled not feared. He's escaped what should have been in store for him."

But there's more to it than that, Kubu thought. I killed a

man. A bad man, a man who deserved to die, but another human being nonetheless. He dragged me to his level.

Joy shuddered. "I don't care. He might've got away. I'm glad you killed him."

Kubu pulled her closer, wishing they could go to bed, make love, put it all out of their lives, but he knew the moment wasn't right. And that this was something he would carry alone.

"Do you want some tea?" Joy asked.

Kubu would have preferred a stiff brandy, but with all the drugs, that might not be a good idea. "Tea sounds good."

Joy went to the kitchen, and Kubu stretched out, allowing the tension to seep out of his muscles, to be replaced by physical tiredness. They would have tea, he would reassure Joy, and they would go to bed. There was much to do in the morning. And the painkillers would wear off at some point.

He heard a scrabbling in the ceiling and glanced up. The mongoose, he thought.

Then Joy came back with the tea, snuggling close to him again, and he knew that everything would turn out all right.

SIXTY-ONE

Despite Joy's protests, Kubu decided to go to work after lunch. He had slept soundly until after ten in the morning, when the painkillers started to wear off. His hand throbbed, and he had a headache, but his determination to tie up the loose ends in the witch doctor case was as strong as ever. He phoned Samantha around noon to ask her to pick him up, so they could go through the witch doctor's house.

"And get the keys we found in his trousers last night from Zanele," he said before he hung up. "I hope they're his house keys. I'm not in the mood to break down a door."

"Rampa seems much better this morning," Samantha said as they left Kubu's house. "The rash seems to be fading. Maybe it was just an allergy after all. And he's being very cooperative now that the witch doctor is dead. We're getting all the details of where and when he buried the extra bodies. We'll be able to exhume those children and give them proper funerals."

"We'll still charge him with whatever we can manage," Kubu growled. "If he hadn't closed his eyes to what was going on—out of fear and greed—the witch doctor would've stopped being invisible long ago."

Samantha hesitated, then blurted out, "Kubu, I have to admit I was really scared last night, and I didn't know why. The witch doctor was dead, but it all felt so wrong. So dangerous somehow." She hesitated. "And I've been sleeping badly. I'm beginning to wonder whether this witch doctor thing is getting to me. I kept hearing something moving in the ceiling."

Kubu looked at her sharply. "You, too? It's rats. Or mongooses. Joy persuaded one of our neighbors to climb up into our ceiling yesterday. I don't do that sort of thing." Samantha could well believe that, and the thought of Kubu putting a foot through the ceiling forced her to suppress a smile. "There weren't any droppings, so it wasn't rats. But he saw a mongoose climbing through the rafters."

"I'm sure that's what it is," Samantha agreed at once. "Anyway, I didn't hear anything last night."

Kubu just nodded, and they drove in silence for a few moments. When they stopped at a traffic light, Kubu turned to her. "Samantha," he said, "I want to tell you what a good job you've done. If you hadn't been so tenacious about following up the *muti* killings, Pilane might still be out there with his mask and leopard skin and scalpel."

"Thanks, Kubu. I thought . . . I thought I'd drive to Mochudi tomorrow in the afternoon and find Dikeledi Betse. I'll tell her what happened to Lesego. We won't really ever know the details, will we? But at least she won't have to wonder about it anymore. Not knowing is the worst."

"Like you with Segametsi Mogomotsi?" Kubu asked quietly. Samantha nodded.

Kubu enjoyed being driven, because it gave him an opportunity to make some calls. Joy had forbidden him to do any work that morning. Now he was eager to move forward. The first call was to the doctor at Princess Marina Hospital. He listened to the doctor and breathed a heavy sigh of relief.

Samantha glanced toward him. "Is something wrong, Kubu?" she asked after he hung up.

Kubu shook his head. "No, everything's fine." The policeman who had been slashed to death by the witch doctor the previous night had turned out to be HIV negative.

Then he called Zanele Dlamini, the forensics expert. She had taken a team to the house that the police had stormed the previous night to look for evidence of the *muti* murders.

"It was a gold mine, Kubu," she exclaimed in a weary voice. "We've worked all night and have strong evidence. The back room was spotless, but it still amazes me that smart people don't know how hard it is to get rid of all traces of blood. The witch doctor must've used the table in the middle for his killing. We found blood in some of the seams of the cover, as well as in some of the cracks in the concrete floor."

"Could you identify any of it?" Kubu asked impatiently.

"Yes," Zanele replied. "Thank God we still have that new DNA machine that South Africa loaned to us. We positively identified that some of the blood was from the albino."

"Excellent! Anything else."

"In the cabinet, we found a variety of medical things, such as stuff for suturing, anesthetics, such as chloroform, a number of scalpels—"

"That's where he got the one that he slashed me with," Kubu interrupted.

"And there were various plastic containers and gourds."

"Anything useful from any of it?"

"Yes! And guess whose fingerprints we found on a scalpel from the cabinet. You're going to love this! Joshua Gobey's. It is a clear match." Zanele could not contain her excitement. "I just received the results. It'll stand up to any scrutiny."

Kubu thought for a moment. "This is what we're going to do. I'm going to call the director and ask him to speak to the commissioner. This is bad news for the police force, and he needs to know. We're going to ask his okay to get a search warrant for Gobey's house. As soon as it's signed, I want you to go through the house and particularly his clothes to see if we can tie him personally to Owido. The print on the scalpel only ties him to the place."

"And then?"

"Then I'm going to interview him later this afternoon to see what his story is. Don't let news of that print get out. I want to surprise him with it."

A few moments later, Kubu ended the call and phoned Director Mabaku to put his plan in place. When he hung up, he turned to Samantha. "I think we've got the bastard!"

A few minutes later, they arrived at the doctor's house on Pela Crescent. Who would have imagined this quiet little street could have seen so much over the past few weeks? Kubu thought.

A constable checked their IDs before letting them go inside the gate. Kubu dug in his pocket with his left hand and pulled out the bunch of keys that had been found the previous night in the witch doctor's civilian clothes. The first one he tried fit the lock, and they opened the door. They decided to do a quick tour of the house to orient themselves. It was a typical suburban home with three bedrooms, one en suite and one that was used as an office.

"Okay," Kubu said when they'd finished their tour. "Let's start! We'll go through everything, leaving the office for last. That's where we're likely to find something, if there's something to find."

For the next two hours, Kubu and Samantha examined every room, every drawer, every cupboard, but found nothing of interest.

"I've never seen a house so neat and well organized," Samantha commented. "Particularly a bachelor's. Even his underwear is folded." She paused. "I assume he was a bachelor. There's no evidence of a woman here."

"Yes, he was unmarried," Kubu responded. "And did you see the walk-in closet in his bedroom? Everything was hung by color. Blues with blues; greens with greens. I hope Joy never gets to see it. My life would end in misery if I had to live like that. I'm perfectly happy that all my clothes are somewhere under one roof."

He looked around. "Have you noticed that there aren't any pictures on the walls or photographs of friends or family?"

Samantha nodded. "It's weird. Almost as though he doesn't want anything giving away who he is. And there is nothing for music, and no TV." She shook her head in amazement.

The two of them walked to the office—the only room remaining to be searched. The wall behind the desk sported two gray metal filing cabinets; the wall to the left of the desk had a single window covered with a thick curtain; and the wall opposite the window was one big bookcase. Kubu turned and looked back at the door. The wall in which it was set was painted a dark maroon.

"What's with the wall?" he asked rhetorically.

Samantha turned and gazed. "Even more weird!" she exclaimed. "Every other wall is white, yet this one is red."

"The one he looked at when he sat at his desk!" Kubu commented, shaking his head. "Will you please go through the filing cabinets while I check out his desk? I've no idea what we are looking for. If something seems out of place, let me know."

He found a key that opened the locked desk, then handed the bunch to Samantha. "I'm sure the cabinet keys must be here, too," he said.

Within a minute, she'd opened the cabinets and pulled out the top drawer of the first one. While she checked the dozens of files, Kubu carefully examined each desk drawer. Here too everything was in order, everything in place. Kubu whistled. "What a strange mind to have—paying such attention to every detail."

"It's the same in the files," Samantha responded. "Everything in order—files by alphabet; contents by date. And an index of contents at the front of each file. Amazing."

When Kubu reached the end of the last desk drawer, he leaned back in the very comfortable chair and took a deep breath. "Nothing so far! And you?"

"Nothing also," Samantha replied. "Most of it is medical stuff. Files of his patients, and so on. I've taken out all of his bank statements and some other financial records. We can look at those later."

Kubu stood up. "Okay, one last place, then we can leave. The bookcase."

In addition to the numerous medical texts and meticulously labeled journal boxes, there was a set of Reader's Digest Classics, an *Encyclopaedia Britannica*, a number of what looked like university texts on biology, botany, and chemistry, and several biographies and autobiographies, mainly of nineteenth- and twentieth-century military leaders. But what caught the attention of both Kubu and Samantha was a single photograph cut from a newspaper displayed in an old silver frame. It was of an older man and a teenage boy in front of a building. They were obviously related. The man was in a suit, and the boy wore a shirt and shorts that looked like a school uniform. He looked as though he was crying. The man was holding the boy's hand, but the boy was turned away from him and seemed to be trying to pull away.

"Pilane and his father, I would say," Samantha said.

Kubu nodded and picked up the frame and scrutinized it. The building didn't look familiar. He looked at the back of the frame to see if there was an inscription. Nothing. He tried to remove the cardboard backing but found it impossible to do one-handed. He handed it to Samantha, who carefully opened the clasps. There was a child's writing on the back of the cutting. She read it out loud.

"December the eighth, 1986."

"What a strange photo," Kubu said. "The only picture we've found in the house, too."

"That date sounds familiar. Maybe we can find out the story behind it," Samantha responded. "It could give us an idea of who he really was. I'll check the newspapers for that day. They may even be online."

Kubu nodded and thought briefly about how lucky he was to have caring parents. "Okay, let's go through all the books. You'll have to do it, I'm afraid." He held up his bandaged hand, wincing as he did so, and sat down at the desk.

It was hard work, particularly for the lower shelves. Samantha took each book off the shelf, riffled through the pages to check whether anything had been slipped inside, and returned it to its same position.

She was halfway through the second shelf when she noticed a safe behind the books. Kubu stood up for a closer look. "I wondered about that," he remarked. "There is one unusual key in the bunch. I thought it might be for a safe."

Samantha took down enough books to give him access and he inserted the key. Sure enough, it turned, and he was able to open to door. There was only one item—what looked like a photo album. He slid it out, took it to the desk, and opened it. On the front page, in neat letters written with a fountain pen, were a name, Jacob Mampe, and the same date: December the eighth, 1986.

Kubu turned the page. On the left was a moth, pressed below the cellophane. Its wings were separated from its body. On the right page was a butterfly, similarly dismembered. Neither Kubu nor Samantha said a word. Kubu turned the page. Two more moths. The next page was the same. Kubu frowned, wondering what the album was all about.

He turned the next page. This time it was a dried frog, with all four legs separated from the body. And on the right, there was a sparrow with its body crushed flat. Again the wings were off. Kubu looked carefully at both the frog and the sparrow. The separations had been done very cleanly, with a knife or something similar.

"This is very scary," Samantha whispered. "He started killing things very young. I wonder why he took off the legs and wings and so on."

Kubu shook his head, but said nothing.

The next page had the furs of a mouse and a rat, again with the limbs separate.

"How did he dry them out?"

"Probably left them in the sun," Kubu replied. "It's so dry here that it wouldn't take very long."

On the next page there was a photograph of the boy with a pet dog. Scribbled at the bottom was the name Tau.

"Doesn't look like a lion," Kubu murmured.

On the right there was a photo of the dog alone, tongue hanging out.

Kubu turned the page. Samantha gasped. There was a photo of a dog's head—clearly Tau's. Underneath was the name Tau again, this time scratched out.

"Well, that may explain one of our cases," Samantha said. "But why did he do it?"

"Maybe he was toying with Marumo." Kubu didn't sound convinced.

"I wonder if he also set up Witness Maleng to murder Marumo then," Samantha continued. "By abducting his daughter and suggesting that Marumo had done it."

"But there's no evidence that the two ever met."

"Maybe he did it through the power of suggestion?"

Kubu glanced at Samantha surprised. "Do you mean through a spell?"

Samantha hesitated, then shook her head. "You're right. It couldn't have been that. Let's go on."

Over the page, there was another photograph of what appeared to be Pilane's father. This time alone. On the right page was a large photograph of a tombstone—quite elaborate.

"They must have had money," Kubu said. "A headstone like that is very expensive."

He peered more closely. "Hold on. This can't be of Pilane's father. The name is Sampson Mampe. Not Pilane. The date of death is December the eighth, 1990."

"The same date!" Samantha exclaimed.

"And the same last name as the one at the front of the book!" Kubu peeled back the cellophane and turned the photo over. In thick black letters was written the word *Amandla*. "Freedom. Freedom from what, I wonder?" Kubu asked.

"Maybe he disliked his father. The newspaper cutting seemed to show that. Perhaps he was happy he was dead."

"Maybe it was his stepfather. It's a different name." Kubu turned the photo over again, and another thought struck him. "Maybe he killed him!"

"Killed his stepfather?"

Kubu glanced at her. "Do you think that date's a coincidence?" He replaced the photo and turned over the page. "At least this isn't strange." They both peered at a University of the Witwatersrand certificate for the degree of MBBCh, awarded on December 1, 1994.

"What's MBBCh?" Samantha asked.

"That means he's a doctor."

"Look at the bottom—in pencil." Samantha pointed. "It's that date again. A week after the degree was awarded. What's going on?"

Kubu frowned. "I've no idea. But it's obviously significant. And look at the opposite page. It looks like the pocket of one of those white medical coats. And it has the same date as the penciled one at the bottom of the certificate."

Kubu turned the page. "This looks like his Botswana Health Professions Council authorization to practice medicine in Botswana." He turned the page again.

"Oh no!" Samantha gasped. Under the cellophane was a small square of fabric—obviously from a dress. Under it, neatly written, was the date: December the eighth, 1998. The next page had a different dress remnant, but this time the date was June the fourth, 2001.

Horrified, the two paged through the rest of the book. "There must be a dozen or more entries," Samantha said.

"Seventeen, actually," Kubu retorted.

Samantha turned back a couple of pages. "That's why the date seemed familiar. This must be Lesego. She disappeared on the eighth of December last year. And the next one is Witness Maleng's daughter, Tombi; and the last one is the day the albino disappeared."

Kubu said nothing, anger and tears welling up.

"It's too bad he's dead," Samantha cried. "He deserves to be tried for each one of these!"

Kubu nodded and continued flipping through the pages. All were blank after the date Owido had disappeared. He reached the last page and under the cellophane was a newspaper clipping. He lifted the cellophane and carefully unfolded the paper. A square had been cut out of it. It was from the *Sowetan* of December 8, 1986.

Traditional Healer's Wife Laid to Rest
Evelyn, the wife of well-known traditional healer

Sampson Mampe, was laid to rest this afternoon at the Avalon Cemetery in Soweto. She was 32 years old. The funeral was attended by local businessmen and politicians, as well as by about 100 other mourners.

Mrs. Mampe was taken ill on the 4th of December and died late that night. Mr. Mampe told *The Sowetan* that she had been suffering from bouts of an undiagnosed illness for about three months. "I gave her powerful herbal potions but they didn't help. When I took her to the Baragwanath Hospital, they said it was too late."

Mr. Mampe rose to prominence after two prominent businessmen publicly thanked him for his assistance in making them successful.

Mrs. Mampe left one son, Jacob, who is fourteen years old.

"Look at that!" Samantha pointed to a caption below the missing square. "Sampson Mampe tries to console his son Jacob after Mrs. Mampe's burial," she read. "The photo at the front comes from this clipping."

"The boy looks more angry than sad," Kubu said, turning back to the photo. "Let's go back to the office. I can't take any more of this." He picked up the book and walked out. "Please lock everything. I'll wait in the car."

SIXTY-TWO

The Caravella is at the dead end of Mokgosi Street, near the city center, and it's one of Kubu's favorite restaurants. He can take his own wine for a small corkage charge, and the fare ranges from excellent Portuguese fish dishes to large succulent steaks. It's not the sort of place Jacob Mabaku frequents, however. He prefers more traditional Batswana dishes, preferably cooked by his wife. So Kubu was surprised when Mabaku walked into his office the day after the discovery of the gruesome photo album and said, "I'll take you to lunch at the Caravella. You're always talking about it."

On the way to the restaurant, Kubu gave the director a full report on progress in the case against Joshua Gobey. "We're certain Gobey was directly involved in the killing of the albino, Owido. Zanele found his prints on a scalpel at the house and blood traces on a pair of his trousers at his home. The blood is a match with Owido's. We think he went to see the witch doctor in order to get rid of the only witness. That would've left him in the clear. Or maybe the witch doctor was blackmailing him. Either would be a strong motivation."

Parking at the Caravella is always difficult, but the parking attendant recognized Kubu and directed them to a prime spot, under a tree, and close to the entrance.

"You've been here a few times, I see," Mabaku commented.

"Once or twice," Kubu responded with a smile.

They chose a table in the walled courtyard in front of the restaurant, shaded by the large trees that share the area with the diners. Mabaku tossed Kubu the wine list and told him to order whatever he liked. Kubu bypassed the French and Portuguese offerings and chose a red blend from South Africa's iconic Kanonkop estate. He added a jug of iced water to the order—the sun was sneaking through the leaf canopy, and the day was already hot.

Once they had ordered, and Kubu had tasted the wine and pronounced it acceptable, Mabaku got to the point.

"The commissioner has decided to appoint someone from the uniformed branch as deputy commissioner. He says he feels the CID is too isolated from the mainstream to make me ideal for the job." He didn't meet Kubu's eyes as he spoke.

Kubu bristled. "He found out how we used him to get to Joshua, didn't he? And he's not big enough to appreciate that we were protecting him by keeping him in the dark."

Mabaku nodded. "I felt I had to tell him the truth. He's satisfied with the outcome but says he can't trust someone who would use him that way. I won't pretend I'm not disappointed but, in many ways, I'm not sorry. The things you and I do are the reason I joined the police force, not to push paper and sit in pointless meetings with senior politicians."

Kubu was not so easily mollified. "You deserved the recognition! The commissioner had no right to treat you that way."

Mabaku took a sip of his wine and rolled it in his mouth. "Kubu, I'll have other opportunities, and so will you. The commissioner will be retiring in the next five years. You're upset because the idea to use Joshua to catch the witch doctor was your idea, so you're blaming yourself. Don't. It was a good idea, and it worked. *That's* what's important."

Kubu started to protest, but Mabaku interrupted. "Mind you, once Joshua found the tracking device, it only worked because you'd already guessed the witch doctor's identity, and we were tracking him, too. What made you decide it was Dr. Pilane?" He shook his head. "A medical doctor was the last person I would've suspected."

In spite of himself, Kubu laughed. "If this were a mystery novel, I'd say that was the reason. Actually, initially I didn't suspect Pilane at all. Like you, I found it impossible to believe a medical doctor could do the things the witch doctor was doing." There was silence for a few moments as they thought about that. Then Kubu continued. "Something about Nono kept nagging at my thoughts." He paused. "Remember that we believed that Lesego and Tombi recognized their abductors? They would never have known Rampa or Molefe, so it had to be someone else. When I was at the assistant commissioner's funeral, Joy greeted Dr. Pilane. I never knew she knew him. When I asked how, she said he was a volunteer medical officer at Nono's day care. That's where my nagging thoughts came from. It turns out he also volunteered at several other schools—including Lesego's and Tombi's. That put him in an excellent position to spot suitable victims."

The *peri-peri* chicken liver starters arrived, so Kubu broke off until they had both cleaned their plates.

"Then I kept worrying about the briefcase. How did it get to Rampa? I was sure Marumo had it with him when he was murdered. At first I thought Witness Maleng must've taken it." He paused, thinking of the lonely, broken man dipping in and out of reality and probably facing a lifetime in a mental institution. Another of Pilane's victims. "But why would he take it, and then how did Rampa get it from him?" He shook his head.

"Once I decided Rampa was telling the truth, it was likely that he was being set up by the real witch doctor. Think back to the night of Marumo's murder. Pilane hears a scream, runs next door, and discovers Marumo dead. He's worried because Marumo has *muti* that's traceable to one of his victims. He takes the opportunity to grab the briefcase—probably takes it with him when he fetches medication for Marumo's girlfriend. He discovers that it contains nothing important, but he can't take it back—too risky with the police on the way. When the dust settles a bit, he tries Marumo's desk. He's very nearly successful, but I interrupt him. Later he has the idea of using the briefcase to frame Rampa in case anything goes wrong. That was a mistake. It was way too clever."

Mabaku nodded. The stupid ones made stupid mistakes; the clever ones made clever mistakes.

"Once I thought it through, it all seemed to fit," Kubu continued. "And it turns out that Pilane was much worse than I ever imagined. We think he probably killed at least seventeen people." He took a mouthful of wine and proceeded to describe Pilane's house and the ghoulish scrapbook they'd found pointing to a stolen identity.

"You mean he wasn't a doctor?" Mabaku asked incredulously.

Kubu shook his head. "We're pretty sure he killed the real Dr. Pilane just after he graduated and took his identity. Nobody here bothered to check. When we contacted the Wits Medical School, they confirmed that a Jacob Mampe had been enrolled at the medical school, but had been expelled the year before Pilane graduated for stealing parts of cadavers. So Mampe had enough background to pull it off."

"But why did he turn to killing?"

"We're not sure, but it looks as though it must have been something that happened at home. After his mother died, he started dismembering insects. Then we think he killed his father. Maybe he thought his father killed his mother or abused her. And all of these happened on the same date—the eighth of December, which was also the date his mother was buried. Then he killed the original Dr. Pilane—also on December the eighth. It is really bizarre."

"And you say you think he killed seventeen people?" Mabaku asked.

Kubu nodded.

Now it was Mabaku's turn to take a gulp of his wine.

Mabaku's main course was a skewer of fish, prawns, and calamari, hanging from an arm over the plate. It looked delicious. Kubu received a plate heaped with thin, succulent pork chops and vegetables, carefully cut by an attentive waiter who noticed Kubu's injured hand. The excellent food lifted them a little from their depressed state.

"What's going to happen to Joshua Gobey?" Kubu asked, when he'd sucked the last morsels of pork off the chop bones.

Mabaku shrugged. "We'll charge him with the murder of Owido. I think we would have had enough to convict him with the DNA matches, withdrawals from his bank account, and the fingerprint on the scalpel. But Zanele found a gourd of *muti* in his house. She just told me that DNA found in it matches Owido's. It's an open-and-shut case." He gulped down the rest of his wine. "Anyway, that is out of my hands now. The commissioner has it, and he's furious that his police force has been tainted by Gobey's actions. He'll push for the death penalty, I think."

"What a waste! Driven by greed—that's all it is," Kubu said.

Mabaku nodded. "At least we've rid the country of one child killer. That's a start."

Now it was Kubu's turn to nod. "And it's thanks to you for letting Samantha follow her quest. With her in charge of missing-children cases, I'm sure we'll see more progress made."

Mabaku nodded. "Samantha had a suggestion, and I think it's a good one. Even with the information Rampa's given us, we won't find all of Pilane's victims. And we won't find the victims of other witch doctors, either. She thought we should hold a service for the parents and relatives of all the people who've disappeared. I think it will bring closure for them—they deserve at least that."

"Good idea," Kubu said. And perhaps it will bring closure for us, too, he said to himself.

The two policemen sat in silence for a few minutes, lost in their separate worlds.

Eventually Kubu signaled to the waiter and ordered Dom Pedros for each of them. Those whisky and ice-cream drinks were one of Kubu's favorites.

Lunch eventually over, they walked to the car. Kubu

stopped, enjoying the sun while Mabaku tipped the car attendant. Pilane is dead, Kubu thought. But the killing of children
for *muti* won't stop until people stop believing in the witch
doctors, their magic, and their promises. And how long will
that take?

He sighed and hurried to catch up with Mabaku.

Author's Note

AUTHORS' NOTE

Although this is a work of fiction, it is, as were our three previous books, set on a background of reality.

Throughout sub-Saharan Africa, witch doctors hold influential positions in society. Most people believe in them and their powers to some extent. Even Western-trained scientists may carry a residue of belief.

Most witch doctors are traditional healers. That is, they use a combination of potions and suggestion to help people. For the most part, these potions, called *muti* in southern Africa, are made from a variety of herbs and plants. Occasionally they add some part of an animal's body, such as the heart of a lion.

However, there are a few witch doctors, regarded as very powerful, who use human body parts in their *muti*. They often choose a victim for a specific reason. If a male client wants to be virile, a witch doctor may kill a young boy and make *muti* from his sex organs to improve sexual energy. If a woman is having difficulty conceiving, a witch doctor may kill a young woman and make *muti* from her vagina, uterus, or breast. Probably all three. In recent years, a number of albinos have been killed for *muti*, because they are regarded as providing particularly powerful *muti*.

Even more horrific is that the power of the *muti* is thought to be enhanced if the body parts are removed while the victim is alive.

The success rate for bringing to justice witch doctors who are involved in *muti* murders is very low, for several reasons. First, the victim is usually not connected to the perpetrator in any way. The witch doctor finds a person who meets a particular need and kills him or her. So, unlike a normal murder, where there is almost always a connection between the victim and murderer, there is none in the case of *muti* murders. And second, because almost everyone believes in witchcraft, many in the police, as well as potential witnesses, are scared of unveiling someone as a witch doctor who kills for *muti*. They are afraid that the witch doctor will put a spell on them, which could lead to bad luck, ill health, or even death.

In this book, we refer on several occasions to the real-life *muti* murder of a young girl, Segametsi Mogomotsi, which happened in Mochudi in 1994. It caused the community to come out in several violent protests, after which one person was shot by a policeman with an AK-47. The government eventually felt it necessary to conduct an independent inquiry, so it called in Scotland Yard from the United Kingdom. Its report was never released.

One of the people to whom we dedicated this book is former High Court judge Unity Dow. Her novel *The Screaming of the Innocent* is a powerful story about a *muti* murder. It is worth reading.

ACKNOWLEDGMENTS

With each new book we have more people to thank for their generous help and support, because we keep leaning on those who have helped us before while finding new ones to impose upon.

We are extremely grateful to Claire Wachtel, Senior Vice President and Executive Editor at HarperCollins, for continuing to support Detective Kubu. Her edits and suggestions always improve our books. We also thank Elizabeth Perrella for her input and Tom Pitoniak for his careful copyediting.

As always we are grateful to our agent, Marly Rusoff, and her partner, Michael Radulescu, for their efforts on our behalf.

We were very fortunate to have a variety of readers of drafts of this book giving us input and suggestions and catching errors. Our sincere thanks to: Steve Alessi, Linda Bowles, Pat Cretchley, Pam Diamond, Pat and Nelson Markley, Steve Robinson, Brunhilde Sears, and the Minneapolis writing group—Gary Bush, Sujata Massey, and Heidi Skarie. With all their comments, it is hard to believe that the book still has mistakes. But it probably does, and we take responsibility for any that remain.

Many people in Botswana have generously given us their time to make the book as authentic as possible. It is amazing to us that so many people in Botswana are willing to take the time to be bombarded by odd questions from two authors about *muti* and *muti* murders, police procedures, and the like. We particularly want to thank Thebeyame Tsimako, previous commissioner of police in Botswana, for taking time from his demanding schedule to give us comments and advice, and for helping with our requests. Andy Taylor, headmaster of the wonderful Maru-a-Pula School in Gaborone, has been extraordinarily patient with all our questions and requests, and invaluable for introducing us to people in the know. We received helpful information from Alice Mogwe, director of the human rights organization Ditshwanelo, and Unity Dow, former High Court judge of Botswana. Their input has been invaluable, and we have dedicated this book to them and the work they do for Botswana.

We were also fortunate to spend time with Senior Superintendent Roger Dixon of the South African Police, who gave us much valuable advice on forensic matters. Similarly, anthropologist Alex Zaloumis provided insights into *muti* and the ways of witch doctors.

Finally, our thanks go to Ken Hall of Nottinghamshire, England, who suggested *Deadly Harvest* as the title of this book.

GLOSSARY

bakkie	Slang for pickup truck.
Batswana	Plural adjective or noun: "The people of Botswana are known as Batswana." See MOTSWANA.
BDP	Botswana Democratic Party.
dagga	Marijuana. *Cannabis sativa.*
Debswana	Joint diamond mining venture of De Beers and the Botswana government.
Dom Pedro	South African drink made by mixing ice cream with whisky or liqueur.
duiker	Small antelope, *Sylvicapra grimmia.*
Dumela	Setswana for hello or good day.
kgotla	Assembly of tribal chief and elders.
kubu	Setswana for hippopotamus.
leswafe	Albino.
melktert	Milk tart. South African dessert.

Mma	Respectful term in Setswana used when addressing a woman. For example, *"Dumela*, Mma Bengu" means "Hello, Mrs. Bengu."
Motswana	Singular adjective or noun. "That man from Botswana is a Motswana." See BATSWANA.
muti	Medicine from a traditional healer. Sometimes contains body parts.
pap	Smooth maize meal porridge, often eaten with the fingers and dipped into a meat or vegetable stew.
pula	Currency of Botswana. Pula means rain in Setswana. One hundred thebe equals one pula. One U.S. dollar equals roughly seven pula. See THEBE.
quattro stagioni	Four seasons. Pizza with four different toppings.
rra	Respectful term in Setswana used when addressing a man. For example, *"Dumela,* Rra Bengu" means "Hello, Mr. Bengu."
seswaa	Traditional Botswana boiled meat dish.
Setswana	Language of the Batswana peoples.
Shake Shake	Common name for Chibuku Shake Shake beer, made from sorghum or corn. The name Shake Shake comes from the fact that solids separate when the beer carton is standing. The drinker needs to shake the beer before drinking.

shebeen	Originally a place serving illicit alcohol. Now usually a licensed establishment.
steelworks	Drink made from cola tonic, lime juice, ginger beer, soda water, and bitters.
tau	Setswana for lion.
thebe	Smallest denomination of Botswana currency. *Thebe* means shield in Setswana. See PULA.
tokoloshe	A short, hairy creature of Southern African folklore—mischievous and evil.
tuck shop	A small shop selling snacks and nonalcoholic drinks.

BOOKS BY MICHAEL STANLEY

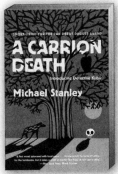

A CARRION DEATH
Introducing Detective Kubu
Available in Paperback and eBook

"Delightful. . . . the Botswana setting has room to breathe and take shape as its own entity, and Stanley's writing style is equal parts sprightly and grave."

—*Los Angeles Times Book Review*

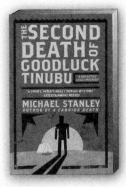

THE SECOND DEATH OF GOODLUCK TINUBU
A Detective Kubu Mystery
Available in Paperback and eBook

"[Kubu is] the African Columbo. . . . This is a smart, satisfyingly complex mystery."

—*Entertainment Weekly*

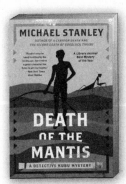

DEATH OF THE MANTIS
A Detective Kubu Mystery
Available in Paperback and eBook

"The best book yet in one of the best series going: a serious novel with a mystery at its core that takes us places we've never been."

—Timothy Hallinan, bestselling author

DEADLY HARVEST
A Detective Kubu Mystery
Available in Paperback and eBook

The fourth mystery in the beloved and critically acclaimed Detective Kubu series tracks a series of murders and the mysterious witch doctor whose nefarious potions might hold the key to a web of missing persons.

Visit www.DetectiveKubu.com and www.HarperCollins.com for exclusive information.

Available wherever books are sold.